Secrets
on the Wind

*Also by Stephanie Grace Whitson
in Large Print:*

Valley of the Shadow
Edge of the Wilderness
Heart of the Sandhills

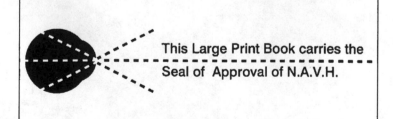

This Large Print Book carries the
Seal of Approval of N.A.V.H.

Secrets

on the Wind

Stephanie Grace
Whitson

Thorndike Press • Waterville, Maine

Published in 2005 by arrangement with Bethany House Publishers.

Thorndike Press® Large Print Christian Historical Fiction.

The tree indicium is a trademark of Thorndike Press.

The text of this Large Print edition is unabridged.
Other aspects of the book may vary from the original edition.

Set in 16 pt. Plantin by Liana M. Walker.

Printed in the United States on permanent paper.

Library of Congress Cataloging-in-Publication Data

Whitson, Stephanie Grace.
    Secrets on the wind / by Stephanie Grace Whitson.
      p. cm.
    Originally published: Minneapolis, Minn. : Bethany House, c2003, in series: Pine Ridge Portraits ; 1.
    ISBN 0-7862-7720-3 (lg. print : hc : alk. paper)
    1. Fort Robinson (Neb.) — Fiction. 2. Women pioneers — Fiction. 3. Nebraska — Fiction. 4. Soldiers — Fiction. 5. Large type books. I. Title.
PS3573.H555S43 2005
  813´.54—dc22   2005007874

Dedication

To my Redeemer,
Who is faithful and true, Who knows
what is in the darkness, and Who
gives hidden riches in secret places.

Daniel 2:22
Isaiah 45:3

As the Founder/CEO of NAVH, the only national health agency solely devoted to those who, although not totally blind, have an eye disease which could lead to serious visual impairment, I am pleased to recognize Thorndike Press★ as one of the leading publishers in the large print field.

Founded in 1954 in San Francisco to prepare large print textbooks for partially seeing children, NAVH became the pioneer and standard setting agency in the preparation of large type.

Today, those publishers who meet our standards carry the prestigious "Seal of Approval" indicating high quality large print. We are delighted that Thorndike Press is one of the publishers whose titles meet these standards. We are also pleased to recognize the significant contribution Thorndike Press is making in this important and growing field.

Lorraine H. Marchi, L.H.D.
Founder/CEO
NAVH

★ Thorndike Press encompasses the following imprints: Thorndike, Wheeler, Walker and Large Print Press.

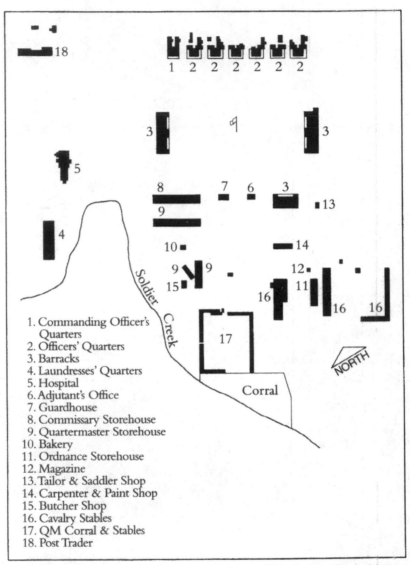

1. Commanding Officer's
   Quarters
2. Officers' Quarters
3. Barracks
4. Laundresses' Quarters
5. Hospital
6. Adjutant's Office
7. Guardhouse
8. Commissary Storehouse
9. Quartermaster Storehouse
10. Bakery
11. Ordnance Storehouse
12. Magazine
13. Tailor & Saddler Shop
14. Carpenter & Paint Shop
15. Butcher Shop
16. Cavalry Stables
17. QM Corral & Stables
18. Post Trader

FORT ROBINSON, September 1879   Map is courtesy of Nebraska State Historical Society

One

Whither shall I flee from thy presence? . . . If I make my bed in hell, behold, thou art there.

Psalm 139:7-8

The acrid scent of burned grass and scorched earth clung to the still air. Fire had blackened the hillside above the half-ruined dugout. He felt his stomach clench. Arrows clung to the dugout's sod face like quills from a porcupine. Dismounting, he pulled one from between the earthen bricks. He could feel the hair stand up on the back of his neck as he touched the tip of the arrow, envisioning what it must have been like in this place only hours ago — the wild rush of painted ponies, the unearthly yelps and cries, the raised war lances, all synchronized into a horrible beauty.

It was so quiet now he could hear the

buzzing of a horsefly as it streaked past him and landed on the crosspiece of the broken window. He took his hat off and slapped it against his dusty thigh. Swiping the sweat off his forehead with the back of his hand, he clamped the hat back on, then handed the arrow up to the grizzled soldier still astride his horse a few feet away. He walked back to peer through the doorway. The carcass of a massive white dog lay toward the back wall.

While his partner examined the arrow, the young sergeant circled the dugout on foot, examining the earth, squatting by a pile of horse manure and prodding it with a stalk of dried grass. Returning to stand beside his horse he said, "Cheyenne arrow. Here about six hours ago, I'd say."

The older man dismounted with a grunt and traced the officer's steps, still holding the arrow in his left hand. He looked at the tracks, grimacing when he squatted down to examine the manure. Grunting again, he stood up and headed back to where his sergeant waited, watching the horizon. He sent a stream of tobacco from between his pursed lips toward the horsefly still crawling along the window frame a few feet away. The fly buzzed off. "Right. About six hours ago. Good tracking, sir."

10

"I told you not to 'sir' me when we're out on patrol, Dorsey," the sergeant said.

Dorsey shrugged. "You earned your stripes, sonny. Guess you deserve the 'sirs' that go along with 'em." He sent another stream of tobacco into the dust.

First Sergeant Nathan Boone looked away from the deserted soddy and squinted at the wiry man next to him. "Is it true you can hit a rattlesnake in the eye doing that?"

Dorsey grinned, revealing almost brown teeth. "You better hope you never have to find out."

"I'll head up the hill in back. Check things out."

Dorsey offered, "I'll do it."

Boone pretended not to hear the old soldier grunt as his arthritic knee crackled. "No need," he said. "You climbed your share of these Sandhills last summer with General Crook."

The older man swore, "I may be older'n you, Sergeant Boone, but I ain't used up yet. Not by a long shot. I'll see you in your grave and still climb a thousand more hills. And don't you think I can't."

Nathan shrugged. "Go on up, then." He turned back toward the door. "I just thought you could check inside and see

11

what you think. It'd help to know if this was a lone squatter or a family." He took a deep breath. "I'm thinking just a lone squatter, but if there's women and children involved. . . ."

Mollified, Dorsey shrugged. "All right, then." He took the reins of Nathan's horse. "Don't get your head shot off up there. We think they're gone, but —"

"I know, I know," Nathan nodded. " 'Just where you don't see any Indians, that's where the most of 'em are.' "

"And where'd you learn that?" Dorsey asked, nodding.

"From some old coot named Emmet Dorsey. Stubborn old guy. Earned a commission in the 'recent unpleasantness' a few years back. Then stepped back into the ranks so he could stay in the army and fight another war out here."

"The man's a darned fool," Dorsey said, grinning.

"You got that right." Nathan headed around the side of the dugout and scrambled up the blackened hillside. Near the top, the smell of scorched earth was overpowered by another stench. Sweat broke out across his forehead. *No women. No children. Please.* He pulled his red kerchief up over his nose and crept forward, willing

12

himself to keep going. He swallowed the knot in his throat and sent it down to his gut where it wreaked havoc with his innards. He tasted bile.

Breathe. Steady . . . breathe . . . steady . . . breathe . . . Beneath the kerchief, he opened his mouth. It helped a little, but now it seemed he could even taste the putrid smell. He reached the crest of the hill and peered over the ridge.

Thankful breakfast had been little enough and long enough ago that there wasn't much to give up, he gazed at the still form only a foot or so away. A man. That helped some. Unless Dorsey found evidence he'd missed inside the dugout. Before they could chase after a captive, they would have to go for help. He started to slide back down the hill, then stopped himself. *Do your job. Look around. Use what Dorsey taught you.*

His dark eyes scanned the horizon carefully. When he was certain he and Dorsey were the lone living humans in the area, he headed back down the hill. Toward the bottom, he lost his footing and finished the slide in a crazy tumble. Just as he scrambled to his feet, Dorsey stuck his head outside.

"Squatter's dead," Nathan said, jerking

his chin toward the top of the hill. He swallowed again to keep from gagging. "You find anything?"

Dorsey shook his head. "You can relax, sonny. Far as I can tell there's no call to go tearing off after 'em. Leastways not without first going back to camp and telling the cap'n what we found. No captive woman to save." He spit. "Most of that stuff is just fodder for dime novels." He grinned. "Guess you'll have to wait to be a hero."

Boone took a deep breath. "I was just thinking how stupid I was going to look back at camp. Glad to know I didn't cost some poor kid's life because I didn't have a company of men ready to move out."

"I been out here ten years and I had no idea of any whites setting up stakes. Whoever this was just made a bad decision, that's all. Probably thought that dog inside could defend him." The man held up a piece of beaded leather. "He tried, though. Got a piece of whoever killed him. My inspection got momentarily distracted." He held up a rattle. "Fell out of the ceiling. Wasn't in a good mood."

"I didn't hear your gun go off," Nathan said, examining the rattle.

"Didn't need a gun." Dorsey spit. "Held him down with my foot and . . ."

He made slicing motions with his hand. Sticking the rattle in his pocket, he motioned toward the side of the dugout. "There's a pile of junk around there. I'll look for a shovel." He pointed at the well. "Get yourself a drink. Clear the smell out of your innards."

While Dorsey retrieved a shovel, Nathan led their two horses toward the well. When he hoisted the first bucketful of water up, a giant bullfrog came along for the ride. Nathan scooped the frog out and offered the water to the horses. The next bucketful was cleaner. After taking a long drink, he doused his face before tying the horses to the windlass and heading to the side of the dugout where Dorsey had found his shovel. A broken rake was the only other tool in sight. But in the pile of rubble he saw pieces of a broken-up trunk. One piece of wood still had a remnant of paper glued to it featuring an idyllic country scene. He closed his eyes. *Just like Lily's.* Rummaging through the woodpile, he found a few more pieces of what he was convinced had been a woman's trunk.

He headed to where Dorsey had started to dig on the other side of the dugout. "There's no more shovels, but I found this." He held up a piece of wood.

Dorsey took it and stared down at the paper.

"You know what that is?" Boone asked.

"Reckon I do," Dorsey said. He spit and thought for a moment. Shrugging, he handed the wood back to his sergeant. "Could mean anything." He stabbed the earth with his shovel. "Suppose you take your giant self inside the dugout and drag that dog's carcass out here. We might as well bury him with his master. While you're inside, look around some. Maybe I missed something."

Nathan headed for the soddy, pausing just inside the door to let his eyes adjust to the dim light. Three crates piled atop one another against the wall to his left must have served as a pantry. The crates were empty now, except for one can lying on its side. To the left of the crates stood a small potbellied stove. Behind the stove Nathan found the base of an oil lamp. There was a wick and a small amount of oil, but no chimney. He set it on the stove. A broad shelf protruding from the base of the right wall must have served as a bed, but no blankets or pillows were in sight. There was no other furniture. The remains of the rattlesnake Dorsey had killed had been tossed in a corner. Nathan shuddered. The thing must have been three feet long before it was beheaded and de-rattled.

Dorsey was right. It was all typical of some lone bachelor's claim. Except for the massive white carcass stretched across the back wall. Nathan would have thought the animal asleep if it were not for the broad red gash that ran the length of its belly.

"So, old fella," he said, stroking the soft white fur. "Dorsey was right. You died defending your master. Good boy." Maybe the white dog was the only friend this settler had. Or maybe he didn't have any friends at all. Maybe he was a heartless thief who deserved what happened to him. *And maybe you think too much. Maybe you should just do your job. Get the burial done and hightail it back to camp. File your report, get a fresh mount, get after the Cheyenne.* He bent down, grabbed the dog's front legs, and started to drag the carcass outside.

"What in — ?!" Nathan dropped the dog's front legs and stared at the dirt floor. His outstretched hand swept away a thin layer of dust to reveal a wood plank. Standing up slowly, he backed to the doorway. "Dorsey," he said quietly, motioning for the other man.

Dorsey looked at his sergeant's face, dropped the shovel, and came to his side.

"There's a trapdoor under that dog." Nathan kept his voice low. The two men drew their revolvers and went back inside.

Nathan pulled the canine carcass off the door.

Dorsey knelt. He pointed down and carefully brushed the dirt away so Nathan could see the iron loop attached to the trapdoor. Signaling for Nathan to be ready, he slipped his index finger through the iron ring. Nathan backed away, positioning himself between the bed and the door so the most light possible illuminated the dugout's interior. He cocked his revolver and nodded. Dorsey grunted and lifted the trapdoor.

An unearthly scream pierced the air. A blur of yellow and brown emerged and flung itself at Nathan, screeching and clawing with such ferocity it was all he could do to keep his balance. Dorsey dropped the door, cursing loudly when it fell back and banged against his knees. He wrestled with it for a moment before finally getting it closed and taking aim at the creature attacking Nathan. What he saw made him hesitate. It sounded animal, it smelled animal, but not only did it appear human, it was wearing yellow calico, meaning it was a human of the female variety. Dorsey dared not fire on a woman. Confused, he holstered his gun and waited for Nathan to subdue the woman-beast.

Nathan would always remember the savagery of the woman's attack as a blurred image of feral eyes and bared teeth made even more repulsive by the terrible smell of a body unfamiliar with soap and water. When she lashed out and raked a swath of flesh off his jaw with her filthy, jagged fingernails, he mustered all the strength in his six-foot-five-inch frame to subdue her. Only when he had finally forced her onto her back and had straddled her and pinned her arms to the ground did he get a good enough look to convince himself that underneath all the filth there was, indeed, a woman. Or at least what had once been a woman.

"Can you pin her legs down?" Nathan looked across the room at Dorsey.

Dorsey howled in agony when she landed a well-placed kick below his beltline.

"Listen," Nathan said to the writhing female. "Do you understand English? We won't hurt you. We won't hurt —" He stopped abruptly when the woman sent a shower of spittle directly into his eyes. "Hey!" he roared and slammed her hard against the earth. She quieted momentarily and stared up at him, defiant, wild-eyed, breathing hard. "That's better," Nathan said. "We aren't going to hurt you."

She stared up at him, then looked past him and concentrated on the ceiling.

"Do you speak English?" Nathan repeated. "Are you . . . ?" The woman eyed Dorsey. "Say something in Cheyenne, Dorsey. She's got dark skin. Maybe she's Cheyenne."

Dorsey complied, but the woman didn't respond. When her breathing slowed, Nathan loosened his hold. The second he did, she launched a new series of savage kicks. She was quick and so surprisingly strong that she managed to turn sideways beneath him. And then, suddenly, she uttered an unearthly, keening, cry.

"Is that your dog?" Nathan asked.

The woman narrowed her eyes to two slits and stared up at him with undisguised hatred.

"We didn't hurt him," Nathan said. "He was dead when we got here." He nodded toward the trapdoor. "We found him sprawled over the door." He looked down at the creature. When a tear trickled out of the corner of her eyes, leaving a smeared trail through the dirt on her temple, he felt the first glimmer of something besides revulsion. She lay quietly, looking at the lifeless white form stretched across the doorway. "He must have been protecting you," Nathan said. "He must have died standing over that trapdoor."

"I'll be," Dorsey said. "You really think that's what happened?"

"It's the only explanation for why they didn't find her. He was so big, they didn't notice the trapdoor. And he took a good chunk out of one of them. They got their revenge by killing him. But they never knew about the hiding place."

"How long you think she's been down there?" Dorsey asked.

Nathan looked down at the woman, who was still staring at the dog. "If I let you up, will you behave?" When she didn't look at him, he shifted his weight. Pinning her arm down with his knee, he reached for her face. The minute he touched her jaw to make her look at him, she bared her teeth and bit down. Hard.

"Hey!" Nathan yelped and slapped her cheek. She let go, and Nathan felt his cheeks blush with shame for hitting a woman — albeit a savage one. "I told you we aren't going to hurt you," he repeated. "But if you're going to fight, I'm going to have Corporal Dorsey bring in some rope, and we'll tie you up so you can't move."

"No!" The woman squealed and began to struggle again. "No!"

"So," Nathan looked down at her. "You do understand what I'm saying?" He could feel her beginning to tremble. Her breath came in short gasps. More tears spilled out. A clap of thunder sounded.

Dorsey moaned. "Now I know why my knees have been giving me such fits. All right with you, Sergeant, if I go back out and try to get the digging done before we got to mess with a mudhole?"

Nathan nodded. "I'll be out directly."

Dorsey chuckled, "Don't count on it, Sergeant, sir," and hobbled outside.

Nathan looked down at the woman. "Your husband didn't make it, ma'am. I assume he's your husband?" The woman snorted and snatched her head to the side again.

"Children," Nathan said. "Did you have children? Did the Indians take them?"

She shook her head from side to side. Nathan relaxed a little. She seemed young, he thought, although it was hard to tell through the layers of dirt. He wondered what creatures had taken up residence in the nasty snarl of her hair. He couldn't even tell what color it was. She was thin. More than thin. Half-starved, really. He wondered how such a scrawny little thing could contain the staying power to struggle against him. Looking down, he noticed bruises encircling both her arms. His eyes traveled up to her face. He should have known she wasn't Cheyenne. Her eyes weren't brown. It was hard to tell in the dim light inside the soddy, but they were some light shade of something.

Nathan swallowed hard. He looked back down at the purple splotches on her arms. "Listen," he said firmly, "I'm going to get up in a minute. There's a storm coming in, and we've got to get your husband — or whoever that is up on the hill behind the soddy — buried. We'll bury the dog too. And then we're heading to Camp Robinson. You ever been there? It's about a day's ride from here." He didn't expect a response, but he kept talking, hoping that something in his voice would calm her down. He didn't want to have to tie her up. "We'll take you with us. If you've got family anywhere, we can send word. You'll be safe." He looked at the dog again. When he glanced back down at the woman she lifted her chin. A shudder passed through her entire body.

"I'm sorry about your dog," Nathan said, and as quickly as he had pinned her to the ground, he stood up, ready to pounce again should the need arise.

This time she didn't fight. Instead, she rolled onto her side and scrabbled across the floor to the still, white form of the gigantic dog. She bent low, caressing the massive head, crooning softly.

"I'm going to help Corporal Dorsey finish digging the grave," Nathan said. Stepping over the dog, he went outside.

The sky was an ugly yellow-gray. Far in the distance, lightning flashed, an occasional bolt of it stretching toward the earth. Before he headed up the hill Nathan looked back through the doorway. The woman had pulled the dog's massive head into her lap and was sitting stroking the broad place between the floppy ears, rocking back and forth with her eyes closed, tears streaming down her face.

"I'll bring him down," he said to Dorsey, who was standing in a waist-high trench digging furiously. Pulling the red kerchief up over his nose again, Nathan headed up the embankment.

The woman was quiet when Nathan approached later. He cleared his throat. "I'll take him now, ma'am," he said, and bent down to grab the dog's front legs.

"No!" she screeched, batting his hand away. "Mine!" She stood up and began to drag the carcass toward the dugout door, panting and staggering with the effort.

"Please, ma'am," Nathan said, still reaching for the dog. "Let me help."

But she would have none of it. She screamed *no* again and flailed so wildly at him with her thin arms that he backed away. "All right. All right. You do it, then. But hurry up. That storm's headed this way."

Nathan retreated to stand beside Dorsey and watch as the frantic little woman pulled her dog across the earth, leaving a broad place swept clean in the dust. She paused at the grave and looked over the edge at the scalped, arrow-ridden body. She got down on her hands and knees.

Nathan had just opened his mouth to express sympathy when the woman leaned forward and spat on the body. She picked up a clod of dirt and hurled it at the scalped skull, smiling when it hit its mark. Dusting her hands off, she pushed the dog over the edge of the grave where he landed with a thud atop the man. Then she sat back and hid her face against her bent knees.

Nathan stepped forward and put his hand on her shoulder. She spun away from him, grabbed the shovel that lay beside the grave, and wielding it like a weapon, backed away from the two soldiers.

"I need that shovel to finish this," Nathan said quietly, pointing to the grave.

"All due respect, sir," Dorsey said in a low voice, "I think the two of us can take her."

The woman looked at Dorsey and backed away again. She lifted her upper lip in derision. "Try it," she said, and raised the shovel higher.

Nathan took his hat off and ran his hand through his long dark hair. "Now listen here, ma'am," he said. "We don't mean you any harm." He nodded toward the grave. "I understand why you might think different, but we're just two soldiers hoping to get back to Camp Robinson as soon as possible. We've spent nearly a week tracking the Cheyenne that visited you. I'm sorry we didn't get here in time to stop what happened, but the fact is, we didn't have any idea there was a white settler within two days' ride of here. So we're just as confused about all this as you are. And we need to get back to camp and file our report so the captain can decide what to do next."

26

The woman lowered the shovel slightly, but she didn't budge.

They stood for what seemed like a quarter of an hour, taking measure of one another. Finally, Nathan broke the silence. "I'll tell you what," he said. "You take the shovel and head for the dugout. Go on inside."

"We need that shovel," Dorsey protested.

Nathan ignored him and continued talking to the woman. "We'll fill in the grave by hand. Maybe by then you'll see your way to trusting us enough to let us take you back to Camp Robinson with us."

The woman seemed to be wavering. At least she was lowering the shovel a little more. "There's other women at Camp Robinson. You can stay with Granny Max. She has her own quarters on Soapsuds Row. She'll see to it you get a good meal. Granny took care of me last winter when I was sick. You'll like her. You can stay with her until you decide what to do next."

Another clap of thunder sounded. Dorsey nodded his head toward the approaching storm clouds. "You got to let us get this grave filled in, ma'am."

Cautiously, the woman backed away. She sidled around the edge of the grave, her bare feet soundless in the dust. Clutching the shovel to herself, she ran for the dugout and disappeared inside.

Corporal Emmett Dorsey and Sergeant Nathan Boone knelt in the dirt and filled in the grave as best they could, using a half-rotten plank to scrape the earth atop the bodies. They worked feverishly, but the downpour began before they could get to the dugout, and by the time they stepped across the threshold and out of the rain, their blue wool pants were smeared with filth. Just inside they saw the woman perched on the bed. At the sight of them, she plastered her back against the wall and brandished the shovel at them.

A clap of thunder and a bolt of lightning made them all jump. Rivulets of water began to run through the door.

"I'm gonna bring the horses closer," Dorsey said. "Maybe we can rig up our India rubber to keep some of the rain away from the door and the window."

"Good idea," Nathan said. He nodded toward the makeshift cupboard. "I'll pull those crates apart. Maybe we can get a fire going in the stove."

Dorsey's stomach rumbled. "I'll cook." He nodded toward the rattlesnake before stepping into the downpour.

Both men busied themselves with their self-assigned duties. Before long, the horses were unsaddled and huddled against the front wall of the soddy, their rumps hunched against the furious storm. Nathan took matches from his bedroll and lighted the oil lamp he'd found on the floor, then started breaking up the empty crates. In a few minutes he had a fire going in the stove.

Dorsey found a way to hang their rubber ground cloths across the door and the window by cramming rocks along the top and sides, forcing the edges of the rubber into the cracks between the sod bricks and then holding them in place with more rocks.

Finally Dorsey began to dig out their rations. He skinned the rattlesnake and chopped it up, then set about frying the pieces in the small tin skillet from his field kit. While Dorsey cooked, Nathan pondered the cellar beneath the soddy. He looked at the woman. "If I come over there to check the cache down below, are you going to brain me with that shovel?"

She shrugged and shuttled to the opposite end of the bed as he reached for the oil lamp, and watched him descend into the hole.

Nathan whistled in surprise as he ran the lamp along the cellar walls. He studied the impressive assortment of traps hung above tall piles of cured hides. *Whoever we buried was a trapper. A good one.*

Then he saw a moth-eaten tick and a tattered quilt tucked back in a corner. When he picked up the quilt, half a dozen field mice scurried across the floor and disappeared beneath the furs. The putrid contents of a rusty bucket told the rest of the story. Nathan looked up at the opening. She'd had to live in this hole. At least part of the time. No wonder she'd spat into that grave.

"You all right?" Dorsey called.

Nathan climbed up the ladder. He avoided the woman's gaze.

Dorsey was chewing on a piece of fried snake. "What about you?" he asked, offering Nathan a piece.

Nathan glanced back at the hole and then at the woman. "I'm not hungry," he said. He grabbed a piece of fried rattler and held it up. Looking at the woman, he said gently, "You must be hungry, though. I'll just set this beside you. I won't touch you. I promise." Gingerly, he stepped toward the bed and tossed the meat so it landed next to her. Resting the shovel across her lap, and still gripping it firmly with her right hand as she watched Nathan, she snatched up the food and popped it into her mouth. Nathan retrieved his canteen. "Think I'll fill this up. Check on the horses."

"In this storm?" Dorsey's mouth was so full, Nathan could hardly tell what he said.

"A little spring rain never did a man any harm." Nathan worked the rubber sheet loose along one side and stepped outside. The first blast of rain shocked his system, but he resisted the urge to hustle back inside. Instead, he clomped through the mud to the well. He pulled up a bucket of water and wasn't surprised when he set it down and a small snake slithered out. As the storm raged, he took off his hat and lifted his face to the skies.

"She's gonna' fall over," Dorsey whispered.

Sitting next to him on the damp dirt floor, Nathan nodded agreement. Opposite them, still perched on the wooden ledge that had once been the trapper's bed, the woman was beginning to fade. Weariness showed in her slumped shoulders. Her eyelids drooped and her chin dipped slightly. Just when Nathan thought she might give in to sleep, a clump of mud crashed to the floor right beside him. The woman started awake and clutched the shovel with renewed determination, suspicion burning in her pale eyes. Rain began to fall in through the hole in the roof. A similar leak had sprung near the wooden ledge.

Dorsey took his turn inspecting the cache beneath the trapdoor. When he came back up the ladder into the pale lamplight, he settled next to Nathan to wait the woman out. He didn't mention overpowering her again.

As time wore on and she gave no sign of relaxing, Dorsey spoke up. "I don't blame you for not wanting to trust us, ma'am. But you got to be mighty tired. Now I'm just gonna spread my bedroll out over here." While he talked he was moving slowly, reaching for his saddle, untying his pack.

As she watched Dorsey's movements, the woman's knuckles grew white around the shovel handle. A leak had sprung above her head. Water was seeping down the sod wall, wetting the earth behind her. She inched forward to get away from it.

"You got to be mighty tired, ma'am." Slowly, he was stretching himself out on his blanket. "We've got a long ride ahead of us tomorrow."

Finally, Nathan decided to follow Dorsey's lead. The leaking roof was quickly turning their shelter to mud. With nowhere dry to unroll his blanket, Nathan tipped his campaign hat forward and leaned against the wall. He had just nodded off when a soft thud sounded across the room. The woman was slumped over on her side, finally asleep, one hand still holding on to the shovel handle.

The India-rubber ground cloth Dorsey had put over the door had blown down. Nathan looked up at the sky. The clouds were beginning to roll off to the east. Without bothering to pick up the sheet of rubber, he grabbed his army blanket and crossed the room toward the bed. When he tried to position her more comfortably, the woman stiffened and cried out, but she never fully awakened. Nathan took the shovel out of her hand and covered her with his blanket before setting the shovel outside the door. He put a couple more pieces of the crates on the fire in the stove before dragging the damp rubber sheet away from the door and, using his saddle for a pillow, stretched out and fell asleep to the sound of mud sliding down the walls around them.

What woke him, he didn't really know. But in the manner of soldiers, one minute Nathan was fast asleep and the next he was sitting bolt upright, the hair on the back of his neck standing up while he held his breath and listened. It had stopped raining and the moon was out. He saw a shadow fall across the threshold.

Crouching down, he moved to the window. *Breathe. Steady. Breathe. Think. Cheyenne? After the horses?* He listened to the footsteps just outside. Only one set. *Please only one.* He chastised himself for sending the rest of Company G back to camp. And for lingering. They should have subdued the woman and headed back to Camp Robinson in the rain. He rubbed his forehead. His childhood penchant for trying to gentle wild things had made him the butt of jokes in school and had caused no end of trouble with his parents as he brought home a steady stream of wounded things. Now it just might get him and Dorsey killed.

He reached for his gun. The holster was empty. So was the wooden ledge. Inhaling sharply, he inched his way to the door. The grass still clinging to the sod bricks brushed against his cheek as he peeked outside.

She was there, her back to the dugout, standing in the moonlight alongside the freshly dug grave, swaying from side to side. *Singing.* Nathan could barely hear it. Almost didn't. He turned his head to listen more carefully and relaxed a little. *She's saying farewell to the dog.* As he watched, she raised her hand. He saw his gun. She pointed it at her temple.

Nathan launched himself out the door and was nearly at her side when she pulled the trigger.

Two

As we have therefore opportunity, let us do good unto all men.

Galatians 6:10

Nathan soared through the night air, strangely removed from everything, blinded by the flash of light and dazed by the roar of a gun going off next to his ear. His left shoulder slammed hard into the mud atop the freshly dug grave and his neck snapped to one side, sending a hot burst of pain across his shoulder and down into his arm. He yelped and reached for his shoulder, but instantly forgot about it at the sight of the crumpled form beside him. In the moonlight he could see the hair on the left side of the woman's head smoking. Pushing himself to his knees, Nathan brushed his hand across the place where the hair was singed, grunting in dismay when a handful of it came away from her head. He brushed his hand clean against his thigh and turned her over. Nauseated by the sight before him, Nathan closed his eyes against the blood. He inhaled sharply at the scent of burned flesh and hair.

"What in — ?" Dorsey was limping toward him.

Nathan put his palm against his left ear in a vain attempt to still the roar. "Shot herself," he muttered.

"Shot herself? How?" Dorsey leaned over to get a better look.

"My gun." Nathan winced, newly aware of the burning pain in his left shoulder.

Dorsey grunted softly. Nathan sat staring at the soiled yellow dress blazing bright in the full moonlight.

"Probably for the best," Dorsey finally said. "Wasn't much woman left anyway." He paused, then said, "We'll need another grave. I'll get the shovel and get to the digging."

She moaned. At first, Nathan thought it was some animal far off across the prairie. Maybe up on the bluffs in the distance. He leaned over her face. He could feel her breath against his cheek. Oblivious to the pain in his neck and shoulder, he gathered her in his arms and leaped up. "Dorsey!

She's alive," he called hoarsely, running for the dugout. "Get that lamp!" He rushed inside, stretched her out on the shelf-bed and turned her head to one side, his heart pounding.

Dorsey brought the lamp and held it close. What the golden light revealed sickened both men.

"Better off if she had died," Dorsey whispered hoarsely.

"Don't say that," Nathan snapped. He reached for the lamp. "Get water."

Dorsey protested. "What for? Nothing can fix that. Even if we had her back at camp, Doc Valentine himself wouldn't know what to do. You can't even see her face under all that blood, son. Maybe she don't even *have* a face anymore."

Nathan set the lamp down to keep Dorsey from seeing how his hands were shaking. "We've got to try."

Muttering to himself, Dorsey headed outside. "All the water in the world can't fix that."

Staring down at the unconscious woman, Nathan was tempted to pray. *If Granny Max were here, she'd pray.* But the last time he'd been desperate enough to pray about something, it hadn't done any good. He looked around the soddy trying

38

to figure what Granny Max might do with such a fearful wound. *She'd pray first.* Swearing under his breath, Nathan descended into the cache and dragged the feather tick up the ladder behind him. Dorsey came in with a bucket of water.

"How can a person bleed like this and still be alive?" Nathan asked. He ripped a strip of cloth off the end of the feather tick.

"Look up," Dorsey said.

"I'm not a praying man anymore," Nathan said.

"And I never was," Dorsey said. "Look up at the crossbeam. See all those cobwebs? My mama used to say there's something in cobwebs that makes the blood flow stop. It's worth a try."

Nathan stepped up on the bed. Positioning one foot on either side of the unconscious woman, he swiped at the ceiling, collecting a gray mass of sticky cobwebs around his hand. Shuddering at the feel of the silk collecting on his fingers, he climbed down.

While Dorsey tore off more strips of fabric and soaked them in the bucket, Nathan lifted the woman's singed hair away from the wound. He dipped the tin cup from his field kit in the bucket and used it to flood the wound with water. Finally he spread the cobwebs on another strip of fabric and lay it atop the wound, pressing down. The woman groaned, but she didn't resist. For a while, the only sound in the dugout was ripping cloth as Dorsey tore the old feather tick apart.

"All right," Dorsey finally said. "Let's see it now."

Nathan pulled his hand away and lifted the bandage. At sight of the woman's skull showing inside the wide gash running the entire breadth of her head, he almost gagged. He looked at Dorsey. "More water?"

Dorsey shook his head. "There's nothing else we can do but wrap her up and head for camp."

Nathan nodded. He felt dizzy, and his hearing still wasn't right. His shoulder and neck burned with a tingling kind of pain he'd never felt before. He wondered if the flash of light from the gun had impaired his vision too. Surely no one could live through something like this. *God, help her.* Maybe God would listen if he wasn't asking for himself.

Dorsey brought in another bucket of fresh water before hoisting a saddle over his shoulder and heading outside to ready the horses for the ride back to camp. With a trembling hand, Nathan lifted the bandage one last time. Maybe the cobwebs were working. There wasn't so much blood now. Rinsing another strip of cloth in the bucket of fresh water, he wiped her face and realized she was quite young. Considering the life she'd led, she might not even be as old as she looked. It was hard to tell. He unbuttoned the cuffs of her tattered dress and rolled them up, then swiped at her arms with another damp strip of cloth. Her hands were crusted with dried mud. He couldn't do anything about the dried blood and filth beneath her broken nails.

"Horses are saddled. I gave 'em the last of the grain." Dorsey's voice sounded from the door. "It's near sunrise."

Nathan stood up.

"Get yerself a piece of hardtack once we get outside," Dorsey said. "It's a natural thing to feel it in your gut when you seen something like that, son. Nothin' to be ashamed of. It'll ease a bit if you chew on something."

Nathan nodded, wishing he could get a long-ago ill-fated ride with an injured woman in his arms out of his mind. "The ride will probably kill her long before we get back to camp."

"Likely," Dorsey said. He shrugged. "But you were right. We got to try."

Together they wrapped strip after strip of cloth around the woman's head. Her breathing was shallow, but regular. Nathan cradled her in his arms and together the men headed outside.

Dorsey mounted his horse. "Hand her up," he said. "Give your shoulder a while to loosen up. Besides, there's no need for you to put up with that stink all the way back to camp."

Nathan lifted the woman up, and Dorsey positioned her across his lap, her head resting against his chest. "Not much to her, is there?" Without waiting for a response, Dorsey urged his dun gelding forward.

Three

If a man have an hundred sheep, and one of them be gone astray, doth he not leave the ninety and nine, and goeth into the mountains, and seeketh that which is gone astray? . . . Even so it is not the will of your Father which is in heaven, that one of these little ones should perish.

Matthew 18:12, 14

By the time Nathan and Corporal Dorsey descended the steep pine-covered ridges looming over Camp Robinson and headed down into the broad valley below, Nathan was convinced God had once again ignored him. Not that he and God were exactly on speaking terms. But over the past few hours he *had* taken the opportunity to fling a word or two heavenward on behalf of the woman. Without any discernible result.

43

He and Dorsey had passed her back and forth several times during the daylong ride, and she'd never stirred. For a creature who had fought so savagely to stay as far away as possible from a man's touch, Nathan thought that was a bad sign. Something inside him felt sick. He scolded himself. *She's not Lily with a rattlesnake bite. She's a crazy woman. Don't forget she nearly blew your head off, too. And you're not some mountain boy saving wounded birds and orphaned calves anymore. You're a sergeant in the United States Army. So just do your duty, and don't get involved personally.*

"All due respect, sir," Dorsey said, riding closer to Nathan. "I'm thinking you might ride west around camp and just take her on down to your Granny Max." He reached inside his shirt and withdrew a leather pouch, inserting a wad of tobacco between his cheek and gum before adding, "No reason to make a spectacle of her to the whole camp."

Nathan turned his head to look at the weather-beaten old man. "You'd better watch it, Dorsey. I'll be thinking there's a gentleman hiding somewhere under that scruffy beard."

In response, Dorsey snorted and spat a

long stream of tobacco between the ears of his horse.

"Duly noted, Corporal," Nathan said. "Good idea, though. I'll take her straight over."

"And I'll get Doc Valentine." Dorsey kicked his horse into a lope, heading south in a line that would take him between the now-deserted Red Cloud Agency to the east and Camp Robinson about a mile and a half to the west.

Taps was being played as Nathan rode along the back side of the row of adobe officers' quarters bordering one side of the square military parade ground. In the still night air he could hear someone strumming a guitar. Charlotte Valentine's strident soprano voice pierced the night air. Hoping he hadn't been seen, Nathan continued around the back of the post trader's log store and the hospital and headed south toward the long line of attached two-room apartments everyone called Soapsuds Row.

Granny Max had just lit her oil lamp and settled into her rocking chair when Nathan's characteristic *rap-rap-kick* sounded at her back door. Laying her Bible aside, Granny hefted her ample frame out of the rocker and hurried through the doorway separating the living area and kitchen from her bedroom.

"Hey, boy, what you doin' scarin' ol' Granny thataway?" she teased as she undid the latch and threw open the back door. Her boy was there all right, and an unconscious woman with her head swathed in bandages lay limp in his arms.

"Dorsey's bringing Doc Valentine," Nathan said, sweeping past Granny into the room. "We were on patrol up on Hat Creek," he explained. "Stumbled on a dugout. Thought it was deserted —"

Granny held up her hand as she peered down at the unconscious woman Nathan had just dumped on her bed. "I need water. Lots of clean water. That downpour last night likely filled the rain barrel out back. I left a bucket by the stove. And stir up the fire." While Granny examined the unconscious woman, Nathan hurried to collect firewood from the stack beside her back door.

By the time Doctor Valentine arrived, Nathan had water heating on the stove and two buckets of fresh water beside the bed. Granny had torn two clean muslin dishcloths into strips. She held the kerosene lamp high while the doctor unwrapped the bandages and examined the wound. Glancing over the doctor's shoulder, Granny caught her breath. When she looked at Nathan, he answered the unspoken question in her amber-colored eyes.

"A bullet deflected off her skull. At least I think it deflected."

Doctor Valentine nodded. "There's no bullet. It's a clean wound."

"We did what we could."

"You did well, Sergeant," the doctor said while he worked. "The bleeding's controlled, too. That's good."

Nathan shrugged. "Dorsey thought I was crazy pouring water everywhere."

"And they thought I was crazy after Bull Run when I insisted on washing my hands between amputations." He finished examining the wound and reached for something in his bag before adding, "But at the end of the day fewer of my patients got gangrene. You can't tell me cleanliness doesn't have anything to do with patient recovery. I can't prove a connection between washing and infection. But I'm convinced somebody will someday."

"Do you think she'll live?" Nathan asked.

The doctor sighed. "It's hard to say. The

gunpowder burned the edges of the wound. I doubt stitches will hold, but I'm going to try. She'll have less of a scar if I can just get it held together a little." Talking more to himself than to Nathan or Granny, he murmured. "It isn't going to be pretty, though. At least she's got plenty of hair. Maybe she'll be able to hide most of it." He looked over his shoulder at Granny Max. "You sure you want to take this on?"

"I never turn away a lamb the Lord brings to my door," Granny said.

The doctor nodded. For the next half hour he worked, doing his best to minimize the damage to the woman's head. As he left he said, "There's nothing more I can do. I'll be back after sick call in the morning. If anything changes before then, you send for me."

As soon as he was gone, Granny sprang to action. "Poor thing. Look at those tattered clothes." She wrinkled her nose. "Whew. She sure needs a bath." She waved toward the front of the little apartment. "Warm me up some more water, Nathan. There's a piece of fried chicken beneath the towel covering that blue crock if you're hungry. Corn bread, too."

"Don't worry about me, Granny. You've got enough to do."

"I'm not worried."

Nathan rubbed his growling stomach. "All right. As soon as I get Whiskey bedded down I'll head back this way." He hesitated at the door and called back over his shoulder, "I'll . . . um . . . get something out of Lily's trunk for her."

Granny's voice was gentle. "That would be kind of you, Nathan."

The woman on the bed moaned softly. Granny laid a huge brown hand across her forehead. No fever. At least infection hadn't set in.

Granny heard Nathan whistle, followed by a soft nicker and the creak of leather as Whiskey came to his master. She smiled. The boy always had been good with animals. She remembered Lily retelling the story she'd heard from Nathan's mother about him carrying a one-legged rooster to school every day for a week, insisting it would learn to get along, just like the three-legged dog on a neighboring farm. He'd cried when the rooster died and conducted quite a funeral behind his father's barn.

Granny looked down at the unconscious woman. Nathan hadn't let his gentle side show in a long time. It was good to see he hadn't lost it.

"My name is Clara Maxwell," Granny said, as if the woman could hear. "Everyone calls me Granny Max. I'm going to take good care of you, you hear me? So you rest easy, little gal. Now we are going to get you cleaned up. Nathan's going to bring you some of poor Lily's things. Lily was Nathan's wife. She's gone now. Been gone two years, Lord rest her soul. Nathan hasn't touched her things in all that time. It's bothered me, him not seeming to be able to let go of Lily's things. Guess now I know why. At least part of it. The good Lord knew we'd be needing them for *you*."

Granny wrung a cloth out and began to clean the woman's face. She lifted her head from the pillow and in one motion swept her long hair up off her neck and across the pillow. "I'm going to need daylight to deal with all that hair of yours." Granny paused. "No, I won't cut it. Not unless I have to. The Good Book says that a woman's hair is her adorning beauty. You've sure got a mess of it, lamb. I'll do my best with it."

Nathan came in with a bowl and the coffeepot. He set the bowl on the bedside table and filled it with water, then set the warm pot on the floor. "You're going to need more than one bowl of water," he said. "I don't think I'll eat just now, Granny. But I'll be back directly. You'll be all right?" He was already heading for the door.

"I'll be fine."

He paused at the door to look back. "Lily wouldn't mind my bringing you some of her things. Would she?"

"Of course not," Granny said. "Lily had a generous heart."

"Well" — he tugged on the brim of his campaign hat — "I'm going to report in now. I'll be back as soon as I can." He cleared his throat. "And I'll make myself some coffee if I need anything. Don't worry about me. Just take care of her."

Granny nodded and turned her attention to her patient. She made short work of removing the yellow calico, cutting it away with a few snips of her scissors. "Now, I know the good doctor would think I am an old fool, to be talking to you this way. But the fact is, those doctors don't know everything. And I am thinking that somewhere past your mind is your soul, and what the mind don't hear, maybe the soul does. So I'll just be talking to you while we are getting you cleaned up. I don't know where you've been or what all happened, but —" Granny paused when she pulled a sleeve away. Even in the dim lamplight she could see bruises. On closer inspection, she saw the scars encircling the woman's wrists. She blinked away tears and laid her hand on the woman's shoulder as she whispered, "Lord bless you, child. What you been through?"

Gently, she washed the woman's body, turning her first to one side, then the other, occasionally laying her broad hands over a bruise or a scar and pausing to pray. By the time she had finished washing the woman and covered her with a soft quilt, Granny was trembling with emotion. She perched on the edge of the bed and stared down at the pale face, the dark shadows beneath the eyes. *Poor little lamb. You can't be even twenty years old. Where you been?*

The lamp burned low. Granny got up. She gathered the woman's tattered clothes in a ball and hurled them out the back door. For a few moments, she let the warm night air blow in, grateful when it cleared out the last traces of the stench of un-washed body and dried blood.

Nathan sat on the edge of his bed in the dark, facing the corner where his dead wife's trunk had sat for the better part of two years. His hand trembled as he reached up, took a chain from around his neck, and ran his index finger along the contours of the key he'd worn since the day he'd returned from Lily's graveside and stowed all her belongings in the depths of the trunk.

Stoic before the men of Camp Robinson at Lily's funeral, he'd wept freely once inside the two-room apartment they had occupied together. He'd fallen to his knees beside that trunk and buried his face in the folds of Lily's blue silk ball gown and soaked it with his tears. Remembering, he inhaled sharply. The pain was still there. Two years, and the pain was still there, sharp enough at times to literally take his breath away.

The last thing he wanted to do was open that trunk and face the memories stored inside. He looked at the wall opposite his bed and envisioned the still form of the wounded woman lying next door in Granny Max's bed. Granny was right. Lily had a kind heart. She would want him to do this.

He could almost hear her gentle voice. *"Sweetheart. Remember that linen nightgown Granny edged with lace? That's just the thing. A lady likes to feel pretty, even when she is slumbering. Why, I bet that poor darling has never had a lace-trimmed nightgown in her life. You give her whatever she needs."*

While he listened to Lily's imaginary urgings in his head, Nathan slid to the floor and half crawled across to the trunk. He put the key in the lock and turned it. Opening the lid with trembling hands, he pulled the top tray out and set it on the floor, grunting aloud in an attempt to control his emotions at the sight of the blue ball gown. Memories swirled through his mind of balls and receptions where Miss Lily Bainbridge was the most sought after dance partner. And then the best memory of all came, sweet in spite of the pain it induced, of the evening Lily crossed a Nashville ballroom to lay her small white hand on his arm and tell a lie.

"I believe you are next on my dance card, Private."

He'd wanted to put his name on her card. Oh, how he'd wanted to. But he'd hesitated, telling himself that the belle of Nashville could not possibly have any interest in a greenhorn private from the backwoods of Missouri. He'd proven the adage about hesitating and being lost, for Lily Bainbridge's dance card always filled quickly, and by the time Private Boone summoned courage to add his name, the opportunity was lost. Except it really wasn't. Lily lied and got her dance. Eventually, she got an adoring husband with a promising military career.

Kneeling, Nathan reached for the blue ball gown. He had memorized the contents of the trunk. He knew the red one lay next, followed by three calico everyday dresses, first gray, then pink, then a green one that made Lily's skin look even paler unless she softened it with a lace collar. He knew every fold, every ruffle, every button of each garment stored here. His heart pounding, he lifted the blue ball gown to his face and inhaled. Tears sprung to his eyes. It didn't smell like Lily anymore. Only two years, and the essence of Lily Bainbridge had vanished.

Gripping the edge of the trunk, Nathan reminded himself, *Breathe. Steady. Breathe.* Feeling calmer, he sorted the trunk's contents, setting aside two nightgowns, the gray calico dress, and a pair of slippers. These he stacked on his bed, then returned to the trunk and blushed as he collected a sampling of undergarments.

Satisfied that he had enough, even if the woman survived a week, which he doubted she would, he returned the top tray to the trunk. Lily's Bible caught his eye. He picked it up, remembering the many Sundays she had lamented the lack of proper church services here at Camp Robinson. In the absence of a regular army chaplain, she and Granny Max had conducted their own makeshift service. But Lily's deep faith longed for more. He opened the Bible and leafed through it briefly before tossing it back into the tray.

The Bible had no more than landed in the tray than he heard Lily's voice. *"Don't let your sorrows come between you and the Lord, darlin'."* She hadn't lived long enough to say much. She'd been in so much pain. But she'd known exactly how he would react to losing her.

"Oh, Lily." Nathan groaned aloud.

A few minutes later, when he finally closed the lid and locked the trunk, Nathan had managed to regain his composure.

By the time she heard Nathan's approaching footsteps, Granny had emptied two bowls of filthy water and rinsed out her washcloths.

"Lord bless you, Nathan," she whispered as she accepted the pile of clean clothing and set them on the stand beside her bed. It was almost midnight and she was weary, but Granny knew that after going through Lily's trunk, Nathan might need some comforting. "Why don't you make us some good strong coffee while I get her into a fresh nightgown."

When Granny finished dressing her patient, Nathan was already sitting out on the front porch, coffee cup in hand. A second cup of coffee sat on a chair. Granny cupped her massive hands around its warmth and sighed with pleasure as she sipped the strong, dark liquid.

"I'm sorry to burden you, Granny," Nathan said. "I didn't know what else to do. I know Doctor Valentine's authorized to take female patients up at the hospital, but . . . well . . . Mrs. Valentine is prone to gossip and I —"

"There is no need to apologize, Nathan," Granny replied. "As I told Dr. Valentine, I would never turn away one of God's lambs from my door."

Nathan leaned forward and let the front legs of the chair drop to the porch. "When I was a boy, there was a woman we called Crazy Jane. Folks in the hills didn't lock that kind of person up the way the city folks do now. Jane's family did their best, but they just couldn't keep her home. They tried just about everything short of tying her down. She always got away. It got to where people set out food on their porches, and Crazy Jane came in the night and ate. Just like a possum.

"I caught a glimpse of her once. She was staring at me from a perch high up in a pine tree. Scared me half to death. Her eyes glittered in the moonlight. When she started laughing I hightailed it home, and it was a week before I would go past the edge of our farmyard." He took another swallow of coffee. "I was just a boy, but I knew then no one should have to live like that."

"That would be a terrible thing," Granny agreed.

"Crazy Jane's family said she was a real bright little girl until she got scratched by some animal and came down with a sickness and a high fever."

"Well, the little gal inside doesn't have a fever," Granny Max said. "And we have Doctor Valentine. I don't think it will be like it was for Crazy Jane."

Nathan stood up. "I hope you're right. I'm going to rouse the quartermaster and get you a cot. I'll be back before long. And don't worry about the company laundry. I'll send someone over to help you."

"Becky O'Malley will help," Granny offered.

"I've got at least a half dozen men complaining about how boring their lives are. They can help, too." He stepped off the porch. "If it will help, I can sit up with her so you can maybe get some rest."

"There's no need for you to do that," Granny said.

"I'd like to," Nathan said. "I feel sort of . . . responsible."

"Well, you aren't responsible for what happens to her now, Nathan. You leave that to God and Granny Max — like the good doctor said."

"God doesn't have a very reliable record with me and mine," Nathan replied. He turned to go and was swallowed by the darkness before he had taken five steps.

Four

Behold, He taketh away, who can hinder Him? Who will say unto him, What doest thou?

Job 9:12

"I had a case something like this during the war." Doctor Valentine talked while he rewrapped the woman's head. It was so early in the morning that they needed lamplight. "I don't mean to worry you, but we must be realistic. She's been unconscious for two days. Her fever has stayed down. That's good. But . . ." He grunted as he finished the bandaging and stood upright. "Everything seemed to be going well with the other case, too. The wound was healing up clean as could be. Then the soldier went unconscious. His fever came up. Next came delirium." The doctor picked up his medical bag and headed toward the front room of

Granny's apartment. "That patient was dead in a few hours."

He set his medical bag on the table and sat down, accepting Granny's proffered cup of coffee. "I don't mean to frighten you, Granny. But the night Sergeant Boone brought her in, I remember him saying *'Nothing that comes to Granny Max ever dies.'* I don't want you to be hard on yourself if this doesn't work out as we all hope."

He sipped his coffee. "When that soldier died it haunted me. There was absolutely no sign of infection. I just couldn't understand it." He set his mug down. "So I did an autopsy. I've never seen anything like it, and I never hope to again. All the infection had gone inside. The poor man's brain was half mush." He swallowed and stared up at the ceiling for a minute before looking back at Granny. "The point of all this isn't to frighten you. It's just to say we never know. And that's the truth. So don't you be blaming yourself if this doesn't work out."

"Nathan was wrong to say that about me — about nothing dying that comes to me. The dear Lord has let me help with many of His lambs. But not every one I care for survives."

The doctor nodded. "Yes. I heard about

Mrs. Boone. Unfortunate. Very unfortunate. You do know, Granny, there was nothing anyone could have done to save her. From what I heard, she wasn't able to get to help for quite some time. The outcome would have been no different with or without a doctor here at the post. I understand the post surgeon had been called away?"

Granny nodded. "He was out on a detail, and they got caught up in a skirmish between some miners and Indians. And I know what you are saying is true. No one on this earth could have helped by the time we found her. It was too late for humans. I knew that the minute I saw her leg." Granny cleared her throat. "Of course, I was still hoping the Lord might look kindly upon the situation and cast a miracle toward Pine Ridge. Rattlesnakes got nothing over the good Lord. He could have healed Miss Lily."

The doctor nodded agreement. "From what I have heard, Mrs. Boone was a delightful young woman. A real lady." He grabbed his black leather bag and stood up, bowing to Granny. "And this young lady's in good hands, too, Granny Max." He saluted her before leaving.

After the doctor had gone, Granny ate a

piece of corn bread before rinsing out the coffee cups and returning them to the shelf that served as her combination china cupboard and pantry. Across Soldier Creek, trumpets sounded guard mount. Nathan would be assigning fatigue details. He'd promised her two soldiers to help with laundry this afternoon and said he would sit with the patient while she showed the men what to do. She pulled the laundry basket closer to the table and set aside three light blue shirts that needed mending. She'd have to hold them out of today's laundry if she didn't get them done.

Heading back into the other room, she touched the woman's forehead. She frowned, then dampened a cloth in the bucket Nathan had left by the bed. Folding the cloth, she bathed the woman's face. The woman began to mutter in her sleep. Her hands twitched. Once she tossed her head sideways, bumping her head against the wall. With a yelp that sounded half animal, she jerked away from the wall, then fell silent.

Granny carried her rocker in from the other room and positioned it beneath a small window where daylight would illuminate her mending.

We need a miracle, Lord. Doctor doesn't think this little gal has much chance of living. And if you are in the mind of doing miracles, could I just remind you, Lord, my boy Nathan is still drowning in an ocean of bitterness. I been prayin' 'bout him for two years now, Lord. And I will keep praying. Not trying to tell you how to do your job. Just reminding you like that widow woman that kept beating on the judge's door in the Good Book. You remember her, Lord. That's me, I guess. Old Granny Max beating on the Lord's door asking Him to open up and give her what she wants. It ain't for me so much Lord as it is for Lily. I just don't think she can rest easy knowing that man she loved is so miserable.

Pondering miracles made Granny think of her own past. She was, in many ways, something of a miracle herself. She had lived all her life on one plantation. While others were bought and sold, Granny had remained at Lily Bainbridge's side. When Lily married her soldier and headed west, Granny rode alongside her, marveling at the beauty of the vast wilderness sky, even while she dried her own and Lily's tears of homesickness.

Granny Max was confident she could make a home anywhere. She had encouraged Lily. *"Where two or three are gathered the Lord is there in the midst of them. He's right here with us. With you and me and your young man, too. We'll be all right."*

And they had been. For a while. Back then, Camp Robinson was nothing more than a collection of canvas tents on the windswept flats a mile north of the confluence of the White River and Soldier Creek. Lily was only the second white woman to live at the camp, and it was obvious early on that she didn't belong. She just didn't have the toughness for army life. Granny had suspected it. But she'd hoped that between her and Nathan and God, Lily would get healthier and tougher, and things would be all right. Certainly if love for a man could have brought it about, it would have happened. Lily Boone had loved her man. There was never any doubt about that. Even that morning they had had the fight and she stormed off toward Pine Ridge alone, Granny knew her anger was only because deep inside she was afraid she was disappointing Nathan.

Granny rocked and remembered, brought back to the moment by the realization that her patient's breathing had eased a bit. She dipped the cloth back into the cool water and laid it across the pale forehead. At her touch, the woman seemed to take a deep breath and settle a little. Granny sat back down. Soon the room was again filled with the rhythmic creaking of her rocking chair.

Five

*Do justice and righteousness, and
deliver the one who has been robbed
from the power of his oppressor....*

Jeremiah 22:3 NASB

What has he done to me this time? She lay
quietly, trying not to move. Sometimes, if
she didn't move for a while, he didn't notice
she was awake. Sometimes it helped. He left
her alone. She had made it a game, lying
still, breathing shallow, drawing in on herself
until she almost willed herself invisible.

He must have hit her again. Only harder
than usual. There was a constant roar between her and the wall, like a wind blowing
past her ear and drowning out all the other
sounds in the dugout. Her head pounded
so hard she could feel tears seeping from
beneath her eyelids. It wasn't the worst of
the pain she had felt since belonging to

him, but it was bad enough.

What has he done to me this time? She wasn't down in the hole. She could tell that just by inhaling. Usually, whenever he had been near her, the stench of him lingered. But all she could smell now was fresh straw. Still, she didn't dare open her eyes because she could sense a presence in the room. She kept her hand from rising to her head just in time, reminding herself not to move. For a moment or two she played the game, concentrating on breathing in time with the pounding inside her head. Inhaling, she envisioned herself placing her fingers on the keyboard at Miss Hart's Academy for Young Ladies and pressing down in perfect rhythm with her own clear, soprano voice. Here, in this place in the wilderness, she could still hear the music of her own breathing, let out in perfect rhythm with the pounding inside her head. She gave herself to the music of her pain and slipped back into unconsciousness.

The next time she woke, she went through the same ritual of shallow breathing and deliberate quiet. The roaring in her ears was less now, and she could hear a soft hissing. There must be green wood in the stove. That meant he wasn't far away. Her head still pounded, but now she was aware of a wide path of searing pain above her ear. Wondering what time of day it was, she relaxed her eyelids a little to let in just enough light to see the doorway beyond the foot of the bed. If it was dark outside, she would have to remain motionless for a long time, for he would be asleep someplace nearby. If daylight shown through the door, he might have gone out. She could try to do something about her head before he got back.

But the doorway beyond the foot of the bed led . . . into another room? And a small window. With . . . curtains? Her eyes flew open. Above her several strong crossbeams supported a roof. There were no cobwebs, no threatening bulges sagging down into the room from the layers of sod above. The scent of new hay and the softness beneath her raised new questions. If she was in a cabin with a window, lying on a mattress stuffed with fresh hay, then where was *he?*

Her mind raced back to the dugout. Slowly, in still-life frames, she began to remember. Cheyenne surrounding the dugout, her retreat to the cellar, the great white dog above her growling, and then . . . the awful sound as he yelped, the thump when he collapsed above her. Then silence and waiting, thirst and hunger, pushing her terror back, willing herself to wait. And then someone dragging the dog away, opening the trapdoor . . . making it impossible for her to do anything but attempt to defend herself.

She clamped her eyes shut and took inventory of her body. She could move her legs. One time he had knocked her into the cellar, and she'd sprained her ankle so badly she hadn't been able to do much more than hobble through the entire winter. Her muscles were sore, but she didn't think anything was really damaged. Without trying to give away her return to consciousness, she thought her way through each joint and each body part, taking stock. Her entire body hurt. Not until she tried to lift her head did she locate the reason she couldn't remember much. Raising her hand instinctively to the place that hurt most, she realized her head was swathed in strips of cloth.

They must have done this to her. Those men who dragged her out. Two soldiers. She thought hard. *Surely not only two.* There must have been more. Didn't they always travel in — companies? That was it.

They called them companies, and there were always several dozen of them. She'd seen them from a distance sometimes and wondered what they would have done if she'd run to them and begged them to help her get away. But she'd always been too afraid.

What else had they done . . . what else. . . ? Even in the dim light she could see that the door in the next room was barred shut. A barred door meant only one thing. He was here. Even if she could not smell him. If not him, those other two. They had her trapped again. They would be waiting for her to wake up.

Something moved across the room from where she lay. Instinctively, she drew her legs up and curled onto her right side. She tried to position her arm to protect her head, but she could not bear pressure above her ear. She lay in a ball, tense, eyes tightly closed, awaiting the first blow.

When a hand closed over her shoulder, she flinched and grunted in anticipation. He was going to use his bare hands. That meant the attack would end more quickly but that he planned to hurt her in a more personal way. She probably wouldn't have any more broken bones tonight. That was something. She could usually block the other out by going back to Miss Hart's in her mind. Or to the riverboat. Already she was halfway there, standing on the stage in a beautiful gown, smiling at the crowd of men and preparing to sing.

"You awake, child?" The voice was deep, but soft, almost feminine. The hand moved from her shoulder to her forearm, gently pressuring her to let down her guard.

She tensed and, in spite of herself, let out a word that sounded too much like a refusal. It was always worse for her when she did that. Her heart began to race.

"Don't be afraid, child. You are going to be all right. Granny Max is going to take good care of you."

Over the last few months, she had conjured up all kinds of memories to help her maintain some level of sanity. But she had never conjured a voice like this. Instinct made her draw away even as she opened her eyes to see what form the voice might take. The hand withdrew from her shoulder even as the voice repeated, "You are going to be all right, child. No one is going to hurt you."

She touched the spot above her ear.

"Yes. I know it must hurt. You were shot. But it only made a path through your beautiful hair. You'll have a scar, of course.

But it didn't hurt anything important. Do you understand, child? You don't have to be afraid anymore."

She pulled her fist down from above her ear and let it rest alongside her jaw so she could squint at the woman looming above her. Were it not for the thick braid dangling across one shoulder and the simple gray dress, she could have been a man. She had broad shoulders and a square jaw. In the dim light of the cabin, it was impossible to discern the features of her dark face. But her large amber eyes were warm with kindness.

"I'm going to get you some of my tea. It'll help with your headache. Make you sleepy, too. You'll heal better if you can rest. Right now that's what you need most. Sleep."

While she talked, the woman headed into the next room toward a small stove where a coffeepot sat, sending a faint trail of steam into the air. A small table beside the stove and a rocking chair in the corner were all the furnishings she could see in the other room. But then a man came into view. Her heart lurched. He was conversing with the Granny-woman in a voice so quiet she couldn't discern the words. While they talked, the old woman took a towel off a hook to use as a hot pad and poured a stream of steaming liquid into a tin mug. She set the mug down on the table momentarily. The man handed her a pillow, then went to the opposite side of the room and out of her sight.

When the large woman came back into the bedroom she was alone. The pillow was meant to help her sit up. She lifted her up and tucked the pillow beneath her shoulders. "I know. Makes you dizzy to sit up. You just take some tea. You've been unconscious for three days. You drink some tea, then go back to sleep. Rest is what you need."

It was drink or have the liquid poured down her front. She drank. As she had feared, the concoction made her even more dizzy. The woman's dark face blurred. She pushed the tea away. With a groan, she lay back down. Before the woman had crossed the cabin to set the half-empty mug of tea on the stove, she slipped away.

Sometime in the middle of the night, she woke again. Moonlight streamed in the window casting a four-paned shadow on the rough board floor. With a soft grunt, she managed to push herself upright. Slowly, she dropped her legs over the edge of the bed and sat up. A savage bolt of pain shot through her skull, and for a moment she thought she might pass out. She waited, concentrating on her breathing until it mellowed a little, then she stood up, weaving back and forth unsteadily.

Grateful when the woman sleeping on the cot against the opposite wall showed no signs of stirring, she crept across the few feet between her and the barred back door. Once she tripped on the hem of the muslin gown. She could feel sweat trickle between her shoulder blades with the exertion of walking. At the door, she leaned her forehead against the frame, grateful for the cool feel of the wood against her skin.

It took nearly all her strength to soundlessly wrestle the bar across the door, up and out of the iron cradle holding it in place. When she had it in her arms, she almost fell over, but she managed to lean it against the wall. Her hand closed over the rope pull. Trembling with weakness and fear, she pulled.

At the first sound of the creaking door, the woman on the cot snorted in her sleep. Her heart pounding, she yanked the door open and flung herself into the darkness beyond the cabin. She willed herself to run even as she realized she was too weak to go far. And then, just as the Granny-woman was calling out from the cabin door, someone grabbed her from behind and wrapped her up inside his arms so tightly she could feel the buttons on his jacket pressing into her through the thin cotton nightgown.

Everything was forgotten in the panic of being trapped in a man's arms. She began to shriek. Kicking and writhing, she spit at his face. She would have bit him, but her efforts to bite through the wool uniform were worthless. She had found a well of unbelievable determination somewhere inside, past the physical pain and the weariness, but it was being drained quickly, and the man holding her wasn't going to let go. He clamped a hand over her mouth.

"Stop," he said calmly. "You're going to wake up the whole camp. Or hurt yourself."

She twitched again and moaned softly, then bit down hard on her lower lip to keep from making another sound. It never went well when she let a man know how much he was hurting her, how much she hated it. She inhaled sharply and began to retreat from the moment, back to Miss Hart's and the music that somehow always got her through.

His grip didn't loosen one bit, even as she felt herself go limp in his arms, even as he picked her up, headed back inside the cabin and to the mattress where she had been sleeping. She wanted to turn her head away, but the wound above her ear was hurting again, so she closed her eyes and willed herself to listen to her own breathing while she waited.

"I can't believe she had the strength to try to run," he said while he reached to the foot of the bed and pulled a quilt over her tense form. She felt his hand brush across her hairline. He smelled faintly of pipe smoke. He must have been outside smoking when she tried to escape.

"I wish you would believe we aren't going to hurt you," he said as he tucked the quilt beneath her chin.

She opened her eyes. It was hard to tell details in the dim light of the lamp the Granny-woman had lit. She had the impression of a handsome face, but when he turned to look at the big woman, the lamp-light revealed four scratch marks along his jaw. That made her even more suspicious. He didn't smile. His eyes were little more than dark pools in the dim light.

"Whoever was keeping you at that dugout is dead. Do you remember that, miss?" He touched the back of one of her fingers just where she gripped the top of the quilt.

She snatched her hand away.

He took a step away from the bed. "My name is Boone. Sergeant Nathan Boone of Camp Robinson, Nebraska. Corporal Dorsey and I were on patrol when we found the dugout. We've brought you to Camp Robinson. Granny Max is going to take good care of you. Maybe you'll tell her your name."

The pounding in her head returned. She raised her hand to her head and squeezed her eyes shut to prevent tears from spilling over.

The man leaned down and put his hand across her forehead.

She flinched.

"She's got a fever." He sighed, then sat down.

She heard a rocker creak and opened her eyes. He had taken his hat off and was sitting in a rocking chair beside her. The lamplight he sat beneath proved her earlier impressions correct. Dark eyes, dark hair. Square jaw. Thick moustache. Handsome.

"We want to help you, miss. Do you understand that?" He leaned forward, resting his elbows on his knees, still holding his hat in his hands. "The man who hurt you is dead. It's over now. All you have to do is rest and get well. You can stay here with Granny Max. Doctor Valentine has been checking on you. When you're better, you can tell us how to let your family know you are all right. There's a telegraph."

She closed her eyes, wearied by his persistent kindness. She might be sick, but she wasn't stupid. She'd memorized her share of little sayings, just like the other girls at Miss Hart's. Things like "Do unto others as you would have them do unto you" and "Love one another." And then she had learned the truth. People did what they did to get what they wanted. And you could never trust a handsome man. Especially not one with fingernail tracks on his face.

The Granny-woman came in with another cup of tea. She didn't need it. Exhaustion closed her eyes once more.

"Yes. He told me the same thing this mornin'." Motioning for Nathan to follow suit, Granny Max picked up a kitchen chair, moved quietly through the back room, past the sleeping woman, and out the back door where she settled within earshot of her patient and within plain view of a glorious sunset. She sighed, and without turning to look at Nathan, said, "If she goes another couple days without a fever, she'll likely make it. I expect she won't even remember trying to run off."

Nathan sat down and leaned back, balancing against the wall, the front two legs of his chair up off the ground. When Granny opened her mouth to scold him, he dropped the chair back to the earth. "Yes, ma'am. 'Don't tip your chair.' " He turned the chair around and, straddling it, crossed his arms across the back and rested his chin on his forearms. "You're still worried about her."

"She has nightmares," Granny said.

"I don't wonder at that," Nathan said quietly. "Has she said anything? Anything at all?"

Granny sighed and shook her head. "She's stopped fighting me. She drinks my tea when I tell her to. She even ate a couple bites of grits this morning. But she's not talking. I almost wonder if she *can* talk. A whole lot more healing needs to go on inside that little gal than what Doctor Valentine can see on the outside of her head. But if she can't talk about it —"

"She can talk," Nathan said. He rubbed

the back of his neck and murmured, "She's been hurt — other ways besides just . . . what we can see."

"I know," Granny said quietly.

Taking the broad-brimmed campaign hat off his head, Nathan swiped his hand through his hair. He began to shape the crown of his hat while he talked. "It was just the usual patrol — wandering around in the hills and not finding much of anything. We'd already headed back for camp when Dorsey thought maybe he'd picked up a fresh trail. At first we didn't think it was much. Only a couple of horses. I sent the rest of the men back and told them we'd catch up. Didn't expect to find anything. We planned on heading back here to camp before noon. Then suddenly the trail that was only two horses joins up with one that looks like it's a huge war party. And just as we decide we'd better come back to camp for reinforcements, we come up over a hill and there's this dugout." Nathan paused. "In three years of patrolling those hills, I never came across anything like it. Arrows everywhere. A man's body at the top of the hill behind the dugout." He shook his head. "There's been talk of closing down Camp Robinson and sending us all up to Camp

81

Sheridan. That won't be happening now."

Nathan spared Granny Max the details of what had been done to the man and went on to describe finding the dead dog and then the woman's emergence from the cache. "We thought we had her calmed down, and so we decided to get some sleep. I don't know what woke me, but I went to the door and there she was standing beside the grave with my gun to her head." He stopped fiddling with his hat.

Granny's hand clamped over her mouth. She spoke through her fingers. "She did that . . . to *herself?*"

He nodded, then looked sideways at Granny. "I don't think Doc Valentine needs to know. But if she's going to live, and with the nightmares and all . . ." He shrugged. "You should know." When Granny was quiet, he said, "I am truly sorry, Granny. I had no right to put this burden on you. There's no way to know if she'll heal up and be all right, or —"

"— or if you've brought me another Crazy Jane." Granny patted his hand. "The Lord gave you a tender heart, Nathan, and now He has used it to rescue one of His lost lambs and bring her to old Granny for some loving. You stop apologizing. Your tender heart is one of the things I love most about you."

Nathan shrugged. "There was no trace of a tender heart when I went down in the cellar beneath that trapdoor. It's a good thing the Cheyenne took care of the —" He swallowed the word. "It's a good thing he was already dead. Or I'd likely be in the guardhouse waiting trial for the cold-blooded murder of a civilian." He was quiet for a moment, watching the sunset. Finally, he asked, "You ever know anyone to be treated like her and be able to be . . . normal . . . again?"

Granny lifted her chin and closed her eyes. Finally, she said carefully, "I've known dozens of women been treated like that." Her eyes glowed with emotion. "Most learned to be normal well enough. Once they were free."

Nathan shifted uncomfortably. He looked down at the earth. "If we'd gone a few rods east or west, I'd never have known that dugout was there. And if it hadn't been for that dog having a piece of some warrior's leggings or moccasin in his mouth, we'd likely have just left his carcass to rot. She would have starved down in that . . ." He gulped. "In that hole." He changed the subject abruptly and nodded toward the sunset. "Beautiful."

Granny nodded. "Mm-hmm. The good Lord is a wonderful artist." She paused before asking, "What do you suppose that looks like from the *other* side?" When Nathan didn't answer, she went on. "I like to imagine Lily just the other side watching like we are. Only her view is unclouded by sinful sight."

Nathan snorted. "I'd like it a far-sight better if God had just stayed out of my affairs and left my wife *this* side of His sunsets."

"I know that, dear Nathan. I know it." Granny laid one great dark hand on his tensed shoulder. "The Lord's ways certainly are not ours, are they? He had other plans for Lily. And now He's brought another of His children into our lives. We can't see His plan, but I know one thing: I'm willing to do whatever He wants. And if she's addled, that don't change a thing. She still needs love and a place to live, and with God's help, we'll give her both."

"I may not agree with you about God's role in it all, Granny. But I do agree with you about this woman. It doesn't matter if she's crazy or not. We'll do our best by her."

Movement out of the corner of his eye

made Nathan look around. The woman was standing at the doorway. The setting sun made Lily's lace-trimmed nightgown glow with golden light. It illuminated the woman's waist-length auburn hair, turning it flaming red. For a moment, she stood looking from Nathan to Granny and back to Nathan again. Her green eyes shone so bright Nathan thought she might be sleep-walking.

Finally, she looked away from him and toward Granny. "Laina," she said clearly. "My name is Laina Gray." She looked back at Nathan. "And I'm not addled."

Six

For God hath not given us the spirit of fear; but of power, and of love, and of a sound mind.

2 Timothy 1:7

Well, she had done the unthinkable. She had tried to take her own life. Standing at the back door and listening while Sergeant Boone told Granny about her had been the catalyst that spurred Laina's memories. She had remembered it all. And according to the preacher who used to visit Miss Hart's on Sundays, those who did such things would never see the Kingdom. They would spend eternity in everlasting fire for having struck at the very image of God himself. Laina only had to close her eyes to see Reverend Fitzpatrick shaking his bony fist to illustrate his rantings.

As the days passed and she considered

her fate, the idea of a life such as hers being the image of God filled Laina with doubt. Surely God had no interest in the likes of her. Surely He put His image into things greater than dance hall girls and gamblers. She didn't really think God had much concern over whether she lived or died or how her life or her death were accomplished. And if He was concerned, then He would just have to understand that she didn't mean anything against Him personally when she took that sergeant's gun and pointed it at her head. She was just taking the only way she knew to make the hurting stop. That night back at the soddy, had someone asked about the idea of fearing hell if she took her own life, she was fairly certain she would have said she had already been there — and would have pulled the trigger anyway.

Now, nearly a month after her supposed rescue, she was trapped again. Not by circumstances like those on the riverboat. Not by ropes that tied her down. Not by a trapdoor too heavy to lift. Now Laina was trapped by her own body. She was too weak to stand up for more than a few minutes. Almost too weak to care what happened.

Here she was, at a place called Camp

Robinson, being cared for by a woman who assured her she was God's little lamb and things would be all right. When Granny talked about God, it was like nothing Laina had ever heard before. Granny seemed to have some kind of special friendship with "the good Lord." She talked to Him as naturally as if He were sitting at the breakfast table eating her flapjacks, waiting to hear her news. Considering Granny's close relationship with God, Laina expected Granny to preach. But even after Laina was feeling better and had begun to go to the table for her meals, Granny did not preach.

Maybe she meant to and just forgot. Or got distracted. Granny Max did a prodigious amount of work. Sergeant Boone's Company G of the Third Cavalry included nearly fifty men. Granny had explained that each company usually had three laundresses, but when the Sioux were moved to their new agency up on the Missouri in '77, the army transferred most of the troops away from Camp Robinson. And with the troops went their wives — the company laundresses. The row of twelve apartments where she lived — called Soapsuds Row — now housed only a few families, and keeping up with the laundry wasn't easy.

Granny had already told her a lot about Camp Robinson. She seemed to think information would help Laina overcome her fear. The long row of attached apartments where she was staying was called Soapsuds Row because the women living here did laundry for the soldiers. The log building to the north was the hospital, and beyond it was the post trader's store. "The Grubers are the only civilians allowed to live on the military camp," Granny Max had explained. "The rest of us are army, through and through."

The first evening Granny Max managed to get Laina outside, they sat on the front porch. From there, they could see the whole of Camp Robinson just across a well-defined trail that ran between their building and the rest of the camp. Laina gripped the edge of her seat with whitened knuckles, trying to control what she knew was unreasonable fear.

"That's Soldier Creek," Granny said, waving her hand toward the winding stream looping between the Row and the rest of camp. "You can see how everything is arranged around the parade ground — that's the big square with the flagpole in the middle. Over on the north, there's the commanding officer's place. And the long row of adobe duplexes is for the officers. We know it as Officers Row. Doctor Valentine and his family live in that one," Granny pointed. "You can just barely see the edge of the front porch." She motioned toward a long building across the trail from the hospital. "That's the back of one of the infantry barracks. There's another one just like it on the opposite side of the parade ground. These buildings right there across the trail are the commissary storehouse and the quartermaster's stores. All the camp supplies come through the quartermaster. Makes him a powerful man. That other building is the guardhouse," Granny said. "Crazy Horse himself was brought there." She sighed before going on. "Past the guardhouse is the adjutant's office and the cavalry barracks. As first sergeant, Nathan has use of a room attached to the front of the barracks." Granny stopped her running commentary on the layout of Camp Robinson and explained how after Lily Boone's death, she had been given her own apartment on Soapsuds Row.

Laina soon learned that while, officially, Sergeant Boone slept and ate over at the cavalry barracks with his men, he'd also been allowed to keep the apartment next to Granny's that he had shared with his wife. Sometimes in the night, when Laina woke from her own bad dreams, she could hear Sergeant Boone pacing on the opposite side of the wall. Sometimes she heard his voice. She couldn't discern the words, but she didn't need words to recognize anguish.

It was apparent that while she had come to Camp Robinson because she was a servant of the sergeant's wife, Granny loved Sergeant Boone as if he were her son. She spent nearly half an hour ironing just one of his dress parade shirts. She creased his pants and insisted on custom tailoring his uniforms. One morning when the sergeant protested what he thought was the unreasonable amount of time Granny spent on his appearance, she argued, "A man has got to look his best. And you know Lily would be very unhappy to see the way that coat hangs on you. *'My Nathan surely cuts a fine figure, Granny,'* she used to say. Now, I don't want Lily scolding me up in glory for letting you go downhill. So you just get over here and let me mark this coat." Nathan acquiesced.

Granny's salary as a laundress was handled by the paymaster and deducted from the soldier's pay. She earned extra for mending shirts and darning socks. But sol-

91

diers got more than clean laundry and darned socks from Granny, who had a reputation for baking some of the best corn bread west of the Mississippi. Laina soon learned that it was the corn bread that afforded Granny the opportunity to do what she considered her real work, which was being a creative combination of drill sergeant and confidante for the men of Company G. While "the boys" sat at her kitchen table waiting for a fresh batch of corn bread to emerge from Granny's tiny oven, they inevitably ended up talking about home. Or about the bully in the company bent on picking a fight. Or their plans for life after the army.

Laina never went into the front room when men were present. Sergeant Boone had mounted two brackets on either side of the door, and Granny had hung two thick quilts across the doorway to give Laina privacy. But she heard nearly every word that was spoken across Granny Max's kitchen table. Occasionally she would hear a man's voice quaver as he fought back homesick tears. Once a recruit, known as the Professor, broke down and cried over a letter from a girl back home. Granny prayed out loud for him.

Laina found herself wondering about

Granny's history. She was old enough to have gray hair. Her skin was the same shade of brown as some of the leather hides Josiah Paine had stacked in the cache beneath his dugout. Even when she was scolding Laina, saying that it was high time she went outside for some fresh air, her eyes shone with kindness.

And her hands. How, Laina wondered, was it possible for hands so roughened with calluses to be so gentle? Granny's hands were always clean, with neatly filed nails and not a speck of dirt beneath them. Laina still couldn't seem to get the grime of that soddy out from beneath hers. Granny's hands patted her shoulder to calm her, stroked her arms to help her awaken from a nightmare, and sometimes combed out the tangles in Laina's hair in the long hours of night when she could not go back to sleep.

And even better than Granny's hands was her voice. It was almost as deep as a man's but was so warm and comforting. Laina could not remember very much of her first days and nights at Camp Robinson, but she did remember Granny singing. Hymns, mostly. Some Laina remembered from Miss Hart's. But there were others she had never heard, with haunting melodies and lyrics about sweet chariots and crossing Jordan and sweet Jesus.

Granny had a prodigious appetite. When she made flapjacks for breakfast, she ate eight. Eight flapjacks and exactly two cups of coffee. If breakfast was grits, Granny smothered hers with blackstrap molasses and so much butter, the grits were barely visible. Although not nearly as tall as Sergeant Boone, Granny towered over most of the soldiers. Once when Laina stumbled and almost fell, Granny picked her up and carried her to bed as effortlessly as a man might have.

As the weeks went by and Laina's waking hours lengthened and her strength returned, Granny seemed to feel a need to fill the silence between them. When some noise from the camp across the creek startled her, Granny would say, "That's just Company G headed out for drill. They got to be sharp so those new recruits that came in yesterday can see what's expected of them. Some of those new boys never even sat a horse. Can you imagine that?"

"You'll get used to the bugles," Granny had said another morning. She counted the various calls that organized the soldiers' days. "Reveille, assembly, morning stables call, breakfast call, sick call, fatigue call. From reveille to taps, a soldier never has to wonder what time it is. Lily's mantle clock quit running a few months ago, and I didn't even notice. You'll learn the tunes soon enough."

One morning, when reveille was sounding, Granny chuckled and sang, "I can't get 'em up, I can't get 'em up, I can't get 'em up at all. The corp'ral is worse than the private, the sergeant's worse than the corp'ral, the lieutenant's worse than the sergeant, and the captain is worse than them all."

On the day Laina first offered to help Granny with her mending, the older woman said, "Now that you're feeling better, maybe we'll have some of the women in for tea. They are all eager to meet you." She smiled encouragement. "Now don't you be worrying over meeting a few old hens. Or young ones, neither. They're nice women. Mostly. Mrs. Doctor can be a little high-minded, but I guess she has a right. She's a real lady from some highfalutin' family back East. Underneath her fancy airs there's a good heart. You'll see."

She was dancing. She was one of many, but

she was the best — kicking her knees a little higher, bending over a little farther, encouraging the men to holler and clap and howl and hoot. Sometimes she even let her hair down. They loved it when she let her hair down.

Wearing his signature stovepipe hat, Rooster pounded on the out-of-tune piano, increasing the tempo until . . . he jumped up on stage — and turned into a monster.

She looked off into the wings for Eustis. But her father was playing cards. Poker. At a table she hadn't noticed before. Odd, that it would be set up right here on the stage. She called for him. "Father." He glanced her way. His black eyes glittered with greed. He waved and grinned, nodding his approval as the monstrous man — with yellow eyes and skin, with rotting teeth and vermin crawling through his beard — grabbed her and —

"NNNOOOOOO!!!"

She gasped, lingering between her dream and the reality of Granny Max's room. She tried to sit up.

"Shh. Shh." A gentle hand on her shoulder. A familiar voice spoke her name. "It was a dream, honey-lamb. Only a dream. Remember? You are here with Granny Max. You are safe. Shh."

She opened her eyes. *One, two, in, out. One, two, in, out.* Counting helped her even

96

out her breathing. Helped her escape the dream and come back.

Granny was humming softly. The woman's kindness had become its own kind of tyranny. Laina squeezed her eyes shut, blinking the tears away. Night after night, Granny Max comforted her, never complaining about the lost sleep. How long had it been now? Over a month, and here Granny sat again, stroking her patient's hair, holding her hand, talking of safety and healing and God's love.

"When I was a child," she said, "I had nightmares, too. I'd just sit up and start screaming. Mama would come and I'd know she was there, but somehow I couldn't get out of the dreamworld and back to her." She paused. "Mama said if I could ever put the dreams into words, they'd go away. And you know, Laina, Mama was right. I had three dreams over and over and over again. And one by one, as I was able to put them into words, they went away." She patted Laina's hand. "There's nobody here in this room but God and old Granny Max. And they both care about you. Can't you give words to the dream? Make it go away?"

The little girl attending Miss Hart's Academy for Young Ladies in St. Louis would have tried. She might even have believed that bad dreams could be willed away. But the grown woman couldn't bring herself to do it. She turned her face to the wall and whispered, "I can't." She couldn't keep the tears from spilling down her cheeks.

"Fear does some strange things to a body," Granny said. "I remember one boy come back from the war and his mama almost didn't recognize him. That boy had snow-white hair." She leaned closer. "He'd been hurt worse than some of the men who'd lost a leg."

Granny smoothed over her own head with the palm of her hand. She leaned back in her rocker, adding its creaking rhythm to the cadence of her voice. "I started to go gray in the winter of eighteen-and-thirty-seven. December. I was fifteen years old. I will never forget that winter. A woman doesn't forget. But sometimes, with the Lord's help and the kindness of others, she can decide to get on with life." She asked, "Do you hear what I am saying to you, child?"

"I hear," Laina whispered.

"I wanted to take a gun and go after him. And I could have, too. He wasn't like some varmints that do their evil and slither away. He stayed right near where I lived for a time."

Laina shuddered. "How'd you ever —"

"My mama got the missus — Miss Lily's grandmother — to take me into the house. That's when I started taking care of Miss Lily's mother. She was just a baby. It helped a little, but I was still afraid.

"One day, I saw some man coming up to the house, and it scared me so that I ran and hid in a closet. I thought it was him. I was shaking and crying and mad all at the same time. Because there I was in that closet when where I really wanted to be was downstairs in the kitchen where Birdie, the cook, was making raspberry pie. I knew she'd give me a taste, if I could just make it down to that kitchen. All of a sudden, it seemed like I could see the hideous face of the very person I feared laughing at me hiding in that closet and missing my favorite food in all the world.

"It was when I got mad — I like to think it was a righteous anger, that the Lord showed me something. He helped me understand that if I didn't get out of that closet, those ugly faces were going to be looming over me all the rest of my days. I realized right then, there was nothing I could do about what had been done.

Someone evil owned my past. I was just a girl, and I didn't have control. But I could keep him from taking my future. And I could sure do something about that raspberry pie."

Laina took in a sharp breath. She lifted her hands and hid her face. "You were just a girl, a slave. I'm a grown woman and free. I should have found a way. I'd seen soldiers in the distance before. I should have —"

"You were afraid."

"But I could have —"

"Stop it, child. Just stop it. Don't go back there and punish yourself and relive it. The good Lord sent them Indians — and Nathan. The *Lord* stopped it. He has given you a new home — if you want it. But there's that battle in here," Granny patted the place over her heart. "The Lord loves you, Laina Gray, and so do I. And we both want you to win the battle going on inside you." She reached up and tucked a strand of auburn hair behind Laina's ear. "You got to come out of that closet in your mind, child. Come out and have some raspberry pie."

Laina turned on her side where she could look up at Granny Max.

"Tell me his name," Granny said abruptly.

Laina frowned. "What?"

"His name. When I was in that closet, I was seeing Spinner's face. Whose face do you see?"

Laina whispered, "Josiah. Josiah Paine."

"Josiah Paine is dead, Laina Gray. Don't bring him back out of his grave. Don't let him rummage around in your life anymore."

"That day you went down to the kitchen and had pie," Laina asked. "Was that . . . was that the end of it? Were you ever afraid again?"

"Oh, plenty of times."

"What did you do?"

"I just kept eating raspberry pie, honey. Or playing with Lily's mama — and later, Lily. Or whatever the next thing was to do. I just did the next thing. And one day I realized I hadn't thought about old Spinner Barnes for a while."

Laina was quiet for a few moments. Presently she asked, "You ever wonder where God was when you were in those dark places?" Laina asked.

Granny nodded. "Everybody that's ever lived has wondered about that."

"Did He answer you? Did He tell you where He was?"

" 'Whither shall I flee from thy presence? . . . If I make my bed in hell, behold, thou art there.' He was there. With me. Whether I knew it or not."

"Then why didn't He make it stop?"

"*Where* He was, I can answer, child. *Why* is a different question. He doesn't always answer *why.*" Granny smiled at her. "Maybe it was because some day I'd be taking care of a girl named Laina Gray, and where I was back then would help me understand where she is today."

"You really think that?"

"I really think that *nothing* is for *nothing.* The good Lord doesn't waste things, Miss Laina. I'd be lying if I didn't say I do a lot of wondering. His ways are not mine."

"Do you wonder about Mrs. Boone? About why she had to die?"

Granny nodded.

"But you don't seem bitter — like Sergeant Boone."

"Well, I have lived a lot longer than Nathan. And I have learned to trust the Lord."

"Even when you wonder?"

"*Especially* when I wonder," Granny said. "That is what faith is, child. Learning to live in peace in the very center of all the things that don't seem to make sense."

Laina frowned as she pondered what

Granny had said. "I don't think I could ever do that."

"Neither did I, honey-lamb, neither did I. I had to take baby steps toward it. Just like I had to practice not thinking about Spinner. And when I took those baby steps, the Lord gave me what I needed to run the rest of the way to His peace."

Granny smiled. "You think that's all just talking in circles, don't you, child. That's all right. You just let it all circle around in your head. Maybe if God's ways circle around in there, those nightmares won't have room."

Leaning back in her rocker, Granny began to hum. From across the creek, reveille sounded. Still humming, Granny rose and got dressed. She went into the front room and started up the fire. A dog barked. Hoofbeats and marching, bugles and yelling all combined into the familiar rhythm of morning at Camp Robinson. Finally, the noise of routine and the swirling thoughts about God and baby steps drowned out the nightmares, and Laina slept.

Seven

For the lips of a strange woman drop as an honeycomb, and her mouth is smoother than oil: but her end is bitter as wormwood, sharp as a two-edged sword.

Proverbs 5:3-4

Beauregard Preston trudged along beside the supply wagon, doing his best not to limp. He'd planned to pull the infernal, ill-fitting army-issue boots off when they stopped to make camp at noon. But now he figured he'd better not. His feet were so raw with blisters, he'd never get the boots back on. If they'd told him that cavalry recruits had to walk the hundred or so miles between the railroad station at Sidney, Nebraska, and Camp Robinson to the north, he — well, he still would have enlisted. But he'd have done something about the boots.

He'd had it with making two dollars a week as a dry-goods store clerk. He'd had it with the uppity wives of the St. Louis rich and their whining daughters, who mooned over choosing between six bolts of fabric — all the same basic color — while they made eyes at him and then pretended shock if he showed any sign of interest. He'd had it with Mr. Cruikshank, the store owner, who made snide remarks about Rebels every chance he got, as if Beau didn't know Cruikshank was a southern sympathizer. During the war, the man had had to get bars put over the windows of his house for fear of what his neighbors might do. Now he acted like he was doing his young southern charge a favor by letting him work eighteen-hour days and providing him a corner in the warehouse across the alley as sleeping quarters.

Yankee customers had annoyed Beau for over two years. As he plodded along, he pondered the other reasons he'd enlisted. He'd been sinking fast and he knew it. It had all begun when he decided the riverboats were a much more entertaining way to fill the long evenings and weekends than pious hymn-sings and church socials. He didn't think there could be any harm in a few drinks and a hand or two of cards. At first there wasn't. Until, little by little, Beau found himself drinking more and more. With the drinking came losing at the tables. To make himself feel better about drinking and losing, he stayed for the entertainment.

Beauregard Preston couldn't remember the first time he'd realized he had a peculiar power over women. Even his mama, ordinarily a strict woman, could be made to forget herself under the gaze of her youngest son's clear-blue eyes. Once, she had literally dropped the switch right out of her hand and rumpled his tawny hair while she laughed, "I declare, Beauregard, you are going to do some damage to more than one girl's heart with looks like that! Go on, now! And please don't call the cook that name again."

The girls on the river were no different than any other girl he had ever charmed. He had his choice of them all, and he was one of the few Riverboat Annie favored with her attentions. She singled him out and looked straight at him when she danced on stage. And later, she backed up her flirtation, which was more than he could say for the rich girls who shopped at Cruikshank's store.

By the time Beau admitted to himself

that he should do something about being more than a little in debt and more than a little enslaved to whiskey and women, something happened that solved all his problems at once. He came into the store early one morning to unload some dress goods and found himself looking down the barrel of Mr. Cruikshank's rifle. It seemed, Mr. Cruikshank said, that Miss Mavis Cruikshank had been found to be in a family way, and since Beauregard Preston was, in Mr. Cruikshank's mind, the only possible culprit, he was informed that he was engaged. The experience went a long way toward awakening Beau to the dangers of residing in St. Louis.

About ten minutes after Mr. Cruikshank lowered his rifle and sent Beau back to his room in the warehouse to "think about his duty," Beauregard Preston of Mecklenburg County, Virginia, was so thoroughly impressed with his need to reform that he had exited Cruikshank's warehouse empty-handed and headed south to Jefferson Barracks to volunteer for the army. The ten-mile walk effected such a complete reform that, upon his arrival, Beauregard Preston had not only sworn off wine and women, he had become Caleb Jackson.

Thinking back over the recent past, Private Jackson realized that, in spite of the unpleasant aspects, army life had its advantages. Yes, he thought, given the alternative of becoming Mr. Mavis Cruikshank, he'd still have enlisted and marched wherever he was told without complaining. But he would have spent his last twenty cents on an extra pair of socks, if he had it to do over again.

The greenhorn next to him wasn't much better off. He was limping, too. The sleeve of his blue army jacket was tinged with sweat and dust where the kid had swiped his forehead as they marched. At least he'd finally shut up. Jackson had done everything possible to stay clear of the kid at the recruit depot in Jefferson Barracks.

Harlan Yates was round-faced and freckled, and he looked to be about twelve years old. He had a crop of the reddest hair Jackson had ever seen, two huge ears that stuck out from his head like flags in a gale, and a bodacious nasal Yankee twang. And he talked. And talked. And talked. Worse yet, he'd picked up on Jackson's southern accent right away and called him "Reb". Well, he'd tried it, anyway. Once. The fist Jackson had planted on the kid's chin had stopped that. You would have thought he'd have backed off after getting knocked to the ground. But, no. Instead of making him stay away, the blow seemed to have somehow galvanized Yates's intentions to make a friend. He'd come up off the ground rubbing his chin and grinning.

"Good punch, Private. So . . ." He grinned sheepishly. "Should I just call you Jackson?" He lowered his voice then and leaned in to say, "Truth is, the accent's almost gone anyway. I'd never have guessed except we got kin south of the Mason-Dixon Line ourselves." Then he said, "You know horseflesh? I seen you ride the other day, and you sit a horse like you know what you're doin'." When Jackson didn't answer, Yates continued, "The reason I'm askin' is . . . well, I signed up for cavalry. But . . . I don't . . ." He blushed furiously. "Of course we had plow horses and all that on the farm. But I never had such a thing as a real horse to ride. And I was thinkin' that maybe you could . . . well, maybe you could help me pick out a good one. Once we get to Camp Robinson, that is." Harlan grinned, and Jackson noticed he had a chipped tooth. And blast it if that chipped tooth didn't remind Jackson of his older brother.

Jackson glowered at the kid. "Why should I care whether or not you get a good horse?"

The kid scrunched up his face like it hurt to think. He peered up at the sky, formulating an answer, then grinned again and said, "Well, it's like this. Say we're out on patrol and we get surrounded." He crouched down and held his arms out to dramatize the imaginary situation. "There's warrin' Sioux on all sides. Somebody has to go for help." He dropped his arms to his sides and straightened up. "If that somebody's me, don't you think it'd work out better for all concerned if I'm on a horse I can *ride* instead of one that's gonna toss me in the nearest dry creek bed and hightail it for Deadwood?"

Jackson stifled his laughter. He shrugged and jabbed his forefinger in Yates's chest. "Listen up, greenhorn. I've had enough jokes about Johnny Reb spoken in my hearing to last the rest of my life. So I'll make you a deal. You forget about which side I was on in 'the late unpleasantness,' and I'll look the herd over when we get to camp and tell you what I think."

Harlan grinned at him. "You do know horseflesh, then?"

"My daddy had about the best stable of

thoroughbreds in Mecklenburg County."

That had been over a week ago. The kid had stuck to him like glue ever since. Of course it could be worse. He could have been paired off with the German who barely spoke English and had breath bad enough to kill a buffalo at fifty feet. At least this kid could take a hint and was learning to keep his mouth shut. He still liked to tease and had played more than his share of practical jokes. But to his credit, he hadn't said another word about the South. Or Jackson's knowledge of horses. Jackson had come to the grudging conclusion that when they got to Camp Robinson, he'd probably even be able to tolerate Harlan Yates as his bunky.

"Whoa!" Corporal Emmet Dorsey pulled his six-mule team to a halt. He stood up slowly, appearing to survey the land around their noon campsite, hoping none of the recruits caught on to what he was really doing, which was giving his knees and back a chance to loosen up a little before he tried to climb off the wagon seat. Gritting his teeth, he worked his way down.

Their time at Jefferson Barracks near St. Louis had taught the recruits exactly what was expected of them, and they made camp quickly. Dorsey made a mental note to tell Sergeant Boone to make sure he got the private called Frenchy attached to Company G. The man could do amazing things with army-issue rations.

After unharnessing his team and filling a nose bag with grain for each mule, Dorsey made his way to the campfire, where Frenchy sat on his haunches tending a skillet. He saw a few bits of something unrecognizable sizzling in the pan, but it smelled so good the corporal's mouth started to water. With a grunt, he sat down by the fire. Before he'd even settled, Frenchy thrust a mug of hot coffee in his hand. "You drink this — you'll feel better, eh?"

"Feel better about what?"

Frenchy rubbed his hand over his knees but didn't say anything.

"What's your real name, anyway?"

"Dubois," the man said, puckering up his lips when he said the *u*. "Charles Dubois."

"Well, *Sharl Doo-bwa*," Dorsey said, doing his best to mimic the Frenchman's pronunciation, "Where'd you learn to cook? I never saw a man who could make something out of nothing like you."

"My family have been chef back to Charlemagne." He stirred what was in the skillet with his fork and pulled it off the fire. "Cooking is in the Dubois blood." He held the pan out to Dorsey, who took a chunk of meat between forefinger and thumb and popped it into his mouth. It was hot, and for a few minutes the corporal alternately sucked in air and tried to chew without burning his tongue. Finally, he swallowed. "You assigned to a company yet?"

Dubois shrugged. "I don sink so."

"We need a cook in Company G. I raised a respectable garden last year, but the men ate the same old same old."

"Garden? You haf a garden?"

Dorsey nodded. "Planted it myself. Lettuce. Beans. Beets. Tomatoes. Onions."

Dubois's brown eyes crinkled at the corners. Dorsey couldn't see the mouth, as it was hidden by a brown moustache that covered even the Frenchman's bottom lip. It was a wonder he could get food past the hairy mess, but as Dorsey watched, Dubois took a bite from the skillet and sat back in the dust, savoring his lunch.

"Between the post trader, the quartermaster, my garden, and your cooking, Company G would do all right."

The greenhorn Yates sidled up. "Couldn't help hearing, sir." He saluted smartly for the corporal. "Any way you could get me and Jackson into your outfit with Frenchy, sir?"

Dorsey frowned and took a sip of coffee. "And why would I care to do that?"

"Well, Jackson's a good rider. Real good. Told me his family had one of the best stables in the county. I figure he's one of them rich boys who's been riding since before they could walk."

"So much for Jackson. Why do we want you?"

Yates worked his eyebrows up and down and made a face. "I, good sir, have the gift of laughter. I know enough jokes to last you all winter. Laughing at me will give you something to do besides playin' checkers when the snow's blowing outside . . . and the wolves are howlin' and . . . you're hankerin' for a little entertainment like they got in that there *Paree*." He winked at Dubois.

"What do you know about *Paree?*" Dorsey asked.

Yates looked at Dubois and worked his eyebrows again. "That's for me to know and him to find out, right *Sharl?*" He jumped up and did a perfect imitation of a

114

dancing girl high kicking and tossing her ruffled petticoats around as he circled the campfire. He wiggled his hips and then, with a loud "whoo-whoo", circled Frenchy's head with one pointed toe while he hopped up and down on the other.

Dorsey snorted, spraying coffee in all directions. Yates added to his routine until the men were howling with laughter. Finally, when Yates dropped to the earth beside the two men, Dorsey wiped the tears away from his eyes and said, "All right, Yates. All right. I'll put in a word with Sergeant Boone. But I make no guarantees."

He got up slowly and stretched his lower back, wincing. "Get Jackson and tell him I need help harnessing up my mules."

When Yates jumped up to obey, Dorsey leaned over and said, "I saw you boys limping pretty bad before we stopped. We'll be crossing a creek in about an hour. When we do, see that you wade in it long enough to get that leather soaking wet. I mean soaking. Then don't take those boots off until they are dry. As they dry, they'll mold to your feet. You'll have the best-fitting boots you can get until you muster out and go to a fancy cobbler in Denver."

"Thanks, Corporal." Yates saluted

smartly. "I owe you."

Dorsey nodded. "You got that right. Now get Jackson over here. We're supposed to be in camp by tattoo — that's 'lights-out' to you, greenhorn."

For the twentieth time in an hour, Miss Charlotte Valentine laid her needlework aside and peered out the front window toward the log barracks to the southwest. Seeing nothing but an empty parade ground and a group of men returning from target practice, Charlotte sighed. It had been a long day of waiting, and she was beginning to think Sergeant Boone might not be coming for dinner after all. There was no sign of the new recruits her father had said would arrive today from Sidney. And Nathan had to meet them, get them inspected, and give them orders before he could think of socializing. "Nathan." Charlotte whispered the name to herself. Not *Sergeant Boone*. He was *Nathan* to her. Of course he didn't know that. Yet.

Charlotte got up and went to the window. Shoving her mother's heavy brocade drapes aside, she leaned against the window frame and let out another sigh. Less than a year ago Camp Robinson had been bustling with activity, with hundreds

116

of Indian camps less than a mile away near Red Cloud Agency, and nearly a thousand men stationed both at Camp Robinson, and a number of makeshift camps scattered around the Pine Ridge area. Now it was almost a ghost fort. With the Indian Wars all but over, and the Sioux moved to their new agency, most of the troops had left Camp Robinson.

There was only the Friday-night hop to attend these days. And the same soldiers to dance with. Not that Charlotte cared for any of *them*. But it was her duty as an army officer's daughter to do what she could to keep morale high. Dancing every dance with a different soldier was something she could do. There just weren't enough women to go around at those things. Even old Granny Max from over on Soapsuds Row got asked to dance every dance, and soldiers still had to tie a white scarf around their arms to designate themselves "ladies" so everyone could have a partner.

Thinking of Soapsuds Row made Charlotte frown. She'd never given the women living there much thought. First, because they were all married. And second, because there wasn't a lady among them. Even when Meara O'Malley's husband got himself killed, thereby providing a single woman for all the soldiers to court, Charlotte didn't worry. Only the lower classes of soldiers would give a laundress any thought at all.

But something had happened a few weeks ago that worried Charlotte. Nathan and Corporal Dorsey had ridden in late one night with a woman they'd found in the wilds. Charlotte's father had been summoned to tend a gunshot wound. He feared the "poor woman" would die. But she had surprised everyone and lived. Which was, of course, a good thing. Miss Charlotte Valentine was not one to wish evil upon anyone, least of all some poor creature drug in from the hills. But with the arrival of that woman, whom her father eventually described as "about twenty and quite pretty, in spite of a terrible head wound," Sergeant Boone had begun dining with his old Granny Max more often than he joined the Valentine family.

Charlotte was only seventeen years old and, therefore, was not privy to her parents' private conversations about the various members of the infantry and cavalry troops stationed at Camp Robinson. But she was not averse to passing beneath the dining room window on her way to gather eggs from the chicken coop out back. And was it her fault if, pausing to inspect a spot old Granny Max had failed to remove from her new apron, she just happened to hear what her parents discussed?

Sergeant Boone had grieved deeply the death of his wife. He had almost resigned his commission. He still visited her grave in the post cemetery across the river several times a week. Rumor had it the Boones' quarters over on Soapsuds Row remained exactly the same as the day Mrs. Boone died, although Nathan rarely slept there. He spent most of his time in the barracks with his men. At least he *had,* Charlotte thought with a frown. *Until he found that woman.*

She had overheard more than one parental discussion about Sergeant Boone's grief. Her father was concerned about the young sergeant, although he never knowingly let Charlotte hear him say it. Mrs. Doctor, however, was not so careful. She let Charlotte know all about her concerns that such a "fine young man" was allowing "an unfortunate first marriage" to impact his military career.

While both of Charlotte's parents were concerned about Sergeant Boone, it was her mother who took action and began extending frequent invitations for him to join the Valentines for dinner. After a few of those dinners, Mrs. Valentine tactfully shared news of a dear friend of hers in the East who had nearly gone mad with grief after losing her beloved husband. She had left everything untouched. Created a shrine to the man. And then one day she had risen from her grief and realized she was destroying herself. She had donated her dead husband's suits to charity and was remarried within a month. "And she's so *happy* now," Mrs. Valentine had said. "I'm just so pleased for her."

When Sergeant Boone did not learn from the example of Mrs. Valentine's friend, when he left things unmoved over on Soapsuds Row and continued to visit his late wife's grave, Mrs. Valentine confided to Charlotte that she was beginning to suspect Granny Max was an obstacle to the sergeant's recovery, and perhaps it would be in his best interest if his wife's servant left Camp Robinson.

"Just think of it, dear," Emmy-Lou had said one evening as she helped Charlotte set the table for dinner. "The poor man doesn't have a chance to get on with his life while Granny Max is there, reminding him daily of poor Mrs. Boone's absence. They were very close, you know." She

120

sighed. "Sometimes it's best just to put the past behind us and not talk about it anymore. But of course Sergeant Boone can't do that. Not with Granny Max living right next door. If he no longer has her to reminisce with," Emmy-Lou continued, "he will be better able to move on." Charlotte thought her mother's reasoning made sense.

But later that evening, when the subject of Granny Max came up at dinner, Sergeant Boone had launched into a litany of praise for the old woman that squashed Mrs. Doctor's plans.

"I assumed Granny would want to head back East after —"

"Yes," Mrs. Doctor echoed. "I've been telling Avery the old dear should be reunited with her own people. Being a laundress is far too grueling for a woman her age."

Nathan chuckled. "Well, I only brought it up once. Granny was stirring soap into a batch of laundry. She put her hands on her hips and just glared at me. 'Are you ordering me to leave Camp Robinson, Sergeant Boone?' she asked. She was mad." Nathan leaned back in his chair. " 'Why, no, Granny,' I said. 'I just thought —'

" 'Good.' That big voice of hers was

121

booming so loud I bet every woman on the row heard her. 'Because I been taking orders from white boys for most of my life. And as I recall, there was a war fought so I would no longer be obliged to do so.' She grabbed up her stick and began to stir that laundry so hard the water sloshed over the side and almost put the fire out.

"I started to apologize, but Granny didn't let me say another word. She said, 'You say I am free to go, and that means I am just as free to stay, and I would kindly appreciate it if you would allow me to decide my own future.' Then she stopped stirring and marched right up to me. She looks up at me and shakes her finger not an inch from my nose. I've never seen her so angry. 'You may not realize it, Sergeant Boone, but the fact is you need me. I don't intend to stand before the Lord God and Lily someday and have them asking me just exactly why I deserted my post. Now I'm going to mend your shirts and keep liniment ready for when you get the quinsy and bake your favorite chokecherry pie come July. So don't you be bringing up my leaving Camp Robinson again!' "

Nathan shook his head and laughed. He looked around the table. "The truth is I'm grateful she's stayed. She makes me feel . . . connected. Keeps me grounded. I'm thankful Granny Max was smart enough to know I need her. It took me a while, but I've finally realized it for myself. And since she does the work of two women, there's no argument about her value to the army, either."

For a moment, the conversation around the Valentine's dinner table had ceased. Then the doctor cleared his throat and offered, "Sometimes I think she's the unofficial camp chaplain too. The men seem drawn to her."

"Unless they've been in the guardhouse," Nathan said. "Then they avoid her like the plague. Granny doesn't put up with mischief."

Charlotte admired how her mother had deftly guided the conversation to other things, how she was sensitive to Nathan's wishes, dispensing with any more talk of Granny Max leaving Camp Robinson. Mama also stopped hinting that Mrs. Boone's things should be removed from Soapsuds Row. But not long after that dinner, she had taught Charlotte how to make Sergeant Boone's favorite chokecherry pie.

Chokecherry pie. Watching out the front window, Charlotte now smiled to herself.

She was becoming a very good cook. Mama said she had heard that Lily Boone couldn't cook worth anything. In fact, Mama said Mrs. Boone hadn't been much use as a soldier's wife at all. "She just wasn't cut out for military life, Charlotte. Mrs. Gruber said so. Sergeant Boone's next wife should be from military stock. If he has any sense at all, he realizes that."

Sighing with impatience, Charlotte went back to her needlework. She was piecing a nine-patch quilt with squares so tiny it would likely take the rest of her natural life to get enough squares to make a quilt. But Mama said that a good military wife realized the importance of letting nothing go to waste. Charlotte picked up two squares of cloth about the size of her thumbnail and began to stitch them together with a neat running stitch.

Charlotte sewed. And thought. She reviewed her many assets, not the least of which was her abundant straw-colored hair and light blue eyes. She was the best dancer at Camp Robinson. She was learning to play the guitar and sing. And she was a good shot, as well prepared as any military wife could be to protect herself against savages. Nathan's career would benefit if he married into an officer's family. All in all, Charlotte could not think of a single thing to keep Sergeant Nathan Boone from falling to one knee and proposing.

The sound of marching brought Charlotte back into the present. She hopped up and ran to the window just in time to see the new recruits marching into camp.

"Dinah! Dinah Valentine! You come here!" Charlotte ran for her parasol and bonnet. When there was no sight of her eight-year-old sister, she hurried to the back door. "Dinah! Dinah, where are you?!"

"I'm here, Charlott-ah," Dinah said, sticking her head out the door of the shed. "I think Maizy's calf is on the way."

"Oh, who cares about old Maizy and a calf! You come here! The recruits have arrived. You come and walk with me."

Dinah frowned. "I don't care about a bunch more soldiers," she protested.

"Well, I can't exactly go strolling up and down the picket fence gawking at the soldiers by myself," Charlotte said. "Mama would have a fit."

"Get Mama to go with you," Dinah said. She didn't budge from the shed door.

"I can't. Mama's over at Mrs. Gruber's seeing if the freighter brought a new supply of canned meat." She hesitated, then blurted out, "I'll give you the rest of my candy from Christmas."

Dinah considered. "You got any horehound left?"

"Three pieces," Charlotte said.

Within five minutes, the Misses Charlotte and Dinah Valentine were promenading up the picket fence bordering along the adobe duplexes.

They giggled about one soldier's fiery red hair. "Won't *he* be a fine target for the Indians." Another seemed so old Charlotte couldn't imagine he'd be much use. Others were declared to be too short, too skinny, or too dirty. Besides the one with the red hair, Charlotte found nothing of interest among the new recruits. Save one.

Standing toe-to-toe with the recruit who called himself Caleb Jackson, Nathan spoke with authority, "Jackson?"

"Yes, sir." The recruit snapped his reply and saluted smartly, shifting his gaze so that he was staring just past Nathan's left earlobe.

Nathan frowned as he looked down at the footsore recruit. "I see you've met Corporal Dorsey."

"Sir?"

"Your boots. Feel better, don't they?"

"Yes, sir."

Nathan folded his arms across his chest. "Civilian experience?"

"I worked in a variety store in St. Louis, sir. Behind the counter."

"Seems to me you should be assigned to the quartermaster, then."

"No, sir!" Jackson barked. He shifted his gaze back so he was peering into Nathan's eyes, pleading. "I joined up to see action, sir."

"Didn't like working in a store?"

"Hated it, sir."

Nathan nodded and let his eyes run down the row of Jackson's shirt buttons. "Can you sit a horse?"

"Yes, sir."

"Really?" Nathan asked. "Seems to me a St. Louis store clerk wouldn't have much call to ride."

"My family owned horses, sir. I grew up riding."

"If your family owned horses, what landed you behind the counter of a store in St. Louis?"

The recruit narrowed his gaze. He swallowed. "We lost it. Everything." His thin lips sneered. "Apparently my father's stables threatened some great moment of military bravery." The slightest southern accent flavored his last sentence. "As did the house, the servant's houses, and the cotton fields. Yankees burned it all."

Nathan cleared his throat. "Camp Robinson is not the place for settling old scores with the Yankees, Private Jackson."

"I'm not here to settle old scores, sir." He stared straight ahead.

Nathan touched the brim of his hat with his index finger and took a step back. "Well, then, maybe you can help some of the boys when we turn them loose with their new mounts."

"I'll do that, sir."

Nathan moved to the next recruit and the next, moving down the line until he had sized up the men to be integrated into Company G of the Third Cavalry. They'd gained a cobbler and a tailor, along with a few farm boys; two railroad workers, who would likely be the first men to discover that Sergeant Nathan Boone would back up his orders with his fists; and a couple of Irishmen whom Nathan expected to desert the first time they ventured north into gold country. But Private Caleb Jackson, though not the only galvanized Yankee in the bunch, was certainly the most intriguing.

Nathan wasn't likely to have forgotten the night he and a fourteen-year-old Confederate drummer boy named Beauregard Preston met. It had been nearly fifteen years ago, but they'd spent the night picking their way through a battlefield so strewn with dead bodies that they could scarcely find a place to step without landing on some body part. They'd seen each other once after the war. Nathan didn't remember Beau talking much about his home or family. But then, Nathan had been so enamored with Lily at the time, he was hardly in his right mind. After that chance encounter in Nashville, he'd never seen Beau again, but he would have known him anywhere.

Jackson. You've got to remember to call him Jackson.

Nathan dismissed his men with orders to report to the quartermaster before afternoon roll call. "If any of you other men have an eye for horseflesh, you can look over the new mounts with Private Jackson here." Nathan nodded toward his old friend. "Mounted drill starts tomorrow."

Jackson hoisted his bedroll and hurried off across the parade ground toward the cavalry barracks on the southeast corner of the post. Watching him go, Nathan wondered what could have happened to make Beau Preston change his name and lose his accent. He had almost decided to say something when Jackson turned and looked back at him. He hesitated a minute, then touched the bill of his cap with one finger and nodded.

Nathan returned the salute. "I'd like to talk to you after you look over those horses, Private," he called out. "Alone."

"Yes, sir," Jackson called back. "I'll be glad to answer your questions, sir."

"Meet me at the corral in half an hour," Nathan called out and turned to go. Reporting in to the captain required Nathan to go by the row of officer's duplexes.

"I see you have some new men to break in, Sergeant Boone," Charlotte called out in her most grown-up voice as Nathan approached the Valentine residence.

Nathan smiled and touched the brim of his hat in a brief salute. "Yes, ma'am."

"The ladies will be even more outnumbered at the next hop," Charlotte observed.

"But there is a bright side to the dilemma," Nathan said, grinning. "At least two of the new men actually know how to dance."

"Oh?" Charlotte opened her fan with a

flick of her wrist. "Let me guess. The flaming redhead."

Nathan laughed. "No. I don't think Yates is much for the quadrille. But keep an eye on the one with the beard."

"Which one?" Charlotte made a show of peering over her fan toward the retreating backs of the recruits.

"The one you were eyeing so carefully as they marched by."

Charlotte's cheeks burned. "Why, Sergeant Boone, I don't know what on earth you are talking about."

"Jackson."

"I beg your pardon?"

"His name. It's Private Caleb Jackson. I'll introduce you at the next hop." He bowed and backed away, hoping Charlotte's flirtation would distract her from wondering just how it was a company sergeant could tell which of his new men knew how to dance.

"Buckskin mare's a looker," Nathan said. He draped his arms over the top bar of the quartermaster's corral and waited for Jackson, who stood next to him, to comment.

"Cow-hocked," was all the man said.

The mare wheeled around on her hind

legs and set off for the opposite side of the corral. Nathan watched her movement and nodded. "You do have an eye for horse-flesh." He looked at Jackson. "Yates said you were going to help him pick out a mount."

"Yates has a big mouth," Jackson said, pulling the brim of his hat down on his forehead.

"He's all right. Green as they come. But he'll do. If he survives tomorrow."

"He will." Jackson pointed at the buck-skin mare, who had crowded up against a scrawny-looking dun gelding and was nib-bling playfully at his withers. "She's cow-hocked, but she's got a sweet tempera-ment. I figure she'll put up with Yates."

"How do you figure that?"

Jackson whistled. The mare's ears went up, and she trotted over to the fence and thrust her nose between the boards.

Nathan nodded, smiling. "You always had a way with the ladies. Even when you were only fourteen. I remember how you sweet-talked those Sanitary Commission ladies into letting you have an extra pair of socks."

"*Two* extra pair," Jackson said, still rub-bing the mare's forehead. He kept his head down as he murmured, "I couldn't believe

132

my eyes when I looked up and saw who my new sergeant was. Thanks for not letting on that you know me."

Nathan cleared his throat. "Look, Beau . . . er . . . Caleb. I've learned not to ask many questions about the men under me. Fact is, I don't even *know* some of their given names. I suspect there's more than just you using a name their own mama wouldn't recognize. That's their business. As long as they obey orders and do the job."

"You won't have any trouble from me," Jackson said quickly. "I won't be expecting any special treatment just because we knew each other in another life. Fact is, I'd appreciate it if nobody ever knew about that."

"You running from the law?" Nathan asked.

Jackson shook his head. "The only crime I ever committed was not marrying a certain young lady back in St. Louis when her papa thought I should."

"Meaning?"

"Meaning I didn't have anything to do with the baby on the way, and I wasn't about to pay for somebody else's mistakes. Even if the papa in question was my employer at the time." Caleb tugged on the mare's forelock and began to scratch behind her ears. "St. Louis was bad for me, that's all. I'd seen enough of soldiers coming up to the city from Jefferson Barracks to know accents and origins don't matter so much in the army."

"You pretty much got rid of the accent. Last time I saw you I could hardly believe you were from the some country as me."

"In some ways Mecklenburg County *isn't* the same country." Jackson nodded toward the horizon. "I never been any place like this — where you can see so far you'd swear you can see tomorrow coming at you."

Nathan chuckled. "It sure isn't anything like home."

"I like it," Jackson said quickly. "A man can breathe out here."

"Or get lost," Nathan added.

Jackson shrugged. He pushed the buckskin mare away and swatted her on the rump. "Go on, now." The little mare trotted off.

Sergeants' assembly sounded. Nathan turned to go. "Well, I guess we're straight then, Private Jackson."

"Yes, sir," he saluted. "Thank you, sir."

Nathan returned his friend's salute and headed off toward the adjutant's office where he'd receive the next day's orders from his commander.

Eight

My heart is sore pained within me: and the terrors of death are fallen upon me. Fearfulness and trembling are come upon me, and horror hath overwhelmed me.

Psalm 55:4–5

The internal music Laina usually summoned to calm herself wouldn't play. Instead, drums pounded against her temples. She felt dizzy. Her heart began to race and beads of sweat broke out across her forehead. She braced herself against the doorway, fighting a wave of nausea.

Across the road on the parade ground, a company of men marched in cadence to the bawled orders of their drill sergeant. Here and there, small groups of soldiers stood or sat in clusters near the bakery and the quartermaster's stores. Over by the stables, a few men had tethered their horses in the morning sun and were making half-hearted attempts to comb out manes and tails.

Nothing to be afraid of. Just soldiers going about their normal day. More than usual because of the recruits who arrived a couple weeks ago. But nothing to be afraid of.

Still, her heart raced.

Sergeant Boone seems nice enough. He's a gentleman. Harmless. Focus on him. Don't think about the others. Nothing to be afraid of.

It didn't help. The drums still pounded inside her head, her stomach still roiled. Pulling away from Granny Max, Laina propelled herself backward away from the door, and fled to the back room, where she wretched into the basin perched on a washstand beside the back door. Wiping her mouth with a trembling hand, she looked up at Granny's reflection in the clouded mirror hanging above the washstand.

"Maybe tomorrow," she said, swiping the kerchief off her head. Making her way back into the front room, she sat down in Granny's rocker and retrieved a shirt from the always overflowing mending pile.

Granny followed Laina's gaze across Soldier Creek to where perhaps a hundred or so men were engaged in their morning routine. "We'll go the back way," she said. "Mrs. O'Malley and the other girls are already in the washhouse working. We can go in the trading post by the back door. Mrs. Gruber won't mind. You'll like her, Laina. She's a good woman. When Lily died, it was Mrs. Gruber who cut up one of her own quilts to line the casket. She spent the night helping me work on it." Granny added, "She'll make you tea, and you can rest while I do some shopping. The freighter was supposed to be bringing in some bolts of calico. I was hoping you'd pick out one for a new dress of your own."

Laina picked at the sleeve of Lily Boone's gray calico work dress. "I've no way to pay for a new dress," she said.

"Mrs. Gruber says when you're better, you can help her out at the store a few days."

"There's nothing wrong with this dress," Laina argued. "Unless . . . unless maybe Sergeant Boone doesn't like me wearing *her* things?"

"Of course he doesn't mind," Granny said. "That's not the reason I want you to go with me. You need some fresh air and sunshine. It's time you got out a little."

Laina sighed. "Later." She put her hand

to her stomach. "I just don't feel good enough right now."

"There is nothing to be afraid of," Granny said gently.

Laina hung her head. Pressing the back of her hand to her forehead she said, "I know that in my head." She looked up at Granny. "But my heart pounds." She spread her fingers across the front of her dress. "It feels like it's coming right out of me."

Granny closed the door and sat down at the table. Taking one of Laina's hands in hers, she murmured, "Like I said the other night, you've got a choice to make. You *can* keep Josiah Paine from taking your future."

Laina pulled her hand away and took up the shirt atop the mending pile, checking for loose buttons. "I can't. It keeps coming back to me." She ran her hands across the layer of buttons in Granny's button box. Selecting a small white button, she compared it to the ones already sewn onto the shirt in her lap. Laying it aside, she looked for another.

Granny reached into the button box and handed Laina a button.

"Everyone will stare," Laina said. "They'll be wondering . . . imagining . . ."

"Imagining what, child? All anyone here

at Camp Robinson knows is that you survived an Indian attack."

"*They* know. Sergeant Boone and that corporal. They know all of it." Laina looked up at Granny. "*Where* I was — *what* I was."

"You stop that." Granny's voice was stern. Almost angry. "That was not your fault. And they both know it." Granny sighed. "What is it that has you so determined to let go of life, child?"

Laina folded her arms across the edge of the table and rested her forehead atop them. "I was so stupid. So stupid." She began to talk. The past spilled out of her, details flooding the room like waves of the Mississippi in a storm, crashing against its banks, leaving empty bottles and rusted cans in its wake.

"The earliest thing I remember is my father — Eustis Gray — sitting at a table playing cards. He was frowning at me. Then he whispered something to the woman who'd brought me to him, and I was taken away. I guess my mama must have died. I don't really know. But I think I must have got my auburn hair from her. My father had black hair. As black as coal. I remember how it used to glisten in the sunlight when he went up on deck." She

139

paused, picking up a large button and circling it nervously with one finger. "I was taken off the riverboat to a place that turned out to be a school — mostly for wealthy girls whose parents did not want to be bothered with them. At least that's how it seemed to me. I don't remember seeing anyone's parents very often.

"When I was about seven years old, a girl named Nellie Pierce got mad at me one day and sneered, *'Don't you think you can order me around, Laina Gray. Everybody knows your father is a no-good gambler. The only reason Miss Hart even let you come to our school is because he pays twice what everybody else does.'* That was the first time I knew why Miss Hart never treated me quite like the other girls.

"When I was about fourteen — that's a guess; I'm not certain how old I am — my father came and took me away from Miss Hart's. He'd begun losing at the tables. Miss Hart had told him what a fine musician I was. He asked me to play the piano and sing for him. When I did, he smiled and said I would do just fine on the riverboat and not to be afraid. But I was afraid. Nellie and the other girls told stories late at night about all the bad people who lived down on the riverfront. I was terrified to go, but when I told my father, he got mad. Told me I could walk the streets by myself if I wanted to, but he had given Miss Hart his last dollar.

"Life on the river wasn't all bad. The women who sang and danced in the saloon were kind to me. One of them named Rose talked my father into letting me room with her. I soon learned that Rose did more than sing and dance to earn her keep, and when my father hinted that I would soon be doing the same, I made plans to run away.

"I was creeping along the deck of the riverboat late one night when suddenly my father stepped in front of me and wanted to know where I was going. He grabbed my arm and dragged me to his room. He told me Rose had filled my head with up-pity ideas and that if I tried to get away again, he'd see to it that Rose was pun-ished. I hid the bruises on my arms and did what he said.

"Performing with Rose and the girls wasn't all bad. The men cheered and waved at us and most of the time they didn't bother me. One night a wealthy man from New Orleans came to the show, and afterward he sent a note to me that he would like to have me join him at a private party up on Locust Avenue. My father had lost a lot of money to this man at the gambling tables that night.

"Rose said this was my chance to get away. She said I would be off the riverboat and that once I was at the private party, I could get away. She helped me stash all the money I had saved inside my corset. So I went to the party with the man from New Orleans. He called himself Pierre Dupre, but I don't know if that was his real name."

Laina paused. She swiped a trembling hand over her eyes. "I woke up the next morning in the back of a covered wagon. My hands and feet were tied. There was a foul-smelling rag stuffed in my mouth. Josiah Paine said he'd won me from Dupre. I couldn't remember anything after Dupre lured me into a back room of his mansion. He gave me something to drink and I passed out." She sobbed. "I actually thought my father might come after me. Might rescue me. So I waited. Until we were so far out in the wilderness, there was no one to run to." She tried to laugh. "Stupid, stupid girl. I should have tried to get away."

Granny snorted. "To where? To some Indian camp? If you're like most women, whatever you heard about Indians was depradation and damnification. No one can blame you for not running." She touched the scars on Laina's wrists. This time Laina endured the touch. "No one blames you, child."

Laina laid her free arm on the edge of the table and hid her face against it. Granny let go of her hand and patted her shoulder while Laina hid her face in her folded arms and sobbed. "Why couldn't Sergeant Boone have been just a second later? Why didn't God just let me *go*."

Granny sat down next to her. "Come here, honey-lamb. Come to Granny Max." Gently, she pulled Laina into her arms. She slid to her knees on the floor and buried her face in Granny's apron, sobbing and shuddering while Granny stroked her back and whispered words of love.

Granny patted her shoulder. "Even now, Josiah Paine reaches out from the grave and harms you. He makes you a prisoner in my house, a prisoner afraid to take a step outside, afraid to hope for better things." Granny's hand covered the back of Laina's bowed head. "You got a choice to make. Maybe the hardest one you will ever make. You can let him keep you a prisoner or you can tell him *no*. You can't change the past. And Josiah Paine owns a big, awful piece of yours. But you do *not* have to give him your *future*."

Laina looked up into the older woman's lined face. Granny's eyes burned with the conviction of what she had just said. "Do you . . . do you think I could really just . . . *leave it?* Stop being so afraid all the time?"

"Yes. Yes." Granny squeezed her hand.

Laina closed her eyes, imagining what life might be like without the nightmares and the day fears. "I . . . I want to try, Granny. I do." She clutched her stomach. "But . . ."

"Baby steps, child. Baby steps." Granny bent down and kissed the top of her head. Instead of urging her out the door, Granny asked, "Where did you learn to sew?"

"Rose taught me."

Granny stood, pulling Laina up off the floor and guiding her back into her chair. "All right, then. That's someone in your memories that did something *good* for you."

She studied Laina's tear-stained face. "You know, Laina, if I could just walk into your head right now and clean up all those evil memories, I would do it. Fact is, I can't. But there is something in my Bible that has helped me." Granny reached for her Bible, still lying open on the kitchen table from her morning reading. Thumbing through the pages, she found the place and read, " 'Finally brethren, whatsoever things are true, whatsoever things are honest, whatsoever things are just, whatsoever things are pure, whatsoever things are lovely, whatsoever things are of good report; if there be any virtue, and if there be any praise, think on these things.' "

Granny closed the book and laid it back on the table. "Now I am not one of those people who thinks you just open that book and read a verse and that makes everything all better. I know the battle is raging inside your pretty head, and I know it is a terrible one. You got people like Rose and you got Josiah Paine — and maybe more than just him. I don't know." She leaned down and hugged Laina fiercely. "But you got a quick mind to help you fight this battle. And the battle for you right now is this: Which one you gonna think on? Josiah Paine or Rose?"

Laina nodded.

"Everybody has sad memories. Some worse than others. Yours are among the worst I've ever heard. But you got good things you can think on too. Rose. Sergeant Boone. Shelter. Food. A new dress —"

145

"— you," Laina interrupted her. Tears welled up in her eyes. "And you, Granny Max."

Granny smiled down at Laina. "Thank you, honey. I am pleased to be one of your *good things*. You got any others that come to mind?"

"Music," Laina whispered. "I always liked singing."

Granny reached over to the table and handed her button box to Laina. "Maybe you will have a song ready for old Granny when I get back from Mrs. Gruber's."

Laina nodded and returned to the seat beside the kitchen table. She bent to the work of sewing buttons on Sergeant Boone's shirt.

Granny slung the market basket back over her forearm and went to the door. "You are going to be all right, Laina Gray. It may take some time. But if you are willing to work at *thinking on these things,* you will be all right." She turned to go, then stopped and turned back, calling Laina's name again.

Laina looked up at her.

"Don't you be worrying about what Nathan and Corporal Dorsey might be thinking when they see you. They are men," Granny said, smiling. "When they see you, all they see is pretty."

Laina touched the side of her head where the gunpowder had burned away her hair. She could feel a blush rising up the back of her neck and spreading to her cheeks. She shook her head and concentrated on moving the button beneath her thumb into position as Granny closed the door. In the quiet, she was drawn back into the past, and just as Granny had predicted, the specter of Josiah Paine returned. Looking up from her work, Laina tried what Granny had said. Instead of retreating into the dugout in her mind, she went to Miss Hart's, to music class. She began to hum to herself, surprised when the words to a song came to mind.

Presently, singing softly to herself, Laina went to the back door, opened it, and peeked out. There was no one in sight. The sensation of the spring breeze against her face felt good. If she angled the rocker just right, she could enjoy the fresh air and a view of the broad valley stretching off toward pine-covered ridges in the distance and still be almost completely shielded behind the open door. She took a few minutes to arrange things before settling into the rocker and taking up a shirt. The same creek that looped between Soapsuds Row and Camp Robinson's main buildings meandered toward the south. Its banks were hidden by low growing brush and scrubby looking trees covered with white blossoms. Laina bent to her task, but not before judging the distance to the nearest clump of trees and thinking that perhaps she and Granny could walk down there this afternoon.

Raucous laughter. *That only sounds close. Those men are over at the stables. Sergeant Boone said the recruits would be riding again today. And at least a few were still saddlesore. That's what they are laughing about. Think on these things.*

Pounding hooves. *The cavalry is drilling. Think on these things.*

Marching. *The infantry. They drill every day. Think on these things.*

More hoofbeats. *Sergeant Boone and Company G are going out for target practice. Today is Monday. They do target practice every Monday. Think on these things.*

Laina had done well at remembering some good things from Miss Hart's. She even had a funny story to tell Granny Max when she got back from the trading post. She willed herself to stay seated in her rocker while the sounds of the military

148

camp assaulted her good intentions with new fears. She recited what she knew about life at Camp Robinson to herself. There was a very good explanation for nearly every noise. She even recognized water call when the bugler sounded.

But in spite of her attempts to replace fears with good thoughts, the empty room began to get on her nerves. She began to feel queasy again. Thinking she heard footsteps coming toward Soapsuds Row, she began to tremble with fear. She reminded herself to notice the beautiful spring day. There was nothing to be afraid of. She knew all these things. She even half believed them. But suddenly all she wanted to do was stop the mental battle and crawl beneath the quilt on her bed and go to sleep.

Someone slammed a door up at the opposite end of Soapsuds Row. Jumping up, Laina quickly closed the back door and lifted the bar into place. She stood with her back to the door. *There. Safe.* She sat on the edge of her bed in the muted light, nervously tugging at one gray cuff.

She could hear muffled laughter. That would be Katie and Becky — the O'Malley girls, likely headed toward the washhouse to help their mother. Granny said Meara

O'Malley and her girls had arrived not long after the Boones and had caused quite a stir when they banged on the captain's front door demanding to see Paddy O'Malley of Company I, Fourth Infantry. Due to O'Malley's being out on patrol, it had been a few days before the family was reunited.

Meara O'Malley had ignored the camp gossip that placed Paddy O'Malley in a Sioux tepee over at the agency instead of out on patrol.

"My Paddy? Takin' up with the savages? The dear Lord preserve me," she'd said, and crossed herself. "I won't believe that until Paddy tells me himself."

Paddy had not told her. He'd come home smiling and seemed completely delighted to have the life nearly squeezed out of him by the overzealous greeting of his overweight wife and the enthusiastic hugs from his two daughters, the youngest of whom did not even remember her father.

When Paddy O'Malley died in a freak accident out on maneuvers, Meara dressed in black and grieved her husband. But it wasn't long before Meara, wide-of-body and sharp-of-tongue, succumbed to the flattery of all the attention she received from a long line of soldiers. Women were scarce on the frontier. None stayed single for long, Granny said. Meara's girls had a new father within three months of Paddy's death. He was gone now, too — a victim of his own affinity for whiskey. He'd been shot in a drunken brawl at one of the hog ranches off the military reservation. But he'd left a lasting memory of himself. Meara was pregnant.

Laina found herself wondering what the O'Malley girls were like. She wondered if they minded living at Camp Robinson. How they felt about losing *two* fathers. If they missed anyone back home.

"Home." There was a word. She whispered, *Chez moi. Ma maison,* pronouncing the French words carefully, strangely satisfied that she remembered them from her French lessons at Miss Hart's. All Miss Hart's students went home for the holidays. It had caused Laina a few sleepless nights the first time she faced the awful possibility of Nellie Pierce sneering goodbye as she walked down the broad front steps of Miss Hart's Academy for Young Ladies, leaving Laina behind.

To avoid the disgrace, Laina had created an alternative scenario. By forging her father's signature on a note asking that she be taken to the train station, Laina succeeded in creating the illusion of *going home* for herself. No one ever guessed that while the girls from Miss Hart's were at *home,* one from among their number was living on the streets of St. Louis. After that first Christmas, when she'd broken out in a cold sweat from the fear of being discovered, Laina had developed a routine of sorts that amounted to her own holiday traditions. She always attended Christmas Eve mass in the Cathedral down on the waterfront. The year she managed to hide in an alcove and get locked in was one of her better Christmases. *A good memory.* Granny would be pleased.

Up the row the same door slammed again. "Kathleen Eileen O'Malley!" Mrs. O'Malley shouted. Laina closed her eyes. "Get that creature *out* of here right this minute! Look at that! He's ruined the handle on my best knife. I declare, Katie, if he chews on one more thing of mine. . . !"

Laina thought of the night Eustis Gray had caught her trying to run away again and cut her with the tip of his knife, just beneath her jawline. Not so the scar would show, but so she would remember. That knife and the realization her father would make good on his threat to hurt Rose ended any plan Laina had to leave. Eventually, when she made a name for herself as "Riverboat Annie," she learned how to keep the real Laina separate from the dancing and drinking and everything else that went on in the narrow hallways and darkened rooms below deck. Not until Josiah Paine came along did anyone manage to pierce the veil between Riverboat Annie's performances and Laina Gray's life. Eventually, his depravity plunged her into a darkness so complete that Laina Gray was nearly snuffed out.

Nearly. But Laina Gray was still alive. She was more than a little crazy at times. She panicked at the thought of going outside. She hid from the soldiers. But she was learning not to hide when Sergeant Boone came for dinner. Two nights ago she had even sat at the table with him and Granny Max. She hadn't said much. But it was a start.

She could remember some of the French from Miss Hart's. She could still sing. And she could, at least part of the time, do what Granny Max said. She could choose to push the bad memories away and replace them with good things. Laina pondered Granny Max's words. *"He has your past. You do not have to give him your future."*

She looked around her, at the evidence

of Clara Maxwell having done exactly what she said Laina must do. The two rooms were tangible evidence of Granny's making things better. Instead of leaving the windows bare, Granny Max had made curtains. She had picked some spring flowers and put them in a tin can on the table. She'd monogrammed the linen towel hanging on the hook above the washbasin. And instead of using plain army-issue blankets on the beds, Granny had made quilts.

Perched on the edge of her narrow bed, Laina looked down at the quilt. It must have a thousand pieces, tiny brown and pink triangles joined to make squares, the squares joined to make bigger squares. The quilt represented hundreds of hours of stitching and a strong determination to make something beautiful. In the long-ago past, Clara "Granny Max" Maxwell had stopped hiding in a closet and started eating raspberry pie. In the present, she had taken two bare rooms and made them a home.

Looking at the door she had just barred, Laina thought, *And I've taken these same two rooms and locked myself inside and made a prison. I might as well still be in the dugout.*

Slowly, Laina stood up. Going to the

window above Granny's bed, she pushed the curtains aside and let the morning light stream in the window. It highlighted a worn spot on Granny's quilt. Leaning down to inspect it, Laina decided that once she was finished sewing buttons on Sergeant Boone's dress parade shirt, she should patch Granny's quilt.

Walking into the next room, she stirred up the fire and set the coffeepot on the stove. It was getting near lunchtime. She'd never learned to cook much, but maybe she could manage flapjacks. Granny liked flapjacks.

While the water heated, Laina took up the straw broom propped in the corner behind the front door and swept the floor. Guiding the dust toward the back room, she swept all the way to the barred door. And then she unbarred the door and swept the dust outside.

Anyone passing by would have had no idea of the battle being waged inside the mound of quilts in Granny Max's rocker. Only a fringe of auburn hair gave witness to the humanity inside the quilt. But having finally opened the front door to the outside world at Camp Robinson, Laina had determined not to close it until

Granny came back. She had made flap-jacks and they were being kept warm in the oven. She had finished sewing the buttons on Sergeant Boone's dress shirt. She had swept a floor. She had opened a door. And she had made a choice. She was exhausted, but as she huddled inside her pink-and-brown quilt, listening to the sounds of Camp Robinson, Laina was deliciously conscious of a newly arrived inner quiet. She had nearly dozed off when she heard the shuffle of childish footsteps approaching from up the row of apartments.

She had wondered what Kathleen O'Malley looked like, how old she might be. About eight, Laina now guessed as she returned the startled gaze of two brilliant blue eyes. Just as their eyes met, the fat white puppy clutched in Kathleen's arms wriggled nearly out of her grasp. Her tangle of blond hair completely obscured her face as she leaned down to deposit the squirming puppy on the ground. Wagging its entire rear end, the pup snuffled along the dirt before padding confidently to where Laina sat.

"No, Wilber, no," the child called. "Come back here!"

To Wilber's credit, he did at least hesitate. He even yapped an answer. And kept going. Straight for where Laina sat. She slipped her feet to the floor. Wilber's tail wagged even more furiously. She held her hand out. Joyously, he kissed her fingers, then wriggled away just far enough so that when he squatted to relieve himself the puddle didn't land on Laina's feet.

"Wilber, *no*." Kathleen rushed for him and gathered him up in her arms. "I'm sorry," she gasped. "I'll clean it up. I'm sorry. Oh, *please* don't tell Ma. Please don't."

"Don't worry. I like puppies."

The child drew away, still clutching her puppy. She nodded and struggled to keep from dropping the impatient dog.

"Puppies can't help it sometimes." Laina let the quilt fall away from her.

Kathleen blurted out, "Why aren't you mad? Ma gets terrible mad when Wilber forgets he's in the house. She said if he does it one more time, he's a goner."

Laina smiled. "You have to watch a puppy every minute for a while."

"How come you know about dogs?"

Laina had gone to the kitchen and was returning with a bucket and a rag. As she bent to wipe up the puddle, she said, "I had a dog. He looked a lot like Wilber."

She reached out and scratched under the puppy's chin.

"What happened to your dog?"

Laina put the used rag in the bucket and set it outside the back door. "He died," she said.

"Wilber came from the Indians. Pa — my *new* pa — gave him to me." She added, "I got to teach him to stay home so he don't get et. He's fat and they like the fat ones. At least that's what Pa said."

Laina touched the soft black nose. Her eyes misted over. "Make certain when he comes to you he always gets something good. He'll be staying close by soon enough."

Kathleen looked doubtful. "Wilber's awful stubborn." The puppy struggled and managed to wriggle out of her grasp. With a delighted yelp, he tore off toward a clump of trees down on the creek. Kathleen shrieked his name and set off after him.

Laina followed.

Nine

But when thou makest a feast, call the poor, the maimed, the lame, the blind: And thou shalt be blessed; for they cannot recompense thee: for thou shalt be recompensed at the resurrection of the just.

Luke 14:13-14

"My mama says you're crazy," the girl said as she plunked herself down beside Laina. "I think you're nice. You can call me Katie. Everybody does. Except Ma, when she's angry about something."

"Thank you," Laina choked out. Discouraged to learn only a short walk made her feel faint, she leaned back against a fallen log and waited to catch her breath. Wilber, who had been exploring the creek bank just a few feet away, bounded over and invited himself into Laina's lap. His muddy paws dotted her skirt with filth.

"Wil-*brrrrrrr*," Katie scolded, reaching for him.

Laina waved her away. She swallowed and took a deep breath. Wilber snuggled into the gray calico folds of her skirt and fell asleep. "It's all right," she said, smiling. "Crazy women don't care about mud on their dresses."

"But you're *not* crazy," Katie said. She brushed her blond curls out of her eyes and looked sideways up at Laina. "I hear you at night sometimes. When you have a bad dream." She nodded. "I have bad dreams, too. You ever hear *me?*"

Laina shook her head.

"Well, I don't always yell. Becky — that's my sister — Becky makes fun of me if I yell." She reached over and touched the top of Wilber's head. "That's why Pa brought me a puppy. He said I could have Wilber sleep with me, and if I woke up scared, Wilber would help. Ma didn't want me to have a dog. Said they are dirty and good for nothing but fleas. But I quit waking her up at night, so she lets Wilber stay. Now that Pa's died, Ma don't mind having a dog so much." She ducked her head and then, leaning over, looked up into Laina's face. "Is that why *you* had a dog? To help with bad dreams?"

Laina looked up at the blue sky. She shook her head.

The young girl kept talking. "They got whole *herds* of dogs over by the Agency. Just running loose all over the place since the Indians left. Pa said there's so many the soldiers use 'em for target practice sometimes. Some of 'em are half wild. Not Wilber, though. Wilber's nice. Are you going to stay with Granny Max?" She didn't wait for an answer. "Because if you are going to stay, maybe you could help me teach Wilber so Ma wouldn't yell at him so much."

"Kathleen! Kathleen Eileen O'Malley!"

"Oh no. Now she's really going to be mad. I was supposed to put Wilber in his cage and sweep the floor." Katie scrambled to her feet. "Here, Ma!" She jumped up and yelled at the top of her lungs. "I'm here!" She turned back around. "I better go," she said, and scooped the puppy up in her arms. "You want to meet my Ma?"

Laina shook her head.

"Come on," Katie pleaded. "She won't be so mad if you come with me. Please." She held out her hand and Laina took it.

"This is . . ." Katie frowned. "What's your name?"

"Laina," Laina said and extended her hand to Katie's mother. "Laina Gray."

"Laina helped me with Wilber," Katie said, completely oblivious to her mother's openmouthed stare. "She can show me how to make Wilber behave, Ma. And he won't make any more puddles inside, and he'll come when I call him. Isn't that so, Laina?" Katie nudged her.

Laina dropped the offered hand, which had been ignored, and looked down at the ground. She could feel her face burning as her cheeks turned red beneath the woman's careful inspection.

"We'll have to see, Katie," Mrs. O'Malley said.

"But, Ma . . . you said if —"

"I said we will see, Kathleen. Now come inside and do the sweeping you were told to do an hour ago." The woman pulled her daughter inside and closed the door without so much as another glance in Laina's direction.

Once back inside, Laina shoved Granny's rocker over and barred the front door before crawling beneath her quilt and falling into a dreamless sleep.

Pounding on the front door roused Laina, but before she could get up, Granny

Max burst in the back door.

Laina sat up, still groggy.

Granny put her hand on her forehead. "You all right, honey-lamb? Why'd you bar the door?"

"I was . . . the noises . . . the marching . . ."

Granny clucked and made her way into the front room where she lifted the bar from the door and admitted a soldier, who dumped packages on the table as Granny bustled about the kitchen. "Now you just sit yourself down for a minute, Private," Granny was saying as she opened the oven door. "I'll pop this in and warm —" Granny stopped abruptly and set the pan of cold corn bread down on top of the stove. She withdrew the plate of warm flapjacks.

"They . . . they probably aren't even edible. But I tried." Laina had pulled the quilt-curtain aside and was standing in the doorway.

Granny didn't answer. Instead, she looked at the soldier who was blushing furiously even as he removed his hat and bobbed his head to greet Laina. "Well, Private Yates, I guess you can eat flapjacks instead of corn bread. This is Miss Laina Gray. Sit down."

The soldier did as he was told.

Laina ducked into the back room, presently returning with a stack of folded shirts in her arms. She placed the shirts on the edge of the table opposite the soldier and retreated to the doorway. Resisting the instinct to disappear into the back room, she stood still, her hands clasped behind her.

Private Yates stammered a thank-you. Blushing furiously, he stood up. "I got fatigue duty to finish up, ma'am," he said, backing to the door.

"I'm not finished with you yet, young man," Granny said. "How much do you owe the canteen?"

"I ain't been drunk again, Granny," Yates said, sidling for the door. "Honest. I told Jackson no more drinking for me."

"You didn't answer my question, Private."

"Now, Granny," the young man looked longingly out the door. For a moment, Laina thought he might make a run for it.

"So how much do you owe?"

"Two dollars." He hung his head.

"Mrs. Gruber said it's two-fifty," Granny said. "And by the time the quartermaster deducts for your laundry bill, are you gonna have anything left to send your mama? You said you stopped drinking with

Private Jackson. But are you still playing cards with him?"

Yates pressed his lips together stubbornly. "I will have some money to send home, ma'am."

"It is a nice thing for you to be buying little Katie O'Malley hair ribbons, Private Yates."

"Yes, ma'am," Yates nodded his head.

"But your own mama has got to come first."

"Yes, ma'am. You are right."

"And you need to remember your mama's lessons and keep away from the poker table," Granny said. "Now I may be an old woman, and you may think I don't have much sense —"

"Oh no, ma'am!" Yates interrupted her. "I know better than that, Granny."

Granny put her hands on her hips and nodded. "Good. Then you listen when I say you need to stay out of the canteen and away from card games. Those men know you are a greenhorn, and they beat you every time you play. Gambling is foolishness, Private Yates. But since your mama is a good Christian woman, I reckon you already know that."

"Yes, ma'am, I do. I just forget sometimes. You know how lonely it is here, ma'am. There's not much to do once fatigue duty is done."

Granny's voice gentled. "Yes, I do know that. Most of you boys come out here to the West with some fool dime novel in your heads, thinking you're going to be Indian-fighting heroes. And then you come to Camp Robinson and end up doing the same thing every day, with lots of free time to fill and not much to fill it with." She smiled. "The next time you are longing for home and your ma, you come sit on my front porch and play me a tune on that mouth harp I hear you bragging about playing so pretty."

With a glance in Laina's direction, Yates pulled on the brim of his hat. "I'll do that, Granny. Truly I will."

"From what I've heard about Private Jackson, he won't be forgiving you any gambling debts. And Mr. Gruber will be there with his hand out the minute the paymaster puts that thirteen dollars in your hand. Now, I don't want to be the cause of your mama not being able to pay her rent. I'll credit you your laundry bill for this month."

"You don't have to do that, Granny."

"I know I don't," Granny snapped. "And it's not a gift. I need some things done around here. You think you could come by after roll call a couple of evenings next week and do a few chores?"

Yates nodded. "Yes, ma'am."

"Don't you be telling any of those other soldiers Granny Max is a pushover about paying the laundry bill now, you hear?"

"Oh no, ma'am. I won't." Yates shook his head from side to side.

"And don't be expecting me to cancel any more debts after this month, either."

"I won't."

"Now git. Sergeant Boone will have your hide for being late for assembly again. And if you're in the guardhouse you won't be any use to me."

Private Yates took his leave of Granny Max and headed for the stables. Once inside, he walked down the broad center aisle to the last stall on the left. Tying a lead onto the halter of a buckskin mare, he led her out of her stall. He brushed her black mane and tail, remembering to spend an extra minute or two scratching her favorite spot just below her withers.

"I saw her, Babe. I saw the woman Sergeant Boone brought in. And Dorsey didn't tell the half of it. She's more'n pretty, Babe. She's an outright angel."

Babe stomped her foot and snorted.

"Oh, I know, I know. A pretty little thing like that isn't going to be interested in me. But she might give me a dance or two at the hop, mightn't she? Even that snooty surgeon's daughter dances with me at the hops. 'Course she acts like she's doing me a favor, but it's better'n bein' stepped on a thousand times by old Corporal Dorsey. That man may be a good soldier, but he's got no music sense at all."

Babe tossed her head and turned it sideways so she could eyeball Yates.

"Oh, go on, Babe. I know what you're thinking. But I got to go on over there at least a couple times. I got to work off the laundry bill. And Granny asked me to play harmonica sometime. There's no harm in that, is there? Who knows, maybe Miss Gray *likes* music."

As it turned out, Miss Gray *did* like music. But Private Yates didn't learn that for a couple of weeks. First, he learned that Miss Gray was shy and awkward around men. He assumed it was because she was self-conscious about the bandage on her head. She wore a kerchief to keep it covered, but she always seemed to reach up and touch the left side of her head when-

168

ever one of the soldiers came to collect his laundry. She had stopped hiding in the back room of Granny Max's as much, but Harlan could tell she was still nervous around strangers. It made him feel protective.

Another thing Harlan learned was that Granny Max didn't really need all that much done. He felt bad about it at first, letting her credit his laundry bill for so little work. He scavenged some lumber and put three more shelves on the wall beside the stove. He begged some whitewash from the quartermaster and whitewashed the kitchen walls. He repaired a kitchen chair leg. Finally, when he realized Granny was trying to find work for him, he insisted that she let him do some of the company laundry.

The first time one of the boys from Company G saw him hanging drawers out to dry, he thought he would die of embarrassment. But that very day Miss Gray brought him a piece of pie, and while she didn't exactly sit down and talk to him while he ate, she didn't run away, either. And when he said "Thank you," she said "You are welcome, Private Yates" before she went back inside. Harlan didn't mind the teasing that night in the barracks. He let the men poke fun at him while he lay on his cot with his hands behind his head smiling.

When it became common knowledge that Private Yates had actually seen "the crazy woman Sergeant Boone had rescued," Harlan acquired new status among the men. In the tradition of soldiers lonely for female attention, they pumped Yates for details and wondered when the woman might come to a Friday-night hop.

It took only two weeks for Harlan to work off his debt to Granny Max, but by the end of the two weeks Miss Gray had stopped acting so nervous around him. He had even told her some of his better jokes and been rewarded with smiles. Once, she laughed out loud when he did a perfect imitation of a rooster and strutted around the kitchen table to illustrate a story.

The Sunday morning at the end of his stint with Granny Max, Harlan was taking special care to make certain his cowlick was plastered down, when Private Jackson nudged him out of the way, teasing, "Give it up, Yates. It's no use. And what are you primping for, anyway?"

"Nothing special," Yates lied. He tucked his mouth harp into his pocket.

"Well 'nothing special' sure has you flustered. You gonna play that harmonica for the horses?"

"I'm just going over to the Row to play some music for Granny, that's all."

"For Granny and who else?" Jackson teased.

"Granny Max and the O'Malley girls and maybe Miss Gray."

"Whoa," Jackson said, holding up his hands. "Harlan Yates and all those females?" He reached for his hat. "You need some help, boy. I'd better come along."

"Y-You're not invited!" Yates stammered.

"Bet you two bits I can *get* invited," Jackson said. He grabbed Yates's arm. "Let's go."

Yates pulled away. "Now wait a minute, you can't just show up."

"Sure I can," Jackson said. "Everybody knows Granny Max has a soft spot. I bet I can find it just as good as you. I'll have her eating out of my hand."

"L-Listen, Jackson. You just can't show up. Miss Gray . . . well, she gets nervous around men."

Caleb arched one eyebrow and peered at Yates. "Aren't *you* a man?"

"She knows me. That's different."

"And she'll know me as soon as you introduce us," Jackson said again.

"You can't go!" Yates blurted out. "You just can't."

Jackson scowled. "You telling me I'm not good enough to be around your precious ladies, Private?"

"No. That's not —"

"Good. I didn't think you meant that." Jackson dragged Yates outside.

"But you still can't go."

"How you gonna stop me?" Jackson said.

Yates gulped. "Look, Jackson, you been a good bunky, but I —"

"You got that right," Jackson said. "Who got you a good horse?"

"You did."

"And who kept you from blowing your own foot off at target practice the other day?"

"You did."

"So now you can pay me back. Introduce me to the ladies. Come on, Yates. It's time to put up or shut up." Jackson headed off toward Soapsuds Row.

"Don't make me stop you," Yates croaked.

Jackson turned around, his head cocked to one side. "What did you say?"

"I said," Yates repeated, doubling up his

172

hands into fists. "Don't make me stop you."

Jackson snorted. "Very funny. As if you could, you ugly carrot-topped jerk."

"No need to call names," Yates said. "It's just that Miss Gray isn't ready to meet new people yet."

"What's her problem, anyway? I heard she's crazy. Do they have to keep her on a leash or something?"

Yates lowered his head and plowed into Jackson, who was caught off-balance and went down flat on his back in the dust just outside the barracks. Instantly there was a crowd around the two men. A minute later, Sergeant Boone and Corporal Dorsey were pulling the two men apart.

"He insulted a lady!" Yates screeched, struggling to pull away from Dorsey while at the same time putting a hand up to his bloodied nose.

Jackson didn't say anything at first, other than to quietly tell Sergeant Boone that Private Yates had started the fight by tackling him without provocation.

"Without . . . what?" Yates protested. "What's that mean, anyway?"

"It means," Boone explained, "that you started it."

"I did," Yates agreed. When Sergeant

Boone looked surprised, he explained. "Well, I couldn't get him to listen."

Boone looked at Jackson. "Tell me something that's news," he said.

"He's going to have a little social with the ladies over on the Row. When I said I wanted to come, he went crazy," Jackson said.

"That's because Miss Gray —" Yates stopped. Looking around him at the crowd of soldiers who had suddenly grown quiet at mention of the mystery woman over on Soapsuds Row, Yates pressed his lips together. He thought for half a second and then said to Nathan, "You know what I mean, sir."

Nathan nodded. He bent down and picked up Yates's hat, which still lay in the dust at his feet. "Is your nose going to be all right?" he asked, handing the private his hat.

Yates put the hat on. "Yes, sir. Nothing to worry about."

Nathan turned to Jackson. "You in the habit of inviting yourself into the company of ladies who haven't requested your presence?"

Jackson thrust his chest out and boasted, "I am in the habit, Sergeant Boone, of having whatever female company I choose.

Even the ones who don't initially request my presence are eventually glad they got to experience it — at least by the next morning."

A number of hoots and whistles went up.

"Well, that sort of female company doesn't exist at Camp Robinson, Private," Nathan snapped. "And you'll remember that, or you'll become very familiar with the interior of our newly appointed guard-house." He thought for a moment. "Suppose you make use of this fine spring afternoon by mucking out all the cavalry stalls, Private Jackson."

"*All* of them, sir?"

Nathan nodded. "You seem to desire female company. There's plenty of fillies over in the stable who will appreciate your attentions to their feed troughs and water buckets. Braid a few manes if you get really bored," Nathan said sarcastically. His voice grew more serious, "But remember that Soapsuds Row is strictly off limits to you until further notice."

"What about clean laundry, sir?"

"Have someone pick it up for you," Nathan said. "Someone who has sense enough to mind their own business and time enough to mind yours."

"Yes, sir."

Turning his back on Jackson, Nathan smiled at Yates. "Private Yates."

"Sir?"

"It's never good to keep Granny Max waiting when she has her mind set on something."

"Thank you, sir," Yates said. Trying not to gloat, he gave Jackson a wide berth and walked away.

Private Yates almost expected Granny to hear his heart pounding before his knuckles rapped on her door. When Granny opened the door and Miss Gray was right there in the kitchen, his face flushed bright red. Years of being the butt of jokes — about his long neck or huge ears or his red hair — had provided Yates with enough internal voices to render him almost speechless around most females. Private Jackson's name-calling a few minutes ago didn't help, either. *I must look like a chicken, bobbing my neck at her that way. I'm gonna scare her if I keep staring.* Harlan turned his attention to Granny. "You said to come and play for you sometime. I was hoping —"

Granny motioned for him to come in. "We're just packing a lunch."

Harlan could see that Miss Gray was

wrapping something in a cloth and settling it into Granny's market basket. Was it his imagination or had she turned just a little bit so her back was to him? He noticed her reach up and touch her head. She didn't have the kerchief on. In fact, her auburn hair had been braided into a thick rope that hung down her back all the way down to her waist. Why, Harlan thought, if she didn't have it tied into that braid, she just might be able to sit on her hair. He glanced at Granny, who was smiling knowingly at him.

"Why don't you join us, Private?" Granny asked. "We're just heading down to the creek for a little picnic."

"Oh, no," Harlan stammered. "I couldn't. I mean, I wouldn't want to be a bother."

"You'd be welcome company. Wouldn't he be, Miss Gray?"

Laina glanced over her shoulder at him. Her hand went to the left side of her head. She didn't say anything, but neither did she frown or disagree with Granny.

"Just get that dried-apple pie down off the shelf for me, Laina. We'll have plenty."

Harlan watched, his mouth watering at sight of the pie Miss Gray was just then taking down and settling into the basket.

"You like apple pie, don't you, Private Yates?" Granny asked.

Yates bobbed his head up and down. "Sure do, ma'am."

"Well, then," Granny said, "that's settled. You just wait around back for a few minutes while we finish, and we'll be out directly. The O'Malley girls will be joining us. Mrs. O'Malley isn't feeling well, and I told her we'd love to have the girls go along. We're going to have a little hymn sing by way of a church service, and you can play your mouth harp for us. How does that suit you?"

Harlan smiled and nodded and made agreeable sounds as he scooted out the door, drawing it closed behind him. Once on the front porch, he allowed himself a huge smile and a glance toward the stables where he pictured Private Jackson mucking out stalls while he, the "ugly carrot-topped jerk," accompanied Miss Laina Gray on a picnic.

While Yates rejoiced outside, Laina was battling the inner demons launching a full-scale attack on her newly acquired determination to follow Granny's lead down the path of normalcy and into an as yet uncharted future. "Just do the next thing, honey-lamb," Granny had urged when Laina felt panic rise inside her at the prospect of facing the world. Granny always knew how to help her face something new. Only Granny appreciated what it had taken for Laina not to crawl beneath her quilts and plead illness at the prospect of a long walk and a picnic with a soldier — even if the soldier *was* Private Yates.

Laina reminded herself that Yates was so shy he could barely form a complete sentence in her presence. Had she ever had a brother, Laina could imagine someone funny and endearing, just like him. He was oversized, clumsy, and amusing — in fact, Laina thought as she wound her long braid around her head, Private Yates shared some of Wilber's finer qualities. And he was housebroken. She smiled at her own joke.

Sergeant Boone appeared at the door. He was talking almost before he stepped inside, "He's just so stubborn," he was saying to Granny, "I can't get him to go to Doc Valentine, but he can barely walk, and I was wondering —" He stopped short and stared at Laina, who was just finishing pinning her hair up.

Laina's hand went to the left side of her head. She smoothed her hair back and reached for her bonnet.

"Good morning," Boone said. "It's good to see you're feeling better."

Granny interrupted. "We are taking a picnic down to the creek. The O'Malley girls are coming. And Private Yates. Why don't you come?"

Laina reached for a stack of blue napkins, counting to make certain there were enough, hoping Sergeant Boone didn't notice her hands were shaking.

"When we get back, I'll mix up some liniment for Corporal Dorsey's knees."

There was a clatter at the door, and Katie and Becky O'Malley tumbled into the room with Wilber yapping at their heels. The dog ran to Laina and, standing on his hind legs, planted his paws on her knees and looked up at her adoringly, yapping and wagging his tail. Grateful for the sudden distraction, Laina smiled down at the puppy and bent to scratch his ears. She buried her face in his soft fur and kissed the top of his head. "Sit," she said.

Wilber sat, staring up at her adoringly.

"Oh my goodness!" Katie exclaimed. "Look at that! I can't believe it! He *did* it! Did you see him Becky? Wilber *sat!*"

"I told you he'd learn," Laina said. She kissed the top of the puppy's head again.

"Good boy. Good boy." She lifted him into her arms and stood up, glancing in Sergeant Boone's direction and feeling the color rise in her cheeks when she realized he was watching her intently. She didn't remember noticing the cleft in his chin before. She looked away quickly and handed Wilber to Katie.

"Will you come on our picnic, Sergeant Boone? Please?" Becky O'Malley was staring up at the sergeant, her gray eyes pleading.

Laina glanced sideways at Becky. If ever a girl had had a crush on a man, Becky O'Malley was mad for Sergeant Nathan Boone. She smiled to herself and reached for the picnic basket, but Sergeant Boone was offering his arm to her.

"I've been hornswoggled into guarding you ladies from wild beasts," he said.

Laina picked up the picnic basket and looped it over the sergeant's outstretched arm. "If you brought that piece of rope," she said to Katie, "we could work on teaching Wilber to walk on a lead." Katie held out the rope, and Laina quickly fashioned both leash and lead.

"You have bait in your pocket?" Laina asked.

Katie nodded and produced a small dark

chunk of meat, which immediately got Wilber's attention.

"All right then," Laina said. She concentrated on Katie and Wilber so hard she barely noticed Sergeant Boone take the picnic basket off his arm. Or Becky O'Malley tuck her hand under the sergeant's elbow.

Laina joined everyone as they made their way out the door and around the side of the apartment to the back where Private Yates waited, hat in hand. At the sight of his sergeant, the private snapped to attention and saluted smartly.

"At ease, Private," Sergeant Boone said gruffly.

"Uh-um." Granny cleared her throat. "Didn't your mama teach you manners, Private?"

Blushing again, Yates offered Granny his arm. Laina walked beside Katie O'Malley, helping her teach Wilber not to fight being on a leash.

Ten

A wise man will hear, and will increase learning; and a man of understanding shall attain unto wise counsels.

Proverbs 1:5

"Well, what did you expect, sonny?" Emmet Dorsey spat tobacco and swiped his mouth with the back of his hand. "Don't you appreciate the fine scenery out here on the plains?" He took off his hand and swept it through the air, outlining the high ridge in the distance.

With a glance in Sergeant Boone's direction, Jackson shot back, "Well, I sure didn't expect to be bored. I had enough of that standing behind the counter in that dry goods store in St. Louis."

Nathan walked up. "There's worse things than being bored, Private," he said.

"Got that right," Dorsey agreed. "When we made dinner out of the hindquarters of a starving mule back in '77, I would have welcomed a little boredom." He laughed. "Now I wonder what Frenchy would have done with *mule* on his menu."

Jackson said, "I was expecting to see some Indians by now. Not be assigned to some half-deserted army outpost where the biggest action is chasing after some rancher's cattle."

"Well, cheer up, sonny," Dorsey interrupted, slapping him on the back. "There's trouble down in Indian Territory. Dull Knife and Little Wolf been makin' noise about coming back up this way. Maybe you'll get some action after all. In the meantime, you better do what you can to make sure you don't end up getting shot at by Cheyenne who aim better than you. Now let 'er rip." He handed Jackson his rifle and stepped away.

Jackson winced as he settled the rifle butt against his shoulder. "Got some bruises yesterday," he said.

"That's what you get for trying so hard to impress those ladies out for their Sunday afternoon drive," Dorsey teased.

"Small price to pay for seeing the look on Miss Valentine's face when I hit that target dead center." Jackson winked at Nathan. "I just bet I'm first on her dance card at the next hop. She likes me. I can tell."

"Well, it isn't ladies' day at the firing range today, Private," Dorsey snapped. He stepped closer, pulled something out of his pocket, and nudged Jackson's arm. "Stick this inside your shirt. Extra cushion." He looked from side to side. "And don't be telling anybody I done this. I don't want the fellers thinkin' I've gone soft." He stepped back and exchanged a smile with Nathan.

Jackson stuck the sock he'd been given beneath his shirt. He raised the rifle to his shoulder.

"Settle it in there good," Dorsey admonished. "It's a Springfield. You're still gonna get recoil. You want that sharpshooter medal, you'll have to put up with a sore shoulder."

Squinting, Jackson took aim and squeezed the trigger. Seconds later he was lying flat on his back in a daze while the seasoned veterans in Company G were pounding Dorsey on the back and laughing.

Nathan did his best to suppress a smile as Jackson, all cockiness at least momentarily gone, staggered to his feet and cupped his hands over his ringing ears.

"Corporal Dorsey," Nathan scolded, "You know we use fifty-five-grain cartridges in the Springfield. It's the Long Tom's that get the seventy-grain shells. Did you switch 'em again?"

Dorsey shook his head and scratched his goatee. "Looks like I did, Sergeant. I must be gettin' old." He looked at Jackson. "What was that you called me, sonny? Old-timer? Guess you were right. I'm old and forgetful."

Shouting a stream of curses, Jackson plowed into Dorsey. Nathan heard a sick popping sound as the old soldier went down, howling with a mixture of pain and rage. Dorsey's hands went up instinctively as Jackson leaped on top of him and began pummeling his face. Nathan grabbed Jackson by his collar and jerked him off the corporal. While three recruits held the enraged private down, Nathan knelt beside the veteran.

"Let me up!" Dorsey yelled. "Let me at 'im!"

"Hold on, Corporal," Nathan said, checking Dorsey's knee.

Dorsey ignored Nathan and tried to get up. His face went white and he sank back to earth. "You idiot!" he screamed at

Jackson. "You broke my leg!"

If Jackson had cursed back at the older man, Nathan would have felt better about what happened next. But Jackson's voice was calm and free of emotion when he said, "Be glad I didn't kill you, you washed-up old —"

"That's enough, Private," Nathan said, cutting him off. He looked at the three recruits standing around Jackson. "Professor. Frenchy. Escort Private Jackson to the guardhouse. Yates. Splint Corporal Dorsey's leg."

"S-Sir?" Yates stammered.

"You heard me. If it's broken he shouldn't be moved without stabilizing that leg."

"But . . . but, sir . . . what do I use for a splint?"

"Your imagination, Private," Nathan snapped. "You think you'll never be out in the field without a surgeon waiting to take care of the wounded? Figure out a way to splint the leg. I'm going for Doc Valentine and the ambulance."

"I don't need no ambulance!" Dorsey roared angrily, struggling to get up.

Nathan planted one foot on Dorsey's shoulder and gently forced the man back to the earth. He looked at Yates. "It'll take

187

about half an hour to get back to camp and get an ambulance headed this way. If he tries to get up again, knock him out." He mounted Whiskey and set out for Camp Robinson. On the way, he passed the soldiers escorting Private Jackson to the guardhouse.

Later that evening, after filing reports and visiting Dorsey in the hospital — where he learned the corporal's knee was only badly twisted — Nathan sat in the doorway of the first sergeant's room at the barracks thinking over the incident. He'd been uneasy about Caleb Jackson since the day the man arrived in camp. It was more than just the name change. Plenty of men in the army were serving under assumed names. As long as they did their job and obeyed orders, no one begrudged a man a second chance at life, but as he thought back over the past weeks, Nathan realized Jackson's fight with Dorsey was only one symptom of more disturbing troubles lying just beneath a thin veneer of mostly good behavior.

Jackson had an obvious weakness for gambling. Nathan had watched him play at the canteen, and when he took a seat at a poker table, Jackson had a gleam in his eye as intense as a hunter about to kill a trophy antelope. The man relished emptying another soldier's pockets, and he had no mercy when it came to collecting debts. He'd even taken advantage of his bunky, Harlan Yates. Happily, Yates was refusing to play poker anymore.

Liquor was another problem. The post trader could sell it, but he had to keep a record of his customers and was only allowed to sell them three drinks a day, and those had to be at least an hour apart. Civilians were always trying to find a way to get contraband liquor onto the post. The summer before, one enterprising gardener had sold the men watermelons at a dollar apiece — ten times the usual price because the melons contained bottles of liquor. Just last week Nathan had discovered several barrels of contraband brew buried a few rods south of the cavalry stables. He couldn't prove Jackson was involved in the attempted smuggling, but he also couldn't explain Jackson's seemingly intimate friendship with the freighters who regularly passed through the area, nor the sudden increase in his available cash for the poker table.

And Jackson was too familiar with the ladies. It was more than just a soldier's good-natured teasing when in female company — more than the usual loneliness and desire for a companion. Jackson played with the ladies like he played poker, with veiled eyes and secretive smiles. Today's comment about Charlotte Valentine especially rankled Nathan. A gentleman didn't brag about a lady being interested in him that way. Not to a bunch of soldiers. It wasn't right to put a young innocent like Charlotte Valentine on display like that. Like she was a trophy to be won.

Nathan blamed himself for that incident. If he hadn't changed his usual Sunday ritual of visiting Lily's grave and then dining with the Valentines, Charlotte wouldn't have been out driving. She never would have witnessed Jackson's impromptu showing off. And she would be less vulnerable to the soldier's attentions. But he'd gone on that picnic with Granny Max and set himself back at least two hours. By the time he got back from the cemetery the Valentines had already dined and were off on a Sunday drive. He'd been relieved. Now he felt guilty. Miss Charlotte Valentine had no idea what kind of attention she might be inviting by flirting with Caleb Jackson.

And then there was Jackson's temper.

No one could begrudge a bored, lonely soldier throwing a punch or two out of frustration. Such fights were actually fairly commonplace at Camp Robinson. But things usually flashed up like a brush fire and were doused quickly with no hard feelings lingering to cause trouble. Jackson's murderous rage at being the butt of a relatively harmless joke was something else again.

The man seemed to be harboring a whole library full of hard feelings against the world in general and several of the men in Company G in particular. Today's attack on Corporal Dorsey was not going to set well with anyone. Nathan had seen it happen at least a dozen times. Raw recruits often quickly sized up the old man and relegated him to a category of "washed up and useless." Then they got to know him. They heard his stories. Saw his grit. Respect flickered and grew into an intense loyalty for the veteran that only a soldier could understand. One by one, recruits inevitably came to a place where they realized that when Corporal Emmet Dorsey played a practical joke on you, he was exercising his right to test you. And when you passed, and Dorsey pounded you on the back and said you were "all right, although a little wet behind the ears," you felt honored.

Nathan thought back to his own initiation into the regular army. It happened at the hands of an Emmet Dorsey twin, who had inked his belt buckle and impressed it into the skin on his thigh so that it looked exactly like a tattoo. When he displayed it and informed Nathan that he'd better report to the surgeon's office for company tattooing, Nathan obeyed orders.

The surgeon played his part in the prank perfectly. Nathan's bare posterior was hanging over a hospital cot ready to accept the "company tattoo" when the surgeon pulled back a curtain around the cubicle and Nathan was backside-to-face with half the company. Scrambling to pull up his pants, he had flushed with embarrassment, but he had the good sense to realize not one of the men laughing at him meant it as a personal attack. It was just a good joke. When he went to buckle his belt and recognized the source of the "company tattoo," Nathan didn't have to pretend to join the men in laughing. It *was* funny.

Thinking back to that event, Nathan puzzled over why Jackson wouldn't just accept his share of hazing in a good-natured way and let it be. If anyone had a right to tease the younger recruits, it was Emmet Dorsey. Jackson had spent enough evenings in barracks listening to the man's war stories to know that. No one could blame Emmet Dorsey for having a little harmless fun at the expense of the green-horns. It was part of army life. Jackson should know that every recruit just had to accept his turn at being the butt of pranks with grace, knowing his turn would come to be on the other side of the joke — *if* he proved himself to his company and won his own place in the ranks. Either Jackson just didn't understand the unspoken rules of army camaraderie, or he was purposely ignoring them. Either way, the men didn't like him. That would be a problem the next time Company G engaged the enemy.

There was no arguing the point that life at Camp Robinson wasn't what recruits usually expected. With the departure of the natives to their reservations and the future of Camp Robinson uncertain, filling the long hours and days of routine probably had led to a little more practical joking than even Nathan would have liked. Still, if Jackson couldn't find a sense of humor, he was going to be a problem. He'd have to talk to him. But not until the private spent a couple of days cooling off in the guardhouse.

"Sergeant Boone?" Dinah approached from across the parade ground, trotting along with her hands raised to hold imaginary reins.

Nathan jumped up. "I'm late for dinner."

Dinah nodded.

Nathan looked down at his mud-encrusted boots. "You know what, Dinah, by the time I get cleaned up that roast your mother promised me is going to be cold. Maybe you'd better just give her my regrets."

"Papa wants to talk to you about something," Dinah said. "And Charlott-ah will be mad if you don't come. She's been primping all afternoon."

He grinned. "Is that right?"

Dinah nodded. She tilted her head and looked up at him. She sniffed. "You've been around the horses too long, Sergeant."

Nathan burst out laughing. "Duly noted, Miss Valentine."

Dinah turned to go. "Put on some of that fancy cologne you wear. Charlotte likes that."

"She does?"

"Oh, yeah," Dinah said, rolling her eyes. "She goes *on* and *on* about it. You should hear her —"

Nathan held up his hand. "I get the general idea, Miss Dinah. If you're sure they don't mind waiting — what does your papa want to talk to me about?"

Dinah shrugged. "I don't know. I just heard him promise Mama he would. They both got real quiet after I came into the room. So it must be important." Slapping her skirt with the flat of her hand, she shook her imaginary reins. "I hope you hurry up. I'm real hungry," she said, and trotted off.

After dinner Doctor Valentine invited Nathan to play chess while the ladies did dishes. The two men proceeded into the parlor, where the doctor's chessboard waited atop a small table in front of the window facing the parade ground. After a few moments wherein Nathan barely managed to stand off a checkmate, Dr. Valentine took a moment to pack and light his pipe. After a couple of satisfied puffs, he asked, "Happy with the new recruits?"

Nathan shrugged. "The usual complement of greenhorns, crooks, and starstruck do-gooders."

Valentine contemplated the chessboard. "I wanted to apologize for Emmy-Lou's prying questions at dinner tonight, Sergeant. I hope you can appreciate that it's just natural curiosity. All the ladies at Camp Robinson are anxious to make Miss Gray's acquaintance."

"Only natural. As you said," Nathan replied.

Moving his bishop, the doctor said, "Check." While Nathan studied the board, he continued, "That head trauma was one of the worst I've ever seen a person survive. Her physical recovery appears to be almost complete. I am, however, somewhat concerned about what appears to be a tendency to reclusiveness. She's been at Camp Robinson for almost two months now, and as far as I know she hasn't taken more than a few steps outside that apartment." He puffed on the pipe. "Do you know if that manifested itself before the incident? Or is it something new?"

Nathan didn't look up when he said, "She's getting better. She went on a picnic Sunday."

"Really? With whom?"

"Granny Max. The O'Malley girls. Private Yates." Nathan shrugged. "At the last minute I went along."

"Well, now. That's fine. How did she seem to you?"

"Nervous. On edge. But I don't think she's a recluse." He looked up at the doctor. "Granny thinks she's going to be all right."

The doctor puffed on his pipe. "If I were a betting man I'd put my money on God and Granny Max to bring Miss Gray around."

"I hope you're right," Nathan said earnestly. "She deserves a chance at some kind of life."

"A word to the wise, Sergeant Boone," the doctor said. "Do not let your men see this side of you."

Nathan grinned and held out his right hand for the doctor to see his skinned knuckles. "The only side of me most of them are likely to see in the near future is the one that barks orders and doesn't back down from a fight."

"Good," Valentine nodded. He picked up his rook and slid it along the board, murmuring as he did so, "A couple of those new men worry me."

"How so?" Nathan asked.

"McElroy is going to bolt," the doctor said.

Nathan agreed. "And likely take O'Brien with him when he does. They're far too in-

197

terested in the subject of Black Hills gold. First time we're on patrol they'll probably hightail it for Deadwood. Or at least try. I'll be watching." He leaned back and stretched his long legs out before him. "Who else concerns you?"

"Jackson."

"He's in the guardhouse for what he did to Dorsey today."

The doctor puffed on his pipe thoughtfully, "That young man is disturbed."

Nathan forced a laugh. "Doesn't a man have to be disturbed to volunteer for the United States Army?"

Valentine pulled his pipe out of his mouth and lifted it as if toasting his guest. "*Touché*, Sergeant. Unfortunately I suspect there's more to Jackson's problems than just that."

"What makes you say that?"

"Instinct. Something in his eyes." He shook his head. "I hope I'm wrong." The doctor puffed on his pipe. "My family took a little drive on Sunday. Watched the men at target practice."

"I'm sorry about Sunday, sir. I've been ignoring Granny's urgings to socialize for so long, that when she invited me on her picnic, I felt obligated."

The doctor gestured, "I wasn't fishing

for an apology, Sergeant. There was never a formal invitation issued, and if you find other distractions you are certainly at liberty to enjoy them." He cleared his throat. "That wasn't the purpose for my bringing this up at all. As I said, we watched some of the men at target practice Sunday afternoon." He drew on his pipe before continuing. "I don't mind telling you I don't like the way Private Jackson looks at my daughter." He gazed evenly at Nathan. "Nor should you."

Nathan shifted in his chair. "If any of my men are guilty of ungentlemanly conduct —"

"Private Jackson never crossed the line of propriety. But he does like to dance along its edge. I've known men like that before. I've just never had one select my daughter as an audience."

"I'll speak to him."

"Oh, I don't think that's necessary," the doctor said. "That's not my point. And besides, Charlotte encourages a certain amount of harmless flirtation. She is no different than any other young woman her age, Sergeant. And being one of the few ladies at a military camp does result in a great deal of attention." He sighed. "I'm afraid it's gone to her head a little." The doctor puffed on his pipe while he peered at Nathan. "Of course, Charlotte also has serious intentions of becoming an officer's wife some day."

Suddenly uncomfortable, Nathan dropped his gaze and began to study the chessboard with new intensity.

Dr. Valentine cleared his throat. "When soldiers behave in a way that makes me suspect they might be contemplating desertion, it is my duty to call that to their commanding officer's attention. I consider I've done that this evening by telling you I suspect McElroy and O'Brien.

"When a man like Jackson shows signs of instability, it is my duty to be concerned. I have expressed that concern. And I've also let you know that Jackson is of special interest to me because I have a daughter who may be vulnerable to his attentions — which I am not convinced are strictly honorable. And that leads me to you, Sergeant Boone."

"Sir?" Nathan frowned. He sat up so quickly he bumped the table and sent several chess pieces tumbling to the floor.

The doctor sighed. He bent his head and with index finger and thumb, pressed the narrow bridge of his nose where his glasses usually perched. "You would have to be

200

blind, Sergeant Boone, not to have noticed that my daughter thinks she is in love with you."

Nathan stared at him, dumbfounded. He frowned. "Sir, I can assure you, I haven't meant to in any way —"

"Oh, calm down, Sergeant. I'm merely trying to ascertain as a father whether it's an unrequited crush or a possibility. I'd like to know what I'm dealing with."

Nathan bent down to pick up the chess pieces. One by one, he set them on the board. "Charlotte is a lovely young woman, Doctor Valentine."

"I'm not asking for an independent review of Charlotte's assets, Sergeant. Are you or are you not interested in courting my daughter?"

Nathan ran his hand along the edge of the chessboard. He moistened his lips. "Sir, I'm not interested in courting anyone." He looked at Doctor Valentine. "And I don't honestly think I ever will have such an interest."

"I see," the doctor said. He looked up at Nathan. For a moment, he held his gaze. "Thank you for your honesty, Sergeant Boone. Now, may I be just as honest with you?"

"Of course, sir."

"For a while, after we lose someone we love, our first thought in the morning is of them. That thought is quickly followed by the pain of their absence. But time passes, and in the normal way of healing, there comes a morning when, perhaps, just for a second, we do not think of our loss. Or if we do, it is a happy memory. In a healthy person, these seconds multiply, until one day we realize that when we think of our loved one, there is more joy than pain. This is as it should be, Sergeant Boone." He paused before saying, "I don't know why, but you seem determined to prevent this from happening in your own life."

Nathan sat forward in his chair. "With all due respect, Dr. Valentine," he said stiffly. "This is not really any of your business."

"Everything that affects the ability of the men of Camp Robinson to perform their duty is my business, Sergeant Boone."

Nathan stood up. "I strenuously object, sir, to your intimation that I am somehow not doing my duty." He bowed. "And if you'll excuse me, sir, that duty requires me to leave now."

"Sit back down, Sergeant." The doctor waved Nathan back to his seat. "We've plenty of time before the day's final assembly. And we *are* going to have this conversation. Whether it takes place here or over at the captain's office is up to you."

"The captain has no interest in my private life, sir."

"Well, now. That's where you are wrong, son. Because the captain needs to know when a sergeant's men are beginning to have questions about a man's leadership because of behavior they consider unusual."

Nathan sat down, his mind racing as he wondered where this nonsense originated. *Dorsey.* Locked away in the hospital with nothing better to do than imagine problems. He had never thought Dorsey was the type to be given to gossip.

"It does not escape notice when you spend several hours a week in the cemetery, Sergeant Boone. And it does not escape notice that things over on the Row remain exactly as they were the day Mrs. Boone died two years ago. That you are maintaining something of a shrine has been mentioned." The doctor looked at Nathan. "Or are the rumors mistaken?"

"Corporal Dorsey is the only man at Camp Robinson who could have let you know about these things, Doc. I've served with him long enough to appreciate that he

203

probably thinks he's acting in my best interest to bring this up to you. But —"

Dr. Valentine interrupted him. "What you are doing, Sergeant — or not doing, as the case may be — guarantees that every single morning of your life you pick at the wound of your wife's death and prevent it from healing. As your physician, I can tell you this is unhealthy behavior. It is unhealthy emotionally for you, and it may be ultimately unhealthy for your men, who deserve better. They are within their rights to wonder if their sergeant may unnecessarily put their lives at risk at some critical moment in a battle because he does not value his own life."

"That's absurd," Nathan said. "Ridiculous. If anything, I'm more motivated to protect my men because I don't want anyone else to ever feel like I do. And what can you or Dorsey possibly know about it, anyway. Especially you, the good doctor with his wife and two daughters in the next room."

The doctor stared across the chessboard at Nathan. His glare softened. He nodded. "That's a fair question. It deserves an answer." He got up. "Shall we take a walk, Sergeant Boone."

They headed outside, slowly making

204

their way down the picket fence toward the hospital. "Emmy-Lou is not the wife of my youth, Nathan. Nor is Charlotte my first-born. My first wife died in childbirth. It was a boy. I named him Avery. We would have called him Junior, of course."

Nathan's anger abated. "I didn't know that, sir. I'm sorry. Truly, I am."

Dr. Valentine shrugged. "I never speak of it. It is part of a past that seems to upset Mrs. Valentine for reasons I won't go into. But when I speak of managing a great loss, Sergeant Boone, I speak from experience." He cleared his throat. "Just because our great love dies, does not mean we cannot go on to have a happy life. Some men were just not meant to live alone, Nathan. And friendship is as good a basis for marriage as passion. Friendship is a comforting thing long after passions burn out. I've overstepped the privilege of my rank this evening, Sergeant Boone. But I don't apologize for it. It pains me to see you using the past as an excuse to stop living. I have been where you are. And I don't recommend any man remain in hell when he has a chance to climb out."

"It was my fault," Nathan choked out. "It would be different if she'd died of cholera. Or in childbirth. Or something else I couldn't control."

"You can control the rattlesnakes of Pine Ridge?"

"We'd had an argument. I could have controlled my temper. And she would never have been out there alone."

The doctor sighed. "What's done is done, Sergeant. There is no profit in lingering over our mistakes. We must accept God's forgiveness, forgive ourselves, and move on. That's all we can do."

"Just like that," Nathan said. He let the bitterness sound in his voice.

"Of course not 'just like that.' But you've had two years to absorb the shock."

"Where is it written that after two years a man should be done with grieving?" Nathan said.

"My dear boy, you'll never be done with grieving. You just learn to contain it. I guess what I'm trying to do is encourage you to start the process of containment so your personal pain doesn't overflow into your daily routine to the point it destroys you."

Doctor Valentine looked toward the opposite end of Officer's Row. "Mrs. Valentine has just come out on the front porch. I've got to get back home."

He put his hand on Nathan's shoulder.

"Look, Nathan. Whether you are serious about my daughter or not isn't my greatest concern. It merely provided the excuse for me to start this conversation. I've been watching you, and I've been concerned for a long time. You should be grateful for Corporal Dorsey. If he hadn't landed in my hospital and brought up his concerns for you, I may never have acted on my own. He's a good friend. You can't control what happened in the past. But you can keep it from ruining your future. I have been down that road and it is not a place you want to travel for long. I trust you'll consider what I've said and take appropriate action." He took a step away, then stopped short. "One more thing, Sergeant," the doctor said.

"Sir?"

"I would appreciate it very much if you would decline the next invitation to dinner with my family."

"Sir?"

"And should you attend Friday evening's dance, perhaps you'll neglect to dance with Charlotte. She's clearly misinterpreted your attentions for something a great deal more serious than they are."

"Yes, sir. I understand, sir."

"Thank you. God bless you, son." He

headed back up the Row where his wife was waiting.

Crossing the parade ground in the dark, Nathan paused and looked up at the sky. *"God bless you." It always comes back to Him.* The moon was rising, looking twice its usual size behind a shroud of feathery clouds. Just the kind of night Lily would have loved. She would have whispered in his ear and led him outside. They would have walked arm in arm down to the creek, where the water would look silver in the moonlight. He would have swept her up in his arms and kissed her. Memories flooded in, sweet and so savagely painful they brought tears to his eyes.

"Well?" Emmy-Lou Valentine spoke as soon as her husband was within earshot. "What did he say about Miss Gray?"

"About Miss Gray?" The doctor stepped up on the front porch.

"Yes. Miss Gray!" Emmy-Lou sounded annoyed. She waved her hand in the air. "Come inside. I declare the mosquitoes in this place are as big as horseflies." Once they were in the parlor, she sat down in the green brocade chair recently vacated by Sergeant Boone. "I asked you to ask Sergeant Boone about Miss Gray. What did he say? Could you tell? Is he . . . does he find her attractive? Charlotte is practically in tears. He scarcely looked at her the entire evening."

Avery sighed inwardly. He knew that tone. Emmy-Lou had latched on to something, and she would hold on until she had shaken a reaction out of him. If he resisted, she would make his life miserable. Feeling not unlike a master trying to get his bulldog to let go of his favorite shoe, Avery packed his pipe with fresh tobacco. He moved deliberately, first lighting the pipe and taking a puff before sitting down, leaning his head back and looking up at the ceiling. "I was thinking, Emmy-Lou. Maybe the quartermaster *could* order that drapery fabric you've been hankering after."

"Avery Valentine," Emmy-Lou glowered at him. "I will not be treated like those hounds of yours. You can't distract me by tossing me scraps."

The doctor drew on his pipe. He smiled at his wife. "According to Sergeant Boone, Miss Gray is shy. She is recovering. And Sergeant Boone really didn't seem too interested in talking about her."

"Well, you talked about *something* half the night," Emmy-Lou wheedled. "I had coffee ready but you never called. The girls finally went to bed. And then I saw you'd gone outside, which I assume was so you couldn't be overheard."

Doctor Valentine was silent.

"You really aren't going to tell me anything, are you?"

"My dear, I have already told you everything I know about Miss Gray. She is recovering from a grave wound. She is able to be up and about, but she is weak with very little energy and certainly not enough energy to accept any callers. Sergeant Boone seems to agree."

"What do you mean he agrees? What exactly is his interest in Miss Gray? That's what I wanted you to find out!"

Inwardly scolding himself for taking pleasure in annoying his annoying wife, Valentine said, "He went on a picnic with her this past Sunday."

"He . . . he . . . *what?!*"

"He went on a picnic with Granny Max and the O'Malley girls and Sergeant Yates. And Miss Gray. Obviously Miss Gray is beginning to gain some strength. She'll probably attend a hop one of these Fridays before long, and then you and all the other ladies can form your own opinions of the elusive Miss Laina Gray."

"What about Charlotte? Did he say anything about Charlotte?"

"Yes. That she is lovely. And that he has no desire to court anyone and does not expect to ever have such a desire." He looked at his wife.

"A handsome young man like him? That's ridiculous. It isn't healthy. I hope you told him so. Charlotte's beside herself," Emmy-Lou fussed.

Why does she have to see everything that happens at Camp Robinson only as it relates to our family? To Charlotte? Can't she be concerned for Miss Gray and Sergeant Boone for their own sakes? The doctor's voice was tinged with impatience when he next spoke. "No, it isn't particularly healthy, Emmy-Lou. But then there isn't anything healthy about death and dying. We all have to manage it our own way. Sergeant Boone has chosen his method." He paused and nibbled on his moustache, a gesture intended to send the message to his wife that what he was about to say was worthy of note and would not be subject to wifely influence. "Just because you may not approve of Sergeant Boone's way of handling grief does not mean it is faulty. Nor does it mean it has to change."

The doctor's words surprised even the

doctor. He didn't even agree with what he was saying. He had, in fact, just challenged Sergeant Boone with exactly the opposite advice. He most definitely did think Sergeant Boone needed to make some changes. But in the face of Emmy-Lou's self-serving "concern," Doctor Valentine felt compelled to put a wall of defense up around the wounded soldier. "Give the man some peace, Emmy-Lou. In fact, I think it would be very wise if you would *not* invite him to dinner again for a while."

"Avery! How can you suggest such a thing? How can you be so blind to your own daughter's charms?"

He felt his temper rising. "It's got nothing to do with being blind to Charlotte's charms, Mrs. Doctor, which, I agree, are many. But they are wasted on Sergeant Boone, and the sooner you and Charlotte realize that, the sooner I will have peace in my house!"

"It is obvious that you are hiding something from me." Emmy-Lou straightened her shoulders and lifted her chin. "You and the sergeant spoke for a long time. It had to be more than just 'Miss Gray is healing nicely.' I demand to know what else he said about my daughter."

The doctor groaned audibly. "You may

not be able to comprehend this, Emmy-Lou, but everything at Camp Robinson does not have direct bearing on Charlotte. To be quite honest, Sergeant Boone and I really didn't discuss Charlotte at length. We talked about him. I offered some unwanted advice, and he was gracious enough not to deck me for giving it."

"If not about Charlotte or Miss Gray, what on earth did you advise him about?"

"About life, Emmy-Lou. About grieving loss."

Emmy-Lou pressed her lips together in disgust. Her nostrils flared. She inhaled sharply. Her tone was accusing. "You *told* him!"

"Yes. I told him." The doctor studied the chessboard. "And I pray to God it helps him."

"I thought we agreed. It won't help Charlotte's chances if people know —"

"If people know what, Emmy-Lou? Why would anybody care one bit to know that my first wife was a cook's daughter? What difference does it make? It doesn't have anything at all to do with Charlotte."

"Well, maybe it doesn't make a difference to *your* people, Avery, but it certainly gave my *father* pause to think someone of your position in society would stoop to —"

213

Doctor Valentine jumped up. Red-faced, he barely kept himself from shouting. "Oh, for goodness' sake, Emmy-Lou. Stop it. This isn't even about Charlotte anymore. It's degenerated into another battle for control of this marriage. You wanted me to pump Sergeant Boone for information about Miss Gray. I didn't. You don't want me to share my past with people. I did. You wanted me to dangle my daughter beneath Sergeant Boone's nose like I bait the dogs. I didn't."

"Avery," Emmy-Lou sniffed, "there's no need to be crude."

Valentine nodded. "You are right. There isn't." Grabbing his hat, he headed for the front door. Before going back outside he turned around. "Why don't you just take Charlotte East to your mother's for a few weeks, Emmy-Lou. Troll for a husband at the lake house. Give Sergeant Boone a rest. Give us all a rest."

Eleven

He that is slow to anger is better than the mighty; And he that ruleth his spirit than he that taketh a city.

Proverbs 16:32

The morning after Private Jackson put Corporal Dorsey in the hospital, Nathan ordered him to march double time around the perimeter of the parade ground shouldering a log. After lunch, he had the recruit put the log down and wait for him at the stables. While Jackson waited, Boone saddled Whiskey. He filled two canteens with water and then ordered Jackson to shoulder his forty-pound saddle and field equipment and head south, while he followed at a distance, leading Jackson's horse and watching the soldier's shirt grow dark with sweat.

When the private finally stumbled and fell to the earth, Nathan rode up to him and offered him a drink. Neither man spoke as Jackson sucked in half a canteen of water, then gathered up his equipment and headed off again.

"A little to the east, Private," Nathan corrected him. "There's a spring just over that hill. That's where we're headed."

Jackson gritted his teeth and regained the double-time pace. Watching him, Nathan couldn't help but admire the determination on the man's face. He would make it to the spring or die trying. Nathan offered to let him slow to regular marching pace, but Jackson ignored him and kept going.

When they finally arrived at the spring, Jackson didn't wait for permission before he threw down his saddle and dipped his entire head in the bubbling cold water, far enough to soak his collar and the front of his shirt. Nathan rode a short distance downstream and dismounted to water the horses. Hobbling both horses and turning them out to graze, he walked back and sat down on the boulder overshadowing the spring while Jackson sopped a kerchief in cool water and tied it around his neck.

"Didn't think you'd have a Sandhills version of the bull ring," Caleb said, panting.

"Bull ring?"

"Big corral at Jefferson Barracks. When we were ornery they had us run around it double time carrying logs." He gave a wry laugh. "How far do you suppose it is from the stables to here?" He nodded toward where Camp Robinson sat inside its fence of cordwood, far enough away the men going about their various duties were little more than insects crawling around a model made of wood building blocks.

"Only a couple of miles," Nathan said.

Caleb bent and picked up the saddle. "Where to now?"

One thing a man had to admire about Private Jackson, Nathan thought. He never shirked hard work. Even in the form of punishment. At times he seemed to enjoy it.

"I brought you out here so we could talk without all the 'sirs' and salutes," Nathan said. He settled his back against the boulder in the shade of a small pine tree growing in a cleft of the rock. "So have a seat."

Jackson took another drink from his canteen, then poured a stream of water over his head. He sputtered and shook his head like a wet dog before walking over and, using a boulder as a seat, positioning himself opposite Nathan.

217

"Doc Valentine says Dorsey's going to be all right," Nathan began. "So as far as I'm concerned, you've served your sentence with the march out here — as long as we can get some things straight between us." He leaned forward. "You've got to get control of your temper, Caleb," Nathan said. "I don't want to have to be part of court-martial proceedings against a friend. But if you keep getting yourself into scrapes, I'm not going to have much choice."

"I know it," Jackson said abruptly. He shrugged. "I've got a short fuse."

"You didn't have a short fuse when we first met," Nathan said. He drew his legs up and leaned forward, resting his elbows on his knees. "Whatever it is that's wound tight inside you, you got to learn to hold it together."

Caleb shot back, "I'm not the only one in Company G with something wound tight inside him."

"That may be," Nathan said, "but the things inside me aren't going to get me court-martialed." He leaned back. "Some of the men already think I'm too soft on you. Think you should have been hazed out a couple of weeks ago after the incident at Gruber's."

"Over *that?*" Jackson snorted. "That wasn't anything."

"Tell Gruber that. You nearly destroyed his store with that stunt. And you could have broken a perfectly good horse's leg."

"I knew that mare could clear the billiard table or I'd have never ridden her in there in the first place."

Nathan laughed in spite of himself. "All right, Beau —"

"Call me Caleb."

"Right," Nathan said. "Caleb. The thing is, this deal with Dorsey isn't just your everyday troublemaking. You could have ended the man's career. Emmet Dorsey has given his heart and soul and body to the United States Army. All he's got to look forward to is a pension, and if any man deserves it, he does. I won't have you ruining a good man just because you can't control your temper."

"Then drum me out," Caleb snapped. "Quit being such a good Christian and be done with it."

Nathan took his hat off and slapped it against his knee. He swore mildly. "I'm not trying to be any kind of Christian. I am trying to be your friend." He paused, then said, "If you don't make it in the army, what's next? You say you hated working in that store. Your family's gone. So what's next for you? Panning for gold?"

The recruit snorted. "There's nothing up in Black Hills for me. I'd head south. That rancher — Bronson, is it? — he could probably use a man who's good with horses."

Nathan agreed. "Until you picked a fight with his best cowhand and broke his leg."

"Dorsey's leg isn't broken." Caleb shrugged. "But I get your point."

"What is it with you, anyway? You can take the orneriest nag in the herd and sweet-talk her until she performs like some harmless circus horse. I've seen you get kicked and bit so many times I've lost count. But not once have I ever seen you lose your temper with a horse. But let a man dare say something that riles you, and you dive in with both fists."

"Horses don't mean any harm. If you watch 'em and get to know 'em, you understand. They are just being horses."

"Well, Corporal Dorsey didn't mean any real harm, either. He was just acting like the old buzzard he is and giving a greenhorn a proper welcome into the army. It happens with every new recruit," Nathan said. He told Caleb about his own experience with company tattoos.

Jackson would not be convinced. "You may put up with that kind of thing, but I won't be made the laughingstock of Company G. I can outshoot and outride every one of 'em, and they'll remember that or they'll pay."

"You're going to kill somebody someday if you don't get control of that temper of yours," Nathan snapped. "And then it won't matter what the men remember. And it won't matter if we were friends or not. I'll have to do my duty. And that means court-martial and time at Leavenworth. Maybe even hanging." Nathan stared off into the distance. "What's eating you up inside, anyway?"

Jackson snorted and jerked the kerchief off his neck. He bent to dip it in the spring again and wiped his face. "You want me to tell you my troubles so you can fix it all up?"

Nathan's voice showed the frustration he felt as he said, "I want you to convince me there's hope of making a soldier out of you." He paused. "Look, Caleb. Since the day I picked up that snare drum and walked into battle with my Uncle Billy's regiment, I've known this is the life for me. I've never wanted anything else." His voice wavered, and he tugged on his hat brim.

"Even when I knew in my gut Lily wasn't cut out for the army, I still didn't give it up. When she —" He swallowed. "After she was gone, I didn't have anywhere else to turn but to the army. Reveille to tattoo, I live by the bugle, and I expect I'll die by it. The fact is, I'm married to the army now. And there's worse things than that. If you came into the army looking to put some kind of order and discipline in your life, the army can do that. But it won't cure any of the demons you're running from."

Caleb's blue eyes narrowed. He stared at his friend. "You know that from experience, do you?"

"Everybody's got demons," Nathan said. "Soon as you learn that, you'll be a long way toward managing yours." He paused. "You spend enough time around company campfires, and you'll learn you're not even close to being the only man in the army who's spent a night walking a battlefield looking for his brother's head so he could write home and tell his mama he buried her son proper. Some of these old-timers out here have stories that'll curdle even your blood. And that's the truth."

Caleb peered off into the distance as he spoke. "You went home from the war to your little cabin in the Missouri hills and saw your mama and family. And then you headed off to Nashville and fell in love and your uncle got you into officer's school."

"That's right," Nathan said, his voice bitter. "I've had a perfect life. Who am I to tell you to get over your troubles?"

"That's not what I mean. I know you've got troubles. I know you don't want anything to do with the fair Charlotte Valentine and that old hen of a mother's plans to get you two hitched. You're tied to Lily as strong as the day she died. It's eating you up inside trying to live without her, but you're doing it. And you are likely bound for a commission and a command. For all I know, I'll be calling you General someday. You've got what it takes."

Caleb took his hat off and, rolling the brim while he talked, continued. "But, Nathan, I didn't have an Uncle Billy. I never met a Lily Bainbridge. And there wasn't any officer's school taking in Confederate drummer boys. I went home to a burned-out plantation, courtesy of the United States government. When I looked at the ruination of everything my pa had worked for all his life, it lit something inside of me. You want to know what's wound up inside me so tight? It's the memory of coming over the hill at home and seeing nothing but charred ruins where the stable once stood. It's finding my mother and father's graves in the family burial ground and seeing they'd been dug into by somebody looking for gold." He paused and wet his lips. When he turned to look at Nathan, Caleb's eyes were red with unspilled tears. He stood up and began to pace.

"I finally figured out that if Beauregard Preston was going to have any kind of life at all, it was going to be up to him to make it. There wasn't anything left for me but ashes and desecrated graves in Mecklenburg County. Most of my friends were dead.

"So I talked Abel Griffin from the next place over into leaving with me. We worked our way to St. Louis, and along the way I learned to talk like you Yankees. By the time I started work at that dry-goods store in St. Louis, you wouldn't have known me for a Rebel unless I wanted you to know." He paused. "So I thought that was it. I was doing good work, and I figured if I just kept at it, someday I'd own my own store and make something of myself." He shook his head. "And then I discovered the riverboats and gambling." He put his hat back on. "I liked the feeling I got sitting at a poker table holding a good hand. It was the first time in my life I felt like I had control over something. Before I knew it, I was playing regular. And winning some."

He laughed. "And then I discovered the ladies. Have you ever seen the women on some of those riverboats? They are something to behold. And they don't play games with a man, either. Those highfalutin daughters of Mr. Cruikshank's customers would flirt and fawn and then act shocked if I took them up on what they were offering. I got to hating them.

"The girls on the river aren't like that. They flirt and fawn and then they make good on what they been promising. There was one called herself Riverboat Annie. She was something else. Better than all the others. Had fine manners and a voice like an angel. In some ways, she didn't seem like she really belonged. Kind of . . . innocent. You know?"

"None of those women are innocent," Nathan said.

"Yeah, well, even if she was sort of innocent when I knew her, I don't expect it lasted, because she disappeared not long after I got to know her. Went off to some rich party. Private entertainment. Never heard of again."

He swiped a hand over his eyes and sat back down. "Somebody told me her papa started off as a big-time gambler. But after she left, he started going downhill. And the last I heard, he was a bum begging for low stakes games across the river." Caleb shrugged. "That's what got me to thinking maybe I ought to change my ways. A girl just drops off the face of the earth and nobody knows — or cares — what happened. And her pa goes from being a high roller to a bum. Just like that.

"About that time Mr. Cruikshank's daughter was making eyes at me. And more. I thought maybe things were looking up. Until Cruikshank points his rifle at me and tells me how I'll be marrying sweet Mavis come Saturday." He shuddered. "I felt like I was drowning."

"And that's when you headed for Jefferson Barracks."

Caleb nodded. "You know it." His voice lowered. He cleared his throat. "But it was more than just Cruikshank's threats that gave me that feeling I was drowning. I'd started having too many mornings with a hangover and no memory of what happened the night before. When I really made myself think about it, I knew I wasn't the one in control at those poker tables.

The gambling and the drinking and the women were beginning to own me — not the other way around.

"But what finally got my attention was that after Mr. Cruikshank lowered his rifle and sent me back to my room to 'think about what I had done,' I thought about how easy it would be to kill him and make it look like an accident. That rifle of his was from the war. He never cleaned it. Who would know the difference if it misfired?"

Caleb shuddered again. He swiped his hand across his eyes. "When I realized I was thinking about doing murder, my blood ran cold. And I had to face something about myself I'd kept inside for a long time. Something that started the night you and I met on that battlefield." He finally looked directly at Nathan. "There's something inside me. Something dark. Something that really could kill a man." He started pacing again. "The army has kept that part of me under control. I hate the bugles and getting up before dawn. I hate it. And I love it all at the same time. I know I drink too much. And I gamble. But there's the guardhouse to keep it under control." He added, "And there's no riverboat women. These ladies here, they

227

expect a man to treat them with respect. And they give respect right back. I know I got a little too familiar with Miss Valentine a couple of times. But I didn't mean anything by it."

He stopped pacing, stopped fiddling with his hat. "You can't drum me out, Nathan. This is all I've got now. I know I've got a temper. I know I've got to control it. And I'll do it. I need the army. I need it."

Slowly, Nathan stood up. He dusted his backside off and went to get the horses. When he came back to where Caleb was waiting, he said, "You say you need discipline. I guess you know by now the army can give you that. What you don't seem to know yet is that these men will be your family and your home if you get them to respect you, and then it won't matter if Company G ends up riding to hell and back in the next few years, you'll have friends who'll risk their lives for you. But you've got to earn their respect and their trust. They all know you can outride and outshoot them. The question you've got to answer for them is, will you ride and shoot for *them?* Will you do it when your own life is at risk?

"Lighting in to one of the best soldiers this army ever had just because he plays a little joke on you is not the way to convince these men you want to be part of their family. But I think you already know that." Nathan pulled his hat on and tugged the brim down. "It's up to you, Caleb. You can either put the past in the past and get control of your demons, or you can let them rip you apart and destroy you. I can't help you with that. What I can do is give you a fresh start with Company G." He handed Caleb the reins to his horse. "So that's what you've got. But if you start any more fights, I won't be able to save your hide. In fact, I won't even try. Are we straight on that?"

"We're straight," Caleb said.

"All right, then. Let's get back to camp."

Caleb saddled up and the two men mounted their horses. As they rode along, Caleb said, "All due respect, sir, I did have one thing to say. If we're still talking as friends. Without the 'sergeants' and 'sirs,' as you put it."

Nathan nodded. "Say it."

"You said every man has his demons. The thing is how we deal with 'em. I raise hell against mine. Or *with* 'em on occasion. But at least I recognize mine and take them on. You're right that I let my feelings drive me too much. But at least I still *feel* 'em. I think my way might turn out better than yours."

"What do you mean, better than mine?" Nathan asked.

"Your way seems to be *not* feeling. Or pretending you don't. Miss Valentine falls all over herself to get your attention. But you mostly look right through her. I noticed that right away, and at first I couldn't understand it. Until I realized that you mostly look right through everybody, Nathan. You said we've all got our demons. I'm trying to get a handle on mine. And with a little help from the army, I think I just might do it. But what about you? Are you trying to get a handle on yours? Or are you just ignoring them and waiting for them to leave you alone? Because if that's what you're doing, Nathan my friend, you can take it from me — they don't leave you alone. They take control. I just told you how they did that to me, one shot glass at a time, one hand of poker at a time, one Riverboat Annie at a time. Until I had to do something to stop 'em."

He pulled his hat down farther over his eyes and sat back in his saddle. "What about you, Nathan? What are you doing to get the demons off *your* back? You're tending the shrine over on the Row, coming out to bugles, doing what they say. You're getting through the day. But you aren't alive. Not really. I know about your little rituals. I see you go across the river every Sunday. You don't just take flowers over to Lily's grave, Nathan. You practically spend the afternoon over there. You see what I am trying to say?"

"I see it's time we got back to Camp Robinson, Private Jackson," Nathan said. He spurred Whiskey and took off toward camp.

Twelve

A foolish woman is clamorous: she is simple, and knoweth nothing.

Proverbs 9:13

Camp Robinson, Nebraska
June 16, 1878
Dearest Mama,

Life for the ladies of Camp Robinson in the year of our Lord 1878 is not at all what you are imagining. While it is true that when Avery first brought us here, things were undeveloped, all has changed a great deal in the past two years. The men have been busy building, and now there is a neat row of adobe officers' quarters on the north side of the parade ground. We have ample room in our little apartment. There is a wide hall down the center of the building, and opposite us is an apartment identical to ours. That apartment is empty now, and so the girls have their own rooms — something I am certain you did not envision when you wrote your last letter.

We have a chicken coop and a cow, and last summer we raised a great amount of vegetables in the garden. Avery has seen to it that we usually have a striker staying in the lean-to at the back beside the kitchen. A striker, dearest Mama, is a soldier who is assigned to help the officers and their families with domestic duties. Most of the men are rough and uneducated, and we have not had a striker for a few weeks, but Avery has introduced us to a new private who hails from France. He is apparently an excellent cook, and I am determined to have him become a permanent part of our household before the captain's wife learns of him.

We have developed a lovely relationship with the sergeant of Company G (cavalry), who will be accompanying our family on a Sabbath day drive. I intend to use all my womanly charms to convince him to give me Frenchy. Just think, Mama, your two granddaughters might learn French right here in the wilds of Nebraska. You need not fret that I am raising ignorant country bumpkins.

The ladies of Camp Robinson maintain all social decorum. In the mornings we make calls on one another. Many hours each day must be relegated to sewing, but that is no different than if we were living with you. Since she finished her linen sampler, Charlotte has begun piecing a patchwork quilt. The scarf you sent us from the Centennial celebration in Philadelphia will be at the center, with tiny squares all around.

Dinah is working on her sampler now, although it is more of a struggle for her, as she is much more prone to want to spend time in the cavalry stables with the animals than in my parlor stitching.

All of the ladies are encouraged to participate in target practice twice weekly. This is perhaps the only part of our week that is much different than yours, Mama. We must be able to defend ourselves — although against what I cannot imagine, as all the Indians have been shipped to their respective reservations, and things here at camp are almost boring. You really must stop believing every news article you read about depradations and danger, Mama. Crazy Horse is dead and with him went the hopes of the Sioux nation. It is perhaps a tragedy, but it was an inevitable

234

one, and now one hopes the natives will adopt a more progressive view and realize that only in giving up their wild ways can they expect to survive into the next century.

In addition to target practice, we ride or take a drive every day, always escorted by one or two soldiers. Avery tells me that one of the new cavalry recruits is an accomplished horseman. Riding lessons for the ladies of Camp Robinson may be in our future.

In the evenings we often play euchre or chess, and on Friday nights the enlisted men usually hold a hop (that's a dance, Mama) that everyone enjoys. On these evenings, social divisions are set aside for the good of all. Even the laundresses and the enlisted men's wives attend, and you would not know there was any difference between us. We ladies are always quick to compliment our dear friends' attempts at finery, and no one cares whether a lady is dressed in silk or gingham. All dance as many dances as possible. Even the old servant of one of the officers finds many dance partners. She is fondly loved by all, and if you could meet dear Granny Max, you would agree that she is as fine an example of her race as ever lived.

Granny has taken in a poor woman recently rescued from abject squalor and conditions too horrible to describe, and according to Avery, her tender care literally rescued the poor creature from the brink of insanity. All the ladies of Camp Robinson are anticipating the opportunity to meet this new resident and assure her of our sincere good wishes. If anything can be said about military ladies, it is that we support one another.

I intend to encourage Avery that perhaps this poor woman would benefit from a position in our household. Certainly I could use help with the housekeeping. The constant wind has a way of dusting furniture and flora with successive layers of grit and grime. It is a challenge to keep a proper home in the West.

From your letter, it seems you think that we are in the wilds, with our lives hanging by a thread. Nothing could be further from the truth. In fact, I must hasten to close this epistle as Charlotte is calling for me to come and join her and her young Sergeant Boone for a Sunday drive.

Sergeant Boone is the subject for another letter, but rest assured that he is one of whom you would approve. His dear wife passed on just before we arrived on the frontier. His recovery from the loss has been quite slow, but we are heartened to see the flicker of life begin to return to his handsome face. He seems to have taken to Charlotte, and nothing would please Avery and me more than to see our eldest make such a fine match.

Your invitation to spend the summer with you at the lake house is tempting, Mama. I have discussed it with Avery, and in his unselfish way he has said I must do what is best for the girls. At the moment, I do not think it advisable for us to leave. Should you want to experience the West for yourself, we would be overjoyed to welcome you to Camp Robinson, where the night air carries the song of coyotes and the star-filled sky is unobscured by the light of gas street lamps.

Your affectionate daughter,
Emmy-Lou

"Come *on*, Mother!" Charlotte pleaded from the doorway. "He's waiting. And Private Dubois came, too."

Emmy-Lou looked up from the small writing desk positioned beside the parlor window. "Where's your father?"

"Driving the carriage, silly. Dinah's already out there, too."

"Calm yourself, Charlotte," Emmy-Lou ordered. "Your blush will make it appear you are too eager. Men do not like for their ladies to wear their feelings on their sleeve."

Charlotte rolled her eyes. "As if Nathan doesn't *know* I care."

While her daughter emoted, Emmy-Lou Valentine was tying her bonnet beneath her chin and making her way back to the kitchen for the picnic basket. "Get the dining cloth from the sideboard, dear," she called. Back in the living room, she reached out to adjust Charlotte's lace collar. She tapped Charlotte's pointed chin. "Now breathe evenly, dear. Calm yourself. Be a lady." While she waited for the blush to recede from her daughter's cheeks, Emmy-Lou lectured. "And don't forget to inquire about Miss Gray. There isn't a man alive whose heart doesn't soften when he sees a woman truly touched with concern for the fate of another. When it comes to permanent attachments like marriage, compassion is a much more endearing — and enduring — emotion than the passions elicited by physical beauty."

Charlotte frowned slightly. "I don't have to *pretend* to care about Miss Gray, Mama."

"Well, of course not, dear," Emmy-Lou said quickly. Taking Charlotte's elbow she headed for the door. "But it never hurts to let the gentlemen *see* evidence of one's tender heart."

Riding along on the opposite side of the carriage from Miss Charlotte, Nathan conversed with Miss Dinah and her father, pointing out flora and fauna to the younger Valentine daughter, while Mrs. Doctor Valentine tried to convince Private Charles Dubois to become a striker for the Valentine family.

"And if you'd agree to instruct my daughters in French, Private Dubois, that would be even more delightful. Of course your remuneration would be increased to make the French instruction worthwhile for you."

"Frenchy eez not a teacher, Meez Valentine," Nathan interjected. He spoke in a terrible imitation of Frenchy's accent, "His family have been chef, all ze way back to Charlemagne."

"Zat is true," Frenchy said, smiling. "But only on ze side of *ma mere, Monsieur Ser-*

geant. On ze side of my father were many *professeurs*." Dubois bowed toward Charlotte. "If *mon sergeant* says I may come, I would be delighted to instruct *les jeunes filles*."

"Oh, Avery," Mrs. Valentine sang to her husband's back as they drove along. "Just think how far it would go with Mama if the girls spoke *French* the next time they went East for a visit!" She glanced at Dubois. "Mama seems to think we are hopelessly lost to civilization."

Doctor Valentine nodded toward Nathan. "Sergeant Boone would have to approve of the situation. After all, he's the one giving up a soldier."

Nathan looked over at Frenchy, who was smiling at Miss Charlotte. "It appears that Private Dubois could be convinced." He raised his voice. "Is that right, Frenchy? Would you care to apply for the position as cook and French tutor for the Doctor Valentine family?"

"French?" Dinah protested. "What use is it to learn French?" She frowned. "I want to learn to *ride*. That's something a girl can *use* out here."

Nathan smiled at her. "We have a Private Jackson who's an expert horseman. You may remember him from your drive that

240

day when the men were having target practice. Tall, with a reddish beard and blue eyes."

Dr. Valentine frowned. "Isn't he the one who tore up Corporal Dorsey's knee?"

"The same," Nathan said. "He's repented of that particular sin. And he really is a fine horseman. Private Yates could go along, too. Perhaps some of the other ladies would want to join in."

"Do it, Papa," Charlotte interjected. "Someone needs to teach her to ride like a lady." She turned toward Nathan. "Dinah wants to go tearing over the prairie like a maniac, bareback, skirts flying, legs exposed!"

"Charlotte!" Mrs. Doctor glared at her daughter.

Dinah tossed her head. "Why does everybody want me to ride like a *lady?*" She pronounced the word as if it were cussing.

"I could drag that old sidesaddle out of the shed and polish it up for you, Dinah," Doctor Valentine said. "It's the very one Charlotte used when she was a girl."

"I'm fairly certain Private Jackson would welcome the diversion," Nathan said. "I'll talk to him before the day is out. It won't hurt him to miss target practice. He's already qualified for his sharpshooter medal."

241

Before they had gone far, it was arranged that Frenchy would take up domestic duties as the Valentine family striker. He would be paid extra for cooking and other odd jobs with a bonus for French lessons. And on Monday morning, any ladies interested in riding lessons with Private Caleb Jackson would report to the cavalry stables.

"Here I was languishing without domestic help, and it's all been solved on one lovely Sunday afternoon drive," Mrs. Valentine enthused. "Thank you, Sergeant Boone, for being so agreeable." She sighed. "A lady needs all the help she can get to keep a proper home on the frontier."

The group rode along in silence for a few moments. Then Mrs. Valentine said, "You know, Sergeant Boone, I will admit to a secret hope that you might somehow arrange for us to make Miss Gray's acquaintance before any of the other ladies on Officer's Row can hire her."

"Hire her?" Nathan asked.

"Well, I just assumed she would be looking for employment. Once she has recovered completely."

With a slight frown at her mother, Charlotte interrupted. She smiled up at Nathan. "We are all anxious to welcome Miss Gray

242

to Camp Robinson. We've been quite concerned about her. We hoped she would be up and about long before now. It's been weeks since she arrived, poor thing."

"Mama," Dinah piped up. "Maybe Miss Gray doesn't *want* to be a maid. Maybe she's a *princess*, and she got lost from her kingdom, and that's when Private Boone found her."

Nathan smiled at Dinah. Something in the child's innocent imaginings was at the heart of his discomfort with Mrs. Valentine's prodding. What was it in human nature, he wondered, that led people like her to automatically assign social position to others. And why did they always assign *inferior* positions? Mrs. Valentine assumed Laina was a servant. Dinah thought she might be a princess. He liked Dinah's way of thinking much better.

Mrs. Valentine spoke up. "Oh, Dinah. Forever dreaming fairy tales. Princesses do not reside in sod dugouts."

"Maybe not," Nathan said, "but dukes and royalty surely visit. Who's to say?" He winked at Dinah. "Maybe one of the princesses did get lost. Just like Dinah said."

"Well," Mrs. Valentine said, "perhaps the princess will honor us with her presence at supper some evening. You'll ask her for us, won't you, Sergeant Boone? As soon as she is able. I hear she is young."

"I don't really know how old she is."

"But she is able now to be up and about? Private Yates said she is helping Granny with the mending."

"Yes. As her strength permits." Nathan pulled his horse up, let the carriage pass, and then moved alongside Charlotte. "Perhaps Miss Valentine would want to recruit interest from the other ladies on Officer's Row for the riding lessons? I'll send Private Yates over this evening to check with you on how many ladies might participate."

Just as they rounded a low ridge that created a sheltered spot along Soldier Creek — and, hence, a favored picnic site — they saw Private Yates of the flaming red hair stand up and stretch. Granny Max was walking along the creek bank with a child in tow. A white puppy tore ahead of them, yapping and darting into the shallow water. Nathan saw Laina glance in their direction before jumping up and hurrying toward Granny Max.

"Sergeant Boone," Mrs. Doctor said, looking up at him with an expression he couldn't quite decipher. "Would you help Charlotte down from the carriage, please?

We've brought enough food to feed all of Company G. We shall invite Granny to join us. And I assume that is the elusive Miss Gray? No one ever mentioned just how lovely she is. How nice to see her so well recovered."

When the carriage bearing the Valentine family approached, Laina had been reaching into the picnic basket to get a piece of Granny's pie for Private Yates. Becky O'Malley had attached herself to the private as completely as was socially acceptable, and he seemed grateful for the female attention.

With Private Yates's attention expended elsewhere, Laina had been able to relax, coming as near to enjoying the outing as was possible for her, given her still-jittery nerves. She and Katie had had another session of training with the puppy, and Wilber had performed almost flawlessly — sitting on command and following along obediently without pulling on his lead. Laina realized she had been away from the protecting walls of Granny Max's quarters for over an hour, and not once had she been overwhelmed by unreasonable fear or panic.

And now the peace of the outing was

shattered by the arrival of unwelcome guests. She heard rather than saw the approach of the carriage and horses. She felt her heart begin to pound and her hands to shake. Private Yates must have noticed. Laina inwardly blessed him for moving so that he was positioned between her and the oncoming carriage.

While the people clamored down from the carriage and the soldiers dismounted, Laina jumped up and headed off along the edge of the creek to where Granny Max and Katie O'Malley were inspecting the tiny white blossoms of some wildflower just peeking above the landscape. The clatter and strange voices behind her sent a chill down her spine. She gazed toward Soapsuds Row.

Granny took her hand. Squinting at the arriving party, she said, "It's only Nathan with Doctor Valentine and his family. Looks like he's brought along someone else from the barracks. That's just one private and two grown women you don't know. And Dinah Valentine. She's about Katie's age." She caught Laina's gaze and held it. "No dark closets, right?"

Laina stared into Granny's loving face. She nodded and forced a faint smile. "No dark closets. Raspberry pie instead."

Granny squeezed her hand and held it close. "That's my girl." She led her along the creek bank toward the group of new-comers.

Not since the moment his wife had seen Camp Robinson for the first time had Sergeant Nathan Boone seen such abject terror reflected in a woman's eyes. Laina only proffered him a fleeting glance, but he registered the emotions roiling inside her as easily as he could interpret the mood of a wounded animal. She was pale, and the knuckles of the hand that clutched Granny Max's arm were white. He didn't need to see her trembling to sense it.

"Miss Gray," he said, bowing low. "It's good to see you've regained some strength." He did his best to communicate peace and encouragement in a lingering glance before turning aside to introduce Frenchy.

Frenchy stepped forward and bowed. With a flourish, he bent over Granny's hand and kissed it. He murmured a greeting and turned to Laina.

"*Enchanté, mademoiselle,*" he said. In one sweeping gesture he removed his hat and bent low over her hand, lifting it to his lips and barely brushing it with his moustache.

Encouraged by Katie's giggle, Laina said softly, *"Enchantée, monsieur."*

Frenchy stood up abruptly. His blue eyes twinkled. *"Vous parlez français, mademoiselle? Mais, c'est incroyable!"*

"Un tout petit peu," Laina said. "Only a little."

"C'est merveilleux!" Frenchy exclaimed with delight. "You must tell me how you learned such good accent. Is beautiful, *mademoiselle.*"

Aware of being the center of attention, Laina blushed and leaned into Granny, who had slipped an arm about her waist.

Dr. Valentine introduced his wife, who extended her hand. "How good it is to finally meet you, my dear." The kindness dripping from her elicited little more than a murmur from Laina.

Mrs. Doctor enthused. "May we impose on you and share this lovely spot and our meal?"

Miss Charlotte Valentine pretended Nathan had offered his arm to her. She tucked her hand beneath his elbow as she nodded at Miss Gray. "Yes," she said. "Please do join us. We've been wanting to welcome you to Camp Robinson." She smiled up at Nathan. "But Sergeant Boone insisted you weren't able to receive callers." She looked at Laina. "What a pleasant surprise it is to see that he was mistaken."

Private Yates trilled a scale on his mouth harp. "Granny invited us out here for a Sunday service. We haven't even started the hymn sing yet, have we, Granny?"

"Well, we got to serve up some raspberry pie first, Private." She shook her head. "Did I say raspberry? I mean *apple*." She grinned at Laina.

"And we've brought Sergeant Boone's favorite. Chokecherry," Charlotte offered quickly.

Wilber nearly ended things when he tore across the picnic cloth in hot pursuit of some imaginary prey. While Charlotte screeched, Laina caught the erring pup by the scruff of his neck, flipped him on his back and, holding his face in her hands, scolded him. "Now sit!" she said sternly. She released the pup, and he immediately planted his posterior upon the earth and stared up at her adoringly.

"What magic do you have hidden up your sleeve, Miss Gray?" Mrs. Doctor asked.

"Oh, Laina knows about dogs," Katie O'Malley offered. "She had one just like Wilber. She's been teaching me how to train him. And Ma don't mind him near so much now." Katie beamed at Laina. "He hasn't peed on the carpet in a long time, Laina."

Laina nodded while she sat down to pet Wilber, who slowly slumped against her, finally tumbling into a white ball at her side and falling asleep.

After lunch, Charlotte asked, "Do you know 'Amazing Grace,' Private Yates?"

Harlan began to play, and Charlotte's reedy soprano joined quickly, albeit slightly off key. Becky and Katie O'Malley's strong duet corrected Charlotte's wavering notes, and on the second verse even the elder Valentines sang. Granny's rich contralto supported them all. And then, Laina joined them. Her clear soprano was pure and sweet and so clear it made all the other voices meld into a garble of background noise.

One by one, the other singers dropped out. Laina was unaware. She sang, "When we've been there ten thousand years, bright shining as the sun, we've no less days to sing God's praise, than when we'd first begun." As the last note rang across the clearing, she opened her eyes. Suddenly aware that she was giving a solo performance, she stopped abruptly.

Doctor Valentine said, "I do not think I have ever heard a more lovely voice in all my life."

Blushing furiously, Laina touched the left side of her bonnet and thanked him.

"Please, Miss Gray. Honor us with another song," the doctor asked.

"You know this one?" Harlan began to play a spiritual.

Laina shook her head.

"Go on, honey," Granny said, nudging her. She whispered, "Best piece of raspberry pie old Granny has tasted in years."

Laina smiled at her. She caressed Wilber's sleeping form. As the music floated out of her, every ounce of fear and stress melted away. Her shoulders relaxed and the line between her finely arched eyebrows disappeared. She opened her eyes and saw Sergeant Boone staring at her. Their eyes met. She looked away quickly, giving Wilber her full attention.

When the song ended, Sergeant Boone got up and retreated from the gathering to check on the horses. Laina saw him take something out of his pocket and look at it.

Charlotte Valentine was watching, too. She rose and followed Sergeant Boone. Laina saw him tuck whatever he was looking at back in his pocket. He said something to Miss Valentine while he undid the knot tethering his bay gelding to the Valentines' carriage. Then, turning around to glance back toward Laina, he tipped his hat before mounting and heading off toward the east.

Charlotte made her way back up the path to join the small group just beginning to enjoy Mrs. Doctor's picnic lunch.

"Sergeant Boone offers his apologies," Charlotte said. "He has some things to attend to back at camp."

Thirteen

As for me, I will call upon God; and the Lord shall save me.

Psalm 55:16

He had come here every Sunday for two years now. Unless he was out on patrol. Most of the time he came with a bouquet of wildflowers. Whatever was in season. It didn't matter. Lily had loved flowers. And color. Especially bright blue and red and yellow. But she had always oohed and aahed over whatever Nathan brought and put them in that fancy vase she'd received from her mother. The one her mother called a *vahz*. So he brought her flowers on Sunday afternoons and pretended he could hear her exclaiming over them.

Now that he didn't talk to God anymore, he tended to stay longer at Lily's grave. He could talk to her. Of course, she didn't answer him. Not so he could hear. But then neither did God, so all things being equal, he'd just as soon talk to Lily. At least he could imagine an answer from her. He'd given up trying to imagine what God thought or said about things over a year ago.

For the first year after Lily died, Nathan had tried to reason things through. He kept Granny Max up until all hours of the night with his questions. She listened and nodded and tried her best to give him counsel. She always had Bible verses that spoke to his doubts. But every conversation seemed to end with the same answer, which was that either he had faith to live with unanswered questions — like why God let his wife die — or he didn't. As it turned out, Nathan didn't.

Granny said he could ask God for faith. She seemed pretty confident God would answer that request with a *yes*. But Nathan didn't really want to have faith in a God who might say *no* when His very own children asked Him for important things. There wasn't anything comforting about that. And besides, when it came right down to it, Nathan could think of only one thing he really wanted. Well, one thing he wanted that he couldn't get on his own,

254

that is. He also wanted a commission. But he could handle that one. He was a good soldier, and all the right people had their eye on him. He wouldn't disappoint them. As Nathan saw it, becoming an officer would not require any assistance from the Almighty. What he really wanted was a face-to-face talk with the woman he loved — and he knew the Almighty wouldn't be helping him with that.

As he dismounted at Lily's grave in the tiny Camp Robinson cemetery, Nathan Boone had new problems to talk over with his wife. He wanted to tell her about Doctor Valentine saying the men might be a little nervous about him. He was worried about Caleb Jackson. Did she remember meeting him? Beauregard Preston back then. Beau had so much anger and hate and bitterness bottled up inside him, Nathan didn't know if he'd make it in the army. Doctor Valentine was what really bothered him, though. He was telling Nathan to move on. Forget Lily. Well, not really to forget her. Just to put her things away.

Nathan laughed bitterly. "He actually said I should give myself a chance to *heal*, Lily. Like I cut myself or broke a leg. He knows it isn't as simple as that. He's been there himself." Nathan swallowed the lump in his throat. "Lily, if he'd loved that other woman half as much as I love you, he'd never tell me to give myself a chance to heal. Not if healing means forgetting you. I'll never do that." He bowed his head and let the tears come.

For the first half hour or so that Nathan sat beside Lily's grave, his mind ran in circles. He would try to talk, then get choked up and stop. He took her picture out of his pocket. He'd never felt uncomfortable about Lily when he was around Charlotte Valentine. But today he'd felt a need to look at Lily's photo. To remind himself. It was, Nathan realized, because of Miss Gray. When she sang, Nathan thought how good it was to see her finally free of all the fear and pain she carried locked up inside her. And he'd noticed she was pretty. Not in the way of Lily's delicate beauty. Laina Gray was small but there was an intensity about her, a raw power that would surprise a man. He knew about that because of what had happened at the soddy. There hadn't been much sign of it when she was sick and afraid to go outside. But today, when she'd made herself greet everyone at the picnic, he thought he'd seen a new kind of strength smoldering behind her green eyes. She'd looked at him, and he'd felt guilty.

"I don't know, Lily," he said to the tombstone. "I just felt like I had to get away and come talk to you about it."

He couldn't find any more words. He'd come here every Sunday and poured out his heart, and now, as he sat by Lily's grave, Nathan had nothing left to say. Life stretched out before him, empty and meaningless. He was alone, and he would be alone for the next . . . What would it be, he wondered? How many years before he rested beside Lily?

And then what?

The thought brought him up short. He'd given up God. What *would* happen when he died? What exactly had happened to Lily? Where was she right this instant?

Whiskey whickered softly. Nathan turned in time to see the horse raise his head and look toward the west, his ears pricked, with liquid brown eyes fixed on a lone figure walking toward the cemetery. It wasn't any use to run away from Granny Max. If she had something to say, it would get said, whether now or next month. He might as well hear it.

Granny didn't waste any time getting to her point. "Why'd you come running off up here? That was rude, Nathan, leaving us the way you did."

"I just had to get away."

Granny studied him carefully. "I saw you take Lily's picture out of your pocket."

Nathan looked at the tombstone. "I'm forgetting her." He looked at Granny, his eyes brimming with unspilled tears. "How can that be? How could I forget?" He took his hat off and held it, staring off toward Soapsuds Row.

"Time moves us forward, Nathan. It's part of God's plan for us to move away from the past. And we do some forgetting of what is back there so we can go into the future and the Lord's will for us." Granny patted his hand. "A little forgetting is good for us. Sometimes we try to remember so hard we stand still. That's not what this life is for. When God's ready for us to stop changing, He takes us to the next life." She sat on a thick patch of grass and patted a spot beside her. "Sit down here, Nathan. I wasn't thinking of saying this at Lily's grave, but maybe it will mean even more to you if I say it here." Granny waited for Nathan to sit and then shifted her entire body so she could look straight at him. "You'll never forget Lily, Nathan. And you will always love her. But maybe you felt a little guilty today when Miss Valentine —"

"Charlotte Valentine doesn't mean anything to me."

"I know that," Granny said. "All the times you've danced or dined with Miss Valentine, I bet you haven't felt you had to take out Lily's photo once. It wasn't Miss Valentine today, either. It was Laina's singing. I saw your face. Just for an instant today, while Laina was singing, you weren't thinking of Lily. That's what's bothering you."

Nathan looked away. He reached over and touched one of the blossoms in the bouquet he'd brought Lily. "People were so smug at her funeral. The way they said 'You're young. You'll find someone else.' I never wanted to smash faces so bad in my life as I did that day." With his forearm, he brushed some tears off his face.

Granny patted his arm. "Tell me your brother's name. The older one."

"James."

"Did your mama love you, Nathan?"

"Of course she did."

"But how? How could she love you? Didn't she love James? And what about your sister? Did she love your sister?"

"Of course."

"But not as much as you."

Nathan frowned. "She loved us all."

"That can't be, Nathan. There's not enough love. She must have loved some less, some more."

"Well, if she did, I never knew it."

Granny nodded. "When a woman has a child, Nathan, her love pours into that child to the extent she thinks her heart will break. She gives it everything. Then the good Lord smiles on her again and she is expecting another child. And not a mother or a father on the earth doesn't worry, thinking, 'I love this baby I already have so much. . . . How will I ever love another child? There's not that much love in me.' They worry. That second baby comes. And you know what happens? God just pours more love into their hearts, and suddenly they are loving that new baby with love they didn't know they had."

Granny reached out to trace Lily's name on the tombstone. "You are acting like you used up all the love you will ever have in this world on Lily Bainbridge. But, Nathan, God doesn't give us just a certain amount of love for all our lives to be parceled out. Your mama didn't have to take some love away from your brother to be able to love you. God is the Author of love. He gives and He gives and He gives. More love. There's never an end to it. It's like He is at the other end of a telegraph line. *His* lines don't ever get cut. They run all day, every day, all year for eternity. Just sending love for us to spread around."

She put her wrinkled hand alongside Nathan's cheek. "You gave so much love to Lily. And since she died you haven't ever asked for more. But He has more. If you will only ask for it. It won't diminish or change what you had with Miss Lily. God would never expect you to give anyone the part of your heart you gave to Lily. But, Nathan, He can give you a *new* heart full of *new* love." She patted his cheek. "There is no shame in whatever it was that happened for that instant today. I've been praying for over two years that the Lord would heal your broken heart, Nathan. You have done everything you can manage to keep that from happening. You've kept things as they were to remind you. From the minute you wake up until the minute you lie down, you have reminders everywhere. They keep you from healing. From moving on. Let it happen, Nathan. Let the Lord heal the crack in your heart. He can heal it and still keep what you had with Lily safe."

"The only thing I want from God is an answer to *why?*" Nathan said.

Granny sighed. She patted his arm. "Don't I know that, child." She shook her head. "I got that question on my list, too. And I've lived long enough to have a lot more *whys* in this old gray head of mine than you have in yours. We all have a list of 'whys.' You. Me. Miss Gray."

Nathan said. "What's *she* think of a God who doesn't answer *why?*"

Granny thought for a moment before saying, "Why don't you ask her?"

"Maybe I will."

Perched on a rock ledge overlooking the valley below, Laina lifted her face to the sun. She smiled. *If you really are there, then thank you for today. I think I did well, don't you?* She inhaled deeply and settled back against a rock, humming to herself.

Happiness was such a new sensation she didn't quite know how to deal with it. She was tired, but it was a delicious weariness — the result of battling and defeating some of her most persistent demons. Being in the company of Harlan Yates, Becky and Katie, Granny, and to some extent even Sergeant Boone, today had helped her claim a small victory over herself, over the past, and perhaps even over Josiah Paine.

A few yards away, Katie was wading in

the creek. On the opposite bank, Wilber was on the trail of something. The others had left long ago, but she and Katie had lingered, wanting to work a little more on Wilber's training. Now as she sat thinking back over the afternoon, Laina almost laughed aloud at the idea of Riverboat Annie at a hymn sing with Mrs. Doctor Valentine and her uppity daughter. They had a way about them that Laina recognized immediately. It was the same attitude Nellie Pierce and the other girls at Miss Hart's expressed toward the gambler's daughter. It was amusing watching them adjust their opinions when Laina spoke French with Private Dubois.

She smiled to herself. God surely had a sense of humor. Sundays in her former life meant sleeping late and less business. And here she was going on a picnic and singing hymns. It felt good. It felt almost right. She'd been to hell, and she'd brought some demons back with her, but she was also beginning to sense that a new life might be possible here at Camp Robinson.

Mrs. Valentine had hinted at wanting a housekeeper. She also seemed to have an interest in Laina's helping Dubois teach the girls French, although Laina doubted the little one — Dinah? — would have much interest in it. Still, Laina smiled. She had handled uppity women before. They didn't scare her. That was the best part of all, Laina realized. Terror had challenged her today. She had met it head on and defeated it. Like Clara Maxwell, she had forced herself out of the closet and had eaten a piece of raspberry pie. And here she was thinking of getting a respectable position with a respectable family. If that wasn't a change for the better, Laina didn't know what was. Maybe Granny's God *was* going to work out something, after all.

"Wilber. No, Wilber. Come!" Katie shouted.

Four men were riding toward them. Wilber had forgotten every bit of training and was yowling and tearing out in pursuit, ignoring Katie's pleas.

Laina stood up. The dog's howls had unsettled one of the horses, who began to crow-hop and buck and finally dumped its rider in a bush. Swearing followed, and then one of the riders pulled a pistol and aimed for Wilber.

Laina screamed. "No! Stop! Wilber! Come, Wilber!" She kept yelling at the top of her lungs, pumping her legs hard and running toward the men.

The man who'd been thrown was

264

drawing his pistol too. He fired and missed. Laina grabbed for his gun just as he cocked the pistol and took aim again. "Stop!" she pleaded. "It's a puppy. Only a puppy."

Wilber was barking and yapping at the horses, chasing hooves and having a grand time, oblivious to the danger at hand. One of the horses finally landed a well-placed kick, and Wilber went rolling. He landed in a semiconscious pile, which Katie immediately scooped up. She ran to Laina's side.

Laina put her hand on Katie's shoulder. She noticed the men weren't soldiers. Maybe cowboys, she thought. She didn't like the way they had circled around her and Katie.

"That cur of yours is a menace."

It was the one who'd been thrown by his horse. He was standing behind her. She turned around. He'd caught his horse, but he hadn't gotten back in the saddle. His dirty blond hair hung to his shoulders from beneath a stained, wide-brimmed gray hat.

"He's mine," Katie said. She thrust her chin out and glared at him. "And you're not supposed to be on the military reservation."

The cowboy arched one eyebrow. "That so, little lady. And who's gonna make me get off? That killer dog of yours?" He laughed, showing brown crooked teeth.

Say something, Laina urged herself. She should speak up. But she was trembling so hard, it was all she could do to hold herself upright.

Katie flinched and pulled away from Laina's terrified grasp on her shoulder.

"Let's go home now, Laina." Katie took her hand.

"Not so fast," the cowboy said. He took a step toward them.

Laina grabbed Wilber from Katie's arms. Together, they began to walk toward Camp Robinson. They'd come too far, Laina realized. Too far for anyone to hear if they called for help. *Oh, God. Katie.*

She could hear the men behind her talking.

"Never thought I'd see a speck of a woman get the best of you."

"You can't handle a couple little gals, what's gonna happen if the Cheyenne head back up this way?"

"The gang's gonna love hearin' how Charlie Bates was throwed by his own horse."

She heard the creaking of leather as the

266

man climbed into the saddle, and then hoofbeats as he came up behind them.

"Hey, you." From behind, he snatched Laina's bonnet off. The ribbons caught beneath her chin. He tugged on her bonnet a couple of times, then let go, leaving it dangling down her back.

"Keep walking," Laina whispered to Katie. "Don't say anything. Just walk."

"I'm talkin' to you." The man said. He rode up alongside them. "It ain't polite to ignore a man when he's talkin' to you."

God. Katie. Please.

He moved his horse in front of them, blocking the way back to camp.

Laina stopped. She put her hand on Katie's shoulder. Wilber had begun to struggle to be put down. Laina gripped harder, and Wilber struggled more until finally he succeeded in wriggling free. He dropped to the earth with a thud, jumped up, and tore off like a shot for Camp Robinson. Watching him go, Laina could only be thankful he had lost interest in barking at horses.

Laina found her voice. "They'll be expecting us back." Surprised at how confident she sounded, she forced herself to look into the cowboy's eyes. The face was handsome in spite of the cruelty etched in the lines around his mouth. She had seen men like him before. They were the ones her father especially watched when he played them at cards. The ones who would play all night and lose with seeming grace — but then return later to hide behind a grain barrel up on deck and take a shot at the winner. You could see evil in their eyes, and when this man looked at Laina, her midsection tightened. She had thwarted his cruelty to Wilber. His buddies were making fun of him. He was going to have to show them some proof of his manhood. Her throat constricted with fear.

God. Katie. Please.

"Run, Katie. Run!" Laina grabbed Katie's hand. Together, they took off. As Laina expected, she got about three steps before the cowboy grabbed her from behind. He tried to drag her up behind him, but his half-wild horse wouldn't cooperate.

"Run, Katie! RUN!" Laina screamed. She saw Katie hesitate, then head out. The men seemed content to hold on to Laina and let Katie get away. She wanted to fight. She wanted to kick and scream and spit. But maybe, just maybe if she didn't — maybe they would let Katie be.

There was the sound of hoofbeats. A horse breathing hard. A rifle being cocked.

"Put the lady down."

Laina landed in the dirt. She sprung up and almost cried with relief at the sight of Nathan Boone.

"Now hold on, Sergeant." One of the cowboys was talking. "We didn't mean no harm. Charlie here gets a little crazy sometimes. That's all. We was just chasing some strays."

"And you strayed onto the military reservation, and into more trouble than you bargained for. Get down off your horses." He spoke to her without taking his eyes off the men. "Miss Gray. Come over by me."

Laina went to Nathan while the cowboys considered their options. When Nathan fired his rifle in the air, Charlie's horse threw him again. Swearing, the man got up.

"He's the one you want, Sergeant," one of the men was saying. "He caused all the trouble."

"And you're the ones who didn't do much to stop it," Nathan said. "Get off your horses."

The cowboys complied. The one they had called Charlie got up and dusted himself off.

"Drop your guns and step away from them."

Laina had come up next to Whiskey. Still watching the cowboys, Nathan said to her, "Can you climb up behind me? I'm sort of preoccupied at the moment."

While Laina scrambled up behind him, Nathan kept his rifle trained on the cowboys.

"All right, boys. Now we're going for a nice Sunday afternoon stroll. You'll find the guardhouse at Camp Robinson to your liking. Much better than camping out under the stars. And we have a French cook. Let's go."

With the cowboys walking ahead of him, Nathan followed astride Whiskey.

"Do you know how to shoot a pistol?" he asked Laina. When she said no, he urged her, "Pull it out of my holster and pretend like you do. Just don't shoot me. And maybe you should attend target practice tomorrow."

"I know you know what you are doing, Lord," Granny said as she waited for Nathan to bring Laina back. "But . . . are you sure about this? She's done little more than hide inside for nearly two months now. Today was such a victory, Lord. She wanted to run and hide when the Valentines drove up. You know she did.

270

But she stayed. She even enjoyed herself a little. And now . . . this. Like I said, Lord, I know you know what you are doing, but . . . are you sure about this?"

She shouldn't have left Laina and Katie back there at the creek. She should have stayed, too. She should have made Harlan stay. They all should have left earlier. Or later. She should be up helping Meara O'Malley calm little Katie, who had come tearing up to the Row screaming for help.

The fact was, Granny didn't know what to do. A dozen mounted soldiers were flying to the rescue even as Granny worried. All she could do right now was wait for Laina to get back. While she waited, she made herb tea. She got Laina's bed ready. She prayed. *Oh Lord, is she going to just crawl back under these quilts and be done trying?*

It was more excitement than Camp Robinson had seen in weeks, and when the four offenders straggled into camp and were locked up in the guardhouse, it provided fodder for a week's worth of campfires and checker games. Rumor had it the cowboys weren't really cowboys at all. Rumor had it Nathan Boone had captured four members of Doc Middleton's gang of horse thieves. Rumor had Sergeant Boone

271

and Miss Gray courting.

Rumor was wrong.

Laina Gray sat wrapped in a quilt at Granny Max's table drinking coffee. She'd asked for coffee instead of Granny's calming tea. "I . . . I need to think, Granny. I don't want to sleep. Not yet."

Harlan had come, red-faced and stammering concern.

Doctor Valentine had checked in.

Sergeant Boone had come, too — after seeing to the arrest, caring for Whiskey, and filing his report.

Laina had greeted them all with an almost unearthly calm. She'd reassured them. She'd even insisted on going up to the O'Malleys' and seeing Katie. And Wilber. As it turned out, it was Wilber who had saved them. Sergeant Boone said he had seen the pup charging toward the Row and for some reason decided to make sure nothing else had been left at the picnic site. Were it not for Wilber, rescue would have been delayed long enough for . . . Well, Granny just wasn't going to think about that.

Granny watched her carefully, but as evening wore on, Laina just didn't seem to need calming. So Granny made coffee. Stirred up some corn bread. Sewed on a button. Watched. Waited.

Laina finally spoke. "Granny, He did it." Her hand trembled when she set down her coffee cup.

"Who did what, honey-lamb?" Granny answered, internally gathering all the forces of heaven to help her handle whatever challenge might be coming.

"God," Laina said. "He answered me." She looked up at Granny. "A prayer, I mean. At least I think He did. I didn't think He'd ever answer one of my prayers. But today I just kept thinking *God. Katie. Please.* I didn't even know I was praying. But I was." She smiled at Granny. "And He *answered* me, Granny. *God said yes.*" Laina looked down at the table. "Wilber took off and Sergeant Boone came. And no one got hurt. God said *yes,* Granny. He heard me." She started to cry.

Granny nodded and smiled.

"You thought I was going to come in here and go back to hiding under those quilts in the back room again."

"The thought occurred to me."

"That's why you made your tea. To help with the nightmares."

Granny nodded again.

"Well, I'm not hiding anymore," Laina said. "I don't know Him like you do. But something in here," she touched the place over her heart, "just feels — better, somehow. Peaceful."

Granny hugged her. They talked long into the night, Laina asking questions, Granny giving answers when she had them. As they talked, Laina moved past *why* into *how*. How could she know God the way Granny did? How could God possibly forgive her all those past sins? How could Jesus love her enough to die for her? And then, with Granny holding her hand, Laina Gray, who had for the first time in her life felt God say *yes* to her, said *yes* to Him.

On Monday afternoon, when the ladies of Camp Robinson gathered for target practice, they were joined by Miss Laina Gray.

Miss Charlotte Valentine thought Private Yates made a fool of himself over her.

On Tuesday, Miss Gray accompanied Granny Max to Gruber's trading post and selected a madder-print calico for a new dress.

Miss Charlotte Valentine thought any woman with *that* color of hair should know better than to wear anything with orange in it.

On Wednesday, Miss Gray could be seen helping Private Yates hang shirts to dry just outside the washing shed where Granny Max and Mrs. O'Malley did Company G's laundry.

Miss Charlotte Valentine was pleased to see that Miss Gray at least recognized her status at Camp Robinson was that of domestic servant.

On Thursday, Miss Gray made arrangements with Mrs. Doctor Valentine to begin working for her the following Monday.

And on Friday. Well, all day on Friday, it was rumored there would be another lady at the hop.

Miss Charlotte Valentine applied a bit of rouge to her cheeks. And her mother, who had *words* for young ladies who painted themselves to gain masculine attention, pretended not to notice.

Fourteen

Be not far from me, for trouble is near; for there is none to help.

Psalm 22:11

The spring and early summer of 1878 in the Sandhills of Nebraska had been nothing special. As they had for years and years, endless lines of birds streamed across the sky, honking and whooping and settling overnight along the banks of spring-fed lakes before rising at dawn to continue their trek north.

The men of Camp Robinson followed their rigid daily schedule, obeying the almost hourly bugles and almost always owly drill sergeants, while they complained about having nothing much to do and wished the army would decide whether or not they were going to close the place down and move everyone over to Camp Sheridan.

Private Frenchy Dubois planted a huge garden and boasted that Company G would raise the best crop of fresh vegetables the army ever had.

Private Harlan Yates became Camp Robinson's all-around handyman. He was always in demand by someone for carpentry or repairs, and thanks to Granny Max's influence in keeping him away from the less virtuous elements of the camp — and Miss Gray's presence, which encouraged his affinity for Sunday afternoons over on the Row — he was able to make a real financial difference for his mother and younger sister back home.

Over on Soapsuds Row laundresses laundered and children played. Meara O'Malley grew great with child. She was miserable most of the time, and her two daughters took on more of her duties. Soon she was spending most of her time in bed, and Katie and Becky were spending most of their time in the company of Granny Max and Laina Gray.

Beginning in mid-June, Laina Gray spent the first three days of every week at the Valentines'. On Monday she did the family laundry. On Tuesday she ironed and mended what she had washed on Monday.

On Wednesday she cleaned. But when asked to prepare a meal, she had to admit she did not cook.

"I'm sorry, Mrs. Valentine," Laina said the first Wednesday. "But you don't want me trying to help in the kitchen. I can't cook worth anything."

"Nonsense," Mrs. Valentine said. "I don't expect anything fancy. Just roast a hen and throw in some potatoes."

"You have to kill and clean a hen to roast it," Laina said. "I've seen Granny do it. But I don't know how."

"That's ridiculous," Mrs. Valentine said. "Even *I* know how to do that. Girls learn this sort of thing when they're in grammar school. Where *did* you grow up, Miss Gray?"

A "Riverboat Annie" retort rose to Laina's lips. Barely managing not to utter it, Laina grabbed the flat iron off the stove behind her and slammed it onto the linen tablecloth she was pressing. "I *didn't* grow up. I was hatched and raised by loons."

"There's no need to be impertinent, Miss Gray," Mrs. Valentine snipped.

Just when Mrs. Valentine had opened her mouth — Laina would never know if she intended to apologize or fire her — Private Charles Dubois knocked at the back door and stepped into the silence looming between the two women. He was bearing a handful of green onions and some herbs from the company garden.

Thank God. Laina smiled to herself. *Yes. Really. Thank you, God.* And she hadn't even prayed about the cooking. At least not consciously. And here was Private Dubois, smiling instead of criticizing, teaching her how to kill, clean, and cook the hen.

"Mais non!" he exclaimed, when Laina tried to stretch the chicken's neck beneath a broom handle. "What are you doing?!"

"Isn't that how you do it?" Laina asked.

"You have seen zis done — with a *broom?"*

Laina nodded. "That's how the cook on the riverboat did it."

"Well, zat is not how to kill a shik-en," Frenchy said, muttering to himself in French. He grabbed an ax. *"Tenez . . . la"* he ordered, pointing at the feet. *"Et la tête, mademoiselle."* When Laina obeyed, he brought down the ax. *"Comme ça."* He explained, "She never know what happen. Ze broomstick is torture. Barbarism." He walked away shaking his head.

Later, when the hen was plucked clean, Frenchy instructed Laina to add potatoes, green onions, and parsley to the cooking pot. Pulling a leather pouch from his pocket, he sprinkled some of its contents over the bubbling liquid. Winking at Laina, he raised his finger to his lips and whispered. "This, I cannot tell you, *mademoiselle. C'est magique.*"

Whatever magic Charles Dubois carried in the leather pouch, it elicited adoration from the Valentine family when they sat down to dinner that evening. Laina had gone back over to the Row long before that happened, but she heard about it Friday evening at the hop where Mrs. Valentine's snagging a French cook was subject of many whispered conversations and enough associated envy that Emmy-Lou's face fairly beamed with joy.

As time went by, daily life took on a monotony Laina adored. For the first time in many years, she felt safe. Her biggest challenge in life was not laughing aloud at Charlotte Valentine's ability to make a tragedy out of something so unimportant as whether or not her father would let her have the money to buy a certain lace for a new dress.

Physically, Laina was almost back to normal. While she bore permanent scars, she'd learned to cover the one on her head and on some days she didn't even think about the others. She felt tired most of the time, and her stomach still rebelled on occasion. But all in all, Laina Gray was content with taking baby steps toward the unknown future and baby steps toward the God she was learning to trust.

Sergeant Nathan Boone came around Soapsuds Row more often for dinner. He found time to teach Katie O'Malley to play chess. He treated Becky much like a younger sister, keeping an eye on her at the hops and steering her clear of the Caleb Jacksons, both in Company G and the infantry. The sergeant occasionally favored Wilber, who it seemed would grow taller than any of Dr. Valentine's greyhounds, with a bone fished out of Frenchy's stew pot. And he spent more than one Sunday afternoon listening to Harlan Yates play his mouth harp while Laina Gray sang.

Anyone inspecting Camp Robinson would have detected nothing out of the ordinary. Unless, of course, they talked to Granny Max, who often looked beyond what she could see and caught glimpses of what was really happening.

What is it about her? Nathan Boone wondered. He was standing with his back to the wall, his arms folded, watching Laina Gray dance with Corporal Dorsey. It was the usual Friday night hop. The enlisted men had planned it and invited the officers and their wives. They'd cleared out the barracks to create a dance floor. The company band was providing music. A table along one wall was groaning beneath the weight of Frenchy's now famous delectables. The air was filled with the mingled scents of dust and sweat, and occasionally a fragrance of lavender or lemon verbena as a woman swept by. Laughter rang out above the stomping of boots on the board floor as first one, then another of the men tied a handkerchief on his upper arm to designate himself as a lady.

And in the middle of the foot stomping and laughter, Miss Laina Gray soared around the dance floor like a bird gliding over the smooth surface of a lake.

Nathan had been sure Laina would withdraw after the outlaw incident. When he went to help her down off Whiskey, Miss Gray had run to Granny Max without looking back. She hadn't even thanked him — which didn't really bother him, because he expected her hasty retreat. He was sure she would disappear inside Granny Max's apartment and never come out again. He'd felt bad for Granny Max and the sleep she was going to lose again. That night, he had even slept in his old apartment next to Granny's, expecting to hear screams from another of Miss Gray's nightmares. He'd been ready to help. And then he hadn't been needed.

In fact, the next day Private Yates had reported that Miss Gray, who had accompanied Miss Valentine and the other ladies to target practice, was a good shot. And then when he himself stopped by Granny's, Nathan had been surprised to find Miss Gray down on all fours, cutting up a length of fabric spread out on the floor. "A new dress," she had said by way of explanation. He'd felt a little guilty, realizing that Lily's gray calico was showing some wear. He should have noticed. He had decided to take her another of Lily's dresses weeks ago. But time had gone by and he hadn't done it. Watching her dance, he decided Lily's pink dress wouldn't really look good with Miss Gray's auburn hair. He'd give her the green one. No. He'd take them both. What good were they doing in Lily's trunk, anyway?

His conversation with Granny beside Lily's grave came back. *Why don't you ask her?* Granny had said when Nathan wondered aloud what Miss Gray thought of a God who was silent when asked *why*. *"Maybe I will,"* had been his reply. But he hadn't done that, either. Maybe tonight he would.

Movement along the opposite wall of the barracks reminded Nathan he wasn't the only man keeping an eye on Miss Laina Gray. He spotted Jackson, who lately seemed to have found a way to avoid the temptations of gambling and drinking at Camp Robinson by volunteering for every escort detail and patrol that came up. He was rarely in camp for longer than a day, and when he was, he requested and was assigned stable fatigue. He spent hours longeing horses around the corral. Corporal Dorsey said Jackson knew the personalities of the Company G horses better than the captain knew the men. He'd even helped Dorsey cure a new mount of a nasty biting habit. With Jackson making peace with Dorsey, Nathan had hoped the recruit's personal troubles had been laid to rest. He had congratulated himself on the success of his own attempts to mold Jackson into a good soldier.

But now, watching Jackson eyeball Miss Gray, Nathan wondered if a new problem was in the making. He had shrugged off

Dr. Valentine's comments about the way Jackson looked at Charlotte. Now, seeing the soldier almost leering at Miss Gray from a shadowy corner of the barracks, Nathan understood what the doctor meant. He was glad he'd ordered Jackson to stay away from Soapsuds Row.

He cross-examined himself. Why should it matter to him if Private Caleb Jackson took an interest in Laina Gray? She was a grown woman. He was going to have to get beyond this proprietary attitude he had toward her. She wasn't some injured puppy he had rescued and needed to find a good home for. And she wasn't his personal possession. It was foolish for him to be so overprotective.

He'd talk to her tonight. Watching her dance and smile made him feel good about his role in her recovery. Tonight he would find out how she was really doing. Maybe ask her that question about the God who doesn't answer *why*. If she was truly doing all right, then maybe he could relax a little about her having to deal with the Private Jacksons at Camp Robinson.

The reasonable Sergeant Nathan Boone had almost won his internal argument, had almost decided maybe he should back off and let Miss Gray handle her own affairs, when Private Jackson took a step in Laina's direction. Even as he scolded himself for doing it, Nathan reasoned that Miss Gray had had more than her share of poor treatment from men. If he had anything to say about it, Miss Laina Gray would never be hurt again. He moved quickly to intercept Jackson.

"May I have this dance?" Nathan bowed low and held out his hand.

Corporal Dorsey winked at him. He swiped his forehead with a kerchief. "Thank goodness," he said, grinning. "This lady is too polite to complain, but I do believe I've trounced on enough of her toes for one evening." He turned to Laina. "Thank you, ma'am." He spun about and immediately asked Charlotte Valentine to dance.

Nathan saw Miss Valentine shoot an icy glare in Laina's direction. He assumed Laina didn't see it, but he was taken aback when, with a quick nod and a smile, Miss Gray guided his hand to her waist. He felt her hand linger over his longer than what he thought necessary before she slid it up his arm to his shoulder. She laced the fingers of her left hand through his. The music began. Not what he expected. A waltz. A slow waltz. The musicians were letting the dancers catch their breath. Why, then, Nathan wondered, was he having trouble catching his?

"Private Yates tells me you're a good shot, Miss Gray."

"Private Yates is a good liar," Laina said.

"You . . . um . . . you finished your dress." *Confound it.* Why'd he say that? Much too personal. But the green fabric *did* bring out the color in her eyes. Sort of made her auburn hair look prettier, too, now that he thought about it. She'd pinned a bunch of wildflowers to the bun at the nape of her neck. They smelled good. She was talking. He should be listening.

". . . thankful you took the notion to check what Wilber was barking about."

Did he imagine it, or had she squeezed his hand just then? What had happened to her? She was acting like . . . well . . . she was acting like a normal lady at a dance. How had she come to *normal,* anyway?

Had she asked him a question? "I'm sorry. What did you say?"

"I was wondering," Laina repeated, "just what's going to happen to those men in the guardhouse?"

Obviously, Nathan thought, she still needed protecting. "We're holding them until the sheriff from Deadwood arrives.

Found out they're wanted up there for horse thieving." He smiled encouragement. "You don't worry about them. The sheriff will be down soon to take them off our hands." He spun her around the dance floor, sensing her relief, feeling a surge of emotion inside him when she smiled and the light came back into her eyes.

He would offer to walk her home after they talked. Just as a precaution, in case Jackson was lingering outside.

"Hey, Jackson!" The recruit everyone called "Professor" was walking toward him from the direction of the barracks. "We're gettin' up a game of poker at Grubers. Low stakes. Why don'cha come?"

Jackson shook his head. "Thanks. I've got to check on a mare that went lame today." He started off in the direction of the stable while the group of men headed toward the trading post. As soon as they were out of sight, Jackson doubled back. Sidling along the barracks's log wall, he pulled his hat down over his forehead and turned his collar up. Then he peered around the window frame, watching the dancers.

"You're a good dancer." Nathan leaned

down so Laina could hear him above the music while he waltzed her around the room.

"I had a good teacher," she said. "In another life."

"Your teacher . . . she taught you French, too?"

She shook her head. "No. That was another part of the other life. And the French teacher wasn't a lady." She laughed lightly, "But he wasn't really a gentleman, either."

He looked down at her. Was she teasing him?

"You are staring, Sergeant."

"I'm sorry. It's just . . . well . . . I can't quite . . ." She probably thought he was flirting with her. Lord, keep him from *that* misunderstanding. All he wanted to do was to have that conversation Granny Max had suggested that day at Lily's grave. "You seem different."

Nathan sensed rather than saw her tense up, but he could tell she was distancing herself from him just slightly. She lowered her voice. "Different as in *no longer a raging animal* or different as in *not what I expected* or different as in *get me out of here — why did I ever ask this creature to dance with me in the first place?*"

Nathan leaned down again so the other

289

dancers couldn't hear him. "Would you mind taking a walk with me?" He felt her hair brush his cheek as she turned her head to look up into his eyes. She arched one eyebrow. He hadn't seen that expression before. She took his arm.

Weaving through the other dancers, they headed outside where the moonlight shone bright enough to cast shadows around them. Here and there, small groups of soldiers stood around, telling tales, wagering on a coming horse race, complaining about army food or their recent fatigue duty. Nathan scanned the shadows. No Private Jackson as far as he could tell. They turned left — Nathan made certain they didn't head toward the cavalry barracks or the guardhouse — and began to walk slowly around the perimeter of the parade ground.

Private Jackson watched Sergeant Boone and Miss Gray promenade along one side of the parade ground. He'd seen them head for the door and ducked around the corner of the barracks just in time to escape Sergeant Boone's notice. Now, as they walked away, he watched, wondering how it could be that the woman he'd known as Riverboat Annie could have found her way to Camp Robinson, Nebraska.

He'd had his doubts when he first saw her. He'd never really seen Annie in daylight. He'd never seen her with her hair up, either. He'd thought maybe he was wrong. Maybe this woman only looked like Annie. But watching her dance with Sergeant Boone convinced him. The way she smiled up at him. The way she slid her hand up his arm right before the music started. The way she laced her fingers through Boone's. Jackson remembered every gesture as if it had been only yesterday she had danced with him as Riverboat Annie. She'd done a skillful job of covering up what looked to be a pretty awful scar. The part that showed on her temple wasn't too bad, but it must be worse above her ear because she'd twisted her hair in a way Jackson couldn't ever remember seeing before. Leave it to Annie to think of a way to cover up.

He smiled to himself, wondering what Rose and the other girls from the riverboat would think if they knew the little gal they'd worried about so much after she disappeared, was out west dancing it up with a bunch of soldiers and romancing a sergeant. At least it sure looked like she had him on the hook and was ready to reel him in.

Watching her walk away with Sergeant Boone, Jackson shook his head. She was up to something — that was certain. Even Dr. Valentine's daughter Charlotte thought so. He hadn't missed the look on her face when Boone asked Annie to dance. Private Jackson had played enough games in his life and caused enough jealousy to recognize it for what it was.

Charlotte Valentine was a pretty little thing though. With a high opinion of herself. It would be a challenge to turn that little lady's head. A challenge that would relieve the boredom of tending horses and riding patrol. And flirting didn't have the addictive risks of whiskey and gambling. Jackson smiled to himself, wondering if he'd be able to overcome the girl's parents' reluctance to let their precious daughter be romanced by a lowly enlisted man.

But I'm not just any enlisted man. I've always been able to turn their heads. I need a little beard trimming and a barber to tame my hair. Or maybe not. Maybe a little of the mountain-man look would give these ladies something different from all the spit-and-polished Sergeant Boones they see. Maybe he'd let just a glimmer of his southern accent back into his speech. He could hint at a tragic past. That always got to the girls' mothers. And he wouldn't have to pretend about that part. With a glance over his shoulder, Jackson removed his hat and slicked his hair back with both hands. Then he pulled a lock of it down over his forehead. Hat in hand, he ducked inside. The band was only halfway through their introduction to "Annie Laurie" when Private Caleb Jackson had his hand on Charlotte Valentine's tiny, corseted waist.

"I'm honored you'd see fit to dance with me, ma'am," he drawled. "Some of the other women on the post don't seem to think a galvanized Yankee has much use. Makes it mighty lonely for a poor boy from North Care-lina." He made sure his face was a picture of regret and sadness.

Charlotte looked up at him. When he squeezed her hand, her cheeks blushed pink. "Well, I'm not those women. And I'm happy to dance with you, Private."

"Thank you, ma'am," Jackson said. "It . . . it helps to have a pretty face to block out the . . ." He shook his head.

"To block out what, Private?"

"Never mind, ma'am. The past is past." He forced a smile and pretended to blink away tears. It worked. The girl was almost crying herself. He moved his hand to her back and applied just enough pressure to bring her closer — but not enough so as to raise a red flag in the mind of the old biddy watching them from near the punch bowl. *The mother.* His next challenge.

"I wanted to tell you how glad I am . . . after those outlaws . . . well . . . I wondered if it would somehow set you back." Nathan slowed his pace, trying to match his long stride with Laina's as they walked along in the moonlight.

She reached up and touched the left side of her head. "I'm just as surprised as you that it didn't." Her voice lowered. "As strange as this may sound, I think it helped me somehow."

"Helped you?" Now he really wanted to hear what she had to say.

They had come to the picket fence that created front lawns for the row of officer's duplexes. Laina paused there. They stood together in the moonlight while she explained, "When those . . . men . . . confronted Katie and me, I was so terrified I could hardly stay standing. I couldn't say anything. All I could do was hang on to Katie. My mind kept going blank. Except for three words. *God. Katie. Please.*" She looked up at him. "And you arrived. Later when I was thinking about it all, the possibility dawned on me that God had used you to answer a prayer." She leaned against the fence. Nathan could see her profile in the moonlight. "Thinking God might actually care about someone like me was . . . profound. Moving."

"Someone like you?" Looking down at her in the moonlight, he wished he could see her eyes, but they were hidden in shadow.

She touched the left side of her head again and smoothed her hair. "You don't need to be gallant, Sergeant. You were there in that soddy." Her hands went to the scars around her wrists. "You know what went on there." Her voice trembled. "I always thought God was for good people. Not people like me."

He touched her wrist. "That wasn't your fault."

She pulled away. "But I made the choices that led up to that — that place." She looked down at her wrists. "To these."

"You're not that woman anymore."

"Well, I'm not so certain that *woman,* as you so kindly call her, isn't still in here somewhere." She raised one hand and patted her chest. "Sometimes fear just sort of sneaks up on me." She looked back over her shoulder toward the barracks. She shook her head and laughed. "But amazingly enough, *that woman* has had an encounter with God. And it's making a difference. In a lot of ways."

"That's good. That's really good," Nathan said. "I'm glad for you. Everyone is."

"Oh, not everyone at Camp Robinson is as caring as you, Sergeant. But that's another discussion. We should be getting back. You have a reputation to uphold."

He moved a little so that he could look down into her eyes. "There's nothing wrong with your reputation at Camp Robinson."

"Now you really are being gallant," she said. "If Katie O'Malley has heard rumors, so have you." She held up her fingers as she talked. "One: I'm crazy. Two: I was formerly a lady of the night in Deadwood. Three: I was formerly the lover of Doc Middleton or Little Bat Garnier — take your pick — and those men were after a bag of gold I stole from Doc or Bat. Four: I am the long-lost daughter of the Grand Duke of somewhere. I was captured by Indians when he was on a hunting trip and languished until rescued by" — she pointed at him — "you."

296

"Rumors die after a while. You'll live them down." He looked up and saw that people were beginning to leave the barracks. "Looks like the dance is almost over. How about if I walk you back to Granny's. There's something I've been wanting to ask you."

"Ask away," Laina said, tucking her hand beneath his arm, allowing herself to be led along the picket fence.

"Just now you said God answered a prayer of yours. You said that helped you. What I wondered was" — he paused just opposite the Valentine's quarters — "did you ever wonder why . . . why God didn't hear you sooner? Why He didn't spare you some of those bad choices? Or where He was when you were in that dugout?"

"Only a thousand times a thousand," she said. "I don't expect I will ever know."

He looked down at her. "And you're okay with that?"

She shrugged. "I'm okay with letting God be God and just trying to get through tonight and tomorrow out here in the middle of nowhere. Just trying to become an honorable woman — God help me. And I really mean that. If God is going to start working on Laina Gray, there's a lot of cleanup to do."

"Stop that," Nathan said.

"Stop what?"

"Stop dragging yourself back into the past. Like I said before, you aren't that woman any more."

Voices at the far end of Officer's Row caught Nathan's attention. He looked up. *Oh no.* Here came Charlotte. On the arm of . . . Private Jackson? He forced his mind back to the conversation with Miss Gray. "No one else knows about that woman in the soddy, and I don't think about her — except maybe to be amazed at how much she's changed."

"Sergeant Boone, Miss Gray," Charlotte nodded, obviously intent on sweeping by them with her escort. The escort swept his hat off his head and gave an exaggerated bow as the couple passed.

Nathan heard Laina take in a deep breath. He could almost sense her counting — *one, two, three, breathe.* Just the way he did when something awful had happened and he needed to regain control. He felt her grip on his arm tighten. She moved closer to him. As they walked in silence toward Soapsuds Row, Laina crowded even closer to him, clutching his arm with both hands.

"What's wrong? Are you feeling ill?" he asked.

She shook her head. "I'm just tired. Could we . . . talk . . . some other time?"

"Of course." He frowned, trying to understand what had just happened.

The minute they were inside the door of Granny's apartment, Miss Gray mumbled a thank-you and disappeared behind the quilt curtain into the back room.

Nathan sat in the amber glow of a kerosene lamp, looking down into the top tray of Lily Boone's trunk. *"Stop dragging yourself into the past."* He'd said that to Laina Gray less than an hour ago. And here he was, plunging back into the past. Reaching into his pants pocket, he grasped the rattlesnake rattle he had carried for the past two years. He ran his finger along it, counting the rattles. *Eighteen.* He tossed it into the tray alongside Lily's personal things: her silver mirror and comb, a cameo brooch, letters from home tied with a faded silk ribbon. The small leather *Book of Common Prayer.* And Lily's Bible.

He picked up the Bible, opening it at random and reading. She'd underlined some of her favorite passages. Lily Bainbridge had been a devout woman with a faith so strong she had faced death with amazing calm.

"Don't blame God, Nate. Promise me you won't blame God."

Sitting here remembering how she'd clutched his hand when she said those words, Nathan realized he hadn't fooled Lily. She'd known his faith was more form than substance. That's why she'd worried about him more than herself. He didn't have anything against going to church. It was something civilized people did. In time he even grew to like the ritual. But he didn't get personally involved, and Lily had known that.

Thumbing through her Bible, Nathan realized that if things had gone the other way, if he had died, there wouldn't be any Bible with underlined passages for Lily to keep. His mother had given him a Bible when he left home, but he didn't even know what had happened to it.

Nathan sat back, remembering how he'd held Lily's small hand between his own and, sobbing, blurted out a promise. "I won't, darling, I won't." He would have said anything she wanted to hear, just to make her passing more peaceful.

He'd lied. He did blame God. Who else was there to blame? After all, God was the One who supposedly had the power to reach down and heal Lily Boone, who believed in Him with all her heart and prayed to Him every day.

At first Nathan only *blamed* God, but as time went on, blame fermented and grew into a full-scale resentment that colored everything to do with faith. He stopped talking to God. He locked Lily's Bible up with the rest of her things. Thankfully there wasn't any church at Camp Robinson, but if there had been, he'd have stopped going. Eventually, he decided to give up on God altogether. He would have been happy to never hear the name of God again. He probably would have succeeded in making that happen — if it weren't for Granny Max.

Nathan liked being around Granny. She provided a tangible connection to Lily. But it was more than that. In the years since he had met her, Nathan had grown to love Granny Max for herself. Military life was hard enough without a man deliberately turning his back on things like fresh-baked pie and a listening ear. Granny Max made Camp Robinson feel like home. He liked eating at her table. He liked spending Sunday afternoons with her and whatever gaggle of Camp Robinson misfits she collected for the day. And Nathan knew that if he was going to continue to be around

Granny, he was going to have to put up with a certain amount of God-talk, because God slipped into Granny's conversations just as naturally as if she were talking about the weather. God-talk was just part of who Granny Max was. Nathan would never expect her to change just for him. Now it seemed that Laina Gray was becoming accustomed to God-talk, too. She didn't seem to be angry at God about what had happened to her. That — more than anything else about her — amazed him. How could she not be angry at God?

Hearing about God from people like Granny Max and Miss Gray was only one thing that prevented Nathan's putting God out of his mind. The other was something Nathan wouldn't have admitted to anyone. But sitting in the lamplight looking down at his dead wife's Bible, he admitted it to himself. He just couldn't bring himself to deny God existed. Everywhere he looked he saw evidence of something bigger than himself. Might as well call it God. He remembered a Bible verse that said something like *the heavens declare the glory of God*. And if the heavens weren't enough to convince a man there was a God, Nathan Boone thought the Nebraska Sandhills surely were.

But seeing evidence of God in the ridges, the valleys, and the sky brought Nathan back around in the circle of reasoning where he had been trapped for over two years. Someone big enough to create the universe had to be powerful enough to keep bad things from happening to good people. But Lily died. And Laina Gray was tied up and abused. So Nathan was caught. He couldn't deny God existed, but he couldn't reconcile what happened to Lily and Laina with a loving God. It was asking too much to expect a man to accept both. And so as long as he couldn't reconcile those things, he *would* refuse to call God *Father* and worship him.

Nathan took a deep breath and let it out again. He was tired. Tired of not having answers. Tired of being alone. Tired of being confused. Tired of coming back to these empty rooms. Tired of looking at Lily's trunk.

Nathan's hand trembled as he began to sort the things in the tray. He had decided to give Miss Gray those other two calico dresses weeks ago. It was time he did it. Maybe it was time he took the advice he'd given Miss Gray earlier — *"Stop dragging yourself into the past."* Maybe it was time he took Dr. Valentine's advice, too. Maybe the doctor had a point. Granny Max believed God could heal the crack in his heart and still keep his love for Lily safe. Nathan wasn't ready to trust God for anything, but Granny was a wise woman. Dr. Valentine seemed to agree with her. And his own way of handling things *wasn't* working very well.

He took his hat off and rumpled his hand through his hair, thinking. He'd keep Lily's Bible and those garnet earbobs. He set them aside and opened a velvet ring box, touching the oval stone of a brooch that had been Lily's grandmother's. He would send it back to the Bainbridges along with the letters Lily had read so many times and then tied into a bundle with a lavender silk ribbon. Sending it all back East would necessitate a letter from him. He would worry over that later.

In only a few moments, Nathan had sorted through the tray and was looking down at the blue silk ball gown. As Granny Max had said, Lily was a giving person. The thought brought him a momentary flash of pleasure. He tried to concentrate on the sense of rightness. *Lily would approve of this.* And Miss Gray's eyes would probably look blue instead of green if she wore this dress.

Thinking about Miss Gray brought a new sensation of guilt. His hand went to his breast pocket and he withdrew Lily's picture. He sat staring at it for a long time. "I miss you," he whispered, touching the face in the photograph. "Sometimes it feels like a thousand years ago you were here. Sometimes I still expect to hear your voice when I come in the door. What's happening, Lily?"

He closed his eyes and let the tears come. After a moment, he put the tray back in place and closed the trunk. When he locked it, instead of putting the chain back over his head and tucking it inside his shirt, he left the key in the lock.

Friday night flowed into Saturday. Nothing of consequence happened over the weekend until on Sunday afternoon, with much stammering, Sergeant Boone appeared at Granny Max's door and asked if Miss Gray might be able to make use of a trunk full of ladies' things, and without waiting for a reply, hauled Lily Boone's trunk in the door. Handing Laina the key, he quickly excused himself, leaving her to sort through the contents while Granny Max praised God out loud for working in her boy's heart.

Monday melded into Tuesday, and still Laina pondered and tried to convince herself she was imagining things. After all, she'd only seen that soldier in the moonlight. Maybe his exaggerated greeting was just evidence of one too many mugs of punch at the hop. He hadn't made any effort to talk to her since that night. She hadn't even seen him from a distance. When she'd gotten up enough courage to ask Charlotte about the handsome young man who walked her home from the dance, Charlotte had called him Caleb Jackson.

But when Private Caleb Jackson arrived to collect the Misses Valentine for a Wednesday morning riding lesson, he didn't realize he was being watched as he helped Dinah saddle her pony with the despised sidesaddle. But from where Laina stood ironing in the kitchen, she had a good view. He had a full beard now. The wind and sun had weathered his face considerably. He wasn't a fresh-faced boy anymore. He didn't swagger quite as much. He might have changed his name, but there was no question that Caleb Jackson was the man Laina had known in St. Louis as Beauregard Preston — one of Riverboat Annie's best customers after she'd been

306

forced to start earning money to pay her father's gambling debts with more than just dancing and flirting.

Dear God, Laina prayed, *what am I going to do?*

Maybe he wouldn't cause any trouble. He'd changed his name. Maybe he wanted a fresh start, too. If that were true, then he might be just as worried about her knowledge of his past as she was about his knowledge of hers. Still, Laina worried. People forgave men their "little weaknesses," but those same weaknesses could ruin a woman's reputation, and with it, her life.

She wondered what Sergeant Nathan Boone would think. He had said *"You aren't that woman anymore."* Of course, he thought he knew everything about her past. When he'd said *"Stop dragging yourself back into the past"* he had only been thinking about the woman he'd found in the cellar. He didn't know anything about Riverboat Annie. What if he knew what her life had been like before the dugout?

"Miss Gray," Charlotte said, rushing into the kitchen. She plopped an elaborately trimmed bonnet on her head and begged, "Help me with this bonnet. Please. I'm all thumbs." She peered out the

307

window. "Oh . . . he's here. Isn't he . . .
handsome?"

Laina tied a bow beneath Charlotte's
chin, and the girl hurried outside.

Jackson greeted her with a smile. He
made a joke, and they laughed.

Laina knew that laugh. And knowing
what lay behind it, she cringed.

*Lord. Dear Lord. What should I do? Please.
Tell me what to do.*

Fifteen

O my God, I trust in thee; let me not be ashamed, let not mine enemies triumph over me.

Psalm 25:2

Laina lay on her back looking up at the rough board ceiling of the Camp Robinson hospital. "Take it out," she said, looking straight at Dr. Valentine.

"What?" He cocked his head to one side, a puzzled expression on his face.

"Take it out. Now. I know you can do it. You can just blame my fainting on the heat. Tell Mrs. Valentine you ordered me to rest here in the hospital for the afternoon. Granny Max doesn't expect me back until suppertime. No one ever has to know." She clutched her midsection. "I'll find a way to pay you. I'll work it off. I promise."

309

The doctor went to a table near the door and poured some fresh water in a basin. He washed his hands and reached for a clean towel. Only then did he turn around and face Laina. "What you are asking is impossible, Miss Gray."

"It isn't," she snapped. She sat up. "I knew a girl who had it done."

"That may be, Miss Gray," the doctor said, hanging the towel back up, "but it is impossible here at Camp Robinson because I am the only doctor. And I won't do it." He crossed the room and put his hand over Laina's. "When you have had time to think about this, my dear, you will change your mind."

Laina snatched her hand away. "Don't tell me what I'll think."

"I know this is a shock," the doctor said.

Was it her imagination, or was he forcing a fatherly tone into his voice? He was getting very annoying. *God, where are you in this?* "I'll hate it."

"You won't," the doctor said. "No mother hates her own child. You won't be alone in this, Miss Gray. Arrangements can be made. I know of a place." He seemed to gain confidence as he spoke. "Really. We can work things out. Everything will be fine."

"Fine? Everything will be *fine?*" Laina laughed, barely managing to stop before the laugh began to sound like hysteria. She was trembling with the effort to keep herself under control.

"We'll work it out. Trust me."

Laina forced a laugh. "That's very kind of you, Doctor Valentine. I suppose Mrs. Valentine will feel the same way and let me keep my job. And of course Mrs. O'Malley won't mind if her girls spend time with me. And the men here at Camp Robinson." She thought about Private Jackson. "Why, the men will all just accept that Miss Gray has had an immaculate conception. They'll all show me the same respect they always have." She hid her face in her hands.

"No one has to know for a while. Although I would advise you to trust Granny Max so she can help you make some plans." He continued trying to reassure her. "Mrs. Valentine shouldn't have had you moving that heavy furniture in this heat. It scared her when you just keeled over like that. I can promise you she'll not be expecting such things of you in the future. And neither she nor anyone else is going to question my ordering you to rest this afternoon. Let me walk you back to the Row. I'll talk to Granny Max. I'll take care of everything. And I won't tell anyone what we've discussed here, so you have time to think."

"Tell anyone you like," Laina snapped. "It'll be camp gossip soon enough. Secrets like this have a way of traveling on the wind, you know." She sat up and straightened her shoulders. "I don't care."

"Well, I *do* care," Dr. Valentine said. "About you *and* about the life growing inside you. And I won't be the one sending any of your secrets out on the wind, as you put it. I am here to help you — whether you believe it or not." He rolled down his shirt sleeves and buttoned the cuffs. "You know, Miss Gray, you might consider this: it isn't all that unusual for women who've been . . . ahh . . . treated as you have . . . to be unable to conceive. For you to be in such good health in that respect is something of a miracle."

Laina laughed harshly. "Aren't you glad it's *my* miracle to deal with and not Charlotte's?"

Dr. Valentine took a deep breath. "It may not make you feel better right now. But it is something for you to think about while you decide what to do. God's hand is at work, Miss Gray. We must believe that. Even when we don't understand what He's

312

doing, He is at work. That's all I meant to say."

"God certainly gets blamed for a lot of messes, doesn't He? A flood comes along and it's an *act of God*. Someone dies and *it's God's will*. A woman gets pregnant out of wedlock and *God has a plan*. That may make you feel better about things, Dr. Valentine, but it doesn't help me one bit." She swung her legs over the side of the examining table and hopped down. "Can I go now?"

Retrieving his medical bag, Doctor Valentine said, "I'll walk you."

"No, thank you." Laina said. She adjusted her bonnet and headed for the door.

"I need to check in on Mrs. O'Malley anyway," the doctor insisted as he took her arm. Laina relented and they made their way south to Soapsuds Row. When they came to the Row the doctor said, "I'll do my best to keep Granny Max busy with Mrs. O'Malley, Miss Gray. I know you'll be wanting some time to yourself."

Back at Granny Max's, Laina curled up into a ball upon her bed. She wanted to pull the quilt up over her head and completely close herself off from the world. But it was too hot. She felt like she couldn't breathe. Sitting up, she unbut-

313

toned the top five buttons running down the front of Lily Boone's gray calico dress, then went to the washbasin and soaked a cloth in water and pressed it to the back of her neck. She closed her eyes.

It had taken weeks, but she had finally clawed her way from the brink of insanity. She hadn't had a nightmare in several nights. She almost enjoyed working at the Valentines'. Mrs. Doctor, while a bit of a snob, made few demands beyond basic housekeeping. Dinah's energy and sense of humor more than made up for Charlotte's whining, and Laina enjoyed Frenchy's cooking lessons very much.

She peered at herself in the clouded mirror hanging above the washstand. "You idiot," she said aloud. "Little Laina Gray, making a new life for herself. Brave soldiers to rescue her, Granny Max to love her, God to make everything better." She tapped the image in the glass. "Happily ever after only happens in fairy tales, little girl. And yours just ended."

Turning sideways, she inspected her midsection. How long would it be before everyone would be able to tell? She shook her head. It didn't matter. Granny had said she didn't have to let the past control her. But Granny Max's past wasn't out at the

314

corral right now giving the Misses Valentine riding lessons. And Granny Max's future didn't include her attacker's child.

To make matters worse, Laina had a feeling Caleb Jackson didn't plan on making life easy for her. As time had passed she'd reasoned herself into believing he might be relieved if they just acknowledged one another and agreed to forget the past. But earlier that day, after lunch, she had been kneading dough in the kitchen when someone knocked on the door. Thinking it was Frenchy coming to help her, Laina had gone to the door all smiles. And there, hat in hand, was Private Caleb Jackson.

"So," he'd said. "I wasn't dreaming. It is you." He motioned for her to step outside and asked, "You ever let your pa know what happened to you? He thinks you're dead, Annie." He drawled the name, looking down at her with a sly little smile.

She touched the left side of her head, wondering if the scar was showing. "Annie *is* dead." She inhaled sharply, trying to organize her thoughts.

But then Charlotte had called out a greeting, her voice warm with pleasure.

Looking past Laina, Jackson smiled. "I was hoping you could accompany me on a walk, Miss Valentine." Charlotte was so quick about getting her bonnet, Jackson only had time to tell Laina he wanted to talk with her before Charlotte was at his side, taking his arm, blushing and chattering something in abominable French.

Laina had thought the day couldn't have gotten any worse. But it had. That afternoon Mrs. Valentine had suggested a thorough cleaning of a bedroom. Trying to move a wardrobe the size of Nebraska, Laina had fainted. And now Caleb Jackson's presence and intentions were only a very small part of an overwhelming, impossible, unbearable reality.

I'm going to have to leave Camp Robinson, Laina thought, turning sideways to look at herself in the mirror. Whether Jackson revealed her past or not, her body eventually would.

She smoothed her skirt over her abdomen and tilted her head as she inspected her profile. *I wonder what Dr. Valentine meant when he said he knew of a place I could go. I wonder how long I have to decide what to do.*

She went into the front room. Standing at the open front door, she looked out on Camp Robinson. Just across the road half a dozen soldiers were standing outside the commissary talking. A shout went up and one of the soldiers shoved another. The rest of the men laughed. It hadn't been all that long ago that roughhousing like that would have sent her scurrying back to her room. She'd come a long way.

All those talks with Granny. All that believing that things could change. All that praying. For what? So *she* could be the one those soldiers over at the commissary joked about? She could just hear them now. Oh, they'd bow and smile at the Friday night dances. For a while. But that, too, would end once the truth about her came out. Mrs. Valentine surely wouldn't want a pregnant housekeeper defiling her daughters. Even Meara O'Malley might have something to say about Katie spending time alone with a scarlet woman. Laina began to tremble. Private Caleb Jackson was the least of her problems.

Get a grip on yourself, girl. You didn't really think you could escape the past, did you? Remember? That only happens in fairy tales. White knights can't always rescue damsels in distress.

Turning away from the door, she thought of Granny's bottle of medicinal liquor high on a shelf above the cookstove. A drink might calm her down. Help her think. Moving a chair to the shelf, she climbed up to get it. But she stepped on the hem of her dress and stumbled. She caught herself just in time to keep from falling, but then she bumped into the table and sent a vase of flowers crashing to the floor. At the sound of breaking glass, anger and fear broke through the thin veil of self-control she'd been clinging to all afternoon. She grabbed the edge of the small table and overturned it. That wasn't enough. Next, she flung one of Granny's rickety kitchen chairs across the room.

As quickly as it had come, the violent rage departed. She staggered toward the doorway to the bedroom, oblivious to the broken glass and water on the floor. Her feet went out from under her, and she landed on her backside on the floor amidst broken glass and scattered flowers. Her anger spent, she rolled onto her side, hugged her knees to her chest, and began to cry.

She was still crying when Nathan Boone appeared at the door. He crouched down beside her and put his hand on her shoulder. "What's wrong, Miss Gray? Are you hurt?"

Drawing her knees even closer to her chest, Laina hid her face in her arms and began to sob. *Oh, God.* She hadn't thought she could feel any worse. She was wrong. Without looking at him, she waved her hand toward the door. "Go away."

He touched the back of her hand. "You're bleeding. Let me help you up."

She jerked her hand away and put the cut to her mouth. "Leave it alone." She inhaled, embarrassed to hear the shuddering sound, like her midsection was shaking and wouldn't let the air come. She sat up, hiding her face with her hands.

"I saw you and Dr. Valentine coming from the hospital. Private Jackson said you fainted."

Laina swiped at her hair, trying to brush it back out of her face. "I just got overheated."

"No wonder," Nathan said. "Jackson and I finished moving that wardrobe. I don't know what Mrs. Valentine could have been thinking expecting a little thing like you to move *furniture*. It's not as if there aren't a hundred men available. You shouldn't have even tried to do that."

She resented the mild scolding. "And you should mind your own business, Sergeant Boone."

"Hey," he said gently, putting his hand on her shoulder. "My friends *are* my business. Let me help you up."

She shrugged his hand off and got up. "Point made. Point taken. Don't make such a huge thing of it. I'm all right." She bent to pick up a chair.

"No," he said, "you aren't." He took her hand off the back of the chair.

"Don't," she whispered and tried to pull away.

When he put his free hand behind her back and pulled her toward him, circling her with his arms, she began to sob. Tears streamed down her face, dampening his shirt.

He pulled away and looked at her with concern written all over his face. "I'll get Granny."

"No!" She clutched his shirt. "Please. Mrs. O'Malley has been feeling so terrible. She really needs Granny Max right now." She closed her eyes, leaning against him and drawing strength from his presence and his arms around her. Finally, she pushed herself away and looked up at him, forcing a half smile. "I'm feeling better. Really. Just an attack of nerves."

He looked around him at the chaos. He picked up the other chair, righted the table. "What brought it on?"

"Oh, well. You know me. Crazy." She

bent down to collect the broken pieces of the vase.

"You're not crazy," he said. He touched her again, this time covering her hand with his so she would stop collecting the pieces of broken glass. Lifting her chin, he peered into her eyes. "And you're not telling me the truth. Sit down for a minute."

When Laina obeyed, Boone took both her hands in his and squeezed them. "This may not be any of my business. And maybe I should just let it be. But I'd rather you trust me with whatever is bothering you so much."

"You can't fix it," Laina said, looking down at her hands in his. "What's the point?"

"The point is, sometimes it just helps to talk things over." He ducked his head and made her look at him. "And how do you know I can't help if you don't give me a chance?"

Part of her longed to tell him. Everything. But just then she noticed a corner of Lily Boone's picture barely showing above the rim of his shirt pocket. She pulled her hand away. "You really do need to get a handle on this knight-in-shining-armor complex you have," she said. "Don't you ever tire of role-playing, Sir Nathan?"

He leaned back in his chair. "I'll make you a promise, Lady Gray." He smiled. "You'll be the first one to know when I want to resign."

Well, you'll be resigning soon, Sir Nathan. As soon as you hear the latest about this damsel in distress. She laughed nervously and looked away from him. She swiped tears away with the back of her hand and forced the tension out of her voice. "If I make you coffee, will you drink it and then go home?"

"I don't want coffee. But I'll make *you* something to drink," he said. "Something cold. Wait here." He took her by the shoulders and urged her out of the kitchen chair and into Granny's rocker. "Close your eyes and try to relax. I'll be back in a minute." She leaned her head back and closed her eyes.

Some of the girls at Miss Hart's had had secrets like this. No one there ever spoke of it. The girls went to class, grew large, gave birth, and left. None of the other girls ever saw a baby at Miss Hart's. Once, when they were whispering after hours, the subject came up.

"I know where they go," Nellie Pierce had said, her mouth turning upwards in the smug little smile Laina hated. "One night I heard a scream, and I woke up and looked outside. I saw a carriage waiting down by the door, and Miss Hart came outside with a bundle in her arms. She looked this way and that, and then she went down the stairs and handed the bundle up into the carriage."

"That doesn't tell us anything," one of the girls whined. "We still don't know where they go. What do they do with them?"

"Oh, who cares?" Nellie said abruptly. She looked pointedly at Laina. "No one cares about orphans or bastards. They are a pox on society. My papa says so."

Laina looked down at her abdomen. "You hear that? You're aren't born yet, but you're a pox on society."

She held out her unadorned left hand. What was it, she wondered, that made it all right for an entire world of people to determine an unborn child's worth based on the presence or absence of a piece of metal around its mother's finger — something the child couldn't control. It made Laina angry. Why should a baby be punished for the circumstances of its birth? It wasn't fair.

Right, Laina. It isn't fair. So why did you want Dr. Valentine to kill it? She answered herself. *I was desperate. I know how this is going to work. What people are going to think. Especially if the good Private Jackson starts telling Riverboat Annie stories in the barracks. Neither Sergeant Boone's friendship nor Granny Max's faith are going to be able to change what people are going to think and say about me . . . and how they are going to treat this child.* "*My* child."

She bowed her head and looked down at her still-flat abdomen. *But I can change it. If I leave Camp Robinson and go where no one knows me, I can create any reality I want. Any past I need.*

Her mind racing, Laina got up and began to straighten the mess she'd made. She worked mechanically, and by the time Sergeant Boone reappeared at the door, she had the nucleus of a plan. She looked up at the tall glass in his hand. "Is that what I think it is?" she asked in disbelief.

"Fresh squeezed," Nathan said, rattling the ice cubes in the glass. "Courtesy of Frenchy. I told him about Mrs. Valentine's idea of 'light housework.' And the aftereffects. He mixed this up special just for you. It's lemonade — mostly."

"I thought all the ice from last winter's cutting was long since gone."

"The men are hoarding a last chunk of it

for the Fourth. They won't miss three little pieces." He plunked the glass upon the table and sat down. "Besides, if rank can't get a man a little ice on a hot day, what good is it?"

Laina draped the wet rag she'd used to scrub the floor over the back of the stove and returned to sit down at the table and sip the cool drink. Raising the glass she said, "Tell Frenchy his 'lemonade — mostly' is delicious." Pressing the side of the glass against her cheek, she closed her eyes, relishing the rare sensation of something really cool.

"You might as well tell me the whole story," Nathan said. He crossed his arms across his chest. "Because I'm not leaving until you do."

His jaw was set and he had a stubborn little smile on his face. Laina wondered if this was the look he gave recalcitrant recruits. She shifted in her chair while her mind raced for something to satisfy his curiosity. She pulled her hands into her lap and looked down at the table. "All right. You win."

She took another sip of lemonade while she mentally organized the story she hoped he would believe. "You remember when you asked me where I learned to dance and I said something about another life?"

He nodded. "That other life doesn't matter anymore, Laina. When are you going to finally realize that?"

She shrugged. "I *was* starting to believe it." She took a swallow of lemonade and set the glass back on the table. "But then the *past* escorted Miss Valentine home from last Friday's hop. And then it came by the Valentines' this afternoon to take Miss Valentine for a walk after lunch."

"You're talking about Private Jackson," Nathan said. When Laina nodded, he continued, "I don't know exactly what it is you're talking about, but I can promise you Private Caleb Jackson won't give you any trouble. He and I go way back, and he has enough skeletons in his own closet to worry over without threatening to bring out anyone else's." He added, "And why would he threaten you, anyway?"

Yes, Laina thought. *Why, indeed.* This story wasn't sounding very convincing. "Maybe I *am* overreacting."

"Has he threatened you?" Laina could see the muscles working in Nathan's jaw. "Because if he has, I —"

"No," Laina said. "No. He only stopped by the Valentines' to see Charlotte while I was over there this morning." She shivered and rubbed her arms. "I'm probably reading things into it. But I knew him. In that other life." *Yes, this is sounding more believable.*

"Whatever he knows about you can't hurt you now," Nathan insisted.

Laina took a sip of lemonade. *Tell him the truth. Not all of it. Just enough to convince him that fear of Private Jackson is the only reason you're upset.* She took a deep breath and swallowed a little more lemonade. If she said this just right, he might believe the only reason she fainted, the only reason she was so upset, was because of Jackson. She focused on the top button of Nathan's uniform as she recited. "Once upon a time, there was a riverboat called the Missouri Princess. On the riverboat lived a gambler. And the gambler had a daughter named Laina." She hesitated. She moistened her lips and glanced up at Nathan, who was staring at her with such sincere concern it sent a pang of guilt through her. She looked back at the button and continued, telling him about being sent to Miss Hart's, about her father's gambling debts and having to leave the school to live on a riverboat, and about being known as Riverboat Annie.

"I still don't see what any of this has to

do with what happened today," Nathan said, "unless you aren't telling me everything. Is that it?" He leaned forward. "Did Jackson say something to upset you?"

Laina shook her head. She cleared her throat. "He didn't have to say anything." She shifted in her seat before reaching out to slide her hand up and down the cool glass. "He doesn't have to say a word, Nathan. Because he knows exactly how Riverboat Annie helped her father pay his gambling debts." She looked him in the eyes. "He knows because when he was still calling himself Beauregard Preston, he was one of her best customers." She could feel the blush rising up the back of her neck. Her cheeks began to burn.

Nathan nodded, and Laina thought his face looked redder, too. "That's an interesting story, Miss Gray. But the fact still remains that no one named Riverboat Annie lives at Camp Robinson. And if Private Jackson has an interest in Miss Valentine, he'll realize that your knowledge of his past gives you a certain amount of power over his future, too." He paused. "Dr. and Mrs. Valentine wouldn't want a man like that anywhere near their daughter. And I'll remind him of that. You can be assured he won't be bringing up anything from the past here at Camp Robinson. We were friends once, but you and I are friends *now*. If he dares cause you any trouble, he'll answer to me."

Laina sighed. She rubbed the back of her neck and forced a smile. "Thank you, but I'd really rather you not get involved. I've had my grand self-pity party. I've thrown my fit. What you said earlier is probably right. I just overreacted. It isn't really fair of me to assume he means to cause trouble. And I certainly don't want to be responsible for coming between old friends." She paused. "I need some time to think. Then I'll talk to him. Perhaps he just needs reassurance that I'm not going to ruin things between him and Miss Valentine." She forced a smile. "Everything will probably work out."

Boone nodded. "Look, Miss Gray. I know a few things about Jackson, too. And I've been keeping my eye on him ever since he arrived at camp. We've had a couple of . . . talks. I think he's sincere about wanting to stay out of trouble here. He hasn't always managed it, but I'd like to see him succeed."

"Well, I don't have anything against him, and I don't plan to stand in the way of anything he wants to accomplish. I'll tell him just that. And if what you're saying about him is true, then there aren't going to be any more problems."

"Or fainting spells?"

"Right."

"I'll bring him over whenever you say."

"I appreciate your concern, but I don't think Private Jackson and I will need a referee."

"I'd feel better if you'd let me come with him," Boone said.

Laina closed her eyes. She took a deep breath. "Don't take this wrong, Sergeant, but I'd appreciate it very much if you would climb down off your white horse and just let me be a grown-up. It may be hard for you to believe, but I am clothed and in my right mind most of the time these days." She stood up. "In spite of what you saw earlier."

After a silence that felt to Laina like it lasted for five minutes, Sergeant Boone got up and reached for his hat. "You get some rest," he said, and let himself out.

Laina took another deep breath. It had been one of her better performances, she thought. She was exhausted. Dr. Valentine would have told Granny Max he wanted her to rest. How glad she was of that as she crept to her bed. She undressed slowly, dropping Lily Boone's worn gray calico dress and petticoats on the floor. She removed her shoes and stockings. Letting down her hair, she dampened another cloth for the back of her neck and slipped beneath a sheet where she lay still, enjoying the sensation as she ran the last fragment of ice from her drink over her parched skin. *God bless Frenchy Dubois.* She didn't know when she fell asleep, but sometime after sundown she heard Granny Max come in. She could sense Granny looking down at her, but she feigned sleep.

"You all right, lamb?"

When Laina didn't answer, Granny went back into the front room. Her rocker creaked as she sat down. Laina could picture the old woman opening her Bible. Granny always read her Bible before she went to bed. The rhythm of her rocking was soon joined with the comforting sound of humming.

Full circle. Here I am hiding again, while Granny rocks and prays.

Her thoughts swirled from Granny to God, from Doctor Valentine to Sergeant Boone to Private Jackson, around and around and back again. Both with Dr. Valentine and with Sergeant Boone, she had performed well. She'd almost convinced herself that she was capable of handling things. But she still had to face her past in the form of Private Caleb Jackson. And now, in the darkness, fear returned. *God. Oh, God. Why are you doing this to me?* She smothered her tears with her pillow.

"Granny Max?" Laina whispered, half hoping Granny wouldn't hear her.

The rocker creaked as Granny got up and came to the door. "Yes, honey-lamb. What is it?"

"Do you remember what you told me about Josiah Paine? About the past and the future?"

"I said he may have your past, but you don't have to give him your future."

Tears welled up in her eyes as Laina struggled to reply. She swiped them away with the back of her hand and clutched her pillow as she looked toward Granny's silhouette in the doorway. "I'm afraid you were mistaken."

"Why do you say that?"

"I'm going to have a baby, Granny. J-Josiah Paine's baby." The fragments of her bravery were washed away when she said that name aloud. In the time it took Granny to cross the room to her, Laina had curled up into a ball and begun to sob.

"Oh, darlin'," Granny said, rubbing her

back. "Oh, honey-lamb. Are you sure?"

She told Granny Max about Private Jackson, about fainting, and about Dr. Valentine. "At least Sergeant Boone believed me when I told him the only thing wrong was Private Jackson's showing up here at Camp Robinson."

"So no one knows about the baby but Dr. Valentine?"

Laina nodded. "But everyone *will* know. You can't exactly keep a secret like this for long, can you?" She began to cry again. "Oh, Granny. What am I going to do?"

She had grown so accustomed to Granny Max having an answer for her questions, Laina was taken aback when Granny didn't respond. Moments went by, with her own sobs quieting, and Granny just sitting on the edge of the bed rubbing Laina's back in the dark.

"Lord," Granny finally said. "This is hard news. Hard." Granny's voice wavered. "It seems, Lord, like this little gal has had enough troubles. She didn't need this. I got to tell you, Lord, I am wondering exactly what you are up to. I know you have a plan. I know you work in mysterious ways. But this is one of the most mysterious yet. She is asking me what to do, and I don't know what to say. Show me how to help her. Show us what to do."

Granny Max stopped for more than a few minutes. Laina waited for her to finally come up with something helpful. Some wisdom. Some answers. She didn't.

"Most of all, Lord, show Laina that your love is just as strong as it ever has been. That Josiah Paine might have meant what he did for evil, Lord, but you can work it out for good. Help me believe that and live it so that Laina can believe it and live it, too. Help us both believe in spite of the way things look. Amen."

After a few more minutes had gone by, Granny said, "I don't expect that was what you were hoping to hear me say, was it, honey-lamb?"

"I don't really know what I expected," Laina said. "I'm sorry I've had to burden you with this, Granny. I really am."

"Don't you be sorry for that. Ever. I love you, child," Granny said. "And love bears all things, believes all things, hopes all things, endures all things. So you and I will bear and believe and hope and endure . . . *together*. I promise."

Laina turned onto her back. She clutched a pillow to her midsection. "I asked Dr. Valentine to end it. Does that . . . shock you?"

Granny answered, "It takes a lot more than that to shock old Granny Max, child." She felt for Laina's hand in the dark. "But that's not an answer you want to live with."

"No. It isn't. Not really."

Granny Max squeezed her hand. "Right. So we will wait on the good Lord to give us an answer we can live with."

"And what do we do while we wait?" Laina wanted to know.

"We just do the next thing, honey-lamb. Just like always."

Laina fell asleep holding Granny Max's hand.

Sixteen

The words of a talebearer are as wounds, and they go down into the innermost parts of the belly.

Proverbs 18:8

"Annie?" someone called.

Laina jumped and turned her head just in time to see Wilber tear across Soldier Creek toward Private Jackson. The dog wasn't barking, which Laina soon realized meant he might be a threat, because with a low growl he chomped on to Jackson's pant leg and began to throw all his weight into keeping the soldier from getting any closer to the woman seated beside the creek.

"Wilber," Laina said firmly. "No." The dog let go. "Come," Laina said, laying her comb on the grass and letting her hair fall down her back. Wilber went to her and sat down beside her, ears alert, muscles tense as he watched Jackson.

Jackson didn't come any farther. Instead, he took his hat off and stood, twirling it in his hands. "I . . . uh . . . I wanted to apologize." He motioned to her wet hair. "But I shouldn't be bothering you now."

"It's not like you haven't seen me with my hair down before," Laina said. She stood up. "But aren't you supposed to be doing some kind of fatigue duty this time of day?" She looked toward Soapsuds Row, wondering if anyone had seen the soldier pushing his way through the stand of bushes that afforded her a measure of privacy, both for drying her hair and for thinking.

Jackson nodded. "Sergeant Boone gave me permission to come over to the Row. I talked Granny Max into telling me where you were" — he grinned — "and into letting me come down here alone." He nodded at Wilber. "She doesn't need to worry about you, anyway. Not with that pup around. He seems to think he's a guard dog."

Laina reached up to smooth her hair back off her forehead. "How did you get Sergeant Boone to give you leave from duty?"

"I told him the truth," Caleb said. "Part of it, anyway." He rushed to add, "Not any part that would cause you trouble, though."

"Sergeant Boone knows all about me," Laina said. She lifted her chin. "You can't hurt me by telling him about St. Louis."

"Hey," Jackson protested. "I don't want to hurt you. You were always good to me. I've got no reason to bring up the past. That's what I wanted to tell you yesterday, but then Miss Valentine came out, and I didn't dare say any more. The next thing I knew you'd fainted." He scowled. "Are you all right?"

Laina bent over and picked up her comb. With studied calm, she pulled a hank of wet hair over her shoulder and went back to combing it. "I'm fine, Private."

"I'm glad to see you are safe," he said, sounding sincere. "And I'm hoping you'll agree that there's no reason for the past to have any part in our lives here at Camp Robinson."

Laina peered up at him. He met her gaze straight on and didn't waver. She let go of her hair and tucked the comb into her apron pocket. "You've worked hard on your accent. I don't hear any southern at all. Except when you let it out on purpose to impress Miss Valentine."

He cleared his throat. "Yeah, well . . . old habits die hard." He took a deep breath. "You remember how it is, playing the game. Smiling, flirting, making them want . . ." He shrugged, then shook his head. "I was just playing when I first asked her to dance. But there are things to like about her. She's not perfect, but she can be really sweet." He grinned. "I haven't been with a girl who was honestly *sweet* and truly naïve since . . ." He looked at her apologetically. "Ever."

"It's all right," Laina said. "I don't take that personally. It's the truth."

He smiled at her. "I'm working to change. You could have made things hard for me — could have told Dr. Valentine some colorful stories. I'm grateful you didn't."

Laina said, "I'll admit to being more than a little worried that night you walked Charlotte home from the hop." She paused. "Of course, some of that was on my own account. You could have made things hard for me, too. And I'm grateful you didn't. I guess we both can agree that everybody deserves a second chance. As far as I'm concerned, we can consider both

Riverboat Annie and Beauregard Preston dead." She held out her hand. "Care to shake on it?"

Caleb took her hand. "Long live Private Caleb Jackson and Miss Laina Gray."

When Laina saw him looking down at her scarred wrist, she pulled her hand away.

"What happened to you, anyway? It was like you just disappeared."

"I thought I found a way off the river," Laina said.

"It looks like you did," Jackson said. "I'm glad for you. Eustis treated you bad. You deserve something good."

Laina reached up to the left side of her head. She lifted the hair away to expose the scar. "See that?" she said.

Jackson touched her temple. "It barely shows."

"That's what Granny says." Laina shrugged. "It doesn't matter, I guess. It's not like I'm competing for male attention anymore. I've had more than my share of that." Impulsively, she pulled her cuffs back so Jackson could see both her wrists. "There's worse things than living on the river. I learned that."

Jackson swore violently. "Who did this to you? Somebody ought to teach him a

340

lesson he won't forget."

"Someone did," Laina said softly. "He's buried up in the Sandhills." She told him about Josiah Paine's sod dugout. "Sergeant Boone and Corporal Dorsey found me. Brought me here." She nodded toward Soapsuds Row. "Granny Max brought me back from the darkness. With some help from God. At least I like to think God was in there somewhere. Although I never was one to think much about God before." She looked up at him. "Never figured God thought much about me."

Jackson's voice was almost gentle. "You were always one of the nicer girls. It doesn't surprise me that God would pick you out to see what He could do with you." He nodded. "And it looks like He's doing all right by you. You even got your own personal guardian angel."

Laina nodded. "Yes. Granny Max would fit that title."

"Oh, I don't mean Granny Max," Jackson said. "I mean the one in the blue uniform." He grinned. "He takes his duties real serious, too. In fact," he said, looking past Laina, "here he comes now."

Wilber tore off again, yapping and chasing after Whiskey's feet.

341

"That dog's gonna get himself killed one of these days chasing after horses that way," Jackson said.

"I know he shouldn't do that," Laina said. "But I don't know how to break him of it."

Just then Whiskey landed a kick to Wilber's midsection. The dog yelped and went rolling, then got up, shook himself, and slunk off.

"Maybe Whiskey will do the job for you," Jackson said, offering his hand and helping Laina up. They stood together, waiting for Sergeant Boone to dismount.

"It looks like I've just missed a real serious powwow," he said, looking in Laina's direction.

Laina didn't respond to Sergeant Boone's comment. "I've got to get back to help Granny with the afternoon chores. Thank you for letting Private Jackson spend some time with me." She smiled at Jackson. "I'll likely see you at the hop Friday night, Private."

"Save me a dance," he said, bowing and waving his hat across his body in an exaggerated flourish.

Laina laughed in spite of herself. "You, sir, are an incorrigible flirt."

"I am," Jackson said. "But I'm harmless. At least to you."

Doctor Valentine had said that time would change Laina's feelings. Whether the doctor was right and time changed them, or Granny Max's prayers changed them, or God himself did it, the reality was that Laina's feelings about the new life growing inside her did change. She thought about how the doctor said her getting pregnant was nothing short of a miracle. The idea of Josiah Paine being part of a miracle repulsed her. But after a few more late-night talks with Granny Max, Laina began to think that maybe it was possible for God to take the evil men did and turn it for good.

One Sunday afternoon Granny Max read her an Old Testament story about a man named Joseph, whose brothers were so jealous they made their father believe Joseph had been killed and then sold him as a slave. Even when things changed, and it looked like Joseph was going to build a new life, he was accused of rape and sent back to prison. Laina could relate to the idea of feeling like the worst was over only to learn the worst was still to come. What astounded her was that when Joseph had the chance to take his revenge on his good-for-nothing brothers, he *forgave* them. Joseph's story was where Granny Max had gotten that phrase *"You meant it for evil, but God meant it for good."*

Laina couldn't quite see her pregnancy as a *good* thing. But Joseph's story did help her not be mad at God. She decided she really didn't want to kick God out of her life. With a baby and no husband, she wasn't going to be able to count on getting a lot of sympathy from most people. If God wanted to work something out, she would be all for it.

Granny said a person's faith could only grow if it was tested. Laina couldn't help thinking that, if this was a test, it sure was a big one for someone with her amount of faith. Granny Max told her she should talk to God about the things that worried her. "Don't wait for me to pray for you, child. Talk to Him yourself. Now that you're in His family, you got the same telegraph line to the Lord God I do."

"What do you mean *now that* I'm in God's family?" Laina asked.

They were standing over a tub of laundry in the washhouse. Granny Max looked around her. "You think everybody's in God's family?" she asked.

"Of course not," Laina said. "Josiah

344

Paine certainly wasn't."

"So how does a person get from outside to inside the family?" Without waiting for Laina to answer, Granny Max grabbed up a pile of filthy shirts. "A person has to say yes to God — like you did after them rustlers bothered you. The Bible says all the good things we can do are just like dirty laundry." Then she put the shirts into the washtub. She took up a piece of lye soap. "Only the blood of Jesus can wash us white as snow. We can scrub and scrub and scrub ourselves, and we never get clean enough to please God." She scrubbed at the collar in her hands. "Just like Harlan Yates's shirt collars. I declare there is no soap in the *world* that will get this boy's collars as clean as they were when they were new. And as soon as I get 'em 'Granny-Max clean,' he dirties 'em up all over again — and worse."

"Just like me," Laina said. "I get my life cleaned up a little, and then something happens to get it all messed up all over again — and worse."

"So the whole point, honey-lamb, is we stop trying to get ourselves cleaned up. We just let the good Lord Jesus take all the dirt. That's what He was doing on that cross. And we say 'thank you, Jesus, I'm gonna trust you to take care of all this dirt in my life.' " Granny wrung Harlan's shirt out and plopped it into the rinse tub for Laina. "And that's it. It's gone."

"Without me *doing* anything to clean it up myself?"

Granny nodded. "He already took care of that for you, honey-lamb — just because you said yes. We can't make a soap strong enough to clean up our dirt, child. Only God can do that. And He did it. Only He didn't use lye soap. He used blood."

Laina grabbed Harlan Yates's shirt and rinsed it as clean as she could. While she was wringing it out, she asked, "Granny, do you think Sergeant Boone is in God's family?" She finished pressing the excess water out of Harlan's shirt and added it to the pile of laundry waiting to be hung outside.

Granny sighed. "I don't know, child. I hope so."

"He seems pretty intent on cleaning up his own dirt. I mean, he likes to manage things for himself. It seems like it might be harder for someone like that to just humble down and let God have at their problems."

Granny nodded. "You've got Nathan figured pretty well, child. That is his struggle, as near as I know. He just doesn't want to humble down."

Laina nodded and stooped to lift the laundry basket. Outside in the sunshine, she went to work filling the clothesline with clean shirts. When she finished and headed back to the washhouse, she looked back toward the row of clean shirts flapping in the breeze.

For Laina, understanding her new faith came in fragments, at places like Granny Max's table or the washhouse. Bit by bit she began to put the pieces together. She finally believed God truly loved her. He would listen to her. He would help her. She was, as Granny Max said, one of God's lambs. Imperfect, sinful, pregnant, scared, unworthy. And loved.

She grew more confident in her conversations with God. She asked Him to help her and her little girl — she was fairly certain the baby would be a girl. She just could not think that God would expect her to mother a miniature version of Josiah Paine. She was still afraid, but underneath the fear was a sense that things might work out. So, while nothing changed in Laina's circumstances, it was as if everything had changed, because she was doing her best to look at everything in a different way: *You meant it for evil, but*

God meant it for good.

It was on a blistering Sunday afternoon picnic late in July when Laina first felt the baby move. Sergeant Boone had taken Katie down to the creek to fish. Harlan and Becky were playing euchre. Granny and Laina, with Wilber stretched out at Laina's side sound asleep, were sitting stitching away at some quilt blocks, when suddenly Laina thought she felt something different deep inside her. She lay her needlework aside and stroked Wilber's soft white fur while she concentrated and waited. It wasn't long before the sensation came again. *Quickening.* She couldn't resist the impulse to place her hand over her abdomen while she sent a message to the baby. *Hello. I'm your mama. I am going to take good care of you.*

In recent weeks, Laina had grown less resentful of her predicament and more determined to see that her baby have at least a chance at a decent life. Whatever it took, she would make it happen. *Her* child was *not* going to grow up an outcast. *Her* child was never going to be the one the Nellie Pierces of the world looked down upon — not if Laina Gray had anything to say about it.

348

Mrs. Gruber had asked if Laina could help out at the trading post a couple of days a week. When another laundress left the camp, Laina took on her job. It kept her working from early morning until late at night, and it took every ounce of her strength, but one coin at a time, her savings account grew. She kept her money tied up in a square of calico in the bottom of her workbasket.

She still didn't have a complete plan, but by fall she hoped to have enough saved to leave Camp Robinson and start a new life elsewhere. She could wear a wedding ring and talk about Army life. People would make assumptions, and if she kept her mouth shut, she could become the "Widow Someone." And the baby would have a chance. Maybe Dr. Valentine was right. Maybe no one would have to know.

"Stop!" Charlotte gasped. She clutched Caleb's hand. "We mustn't. Mother and Papa will be back soon from their ride. And I'm supposed to be sick with a headache. I'm supposed to be home taking a nap."

Caleb lowered his head and nuzzled her neck. He kissed her ear. "Good idea. Let's take a nap. Right here." His hands encircled her waist for a minute, then he traced her jaw with his fingertip. "I care for you, Miss Valentine," he whispered, bringing a slight southern drawl back into his voice even as he was backing her into an empty stall.

"I love you, too, Caleb. But — stop it!" She slapped his hand away and reached for the button he had just undone.

"You don't love me. You're just saying that." Jackson slumped down onto the clean straw. He removed his cap and swiped his forehead. He held his head in his hands for a minute. When he looked up at Charlotte, his face was streaked with tears. "I'll make Sergeant someday, Charlotte. I promise I will." His voice was dejected, "But by that time you'll be out of my life. You'll be married to someone else."

"I won't," Charlotte protested. She stroked his bowed head with her gloved hand. "Don't say that, Caleb. Please. I do love you. And I'll wait. For as long as it takes. I'll wait forever."

Jackson snorted. "Forever?" He leaned back on the straw. Without looking up at her he said, "Or just until Sergeant Boone stops mooning over his dead wife?"

"I don't care about Nathan Boone anymore," Charlotte said. She sat down next to him on the hay. "And he doesn't care for me, either. He's much too caught up with rescuing people over on the Row to even think about love. First there was Laina Gray with all her troubles. And now it's those O'Malley girls. And just because their mama is sick. You'd think Nathan Boone was personally responsible for Becky and Katie, the way he pampers them." She pouted, ducking her head and peering at Caleb from beneath the brim of her straw bonnet. She smiled at him. "And besides, the *crush* I had on Sergeant Boone wasn't *anything* like what I feel for you."

Charlotte only meant to comfort Caleb when she kissed his cheek and leaned over to put her head on his shoulder. She didn't expect what happened when he kissed her back, in a way that wasn't anything like the kisses he had sneaked before. There was nothing prim or shy about it. Before she quite knew what had happened, they were lying close together in the hay. She tried to tell herself she should be shocked. She tried not to like it. But he kept kissing her, and in a matter of minutes Charlotte had quite forgotten to care about her virtue.

She would never be able to recall exactly what it was being shouted that brought ev-

351

erything between her and Caleb to an abrupt halt. She would only remember an unbelievable roar and the rage behind it. And she would remember being afraid of her own father for the first time in her life as he shook Caleb Jackson by the neck and shouted at him. "What do you think you are *doing* with my *daughter?!*"

He followed the question with expletives so vile, Charlotte would never be able to repeat it to anyone. She had no idea her father even *knew* such words. They didn't frighten her, because she didn't know what they meant, but her father's rage most certainly did frighten her. For a moment, she feared for Caleb's life. But then her father turned his white-hot anger on her.

"Get yourself put back together, young lady," Doctor Valentine snapped.

It seemed to take an eternity for Charlotte's trembling hands to button the dozen small buttons Caleb had managed so easily. Finally, she fastened the last one. She pulled her hat back on and caught the elastic strap beneath the loose bun at the back of her head. Then she stood up, slapping at her dress to rid it of the last vestiges of hay.

Dr. Valentine was calmer by the time she had reassembled herself. But calmer was even more frightening, because with deliberate intent, he lifted his left leg and planted the bottom of his foot against Caleb's midsection with such force the private fell backward on the hay, arms and legs flung out in all directions. He gasped and clutched his stomach, rolling onto his side.

"Papa!" Charlotte pleaded. "Papa, please. Don't hurt him!"

"Avery."

For the first time, Charlotte saw her mother. She must have been waiting outside by the carriage. Or had she retreated there after seeing into the stall for herself?

"Avery, we need to handle this in private."

Without looking at his wife, Dr. Valentine pointed at Charlotte. "You," he said, lowering his voice with great effort. "You get yourself home before I take a notion to rattle your teeth! *One* unwed mother at Camp Robinson is quite enough! God forbid that *my daughter* join the ranks! Do you want to live out your life over on Soapsuds Row, too?!" Grasping Charlotte by the shoulders, the doctor spun her around and shoved her none too gently toward her mother. "Go home. And you'd better be waiting in your room when I get there."

When her mother slipped an arm about her shoulders, Charlotte leaned against her and allowed herself to be led away.

As the two women scurried across the parade ground toward home, Dr. Valentine took a deep breath and turned to face the stall where Caleb Jackson still lay on his side, afraid to move.

"If you know what is good for you, Private Jackson, you will still be in this stall when I get back."

"Sir," Caleb stammered. "Sir, please. I . . . I've done some stupid things in my life. This is one of the worst. But, Doctor Valentine, I . . . I do care about your daughter."

Valentine glared at the soldier, who had scooted to sit up and was staring up at him clutching his side. "How dare you. *Caring* does not drag a young girl into a barn and treat her like a common harlot. *Caring* doesn't sully an innocent girl's reputation. Do you have any idea the price Charlotte could pay for your kind of *caring*, Private?"

"Look, I was wrong. It won't happen again, sir. Please." He hung his head and murmured, "You've got to believe me."

"No, Private. That is where you are wrong. I do *not* have to believe you."

Doctor Valentine closed the bottom half of the stall door. He peered down at Jackson. "If I can figure out a way to see you drummed out of the army without dragging my daughter's name through the mud, I'll do it, Private. And *you* can believe *me* about that!"

Dr. Valentine kicked the stall door and stormed off to find Sergeant Boone. His rage made him want to skip talking with the sergeant and take the matter directly to the lieutenant. But it had long been the tradition in the army for officers to trust most of the company discipline to their sergeants. And as he walked along the trail curving behind the log ordnance storehouse, around the quartermaster's corral and toward Soapsuds Row, a doubt that had been flickering beneath the doctor's rage finally took form.

What if, he wondered, his flirtatious daughter had done something to *invite* the private's attentions. What if — and he didn't want to believe it, but he had to think it was a possibility — what if Charlotte was a willing partner to what was going on in that stall? The handsome Private Jackson had certainly gotten more than his share of dances at last Friday's hop. He'd been invited to dinner more than once. And Charlotte hadn't mentioned Sergeant Boone in a while. Could there possibly be some truth to the young man's stammered protests just now? And, Dr. Valentine wondered with a growing knot in his stomach, what if what he discovered today had happened before? What if, as he had shouted at his daughter, there was already a second unwed mother-to-be residing at Camp Robinson?

Emmy-Lou was right, of course. The whole thing must be handled in private. What was left of Charlotte's reputation had to be protected. She didn't deserve to have her life ruined because of one mistake. As he walked toward the barracks in search of Sergeant Boone, Dr. Valentine decided two things. First, he would inform Sergeant Boone of the situation, but he would insist on no public punishment of Private Jackson. He would leave Private Jackson to stew for an hour or so and then go back and tell him to resume his regular duties until Sergeant Boone decided what to do. Second, it was high time Dinah and Charlotte paid a visit to their grandmother. August had to be cooler — in more ways than one — on the shores of Lake Michigan, where Emmy-Lou's mother summered, than it was here in the West.

He'd had his share of run-ins with military authority since enlisting, but if there was one thing Private Caleb Jackson understood about the frontier army, it was that guard duty was not to be taken lightly. He'd recently been present when another recruit was sentenced to six months in the guardhouse after the officer of the day discovered the young private asleep at his post. Jackson had determined that while he might be on metaphorically "thin ice" because of other infractions, he would never be caught for anything so stupid as falling asleep while on guard duty.

Other men might grumble about the long, lonely hours spent guarding a post where nothing happened, but Jackson never felt alone at his post near the cavalry stables. After all the hours he'd spent handling the Company G horses, being around the stables was like being with some of his best friends. He recognized Whiskey's unique, trumpeting whinny and Renegade's rumbling complaints against the horse in the next stall. And he knew just when to expect Dinah Valentine to slip into the stables to feed her pony dried apples or peppermint candies. Private

Jackson almost enjoyed guard duty.

But tonight, Jackson found no joy in his assignment. He was, in fact, as close to becoming a nervous wreck as he had ever been. Even when he'd lost two weeks' pay at the poker tables in St. Louis, he had not felt this bad. As he paced back and forth, his mind reeled between the past and the future.

About an hour after he and Charlotte were discovered, Dr. Valentine had returned as promised. He'd grasped the top of the stall door in both hands and said without emotion, "Sergeant Boone has been informed of the situation. He will deal with you later. In the meantime, you are to resume your duties." His usually kind eyes became hateful slits as he added, "And *stay away from my daughter.* Do not discuss this with anyone. Is that clear, Private?"

It had taken every ounce of courage Caleb Jackson had to look Doctor Valentine in the eye, but he'd done it. "Yes, sir. Perfectly clear, sir." He held the doctor's gaze until the man nodded and left. Then he had clamped his hat back on his head, brushed the straw off his uniform, and answered the day's second water call with the rest of Company G. He'd gone to the mess hall with everyone else and waited through one of the longest evenings of his life until his turn came to relieve the sentry posted near the stables. And now, here he was, pacing back and forth, cursing himself — for his stupidity, for not controlling himself with Charlotte, for taking advantage of her inexperience, for losing what little self-control he had — and feeling terrified by the very real possibility that tomorrow he would no longer be in the United States Army. He didn't think Dr. Valentine could do that without a formal inquiry, which he wouldn't call to protect Charlotte, but then Jackson hadn't thought he'd get so carried away with Charlotte, either.

Sergeant Boone had once asked him what he would do if he couldn't be in the army. He'd displayed bravado and a self-assured attitude when he said he'd get a job on a ranch. But the truth was, he wanted to make the army his life. While other men complained about the endless rolling Sandhills, Jackson reveled in the open country and the canopy of sky above him. He wouldn't have admitted it to anyone, but he had come to admire men like Corporal Dorsey, soldiers who had given themselves to a cause and made good on the gift. Men who would throw themselves into a battle with all they had and win. Private Caleb Jackson hadn't ever made good on anything, unless you counted his keeping that promise to Annie about not yapping about her past. Protecting Annie had been pretty well cancelled out by what he'd almost done with Charlotte today.

The only winnings he'd experienced in life had been at a poker table when he cheated better than anyone else in the game. It wasn't much to be proud of. He had begun to wish that when he looked in the mirror, the man who looked back at him would be someone who had a sense of honor, and the self-respect that went along with it.

Being in the army had helped him begin to control some of the demons inside him. He wasn't drinking as much and he hadn't been in a fight in a long time. He even had some of last month's pay left. He hadn't gambled it all away. As a result of forced military discipline, he was beginning to see signs of a developing self-discipline.

A wolf howled, and Jackson shivered. Boone would be coming any minute now, and he had to have a defense ready. Charlotte Valentine had gotten under his skin, and now, having almost conquered his worst vices, he was about to lose everything because of her. He shook his head and cursed himself. *You really can pick 'em, you idiot. Why'd you have to go and pick an officer's daughter? And the very same girl a sergeant's been squiring around. And not just any sergeant. Sergeant Nathan Boone, the unofficial guardian of all that's good in Camp Robinson.*

He wondered what Boone would think if he knew Miss Valentine had been a more than willing participant in their romance. At the thought, he could almost hear his own father saying *"It isn't honorable for a man to hide behind a woman's skirts."* To his surprise, Caleb realized that he wanted to at least try to do the honorable thing when it came to Charlotte Valentine. The truth was, she didn't deserve to have her life ruined because of one mistake. And if the doctor hadn't interrupted them, it could have happened. Maybe he hadn't exactly planned things, but once he and Charlotte were in that stall together, Beauregard Preston had taken over, and Beauregard Preston never stopped with the undoing of a few buttons.

By the time Whiskey gave his signature welcoming whinny to his master, and Boone's voice boomed for the sentry,

Jackson had decided to take the blame for the incident. He hoped he wouldn't have to beg for his career, but he was almost ready to do that, too. He answered Boone's call and braced himself for the worst.

"I know you've probably been practicing your explanation for the situation with Miss Valentine," Boone said.

"There's no reason you or the doctor should believe me, but it won't happen again. I swear it. I'll give the same assurance to Dr. Valentine, if he'll only give me the chance." He could feel the sweat trickling down his back as he spoke.

"Unfortunately, Private Jackson, your assurances are not something people around here can depend on."

"But I mean it this time, sir," Jackson said. "I make no excuses. I behaved badly. Dr. Valentine was right. If I cared for Charlotte, I'd never have led her into that situation. It won't happen again. I mean it."

"Dr. Valentine has already seen to that," the sergeant said. "When he told me about this situation he informed me he's sending Charlotte back East to visit her grandmother."

"He doesn't have to do that," Caleb said. "I'll . . . I'll stay away." He swallowed.

"Come on, Sergeant — Nathan. You know how it's been with me. I've never had much experience with a girl like Charlotte. The rules are different with girls like her. You can't treat them like —"

"Like you treated Riverboat Annie?" Boone folded his arms and looked down at Jackson, rocking back on his heels as he spoke.

"What . . . what's *she* got to do with anything?" Caleb frowned. He glanced in the direction of Soapsuds Row. Why would Nathan even mention Riverboat Annie? He'd kept his promise and kept his mouth shut about all of that. It didn't make any sense for that to be brought up now. Unless . . . Caleb's mind raced to rewind the confrontation in the stable. A light went on when he remembered Dr. Valentine shouting *"One unwed mother at Camp Robinson is quite enough. God forbid that my daughter join the ranks! Is it your ambition to end up on Soapsuds Row, too?" Is it possible? . . . Annie's pregnant? . . . and they're looking for someone to blame?* It was as if Caleb were looking down the barrel of Cruikshank's rifle again. Only this time, he couldn't run off and join the army to get away.

"Listen, Nathan. I don't know what Annie's told you about me, but I've had nothing to do with her since I got to Camp Robinson, beyond a couple conversations and a dance or two at the last hop. I promised her I'd keep my mouth shut, and I have. I told you I came out here to get myself a new life. I messed up a few times at the beginning, and I paid for it. But I haven't had anything to do with Annie since those times in St. Louis. I swear it. If she wants to call herself Laina Gray, that's fine with me. I told her that. And I haven't touched her." He grabbed Boone's arm. "That's the truth. I'd swear on a stack of Bibles I haven't touched her. I don't care what she says."

The sergeant jerked his arm away and smoothed his sleeve. "What makes you think Laina has said anything at all about you, Private?"

Desperation took over. All of Caleb's best intentions faded. "Look," he said hoarsely, "I know what's going on here. Valentine is just mad enough to do it, too. He's just like all the other high-class jerks who enjoy putting the screws to any lowly private who dares to touch his precious daughter. He won't drag Charlotte's name through the mud to get me drummed out, but Riverboat Annie is another story. She doesn't have a reputation to protect in the first place."

"What are you talking about?" Boone asked.

"Come on. As if you and I don't both know Annie's 'in the family way.' Lord knows *somebody* has to take the blame." Caleb laughed harshly and shook his head. "I walked right into this one, didn't I?"

Boone grabbed him by the front of his shirt and nearly lifted him off the ground. "You watch your mouth, Private."

Caleb jerked away. He thrust his chin out and stepped toward his sergeant. "All due respect, sir, I'll grovel all you want. I'll serve time in the guardhouse. I'll tote a log from here to Sidney and back. But I am *not* taking the fall for a riverboat whore." One second he was on his feet, the next he was on the ground looking up at an entirely new galaxy in the night sky.

Boone crouched down next to him and grabbed him by the throat, nearly closing off his windpipe as he growled, "You listen to me, you good-for-nothing — I came out here tonight for two reasons. One was to tell you Doctor Valentine isn't going to make a public spectacle of his daughter just to teach you a lesson. The other was to hear your promise that you won't bring up

365

Laina's past. In light of the *first* item, which grants you yet another chance to make a career of the army, I thought you'd be able to agree to the *second,* thereby giving Miss Gray the same chance you've been given. It appears," he growled, closing his hand around Caleb's throat, "that I've overrated your worth as a human being. You've sunk to an all-time low, Private, bringing an innocent woman into your own troubles — in the worst way possible."

Caleb struggled and gagged. He clamped his hands around his sergeant's wrist. Just when he was about to pass out, Boone let go. Coughing and sputtering, Caleb choked out, "You didn't know?" He sat up, rubbing his neck. "You didn't know."

Boone spat out, "You don't have to be spreading lies about Laina Gray just to make yourself look good."

Caleb rubbed his jaw. "Okay. Okay. I earned that. But, Nathan, I swear . . . Dr. Valentine *said* it. I didn't make it up. He was yelling at Charlotte, and he said something about Camp Robinson not needing *two* unwed mothers — about her ending up being a laundress over on Soapsuds Row, too." Caleb held his hands out, palm up.

"He didn't name Annie. But it didn't take any imagination for me to figure out who he was talking about." He rubbed the back of his neck. "Look, if you want to know, I felt kind of bad for her when I figured this out. We had that talk, and I thought we had things all settled. Then you come down here talking about Annie and honor and . . ." He shrugged. "You can't blame me for jumping to conclusions. Like I said, if somebody's going to take the fall for anything with the ladies around here, I've pretty well opened up myself to be the one."

"Get up," Boone ordered. When Caleb obeyed, he said, "I've got to do some thinking. When you get off guard duty, I want you to report to my quarters over on the Row."

"What are you going to do?"

"I'm going to take a walk," Boone said. He spun on his heels and headed off toward the river.

Caleb shouldered his rifle and marched along the southern perimeter of the camp. He wasn't sure, but he thought the worst was over for him. Boone was now distracted by a bigger problem — Annie. So Valentine was sending Charlotte away. He'd miss her, but if he had to choose between Charlotte and his career, he'd choose the army. Why, then, he thought as he marched along, didn't he feel relieved? He felt something, but it wasn't relief. It took Jackson a few minutes to recognize the emotion clenching at his gut when he thought about Laina Gray. *Guilt.*

Seventeen

For what is your life? It is even a vapour, that appeareth for a little time, and then vanisheth away.

James 4:14

Even as a small boy, Nathan had been drawn to cemeteries. If that was weird, so be it. In cemeteries people left you alone. If you cried, they didn't interrupt you. If you sat with your head down, thinking, no one asked what the matter was. A cemetery was a good place to just be alone with your thoughts. And sometimes the thoughts had nothing to do with death and dying.

The cemetery at Camp Robinson was nothing like the one back home in Missouri. It wasn't very well tended, and there were only a few graves. Lily's grave was the only one with a stone marker, and he'd had to spend nearly two months' pay to have it shipped from Grand Island into Sidney. The freighter who had brought it to Camp Robinson clearly thought Nathan Boone was crazy. Nathan didn't care. Leaning against the tombstone tonight, Nathan was glad he had done his best to do right by Lily Boone. She'd certainly done her best to do right by him, following him out here when the whole idea of Indians and the Wild West terrified her.

He had spent a lot of time at Lily's grave in the past two and a half years. But he'd never come up here to think about another woman. Somehow, it seemed to Nathan that Lily wouldn't mind. She knew his heart, and like Granny had said, he would never give the part of his heart that belonged to Lily Bainbridge Boone to anyone else. So, Nathan reasoned, it was all right to come out here to think about Laina Gray. If Lily was aware of what was going on here below, she also would know that Laina Gray had no chance of usurping Lily's place in his heart. What the two of them had shared was part of a past that he'd always be able to revisit. Nothing could change it or tarnish it.

People certainly did crazy things for love. Well, Nathan thought, people just did crazy things. *Crazy.* Miss Gray used that excuse a lot when she did things he didn't understand. She'd used it as the excuse for him finding her in tears last month when she'd broken that vase. She'd babbled on about Caleb Jackson and her past as some riverboat girl as if that mattered to anyone now. Nathan looked up at the sky and shook his head. He'd sensed that wasn't the whole story. But he'd let it go. Thinking back, he realized he'd maybe even been relieved that she didn't seem to *need* to tell him the rest. It was easier to be someone's friend when the problems were simpler.

She couldn't be pregnant. Could she? It just had to be some sort of misunderstanding. Something Jackson *thought* he heard. He'd said himself that Valentine was raving mad. In that situation, people could easily misunderstand what was being said. *Shoot,* Nathan thought, *ask fighting men to describe a skirmish with the Sioux, and you'll get as many versions as men you asked.* It wasn't that they lied intentionally. They just saw things through fear, and that wasn't exactly an objective view. That was probably what happened in the stable. Jackson was listening to Valentine through his own fear. He didn't hear exactly right.

She couldn't be pregnant. He counted

back on his fingers. *God, wasn't it enough to let that monster get hold of her in the first place? Did you have to get her pregnant, too?*

He thought back over recent weeks. She wasn't hiding at Granny's anymore. She spent time with Katie and Wilber, who was being transformed from a bumbling puppy into a well-behaved dog. She helped Charlotte and Dinah Valentine with their French lessons. She cleaned for the Valentines. She had even started working at the trading post for Mrs. Gruber a couple of days a week and had taken on Mrs. O'Malley's share of infantry laundry. She picnicked on Sunday afternoons and sang hymns. She went to the hops. She danced. But in some ways, Nathan suddenly realized, Laina did seem different.

He hadn't seen her wear any of the things from Lily's trunk. Of course, he couldn't exactly ask Granny Max if Miss Gray was using Lily's unmentionables. But now he wondered if the reason Miss Gray wasn't wearing Lily's dresses was because they wouldn't fit. He didn't *think* she looked pregnant, but . . . He counted on his fingers again. When could you tell just by looking?

He remembered more changes. More than one evening, when he stopped in after taps for a chat with Granny Max, Laina had already gone to bed. And just today, when they had taken the picnic lunch out to the White River, when Miss Gray was singing hymns with Private Yates, she cried. It didn't affect her singing voice much, but by the time she finished the song, tears were running freely down her cheeks. His mother had cried a lot when she was expecting Nathan's little sister. Nathan wondered if Miss Gray was crying a lot more than anyone knew.

"Why didn't she tell me? Why doesn't she ask for my help?"

And exactly what are you going to do to help her, Sergeant Boone?

Nathan's head came up. *I could marry her.* He dismissed the idea as quickly as it came. Stupid idea. Ridiculous. But was it? A man could do worse than Laina Gray for a wife. A lot worse. They got along. They were friends. Plenty of people built good marriages on friendship. Look at the Valentines. You didn't have to be in love to get married. He'd already married once for love. Maybe he *could* marry again. For friendship. It would solve all of Laina's problems. And some of his. He'd have a home again. Single women would stop batting their eyelashes at him. Even the idea

373

of the child didn't seem all that much of a problem. He'd be a good father. He felt sure of it.

He laid his open hand on the earth beside Lily's tombstone. "Well, sweetheart, if you can hear me and if you have any wisdom to share, I am open to anything you can send my way. I've been thinking some pretty crazy things tonight." His voice wavered. "I love you, Lily. Always will." He rubbed his face with his hands, trying to scrub the tears away. "I'm lonely," he whispered. "The fact is, Lily, I'm a mess. And I wish you could tell me what to do."

He got up and stretched his legs. He kissed the inside of his fingertips and laid them on the top ridge of the tombstone.

Nathan was in his quarters on Soapsuds Row waiting for Caleb Jackson to show up when he heard someone pounding on Granny Max's back door. He recognized Katie O'Malley's voice calling for Laina.

He opened his own back door just in time to see Laina kneel down and pull Katie into her arms. She closed her eyes and rocked back and forth.

Katie pushed away and looked up at her. "He just wouldn't breathe. Doctor tried and tried, and then Granny tried while Doctor helped Mama, and then she d—" Katie threw herself onto Laina's shoulder sobbing.

"Where's Becky?" Laina asked.

"With M-Mama," Katie sobbed. "They said I should come up here."

"Come inside," Laina said, taking Katie's hand.

Nathan walked over to them. "What can I do?" he asked.

Laina sat down in Granny's rocker and invited Katie into her lap. "I guess you could warm up some milk." She motioned toward the shelf on the wall. "From the blue crock."

Nathan stoked the fire. Before long Katie's sobs were fading, and Laina was coaxing her to drink some warm milk.

"Wilber," Katie said drowsily. "Mama's gonna get mad again if Wilber —" She opened her eyes wide and looked up at Laina. "I g-guess Mama don't have to worry over Wilber anymore." She burst into fresh tears.

"Shh." Laina looked up at Nathan. Her eyes pleaded with him as she said, "Sergeant Boone will find Wilber. He can come sleep with you here tonight. In my bed."

Nathan smiled at her and headed off to

find Wilber. When he returned with the dog, he paused beside Granny Max's kitchen window to look in. Katie O'Malley was asleep in Laina's lap, her body occasionally wracked by a sob or a shudder. Laina held the child close. Her head was leaning back against the rocker's high back. Her eyes were closed and she was singing.

Nathan stood still and watched. *That's beautiful. She's beautiful.*

Nathan listened through an entire chorus before heading inside. When Laina rose and led a groggy Katie into the back room, Wilber followed, wagging his tail. While he waited for Laina to return, Nathan put on the coffeepot. When Laina came back into the room, he said, "Thought I'd just get it going. It's probably going to be a long night." He reached for Katie's cup.

"Here," Laina said. "Let me."

When her hand brushed his, he pulled away. He could feel color rising up the back of his neck. "I'll go see about things up at the O'Malleys'," he said. But he didn't move. Instead, he asked, "Have I . . . have I done something to offend you?"

Laina frowned. "Why would you think that?"

"Something's different. With you. Is something wrong?"

"There's nothing wrong with me, Sergeant Boone."

"Dang it, you are a stubborn woman."

"Don't swear, Sergeant Boone," she said. "I'll go see if Granny Max and Becky need any help."

"Then I'll rouse Yates and get him to making a coffin." He looked toward the back room. "What about Katie?"

"Oh, don't worry about Katie. She has Wilber. He's a good listener. And I won't be gone that long."

"All right, then," Nathan said. He followed her outside and stood watching as she made her way up the Row toward the O'Malley quarters.

Eighteen

How long, ye simple ones, will ye love simplicity? And the scorners delight in their scorning, and fools hate knowledge? Turn you at my reproof: behold, I will pour out my spirit unto you, I will make known my words unto you.

Proverbs 1:22-23

Relieved of guard duty, Caleb headed for Sergeant Boone's quarters. He had just stepped up on the board porch running the length of Soapsuds Row when Boone opened the door, not to his own quarters, but to those of Granny Max. *Lord help me, he's been talking to Annie.* Caleb took a deep breath and steeled himself for whatever might be coming his way.

"I need you to head over to the barracks and rouse Yates." The sergeant stepped outside and closed the door behind him before saying, "There's need for a coffin. Meara O'Malley's died in childbirth. Come with me. We'll take some measurements." Motioning for Caleb to follow, Boone headed around back and up the Row toward an oblique splotch of light being cast outside the O'Malleys' back door. Caleb followed with a sense of dread.

Sergeant Boone stepped inside Mrs. O'Malley's back door. Caleb lingered just outside, his heart pounding. He'd picked his way across battlefields strewn with bodies and body parts and thought that was what made death awful. But the orderly scene inside that apartment was just as awful in its own way. Mrs. O'Malley and the baby were dressed and laid out, their bodies surrounded by quart jars filled with ice water. Candles and lamps lighted the room where mourners would spend the rest of the night sitting with the remains, both as a ritual of respect and as protection against insects and rodents. The thought sent shivers up Caleb's spine.

Laina Gray came to the door. "Sixty inches," she said to Boone. "A little extra width." She swallowed hard. Her voice wavered. "We thought she'd want to be holding . . . the baby." The sergeant put his hand on her shoulder. She glanced at Caleb, then back up at Boone.

"I'm sending Jackson over to get Yates," Boone said. "He can get started right away on the coffin."

Granny Max came to the door. "Dr. Valentine said to plan for noon tomorrow." She lowered her voice. "The girls can have the morning with their mama and the baby. Doctor says the heat just won't allow them any more time than that. Thank you for getting the ice, Nathan."

It was well past midnight when Caleb roused Private Yates, who in turn roused the quartermaster to help scrounge up enough good lumber to build a coffin. They ended up tearing the sides off a freighter's broken-down wagon. Yates lamented not having time to smooth the lumber and build a properly shaped coffin. He told Caleb the best he could do quickly would be a long rectangular box.

It didn't cool off much overnight, and at dawn, when Private Dubois and Corporal Dorsey shouldered shovels with Jackson and headed across the river to dig a grave in the camp cemetery, the heat was oppressive. The parched earth made the digging go slowly, and it wasn't long before all three men were drenched with sweat.

Caleb welcomed the hard labor, relieved to be granted at least a momentary reprieve from disciplinary action over the incident with Miss Valentine. But he was still struggling with guilt over having brought Laina Gray into the mess he'd created. He didn't look at her once through the forty-five-minute service.

After Mrs. O'Malley's funeral, Caleb volunteered to stay behind and fill in the grave. He figured it couldn't hurt his cause if he volunteered, and shoveling dirt alone down here by the river was better than toting a log around the parade ground in full view of the entire garrison. He hoped it might buy him a little more time to think over his situation and come up with a plan before the inevitable boom was lowered.

Looking off toward where the mourners were filing over the bridge, he saw Laina Gray stop. She said something to Granny Max. The old woman looked back at Caleb and patted Laina on the shoulder. Then, putting one arm around each of the O'Malley girls, Granny continued on her way while Laina turned back toward the cemetery.

Caleb's heart began to thump. His mouth went dry. He bent to the work, still keeping an eye on the doings at the bridge. Sergeant Boone seemed inclined to accompany Laina, but she put her hand on his arm and said something. He glanced toward Jackson, then headed off in the direction of the Row. Caleb gave a little sigh of relief, until he saw Boone hurry to catch up with Dr. Valentine.

Charlotte had been conspicuously absent from Mrs. O'Malley's funeral. Caleb had overhead the doctor tell Mrs. Gruber his daughter had a terrible headache and needed to rest before her departure the next day for the East. His heart pounding, Caleb resumed shoveling as Laina Gray approached. He tried to steel himself for what was coming. He thought of a few excuses he could give for his behavior. None of them were very good, but he'd never let that keep him from trying to avoid taking blame before.

"I'm not certain this is a good idea," Laina said as soon as she was within earshot.

Caleb stopped shoveling. He removed his cap and mopped his forehead with a dirty kerchief. Looking at her, he hesitated. She really had changed. Riverboat Annie would have charged up here with her hands on her hips, and let go with a stream of profanity that would wither a man faster than the Sandhills' heat could kill a fresh daisy. But this woman seemed almost shy. There was a gentleness about her that made him uncomfortable. She wasn't angry. He was surprised at his own words when he motioned to the grave and blurted out, "I wouldn't blame you if you pushed me in and started shoveling." He felt like a boxer warily circling his opponent. Except that she didn't seem inclined to fight.

"Now, why would I want to do that?" she asked. "I just walked up here to invite you to join us. Mrs. Gruber is going to set out a supper for everyone. I thought you might want to come."

Is it possible Boone hasn't talked to her yet? Maybe he's waiting until later. He felt a brief surge of relief, but it lasted only a second or two before his conscience broke in.

You've got to tell her.

I can't. She'll want revenge. She'll tell Doc all about my past. And that'll be the end of me. He won't believe I'm trying to change. He'll see me drummed out or die trying.

So just go on being a coward. Slink around and wait while everybody else decides things for you. Run off and change your name again. How many times you going to do that? You're disgusting. You're not even man enough to own up to this. What did she ever do to you? She didn't have to come back and invite you to supper. She didn't have to promise not to say anything about your past. You could at least warn her that Boone knows about the baby.

While Miss Gray waited for his answer, he argued with himself. Finally, he cleared his throat. "Thank you. Sure. That'd be nice."

"Dr. Valentine will be there. And maybe Charlotte." She smiled as she turned to go. "We'll see you this evening, then."

Jackson tipped his hat and let her go, all the while arguing with himself. Finally, he threw down his shovel and ran after her, catching up at the bridge. "Wait, Miss Gray. Wait." She turned around. He took his hat off and began rolling the brim nervously while the internal argument continued.

Finally, he spoke up. "There's something you've got to know." He tugged on his beard nervously. "Look, you're never going to want to hear the name Caleb Jackson again after this, but . . ." He began to pace back and forth. Her calm was worse than any anger she could have rained down. Seeing her just standing there waiting drove him crazy. Finally, he said, "Look. I've made a lot of mistakes in my life. Most of them from pure meanness. But the truth is, I really have been trying for a fresh start out here. But it's hard to change. You may not have seen him lately, but Beauregard Preston is still in here." He tapped his chest.

"I know what you mean," Laina said. She smiled. "Riverboat Annie is still inside of me, too. It's not that easy to get away from the past we've had."

Caleb blurted out, "Well, Riverboat Annie wasn't caught in the stables yesterday in a . . . uh . . . compromising situation with a member of the opposite sex."

Laina closed her eyes. Her voice was miserable, but sympathetic. "Oh, Private Jackson. Charlotte?"

He nodded. "Old Beauregard Preston stuffed a sock in Caleb Jackson's conscience and did some serious . . . you know."

"So *that's* why Charlotte didn't come to the funeral." She nodded. "And that explains the sudden trip East." She looked puzzled. "But why are you telling me this?"

"It gets worse," Jackson said. "Dr. Valentine and his wife caught us."

Laina studied his face. "Maybe that was

good. I bet it put Private Jackson back in control of Mr. Preston in a hurry."

He shrugged. "Maybe. Maybe not." He looked away. "The thing is, Dr. Valentine was raving mad. He hollered. A lot. He was so mad, he didn't trust himself to even be around me just then. I think he could have just as soon killed me as look at me. He ended up just telling me to get on with the day. Said he would handle it later. That he and Sergeant Boone would discuss 'the situation.' He wanted it kept quiet for Charlotte's sake. He let me stew all the rest of the day and into the night.

"I was on guard duty last night when Sergeant Boone finally came to lower the boom." He paused and moistened his lips. "You know how it's been for me here. I've had just about every discipline there is. I've probably spent more time in the guardhouse than I have in the barracks. But I've been trying. I kept volunteering for patrol. Worked with the horses. And I've been changing. At first with Miss Valentine, I was just playing. But then I started to think maybe I had a *reason* to make it all work out." He put his hands to his waist and stood looking off into the distance as he talked. "But I messed that up, too. And I thought Sergeant Boone was getting ready to tell me my army career was over. I was feeling pretty desperate, and I blurted out something." He swatted at a fly buzzing around his face. His voice was miserable when he finally looked back at Laina and said, "All I was thinking about was me. As usual. I wanted to shift the attention away from myself. I thought maybe I could at least save my career."

"What are you talking about?"

"It's about you. About the baby."

"What?" She sounded like he'd knocked the air out of her. She clasped her hands against her midsection and her face paled.

He reached for her arm. "Let's go down to the river where there's some shade. You're going to faint."

"Tell me what you said," she said, pulling away from him.

"You're going to have a baby. Right?"

"Who . . . who said such a thing?"

"Look, he didn't come right out and say it. Not like that."

"He?"

"Dr. Valentine. He was raging mad. He was yelling at Charlotte about his daughter not ending up as the second unwed mother on Soapsuds Row. Something like that." He paused again. "It wasn't until later I realized exactly what he said, and that he must have been talking about you." He mumbled, "Something Sarge said made me think they were going to make me take the blame for your situation, so they could discipline me without mentioning Charlotte." He took off his hat and swiped his forehead. "So now Sergeant Boone knows about the baby."

"Charlotte . . . and Mrs. Valentine . . . heard this?" Laina's voice was almost a whisper.

"No!" Jackson shook his head. "No. Not what I said to Nathan."

"But they heard . . . they heard what the doctor said?"

Caleb shrugged. "Well, they were there. But they probably didn't *hear* it. Not so as to connect it to *you*. Not the way I did." He slapped the side of his thigh with his hat. "I'm really sorry."

"Tell me what you said to Sergeant Boone." She barely croaked out the words.

He'd expected rage. Swearing. Defensiveness. Maybe even a physical response. He'd seen her go after an especially lascivious customer once with a kitchen knife. But this . . . hurt . . . the fright in her eyes, the lostness. Facing Laina's despair, Jackson didn't know what to do.

Feeling sorrow for others was a new sensation for him, and now he'd felt it three times in rapid succession. At first he'd only been sorry he got *caught* in a compromising situation with Charlotte Valentine. But then he'd realized he really could have destroyed her future, and he'd felt truly sorry for taking advantage of her.

He was sorry for the O'Malley girls losing their mother and baby brother. He had even wondered what would happen to them and felt sorry about that.

And now, standing before Laina Gray, he was sorry again. She really did seem to be doing her best to escape the past and get herself a new life. And, from what he could tell, she was doing a respectable job of it. She didn't deserve the trouble he was causing her. Being pregnant was trouble enough.

For the first time since he'd been a Confederate drummer boy, the desire to do *right* conquered Jackson's overactive instincts for self-preservation. As accurately as he could, he told Laina about his encounter with Sergeant Boone. He didn't make excuses for himself. "All I cared about was getting myself out of this mess. I didn't think. I didn't *care* what it might mean for you. And after you've kept quiet about *my* past." He hung his head. "I'm sorry. Please believe me."

Laina let out a huge breath. "Get back to work, Private."

Her response was so abrupt Caleb hesitated until she repeated herself.

"I need to think. Please. Just let me be alone for a while."

Caleb watched her walk away along the riverbank. When she came to a depression in the shore, she sank down in the shade, drew her knees up to her chest, and bowed her head. Caleb did as he was told. *Where you gonna run to now, boy? Where you gonna run?*

Can it get much worse, Lord? How can things possibly get much worse? Laina crossed her arms over her knees and let the tears flow. Maybe she should just give up altogether. What was the use of trying to build a new life when things like this could blindside you at any minute.

I don't even know how to pray about this. I'm tired, Lord. I'm tired of being the Tragedy of Camp Robinson. The Crazy Woman. Granny's Patient. Nathan Boone's Latest Stray. And now it seems I get to be the Scarlet Woman of Camp Robinson, after all. I was going to leave and start again somewhere else where no one knew me. I only needed a few

*more weeks' income before I could do that.
Granny even thought it might work, just letting people think I was a military widow. But
now Meara is dead. And with the girls
needing us, and Granny not getting any
younger . . . I think she really needs me to help
with the girls. They don't have family anywhere else. There's nothing for them to do but
stay. But how can I stay? How can I stay here
and let this baby become the Bastard Child of
Camp Robinson? She won't have a chance in
life. You can't mean for that to happen, Lord.
You just can't.*

The longer Laina thought, the more confused she became. Nothing made any
sense.

*You said if anyone lacks wisdom they should
ask you. Granny just read me that verse a
couple of days ago. You said your plans for me
include a future and a hope. Or was that just
for Jeremiah? Isn't that for me? Maybe that
promise isn't for the Riverboat Annies of the
world. If you love me, Lord, why are you letting this happen?*

Her body was wracked by sobs as she
looked up at the blue sky and shouted,
"WHAT AM I SUPPOSED TO DO?!"

"Miss Gray. Laina." Caleb Jackson had
walked down to the river. "That was stable

call a minute ago. They'll be bringing the horses down here to water them before too long. What do you want me to do, ma'am?"

"I don't know." She made no attempt to hide the misery from her voice. She swiped the tears off her face and started to get up.

"I wish I could take it all back."

Laina shrugged. "It doesn't matter. I was going to go away, but Meara's death complicates things. I can't just leave Granny Max with two girls to raise. So people were going to find out anyway. Sergeant Boone would likely have been one of the first we told. Doctor Valentine's outburst just started things sooner, that's all."

"But I'm the one who made him mad enough to say those things in the first place."

She sighed. "It's not as if you meant to hurt me personally." She forced a smile. "I believe you about that. I know you didn't mean to cause me trouble."

"Maybe not," Jackson said, "but I usually do whatever it takes to cover for myself, and I don't usually care what happens to anybody else." He shook his head. "In fact, I'm surprised this bothers me at all. But it does."

Laina smiled at him. "Listen to yourself,

Private Jackson. Those words were a foreign language to Beauregard Preston. As I recall, he was all about blaming someone else for everything bad that ever happened to him."

"Yeah," Caleb nodded. "First it was the Yankees. Then it was the Yankees again. Then it was a storekeeper named Cruikshank and his Yankee customers. Then . . ." he shrugged. "What I was missing my whole life was the idea that my biggest problem is me. And *me* has sunk to an all-time low — and dragged you down with him."

"Granny says you can't sink lower than God can reach," Laina said. "Just look at me."

"You were never all that bad," Caleb said.

Laina touched the scar at her left temple. "You've forgotten about this and what it represents. There's nothing attractive about *me* to make God pick me out."

"That scar's nothing," Jackson said. "It barely shows. You're still a beautiful woman. To hear Yates talk, you're as good as they come."

"Granny said all the good deeds we do are just like filthy laundry, anyway." She smiled. "So don't think you're out of

God's reach. And besides that, you've been trying. You joined the army."

"There's plenty of booze and gambling — even women — in the army, if a man knows where to look. And Caleb Jackson, God help him, knows where to look." He shook his head. He was quiet for a minute, then he asked, "What are you going to do?"

"I don't know," Laina said. "Keep hollering at God, I guess. Ask Him to show me what to do."

"Wasn't that you shouting at God a minute ago? It sounded like maybe He wasn't answering."

Laina nodded. "Sometimes it does feel that way."

"What's your Granny Max say about that?" Caleb asked.

"To just keep pounding on the door," Laina said. She cocked her head and looked up at him. "Want to do some pounding with me?"

Jackson frowned. "What?"

"Well, I believe you're sorry about all of this. And I believe Miss Valentine brought out something good in you. Maybe something you didn't even know you had. Maybe we could ask God about all that together."

"You mean . . . pray? Me?" He laughed.

"Sure. Why not?"

He shook his head. "Hey. This is me. You really think God wants to hear from me?"

"Granny Max says —"

"Yeah, yeah. We can't sink lower than God can reach." He snorted. "Wanna bet?"

"All right, Private," Laina said. "You don't have to say anything. You can just listen." She bowed her head. "God, I'm worried about the baby. I had a plan that would give her at least a chance at a good life. But now Meara is dead, and how can I leave Granny Max to take care of those girls all by herself? Private Jackson doesn't have much hope for things getting better for him, either. We both have reason to believe you might not care to answer us." She tried to swallow the knot in her throat. Tears were welling up, and she was embarrassed, but she let them spill out and went on. "So I don't even know what to ask for because I don't see any clear way for this mess we have gotten ourselves into to get fixed. Thank you for listening. Amen."

They both looked up just in time to see a small herd of horses headed down to the water on the opposite side of the bridge.

"I've got to go," Caleb said. He stood up and held out his hand to Laina. She took it and let him help her up. Together they walked toward the bridge. "Wait a minute," Caleb said, and he ran to the graveside to get his shovel. When he came back, he shouldered the shovel and offered Laina his arm. As they walked along, Laina said, "I don't know what Sergeant Boone has in mind for you, but it will be fair, and I'm thinking you'll be able to handle it. I'm not so sure you've ruined your life. Not yet, anyway. Maybe you don't want to come to dinner up at the trading post. But you can always write to Charlotte."

"Oh, I'm certain her father will allow *that!*" Jackson exclaimed.

"You might be surprised what Dr. Valentine will allow," Laina said. They started across the bridge. "Give it a couple of weeks and then go to him. Ask him what he would do if you brought him a letter for Charlotte. Ask him if he would consider reading it and then maybe sending it on to her." She patted his arm. "If you really care for her, don't give up. And don't give up on Caleb Jackson, either. For whatever it's worth, his old friend thinks he has promise."

Jackson looked down at her. "Maybe you

are crazy. At least a little. I spread that news about you, and now you're *praying* for me, for heaven's sake."

"No," Laina chuckled. "The praying is for *your* sake, Private Jackson."

"So," he said. "You know what *you're* going to do?"

Laina shook her head. "Maybe you could tell Sergeant Boone we've had this talk and that things are all right between us. Maybe he'll respect my privacy. In fact, please tell him that's what I'd like. If the Valentine women are leaving tomorrow, maybe that will keep them from talking behind my back and give me more time to think things through."

"Like I said earlier, they might not have even understood what the doctor was talking about. As for Sergeant Boone not saying anything to you, I wouldn't count on that. He's not going to want me telling him what to do when it comes to you. Especially if I'm telling him to leave you be. He's been fixing everything for everybody around him since I first met him. And that was a lot of years ago." He shook his head. "Too bad he can't fix himself as well as he fixes everybody else."

"Yes," Laina agreed. "It is." She patted his arm. "Well, don't give up on Charlotte.

Love hopes all things, you know."

"Is that a little Sandhills wisdom?"

"It could be, I suppose. But I think it's from the Bible." She smiled up at him.

He touched the brim of his cap, saluting her. "People have told me to go to a lot of places in my day, Miss Gray — mostly to regions below the earth. You're the first one who's ever suggested I go to God with my troubles. I don't know exactly what just happened, but I do feel better. And I'm grateful to you. I'll do what I can to convince Sergeant Boone you'd like some time to yourself before the two of you talk this over."

Caleb headed off toward the stables. Halfway there, he turned around to watch Laina. Ever since that night he'd first recognized her, he'd been watching, waiting for her act to slip, expecting to catch a glimpse of the real reason behind her play-acting at respectability. But the woman walking away from him toward Soapsuds Row was no actress. He was convinced of that. Laina Gray was the genuine article. He'd hurt her. Misused knowledge against her. Caused her the worst kind of trouble. And she'd prayed for him. *Prayed*, for heaven's sake. He smiled, hearing her voice when she said *"No. The praying was for your sake, Private Jackson."*

She seemed to want to see things go well for him. She thought he still had a chance with Charlotte Valentine. She even gave him good advice on how to make that happen. Jackson turned back around and headed for the stables. *Maybe she is crazy, but it's a good kind of crazy.*

Nineteen

Lo, children are an heritage of the Lord: and the fruit of the womb is his reward.

Psalm 127:3

"Good-bye, Papa." Charlotte kissed her father on the cheek and climbed up into the stage beside Dinah. Once seated, she leaned over and looked out the window, dabbing her eyes with a handkerchief.

"What's the matter with *you?*" Dinah teased. "Disappointed because there isn't an honor guard of former beaus waiting to announce the queen's departure?"

"You hush," Charlotte snapped. She dabbed at her eyes again and looked mournfully out the window.

"Don't be sad, Charlott-ah. We're going to *like* it at Grandmother's. Remember what Mama said about it? Big porches and cool night breezes and lots of trees and a lake and a beach and swimming! We're gonna learn to swim and . . ."

While Dinah babbled, Charlotte stared toward the cavalry barracks off across the parade ground. If wishing could conjure it, there would be a blue uniform or two emerging from the doorway any minute and coming toward the trading post. Surely Sergeant Boone would say good-bye to her. If not Private Jackson, then certainly Sergeant Boone. *Please.*

Outside the stagecoach, Doctor Valentine bent to kiss Emmy-Lou on the cheek. "Give my best to your mother," he said. His embrace communicated what he did not say — *We are doing the right thing.*

Emmy-Lou echoed her husband's unspoken sentiment. "I know we are doing the right thing, Avery. I just feel like a fool when I've been writing letters singing the praises of Camp Robinson and giving Mother a hundred reasons why we can't possibly come back East." She looked toward the cavalry barracks. "It seems that Sergeant Boone could have at least come to say good-bye," she muttered.

"I expressly asked him not to," the doctor said. "He's busy finally moving the

401

last things out of his old quarters over on the Row so the O'Malley girls can live next door to Granny Max."

Emmy-Lou's eyes brightened. "Then there's hope. He's moving on."

Dr. Valentine took his wife by the shoulders and peered down at her. "What you hope for is impossible, Emmy-Lou. It never has and never will enter Sergeant Boone's mind." He shook her gently. "Move on, Emmy-Lou. Move on. Have a *wonderful* visit. I'll write you every day." He hugged her. "And I will miss you." He helped her step up into the stagecoach and, closing the door, peered through the window at his daughters.

He pointed to Dinah. "Don't go near the water until your mother has hired a swimming instructor."

He patted Charlotte's hand. "Don't go near any young men your mother doesn't approve."

He blew a kiss at his wife. "Don't forget I love you."

The stage driver laced the reins through his hands and, in a flurry of colorful language and slapping of reins, urged his team off. Dr. Valentine watched the stage until it was out of sight. On his way to the hospital to make his rounds, he was intercepted by Sergeant Boone.

"I wanted to talk to you about a . . . uh . . . delicate matter." The two men paused in the shadow of the hospital. "It's about Miss Gray. I know about the baby."

"She's told you?" Dr. Valentine made no attempt to hide his surprise.

"Not her," Nathan said. "Private Jackson told me."

"How on earth would Private Jackson know about this?"

"He deduced it from something you said day before yesterday in the stables." Nathan repeated the doctor's angry words back to him.

Dr. Valentine closed his eyes. *Thank God Charlotte and Emmy-Lou didn't make that connection. And thank God they are gone.* He looked at Nathan. "Is Jackson making trouble for Miss Gray now?"

"I would have handled that without bothering you," Nathan said, frowning. "Actually, it's strange. Apparently they've made peace."

"Really," Dr. Valentine said. "Well, I hope you are right, for Miss Gray's sake. But I don't have quite the faith you do in Private Jackson. He has a self-serving talent for explaining things so that he comes out looking like an innocent — or almost innocent — victim of even the most suspicious situation."

"I really wanted to talk about Miss Gray," Nathan said. He shifted his weight and tugged nervously on the brim of his hat. "Is everything all right with her? Her health, I mean."

"She's in excellent health," Dr. Valentine replied.

"It's a shame," Nathan said. "I'm just wondering what she's going to do now."

"You should be discussing this with her, Sergeant. I've made a few suggestions. I've offered to help. But it's up to her to decide."

"Just when she gets a start at a better life. It isn't fair."

"Life isn't fair, Sergeant. You of all people know that. But once again, I have faith that, between God and Granny Max, Miss Gray is going to be all right."

Nathan snorted. His voice dripped with sarcasm. "How could I forget? Granny can explain just what God is doing, and that will make everything turn out just fine."

"Or perhaps Miss Gray will follow another example she's had lived out before her," Dr. Valentine said abruptly. "Perhaps she'll curse God and spend the rest of her life reminding Him about the horrible mistake He allowed that ruined her life." He gave Nathan a pointed look and turned to go. "I hope you are right about Private Jackson and Miss Gray making peace. I deeply regret that my personal anger caused Miss Gray further troubles. I'll speak to her later today and offer my apologies." He walked away.

Feeling like a child just scolded by a parent, Nathan walked down to the Row and finished moving out of the apartment he and his wife had shared. He swept a few things — including Lily's Bible and garnet earbobs, the packet of letters, and the heirloom ring — into a pillowcase. Back at the barracks, he asked Emmet Dorsey to help him take over an empty trunk, which he then filled with the rest of his things.

While Boone and Dorsey were moving Nathan's things *out,* Private Harlan Yates was helping the women move the O'Malley girls *in.*

"I've taken what I need, Granny," Nathan said as he and Dorsey lugged his trunk out the front door. "Do what's best for the girls. I don't want anything else from here." He didn't stay to witness the change.

Unbeknownst to Katie O'Malley, during

the week after her mother's death, there was much discussion about the future of the O'Malley sisters, who had no family this side of the Atlantic Ocean. Granny Max ended the discussion, at least for the time being, by presenting herself at the post commander's quarters and making a very convincing argument for how fifteen-year-old Becky O'Malley was more than capable of taking up her mother's duties as laundress and that, between Becky and Granny Max and Miss Gray, the O'Malley girls would be all right.

"Mrs. O'Malley was quite ill for some weeks. Those girls have become like family for both Miss Gray and me," Granny Max said. "They love us and we love them. There's no need to send those girls away. I've been mammy to a whole flock of children since I was not much more than a child myself. There's plenty of love left in this old heart for Becky and Katie O'Malley."

"I don't doubt that, Granny," the commander said. "But the fact remains that a child should have an education, and Katie especially is of an age to take advantage of schooling if we can find a good placement for her. Dr. Valentine has mentioned a possible position with his mother-in-law. He said he and his wife are thinking of Dinah's remaining with her grandmother to attend a school in Michigan. The doctor has offered to investigate the possibilities for Katie. The girls are the same age. They might get along."

"Miss Gray attended a fine school in St. Louis until her fourteenth year," Granny replied. "She can teach Becky and Katie all they need to know. You can ask Dr. Valentine about Miss Gray's teaching. She was helping Dinah and Miss Charlotte learn French before they left on their trip."

When the commander wanted to know if Miss Gray might be willing to teach a morning school for any children at the camp whose parents might be interested, Granny Max was noncommittal. Once again, Josiah Paine was reaching into the future and taking things away from Laina Gray. Once it was known Laina was expecting a baby, no one would be sending their children to a school where she was the teacher. But Granny couldn't tell the commander about that. She could only promise to ask Miss Gray about the idea of a small school.

Granny Max's meeting with the camp commander didn't solve much. In fact, Granny thought later, it complicated matters. It was going to be hard to explain why Miss Gray couldn't teach a few children some basic skills. And it was going to be even harder to talk Dr. Valentine out of putting pressure on everyone to let Katie go back East to attend school with Dinah.

It just seems to me like things are getting harder, not easier, Lord. When are you going to let up on Laina Gray?

"You invited *who?!*" Granny Max exclaimed as they packed their Sunday picnic.

"Private Jackson," Laina replied, smiling at Granny's reaction.

"He's handsome," Becky O'Malley added.

"I don't like him," Katie said. "He kicked Wilber once."

"Well, he won't be kicking Wilber today," Laina said. "Wilber's big enough to bite his foot off if he tried it. Isn't that right, Wilber?" Hearing his name, the dog stood up and wagged his tail. He walked to Laina and thrust his nose into her hand and nudged it. "See how ferocious you are," Laina laughed, grabbing the big dog's snout in her hands and kissing him on the head.

Granny Max peered at Laina with a

question in her eyes. She lowered her voice so the O'Malley sisters couldn't hear her. "This wouldn't have anything to do with that little prayer meeting you told me about up at the cemetery would it?"

"It might," Laina said. "I just thought it wouldn't hurt to give him something to do besides playing cards. He said he'd come."

Granny nodded. "What's Private Yates going to think? They don't exactly get along, as I recall."

"He said he owes Jackson. Credits him for keeping him from breaking his neck that week they were all learning to ride. Harlan says Jackson hasn't had a fistfight in a long time."

"All right," Granny Max said. "He's not the first black sheep I've tried to get into the Lord's fold. And Lord willing he won't be the last. Does he like chokecherry pie?"

"No," Yates answered from the doorway. He nudged Private Jackson, who was standing next to him. "He hates it. Said I could have his share."

Wilber's ears went up at the sight of Jackson. He approached the uneasy soldier tentatively. Jackson backed away, his hands in his pockets.

Wilber stalked forward, a low growl sounding deep in his throat.

"Don't kick him," Katie warned.

"I've got no intention of kicking him," Jackson said. He swallowed. "But it looks like he's planning to have me for lunch." He looked at Katie. "You won't let him do that, will you?"

Katie shook her head. "Of course not." She walked to Wilber's side and put her hand on the dog's head. "It's all right, Wilber." She went to Jackson and held out her hand. "Shake. Show him you're friendly."

Pulling his fist out of his pocket, Jackson shook Katie's hand. Wilber stopped growling. "Come here, Wilber," Katie said. The dog marched forward slowly. Holding Jackson's hand, Katie encouraged the dog to sniff. "Friend," Katie said. Wilber sniffed. His tail moved slowly from side to side.

"Pet him under his neck first," Katie instructed.

Jackson obeyed and Wilber stretched out his neck and leaned against him. When Jackson's hand went from the dog's neck to his ears, and then down his broad back, all tension between man and dog relaxed.

"Whew," Jackson said. "That's the scariest introduction I've ever survived," he

410

said. "Except for maybe the time I met my first Yankee."

"Your first Yankee?" Katie asked. "Why'd you be afraid of a Yankee?"

Jackson grinned at her. "Cause they spoke a foreign language," he said. In his thickest Southern drawl, he added, "Y'all jus' don' know how hahd it is fer a southern chile tuh unnerstan' y'all."

Katie eyed him for a moment. "Can you teach me to talk like that?" she asked. "Laina knows French. I'd rather talk Southern. It's prettier." She added, "I was worried about you. You kicked Wilber once."

"I'm sorry," Jackson said.

Katie shrugged. "It's okay. He was barking at the horses. He shouldn't do that." She put her hand on Wilber's head. "Private Yates says you know about horses. Could you maybe help Laina and me teach Wilber to behave around horses?"

Jackson was quiet for a moment. "I could try."

Watching Jackson and Katie talk, Laina was reminded of Katie's helping her come out of her shell. It was good of the Lord to put children in people's lives, she thought. They were so much more open and honest about their thoughts. They could often break down barriers no one else could. *Thank you, God, for Katie O'Malley.* Her own baby moved. Yes, Laina thought. Children could be a blessing. She had to believe that. Even about her own. Even when it looked like an impossible situation.

Twenty

Wait on the Lord: be of good courage, and he shall strengthen thine heart: wait, I say, on the Lord.

Psalm 27:14

The stench of sweat and body odor rising from the pile of filthy uniforms and drawers on the floor opposite the washpot nearly knocked Laina backward. It was only four in the morning, but the air was still, and the August night was so hot Laina had given up on sleep and decided to tackle the day's laundry before the sun rose and the temperatures climbed even higher. Now, just inside the washhouse, she was having second thoughts.

She'd spent most of the night trying to soothe Katie to sleep. The freighters still hadn't delivered the mosquito netting Mrs. Gruber had ordered from Omaha, and the steaming summer nights on Soapsuds Row had become a long battle against the swarms of mosquitoes that seemed to find young Katie especially delicious. Granny had concocted a salve to ease the itching of some of the welts that covered her arms and legs, but Katie was still miserable.

Laina didn't have the heart to wake her to come help with the laundry. Even Granny Max had complained of feeling "frazzled and plumb wore out" yesterday. So here Laina stood, facing hours over pots of boiling water, when she already felt like she herself was boiling. The smells in the washhouse overwhelmed her good intentions. Inhaling sharply, Laina staggered back to the door and sat down abruptly, trying to catch her breath.

"What you think you're doing, child?"

Granny Max was headed toward the washhouse.

Laina sucked in a breath of stinking air. "Just trying to get a start on the day," she panted. "Before it gets too hot."

Granny sat down beside her. "It's already too hot for *you* to be doing this, honey-lamb." She patted Laina's shoulder. "I don't want you passing out and falling into a lye bath."

"And I don't want *you* wearing out, either," Laina protested. "You seemed so exhausted yesterday. *You* even complained about the heat, and that's not like you."

"Don't you worry 'bout me," Granny said. "I'll be all right." She looked behind her at the waiting uniforms. "I do wonder sometimes, though, at the great minds that dictated these men wear *wool* on hundred-degree days. Seems there ought to be a way to get around that." She sighed. "But I guess that's not a decision the army will be putting on its list of things to worry over in the near future."

Laina stretched and reached up to rub her neck. She felt a seam give way.

Granny heard the rip, too. She chuckled. "You can get to adjusting that other dress while I get to the laundry. Sounds to me like you need a little extra room."

"I didn't think it would happen this soon."

"Every woman's different, honey," Granny said. "It seems you are one that blooms early." She added, "And one whose nose gives her trouble."

Laina shuddered. "It's a wonder the soldiers didn't faint dead away when they were fighting that prairie fire. We'll never get those things clean. The way the wind blows all the time, it drives grit into every seam and crease. And now there's smoke, too." She raised her hand to her cheek. "I haven't felt really clean in a long time." She paused. Her voice lowered. "I'm sorry, Granny. I'm turning into a grumbler. Something you said the Lord just doesn't abide."

"Nathan says the men are in a state, too." Granny sighed. "That baseball game yesterday was supposed to get some of the grumbles out of them. And then they couldn't even play."

Laina shook her head. "I never would have believed anyone telling me a ball game had to be cancelled because the ball kept blowing away." She laughed. "All those fine ladies' parasols getting turned inside out."

Wilber came ambling up. He submitted to one pat on the head before slumping into the dusty pit he'd dug for himself just beside the washhouse door. He sighed deeply, looking up at Laina.

Granny laughed. "Even God's creatures are praying for a break in this heat." She put her hands to her knees and pushed herself upright. "Well, I guess there is no putting it off." When Laina started to follow her inside, Granny stopped her. "I meant what I said, child. I won't be responsible for your fainting, or Lord forbid, falling into the fire. You can't help what your nose can't stand." She smiled. "But you can rouse Becky and Katie and send them out here. Maybe we can get a load or two done before daylight."

As Laina walked the path back to the Row, she paused and looked up at the dark sky. She closed her eyes, imagining she could almost hear the heat waves rising from the earth around her. There was just no way to describe August at Camp Robinson other than miserable.

"Maybe you'll see some action after all, sonny," Emmet Dorsey said. He was sitting on a hay bale watching Caleb Jackson curry a horse. The men had been discussing the latest round of rumors from the Indian agency down south. Rumors that Dull Knife's band of Cheyenne — and maybe more than just Dull Knife's band — might soon defy the United States government and head north toward their home in the Powder River country.

Jackson nodded. "I'm ready." He peered over the horse's withers at Dorsey. "Just hope I can remember to load the right size shells in the Springfield."

Dorsey raised his eyebrows. Was the

young troublemaker actually making a joke about their altercation? He rubbed the knee Jackson had injured.

Jackson didn't look up. He seemed to be concentrating on a snarl in his horse's tail. But when Dorsey went to get up and the knee popped, the young private said, "Granny Max has a good liniment for that. I could bring you some."

"I don't need no nursemaid, sonny," Dorsey snapped. "And even iffen I did, it wouldn't be you."

"Suit yourself," Jackson said and untied the horse's halter to lead him into his stall.

Dorsey's grunt filled the air. "What's in it, anyhow?"

"I think she said something about grumble weed and graybeard," Jackson said. "Sounds like it was made just for you."

"Don't go to any trouble," Dorsey said and limped off.

That night Corporal Dorsey found a blue jar of vile-smelling grease on his cot. While he was rubbing it on his knee, Private Jackson walked by.

"Don't get any ideas about us being friends just because I'm trying this," Dorsey said.

"Who said anything about being your

friend?" Jackson retorted. "I'm just sick of hearing you grunt, that's all." He tossed Dorsey a small muslin bag tied with a piece of string. "Granny said you should make strong tea with that. Between the tea and the liniment, she claims you'll be winning footraces in no time."

"Well, that would be something," Dorsey said, tucking the bag in his shirt pocket. "Seeing as how I never could run worth a darn."

Laina turned onto her back and stared up at the ceiling of the room that used to house the Boones. She prayed for Katie, who lay at her side, her childish body wracked by an occasional shudder in her sleep, the remains of a long cry she had had in Laina's arms that evening. Wilber lay curled up by the back door, but the minute Laina lifted her head, he raised his. His tail thumped the floor. His ears came up.

Laina sat up, careful not to disturb Katie's sleep. She headed for the back door. It was the third time tonight she'd had to make this trip. Along with what Granny called "early blooming" and Laina's inability to abide certain smells, she was now "enjoying" frequent trips to the outhouse in the dead of night. She was thankful Granny Max was here to explain what was going on and to assure Laina "it's just part of growing a new life, child." Wilber followed her outside and then back into the kitchen.

In the kitchen, Laina pulled out a chair, grateful for the rug that muffled the sound. She looked down. *Lily Boone made that rug. Granny said they gathered rags for weeks and spent most of their first winter working on it.*

Being surrounded by Lily Boone's things made her uncomfortable, almost as if when she touched them she sensed Nathan's despair. It hadn't really bothered her to wear Lily's calico dresses. Laina wondered what was different now. Maybe it was being in the apartment the Boones had shared. It made her more aware of what Nathan had lost. And how lost he was.

She went to the front door and opened it, then stepped outside in her nightgown, looking off toward the cavalry barracks.

Granny's door opened. "Is Katie all right, honey-lamb?"

The familiar voice seemed unusually weary. "She's asleep," Laina said. "Get yourself some rest. It'll be dawn soon."

Instead of going back inside, Granny

Max stepped out on the porch. "It *is* a hot one tonight."

"I thought maybe there would be a cool breeze. But it's as still as can be," Laina said, settling down on the steps. Granny came to sit beside her, grunting a little as she lowered herself and leaned against one of the posts that supported the roof and created a porch across the front of the Row.

"Granny, I still don't know what to do. Time's running out. I have to decide whether to go or stay before this baby grows too much more." She took a deep breath. "I remember you reading something about how we should ask in faith believing. Maybe my faith just isn't strong enough for me to see God's answer. Sometimes I think maybe it's right in front of me, and I just can't see it." She sighed. "I think I'm beginning to understand a little bit of how Sergeant Boone feels. All questions and no answers."

"But what dear Nathan doesn't understand, Laina, is that sometimes it takes more faith to stay put and wait than it does to act out and demand answers." Granny reached over and took her hand. "If you don't have peace yet, wait on the Lord."

"Do *you* know what I should be doing?"

Laina said. "Do you know and you just aren't saying?"

"If I thought I knew what you should do, honey-lamb, I wouldn't hold it back." Granny Max took Laina's hand. "But the fact is, you can't always depend on me to tell you what to do. You've got your own faith. I've seen it growing."

"Well, it needs to grow faster," Laina said. "So I can be more like you. You're a rock, Granny."

Granny chuckled. "I been called a lot of things in my life. Never a rock. But I will take that as a compliment and tell you the only thing I know to do is what we've been doing. Keep praying and asking the Lord to show us what to do. He trusted this baby to you. I think you can be trusted to make the right decision."

"My head tells me a thousand reasons why it's better for the baby if I start over somewhere else. I could keep house for someone. Thanks to Frenchy Dubois, I can even *cook*. Or I could go to that place Dr. Valentine knows about. Either way, no one would have to know any details. They could assume I'm a widow, and that would change everything. It seems like a perfect solution. But when I think about actually doing those things, the old feeling of panic tears through me. The only thing I want is to stay here with you and Becky and Katie. But that doesn't make any sense. If I stay here, where everyone knows, what happens to *her?*" Laina looked down at her stomach.

"We funnel love to her. Love straight from heaven. So much love she can't keep it all in her," Granny Max said.

Laina leaned over and put her head on Granny's shoulder. "I don't *want* to go anywhere, Granny." She started to cry. "I can't imagine being anywhere without you and the girls."

"Then I have something to say to you," Granny said.

"What?" Laina asked, stifling a sob.

Granny wrapped her long arms around Laina. "Welcome home, honey-lamb. Welcome home."

Twenty-One

For as the heavens are higher than the earth, so are my ways higher than your ways, and my thoughts than your thoughts.

Isaiah 55:9

The weather broke the first week of September with a ferocious hailstorm that shredded trees down by the river and destroyed Frenchy Dubois's fall garden. The hail damaged buildings and broke windows over on Officer's Row. Private Yates needed an apprentice to help him manage all the repairs, and Caleb Jackson volunteered.

"What do you know about carpentry, Jackson?" Sergeant Boone asked when the private requested special duty to assist Yates.

"About as much as he knew about horses when he signed up for the cavalry, sir," was the answer.

"Is this agreeable to you, Yates?" Nathan asked.

Yates bobbed his head and grinned. "It is, sir."

"I thought you were sick of this greenhorn," Nathan asked Jackson.

Jackson shrugged. "I'm getting used to him."

"That doesn't mean you're going to want to take orders from him," Boone said. "We both know you sometimes have problems following orders."

Jackson nodded. "But we've settled our differences. And you'll notice I've stayed clear of the guardhouse, too."

"You telling me all your troubles are behind you?"

Jackson shrugged. "I'm just saying, sir, I'm doing my best to be a good soldier. And I'd like to learn a trade. Harlan and I get along. Carpentry makes sense. And there's a lot of work to be done." He looked at Nathan. "I need to keep busy, sir."

"Then get out of here and get to work," Nathan said abruptly. "I'll have to clear it with the lieutenant, of course, but as far as I'm concerned you can both consider yourselves excused from regular fatigue

425

duty in favor of making repairs around the camp."

Between the cooler temperatures, which seemed to have a positive effect on everyone's temper, and the time he spent with Harlan Yates, which kept him out of the canteen and away from the card tables and liquor, Caleb was keeping his promise to stay out of trouble. Dr. Valentine noticed and said he would consider forwarding a letter to Charlotte if Jackson kept it up for a while longer. Yates's increasing interest in religion didn't bother Caleb. In fact, as the days went by and the two men spent more time together, Jackson was surprised to realize he actually enjoyed Yates's company.

Granny Max seemed to have a special interest in Harlan Yates. Jackson didn't get it. The private was ugly as could be, and no one would ever accuse him of being intelligent. Yet Granny's face crinkled into a wreath of smiles every time Harlan Yates showed up. Jackson suspected it was no coincidence that Granny Max's roof got fixed first. Nor was he surprised when the first precious glass panes that arrived at Camp Robinson via a freighter from Ogallala found their way into Granny's windows instead of one of the officer's duplexes. And it wasn't long before Caleb realized that Harlan Yates had a deep and abiding crush on Miss Laina Gray. He was tempted to make merciless fun of Yates. But something held him back. The something was Miss Gray.

The more he observed her, the more Caleb was amazed by the ongoing transformation of the woman he had known as Riverboat Annie. When Laina confided in him her decision to stay at Camp Robinson and brave the inevitable judgment and gossip, Caleb's respect for her blossomed into admiration. One evening after a hop, he asked permission to walk Laina home.

"You've changed so much, no one back on the river would even recognize you, Miss Gray," he said. "They'd think maybe Annie had a twin or something. I've got to tell you I admire you for staying here. Putting myself in your shoes, I'd be worried to death. Shoot, I'd be choosing a new name and the next place to run to. You just seem to be calmly going about your life."

Laina objected, "Don't give me too much credit. I may be different from the girl you knew, but I'm still very human."

"So what's happened?"

"If you really want to know, this is going

to be a fairly religious talk and a longer one than we had that day at the cemetery. Are you sure you want to hear it?" When Caleb insisted he did, Laina did her best to tell him.

"I believe you," he said when she was finished. "But I still have questions."

Laina nodded. "So do I. I just try to keep learning."

"So how do you learn about these things?" Jackson asked. "We don't have a chaplain and there's no church services."

"Granny and the girls and I read the Bible together," Laina said.

"That's it?"

"That's it," Laina said. "We read and pray. Want to join us sometime?"

Caleb shook his head. "I don't think so."

"You ever change your mind, you're welcome. Does being on special fatigue duty mean you have more say about how you spend your time?"

"It means we have something to keep us busy," he said. "Something besides poker and trying to smuggle whiskey into camp." He hurried to add, "Of course, Yates was never involved in any of that. He's been a good guy since I met him."

They stepped up on the porch together. "Thank you for walking me home, Private," Laina said. "And thank you for the roof repairs and the new window panes." She teased, "I suspect there's a wife or two among the officers who doesn't think too highly of you at the moment."

Jackson shrugged. "From what I've been hearing, there's not a person here at Camp Robinson that hasn't benefited one way or another from knowing Granny Max. I don't think anyone is going to holler too loud when they find out just who we gave those first pieces of glass to. And besides, if they do, they can take it up with Sergeant Boone. He authorized it."

Laina nodded. "He would. He's always been loyal to Granny."

"Oh, it wasn't Granny he was thinking about when it came right down to it."

Laina frowned. "I beg your pardon?"

"All due respect, ma'am, you *can't* have forgotten everything Riverboat Annie knew about men. Don't you see him glaring at me every time I ask you to dance?" When she shook her head, Jackson said, "Good. Because you're a good dancer. And with my reputation, you're about the only woman left in camp that'll trust me — even for a dance."

Laina smiled. "You're fairly harmless from what I can see."

He leaned his head back and looked down at her from half-closed eyes. "I'm not sure I like you thinking I'm harmless," he said. "I may be trying to be honorable, but don't take it to the point of stupidity. You're a beautiful woman, Laina Gray. A man would be a fool not to take notice."

"I'm a pregnant woman, Private Jackson. A man would be a fool not to take notice of *that*." She spread her hands over her waist.

Jackson took her hands. "I don't have a right to say this, Laina. Not with my history. But some man, some day, is going to be very fortunate to have you as his wife. I don't mean me. You'll do lots better than me. I've got a feeling that God of yours is going to come through for you in a big way." He leaned down to kiss her on the cheek. That was when someone tackled him from behind and sent him spinning off the porch, face first into the dirt.

"You get your filthy hands off her!" Nathan Boone roared. He stood over Jackson, his fists clenched.

"What do you think you are doing?!" Laina charged him and hit him full force in the chest, knocking him backward and nearly putting him off balance.

"Defending you," Nathan said.

"When I need defending, I'll let you know!" Laina said, barely controlling her anger. "Were you *following* us?"

Nathan glanced away.

"You were! You were following us." Laina turned around and offered her hand to Jackson. "Are you all right?" she asked as he picked himself up off the ground.

"I'm fine," he said, dusting off his backside and bending down to get his hat.

"Get yourself back to barracks," Nathan ordered.

"This is absurd," Laina said.

"Well, it's going to get even more absurd if he doesn't obey orders."

"It's all right, Miss Gray," Jackson said when Laina opened her mouth to defend him again. "Sergeant Boone is right. You probably shouldn't be seen with me this time of night. At least not without Granny Max or one of the girls in tow." He put his hat on and nodded. "Thank you for letting me walk you home. I enjoyed our talk."

Saluting smartly, he spun on his heels and headed for the cavalry barracks.

Nathan reached for Laina's shawl, which had fallen to the ground when she charged at him. She bent down and snatched it up. "Thank you, Sergeant, but you've helped

431

me quite enough this evening."

"Are you . . . are you *interested* in him? Please tell me you aren't."

"I beg your pardon?"

"He was kissing you."

"He was kissing me on the cheek to say good-night. As a friend. Not that it's any of your business. And why do you care anyway?"

"Because I —"

Laina stepped closer. Her eyes blazing, she lit into him. "You listen to me, Sergeant Boone. I will never be able to repay you for what you did for me. Never. I know that. If I could think of a way, I would. But I can't. What you don't seem to realize is I'm better. You can go off duty now, Sergeant. I'm not crazy, and I don't need to be your project anymore."

"I know that," Nathan said. "I don't think of you that way."

"You *do*. You watch me at the hops like some brooding father-figure in the corner. You're always trying to make everything better. You can't *make* it all better, Sergeant Boone. Some things are just out of your reach. And I don't expect you to solve my problems. So, please, give yourself a break. Give *me* a break."

"I think I can solve your biggest

problem. That's why I was coming over here. I didn't follow you. I was up at the trading post playing cards."

"You don't play cards."

"Well, that's something else you don't know about me," Nathan said. "As a matter of fact, I do. From time to time. And tonight, when we were finished, I realized I don't even like playing cards. I just do it to fill time. And I've been thinking maybe there's a way to help us both. And so I came down here, and I saw Private Jackson, and I made an assumption —"

"A *wrong* assumption," Laina interrupted.

"All right. A wrong assumption. I'm wrong, and Private Jackson's turned into the precious golden boy of Camp Robinson. The demon turned archangel."

"You don't have to be sarcastic, Sergeant. Private Jackson's just like you. He's searching."

"And I suppose you're just the woman to satisfy the search," Nathan said.

Laina slapped him.

"I'm sorry. Oh, Laina. I'm —" He pulled her into his arms and kissed her.

She pushed him away and they stood, both of them breathing hard, staring at each other in the moonlight.

"Marry me," Nathan said.

"*What* did you just say?"

"I said marry me," he repeated. His voice was calmer, his breathing steadier.

"*That's* your solution to my problem?"

"Well, think about it. If you're married, then all your problems with the baby coming are solved. The baby has a family. You have a husband. And a home."

"I already have a home, Sergeant Boone. Right here with Granny Max and Becky and Katie."

"Are you telling me no?" Nathan asked.

He seemed so amazed, Laina felt her anger boiling up again. "Is that so unbelievable?"

"It doesn't make any sense," Nathan said. "I mean, it solves everything."

"For whom?" Laina wasn't letting him off the hook. "Tell me something, Sergeant Boone, just what does it solve for you?"

"I . . . I'm not sure I know what you mean."

"What do you get out of the arrangement?" She watched his expression. "I see. And how is that different from what I did for a living before the honorable Josiah Paine came into my life?"

"Surely you aren't suggesting —"

"No. But you are. You don't love me.

434

You've never loved anyone in your entire life but Lily Bainbridge. And to this day, you are still tied to her."

"My feelings for Lily are none of your business," he barked.

"Get away from me," Laina said.

He reached for her. "No. Wait. We can . . . we can make this work."

"Did you think I'm so helpless and so desperate that I'd just fall to your feet and bless you for saving this poor hopeless wretched woman?"

"Of course not. It's not like that."

"Well, then, how about you tell me what it is like? What were you thinking?"

"All kinds of people have good marriages based on friendship."

"Really? Name one."

"Doctor and Mrs. Valentine."

"Is that what you want? You want a life like Doctor Valentine's?"

"A person could make it work. If they wanted to."

"Well, I don't want to."

"Look," Nathan pleaded. "This isn't the way I meant for this to happen. You think I just blurted that out. All right. I did. But I've been thinking about it ever since I found out about the baby. I've respected your wishes, and I haven't said anything.

But —" When he spoke again, his voice was calmer. "It would work. We could make it work. I like you, Laina. Really, I do."

"And I like you. Which is exactly why it would never work. You may be content with half a life. Half a love. But I'm not."

"Well, maybe you should be," Nathan said abruptly. "Maybe you should be grateful for what God's put in front of you, and stop daydreaming about the impossible."

Laina nodded. "Thank you for the advice, Sergeant."

"Hey. I didn't mean that the way it sounded." He reached out to her.

She waved her hand in the air and backed away from him. Hot tears were stinging her eyes, but she didn't want him to see how deeply his remarks had cut. "Actually, I think you did. And that's exactly the reason I have to say no. I'll never be anything to you, Nathan, but a rehabilitated version of that creature who came at you from beneath the trapdoor in Josiah Paine's dugout."

"That's not true. You . . . you've turned into someone amazing."

Laina smiled and shook her head. "Look, I've done all right. With a lot of help from my friends. And you are one of those friends. Goodness, Nathan, you've gone so far as to offer to mortgage the rest of your life just to help me out."

"We'll learn to love each other," Nathan said again.

Laina nodded. "We could. We already have in some ways. But I repeat: part of you — most of you, I fear — will go to your grave as Mr. Lily Boone. I don't know if you can help that or not. But the fact is, I don't see any evidence of you being willing to even try to love someone else. I'm not willing to live with a man who married me just to be the savior of the downtrodden. If that sounds harsh, I'm sorry. But it's the truth. That's why you'd be doing it, Sergeant Boone. And when you cool off, you'll know it."

"You really are turning me down, aren't you?"

"Yes, Sergeant Boone, I am. And with — as Corporal Dorsey would say — all due respect."

"Well, then," he tipped his hat, "I guess that's it."

"Can we still be friends?" Laina asked.

He laughed. "You're the only woman I know who would turn down being my fiancée and ask to still be my friend."

"Well, maybe that's why God put me in your life," Laina said. "Maybe you need a woman with the guts to say no to you once in a while."

He nodded slowly. "I'll think on that one. You think on the proposal. The offer stands if you change your mind."

"You sound like you're making a deal to buy a horse," Laina said.

He closed his eyes and shook his head. "I think I'm going to quit before I make you mad again," he said, rubbing his cheek as if it still stung. "Good night, Miss Gray."

"Good night, Sergeant Boone."

Are you out of your mind? How could you say no?

He doesn't love me.

Look at him. Are you blind? Half the women at Camp Robinson practically swoon when he walks by!

He doesn't love me.

So he learns to love you. Later. Or even if he doesn't, he'll provide for the baby. He was right, you know. Marrying him would solve all your problems.

But he doesn't love me.

He'd be a great father. I bet he'd dote on a little girl.

438

He doesn't love me.

And who ever promised a man would love you? Look at yourself. Look at that scar. The minute you tell them about your past, they'll all run screaming the other way. Nathan knows about all that and he still proposed. He's willing to give you a home. You've been praying about this for weeks. God sends you the perfect answer, and you turn him down. You know what I think? I think you are *crazy.*

God didn't send this answer.

Right. How can you say that? Because Nathan doesn't love you?

Because he doesn't love God.

Laina Gray second-guessed her refusal of Sergeant Nathan Boone on an hourly basis the day after their encounter. But as she thought and prayed over the next few days, she grew more confident. Gradually, she stopped questioning her refusal and began to really believe she had done the right thing. It would have been logical to marry him, but it wouldn't have been right. Somehow, Laina knew. One of the things that confirmed the rightness of her decision lay in the fact she didn't feel the need for Granny's approval. From somewhere deep inside came faith to trust in things not seen — without first discussing it with Granny Max. God had a plan. He had a purpose. Laina clung to the truth in spite of logic. *"Faith isn't always logical, honey-lamb,"* Granny Max had once said. Laina had gained a new appreciation for just how right Granny was.

Twenty-Two

Precious in the sight of the Lord is the death of his saints.

Psalm 116:15

The first time Doctor Valentine had warned Granny to be careful was about a year after Lily Boone died. Granny hadn't exactly gone to the doctor for attention. He'd discovered her plopped down in a corner in the washhouse clutching her chest and insisted she let him check her over. "Clara Maxwell, I don't like the sound of your heart. It seems to skip a beat every now and then, and it isn't as strong as it should be. You need to slow down."

"When the Lord wants me to slow down, I expect He will let me know," Granny Max had said.

"Maybe He is letting you know through me," the doctor replied as he took the

441

stethoscope from around his neck.

"I don't think so, Doctor Valentine," Granny said. "I think His voice on this subject is much more definite than that."

"Oh, really?" Doctor Valentine said.

Granny nodded. "When He wants me to slow down and stop feeding His lambs, I expect He'll just swing down with one of His chariots and carry me home." She hadn't mentioned feeling poorly to anyone again. She'd tried to rest a little more and had asked for help hauling water and washtubs more often than in her younger days. But she hadn't had any more "attacks" of pain worthy of mention. She'd just continued working and fulfilling her calling to feed God's lambs.

On the night of September 9, 1878, a chariot was sent from heaven to collect Granny Max. She was sitting in her rocking chair reading her Bible by lamplight when she was overwhelmed by the urge to just lean her head back and close her eyes for a minute. And that is where Laina Gray found her, well before dawn the next morning.

Laina assumed Granny was sleeping. "Oh, Granny," she scolded, "let's get you to bed." The hand Laina touched was cool.

Laina leaned her head down to listen for Granny's heartbeat, but her own heart was racing so hard she couldn't be sure if she heard it or not. She tore out the door, across the trail, past the infantry barracks, and down Officer's Row to the Valentine quarters. She pounded on Doctor Valentine's door and begged him to come to Granny's apartment.

Together, they ran back. Together, they moved Granny to her bed. Together, they sat at her table for a long time before either of them said a word.

"You said it was her heart," Laina said.

"She was having some early signs of trouble. I advised her to slow down over a year ago."

"She never said anything," Laina choked out. "All those nights I kept her up — and she never said a word." She bowed her head and let the tears spill down her cheeks.

Doctor Valentine patted her hand. "If you hadn't been here, it would have been someone else. Granny Max had an inherent need to nurture others. That was her gift. And *slow down* was not in her vocabulary. It was just her time. There's no need for anyone to go blaming themselves." He paused. "There really is no

443

better way to die than to wear yourself out loving and serving other people. Granny Max died a happy woman."

Laina nodded. After a moment she said, "Poor Private Yates is going to wish he'd never shown a talent for carpentry. It's going to break his heart to make this coffin." She sighed and looked around her. "This is impossible. It *can't* be true. How am I going to tell Becky and Katie? And Sergeant Boone." She swallowed hard. "He's going to be devastated."

Doctor Valentine nodded. "I'll come with you. Becky and Katie are young. And they have each other. Grief is a lighter load when shared." He smiled warmly at Laina. "I know your head is swimming with questions. I just want you to know you won't have to find the answers alone. I hope you'll allow me to be of service in the coming days."

Laina sighed. "I'm numb. I can't even think. This changes . . . everything." She spread her hand over her abdomen. "Everything." She shook her head. *What now, Lord? What next?*

The doctor patted her shoulder. "This must feel overwhelming. But take one thing at a time. Right now, that's Katie and Becky. And Sergeant Boone."

Laina nodded. She inhaled sharply. "All right." She got up. *Lord. Help. Katie. Becky. Nathan. Help. Help me. Please. Help me.*

Laina opened Lily Boone's trunk. Reaching for the blue silk ball gown, she hesitated. From behind her, Nathan said, "It's the best use possible. Do it. Use them both. I'll get Mrs. Gruber to come down and help you."

Laina rose and carried the ball gown into the kitchen. She had Granny's sewing scissors in her hand, but something made her hide them behind her back. *Wait until he's gone.*

Nathan was kneeling beside Katie, who was sitting on the floor crying. Wilber had come inside to lay beside her and was giving mute comfort, his massive white head in her lap. Nathan put his hand on Katie's head and rumpled her hair gently. "Things are going to be all right, Katie. I promise. Don't you be afraid. You hear?" Katie looked up at him. She sniffed and nodded.

He rose and turned around to nod at Becky, who was just coming into the kitchen with Lily's red ball gown in her arms. He repeated the same promise. "Things will be all right, Becky. We'll work it out. I don't want you to worry about anything."

Out of the corner of her eye, Laina saw him pause at the doorway. She tucked the scissors beneath her apron.

"We'll need to talk," he said. "Later."

Laina nodded.

He seemed to have more to say and stood for a long time just staring at her. Finally he cleared his throat. "After I talk to Mrs. Gruber, I'll get Yates started on the coffin."

"You might ask Private Jackson if he'd want to help," Laina said.

"I'll be helping Harlan," Nathan said. His voice was strained. "We won't need anyone else."

"It's not a question of you needing the help," Laina said quietly. "It's a question of Private Jackson needing to do it." She looked down at the dresses for a moment before adding, "He and Granny have had some good talks lately. I think he might feel better if he helped."

Nathan seemed to be about to protest.

"Please," Laina said. "Just ask him."

"Whatever you want," he said, and he turned to go.

Becky and Mrs. Gruber and Laina worked in silence, cutting the skirt of the blue gown away from the bodice, snipping seams, undoing the work of some long-ago dressmaker to create straight panels of the exquisite Prussian blue silk. Katie rose from the floor. Sniffing, she demanded to help. Laina paused, thought, and then handed her the red gown. "Mrs. Gruber and I are going to do Granny's hair." Her voice wavered. "You and Becky work together and make a pillow cover." She handed Katie her needle and thread.

Privates Yates and Jackson, along with Sergeant Boone, arrived with the casket. Laina suggested to Nathan that Doctor Valentine direct Granny's graveside service. Nathan thought that would be fitting and went to ask him. Laina heard assembly and roll call sound while she and the others worked on the casket lining. By morning fatigue call, the casket was lined, the body was ready, and the women led the funeral procession as it wound its way down to the bridge, across the White River, and into the Camp Robinson cemetery.

"She fought the good fight. She kept the faith."

"She loved me when no one else did."

"She made the best corn bread I ever ate."

"She held me when I cried."

"She gave me a home when my mother died."

"She sang."

"She always read the Bible before starting her day."

"She didn't put up with gambling or drinking."

"She made sure I sent money home."

"Because of her, I know how to love."

"Because of her, I know how to make a home."

"Because of her, I pray about everything."

"Because of her, I value the Bible."

"Because of her, I've stayed out of trouble."

"Because of her, I know Christ."

The good about Clara "Granny" Maxwell would long be spoken of and long be carried in the hearts of those who knew her and in the lives of those who listened when she gave advice.

When the doctor opened Granny Max's Bible as they stood at the graveside, two envelopes fluttered to the ground. Katie picked them up and handed them to Laina, whose eyes filled with tears when she saw Granny's tiny handwriting on them. One was addressed to her, the other to Nathan. From where he was standing behind her, Sergeant Boone must have seen the names. He put his hand on her shoulder and stepped closer. She tucked the envelopes into her apron pocket, gleaning comfort from Nathan's closeness.

"Granny Max had a prodigious knowledge of the book in my hands," the doctor said. "I wish there were some way to know what she would say to us today if God allowed her the opportunity. But as He has not, I have chosen for her. Granny Max was, above all, a gifted comforter of souls. Every single person standing here has, at some time in their stay at Camp Robinson, benefited from Granny Max's gift of mercy. She would want us to be comforted. She would share something from God's Word, not as some potion where the reciting of the words would fix everything, but as something that had become a part of her life. We saw God's Word become flesh in Clara Maxwell's life. May we continue her legacy by taking this message to our hearts."

Then Dr. Valentine began to read, " 'But I would not have you to be ignorant, brethren, concerning them which are asleep, that ye sorrow not, even as others which have no hope. For if we believe that Jesus died and rose again, even so them also which sleep in Jesus will God bring with him. For this we say unto you by the word of the Lord, that we which are alive and remain unto the coming of the Lord shall not prevent them which are asleep. For the Lord himself shall descend from heaven with a shout, with the voice of the archangel, and with the trump of God: and the dead in Christ shall rise first: Then we which are alive and remain shall be caught up together with them in the clouds, to meet the Lord in the air: and so shall we ever be with the Lord.'

"If Granny Max were able today, I feel certain she would tell us not to sorrow for her. She would remind us to have hope, and she'd likely be angry with us if we made a big show of grief over her home-going."

Laina reached down and took Katie's hand.

Dr. Valentine continued. "This passage of Scripture promises us that we can see Granny Max — indeed, all of our loved ones — again. The promise is for all who believe that Jesus died and rose again."

Looking up at Dr. Valentine, Laina met

his gaze and nodded. She could almost hear Granny Max saying *"Amen, brother."* She wondered if the man standing behind her was listening.

"So the best way for those of us who respected and loved Clara Maxwell to honor her life, is to ask ourselves if we believe. If we believe, then we must not sorrow as others who have no hope. If we do not believe, certainly hopelessness is an appropriate response to this loss, for there is no hope apart from Christ. Let us ponder that reality in honor of Granny Max and the Christ she served.

"The passage of Scripture I have read provides the best conclusion possible for our memorial of Clara Maxwell. It says — because if we believe Jesus died and rose again, we shall also rise again, because Christ is coming back for us, because the dead in Christ *shall* rise, because one day we shall be with the Lord *forever,* never again to be separated from those we love — 'comfort one another with these words.' "

Doctor Valentine paused and looked at the crowd gathered around Granny Max's grave. "Let us pray," he said, and began to lead the group in the Lord's Prayer.

At some point during the prayer, Sergeant Boone stepped to Laina's side and took her hand. When the prayer was finished and people opened their eyes, they seemed to take Nathan's holding Laina's hand as a kind of signal, and in a moment or two everyone was holding hands. Laina began to sing. Others joined in. "I looked over Jordan and what did I see, comin' for to carry me home. A band of angels comin' after me, comin' for to carry me home."

When the song was done, everyone hesitated. Laina closed her eyes and swallowed, choking back the sobs of mingled joy for Granny Max and the sadness for herself that threatened to conquer her self-control. Finally, after Dr. Valentine handed Granny Max's Bible to Laina and took his leave, the small group began to break up and head back toward the bridge. Only Privates Yates and Jackson lingered behind, waiting to fill in yet another grave.

Sergeant Boone kept hold of Laina's hand. She held out Granny's Bible. "You should have this."

"You keep it," he said, stepping forward and crushing the book between them as he wrapped his arms around her. "I'm so sorry about this, Laina. I . . . I hope you know . . . I loved her, too." His body shook as he gave way to his own tears. For a moment they stood together crying.

A soldier came running from across the river. "You're wanted at the commander's office, sir. Big news from down South."

Nathan smiled sadly and left.

Laina looked across to where Yates and Jackson waited, clearly feeling awkward about the scene they'd just witnessed. "I hope you'll both come by this evening," she said to them.

"Mrs. Gruber took Katie and Becky back over to the Row. Said there was some things needed cleaning up," Yates said.

Laina nodded. "Yes. The fabric from . . ." Her voice wavered. She shook her head, swiped away a tear, and forced a smile. Looking from Yates to Jackson, she said, "Thank you for all you've done."

Yates bobbed his head. "Granny was a good woman."

"As good as they come," Jackson added. He looked at Laina. "I'll walk you back to the Row if you'd like." When Yates looked at him in surprise he said, "I mean, if you don't want to be alone, that is."

"Thank you," Laina said. "I'd like that. Very much."

Stabbing the loose earth with his shovel, Jackson offered his arm. He looked at

453

Yates. "I'll be back to help. Don't kill your-self shoveling."

Yates nodded.

Together Caleb and Laina walked toward the bridge.

"I never heard a service quite like that before," Jackson said as they walked along. "I mean, preachers always read the Bible and all, but Dr. Valentine sounded pretty convinced he was reading something special." He cleared his throat. "I never thought about things like that as much more than just 'pie in the sky.' You really think you're going to see her again?"

"I really do," Laina said.

"You think that Book is more than just some wise sayings?"

"It's not a great leap of faith to go from believing there is a God to believing He could write a book and protect its message for a couple thousand years or so. What's a thousand years to the God of the universe?"

Caleb was quiet for a while. They were almost at Granny's front door when Wilber came bounding up out of the brush beside the creek to greet them. Jackson patted his head. "Well, you take care."

"You come for coffee tonight, all right?" Laina said.

"As long as Sergeant Boone allows it, Yates and I will be here." He headed back toward the cemetery.

Katie and Becky and Mrs. Gruber had finished straightening Granny's apartment. There was no sign of blue or red silk, and Mrs. Gruber was urging them all to come to the trading post. "We'll make a lunch and find out what the commander told Sergeant Boone." Mrs. Gruber smiled down at Katie. "I might even be convinced to give that pony you call a dog a special treat," she said. "And at least we'll be together." She blinked back tears. "I just can't quite grasp it."

Laina looked around the room. "I keep waiting for Granny's voice to say something wise and wonderful, to tell me what to do next." The minute the words were out, she smiled. Through her tears, she said, "But I know what she'd say. She'd just say 'Do the next thing, honey-lamb. Just do the next thing.'"

"And what would that be, Miss Gray?" Mrs. Gruber asked.

"Making lunch," Laina said. Laying Granny's Bible down on the table, she led the way to the trading post.

Twenty-Three

Behold, thou desirest truth in the inward parts.

Psalm 51:6

Katie and Becky had gone to bed and Laina was sitting up drinking tea with Nathan Boone when she opened Granny's Bible and took out two small envelopes. She placed the envelopes side by side on the tabletop so Nathan could see the cramped handwritten names on each one. *Laina. Nathan.*

"Dr. Valentine said he'd warned her to slow down over a year ago," Laina said.

Nathan nodded. Laina saw his jaw clench as he reached for the letter. "I'll read it later," he said. "Have you read yours?"

Laina shook her head. "As long as I don't read it, there's still a way to hear her voice. Something to look forward to." She ran her index finger across the letter penned by Granny Max's hand.

Nathan nodded. He tucked Granny's letter inside his jacket. "You going to be all right?"

"I think so," Laina croaked. She covered her mouth with her hand and closed her eyes, fighting for control of her emotions. "Just when I think I've cried all I can, it washes over me again."

"Maybe you and the girls should have stayed next door," he said, looking around him. "It can be terrible looking at all the things your loved one touched and held. The cup she drank out of. The quilt she made."

"I wondered what that would be like," Laina said. "So far for me, it's comforting being surrounded by Granny's things. Becky and Katie said that, too. They wanted Granny's quilt on their bed." She sighed. "I don't know how to explain it. It's like she's still here, in a way." She could feel tears gathering again beneath her closed eyes. She swiped them away. "I thought we might read the letters together," she said. "Kind of our own private memorial."

"I don't have to read my letter to know

what it says," Nathan said. He pulled it out of his pocket and held it up. "It says I shouldn't be bitter. It says I should trust God." He looked over the top of the envelope at Laina. "It probably says I should think about marrying again. And although I doubt she actually wrote your name, you're the one she'd have been thinking about when she wrote the letter." He tapped the corner of the envelope on the table. "If you want to read yours, you go ahead. I'll wait."

Laina shook her head. "It's all right." She got up. "You'll be wanting to get back to the barracks. Is it true what I heard? That there's a band of Cheyenne headed this way?"

Nathan nodded. "Dull Knife and some others. They never really settled in down South. Couldn't seem to get along with the tribes already there. Doctor Valentine said the doctor at that agency is one of his old war buddies. He's written Doc about it. He's supposed to take care of five thousand Indians, and he'd had nothing but delayed supplies and other troubles. The northern tribes, especially, aren't doing very well. They've never had to handle the heat and humidity. They've had malaria, measles, ague." He shook his head. "Can't blame them for wanting to come home. I can imagine the Powder River country sounds like heaven to a warrior boiling under an Oklahoma sun."

"But it's cooler down there now," Laina said. "Won't that make a difference?"

Nathan shrugged. "It could. Or it could just make them more desperate to get up north before snow falls. Captain says there are a lot of other problems besides the sickness. I guess they're starving half to death. Like I said, I can't blame them for wanting to come back North."

"Why can't that be allowed?" Laina asked.

"Probably because the people making the decisions aren't making decisions based on *people*. They just see a *problem* to contain. Not people to care about."

"How do you see it?" Laina asked softly. "As a problem or people?"

"All I know is we're being put on alert. Captain doesn't seem to think we'll have to get involved at all. It's expected they'll all be rounded up and returned to the agency before long. They're crossing the plains, in unfamiliar territory. No place to hide. And they can't travel very fast with their women and children and old folks along." He smiled at Laina. "Nothing to worry about."

He scooted his chair back and stood up. "You get some rest," he said.

She nodded. "I'm fine. You take care." As he turned to go, she said, "We should still do the Sunday picnic. It's getting cooler. There won't be many more Sundays when we can." She shrugged. "I don't feel like it, but . . ." She looked behind her toward the back room where Katie and Becky were sleeping. "It's reassuring if some things stay the same." She looked up at him with a question in her eyes. "Do you think?" She felt the baby moving, and with that quivering deep inside, she began to tremble.

"Hey," he said. "Hey. Come here." He pulled her into his arms.

Laina relaxed against him and let another wave of grief wash over her.

When she was quiet, he released his grip and, looking down at her, said, "I'll ask Frenchy to make something for a picnic lunch. You try sleeping a little later than usual." He lifted her chin. "You hear?"

She nodded.

He touched the tip of her nose lightly and smiled down at her. "We'll be all right."

After Nathan left, Laina reached for her envelope. There was no good reason to

wait. She needed to hear Granny's voice —
now.

Dear Laina,

*I can imagine Dr. Valentine saying
he was right — I should have slowed
down. And I imagine you wondering
what to do now. When I thought
about writing these letters just in case
something happened, I imagined
putting all kinds of advice in them.
Things I've wanted to say but didn't.
But the fact is I've no right to try to
take the Lord's place in your life and
guide your future. These past weeks I
have wondered just as much as you
what the Lord was doing. And I will
tell you that I was none too happy
with Him expecting you to raise a
child by yourself. Maybe it won't be by
yourself. But you've got to be prepared
to do that. In the end, we all just have
to rest ourselves in the everlasting
arms of the Good Lord and do the
next thing, all the time believing. You
have been one of the sweetest lambs
the Lord has brought me, Miss Laina,
and He's brought me a good flock of
lambs in my day.*

You talk to the commander about

461

staying on at Camp Robinson. He's a good man, and you and Becky are hard workers. He won't send you off without a place to go to. If you want to go to that place Dr. Valentine knows, I hope you will take Katie and Becky with you. But in my heart I hope you stay and watch over Nathan for me. Give him time, Laina. I think he will finally come to healing and some kind of peace, if he only has someone around him living the love. You could be that person for him. I have prayed it might be so.

The best advice I can give you for life, Laina, is written inside my Bible cover.

Never forget, honey-lamb, YOU ARE LOVED.

I will be waiting to welcome you. Give your little darling extra hugs and kisses from her Granny Max. Maybe you will tell her about me.

On Sunday morning, in spite of Sergeant Boone's advice that she try to sleep later than usual, Laina woke with a sense of urgency. She sent Wilber outside. Quickly, she made a batch of flapjacks for Becky and Katie while she downed a cup of coffee. Leaving the flapjacks wrapped in a towel on the stove, she dressed and headed off toward Officer's Row, where she let herself in at the Valentines' back door and set to making breakfast for the doctor.

He appeared in the kitchen, slightly rumpled and not a little surprised. "Miss Gray? I didn't expect you this morning. I can fix my own breakfast, you know. You shouldn't feel obligated to —"

"I don't feel obligated, Dr. Valentine. I've got to get some things settled, and I've come to ask your help."

"Give me a moment to wash up," the doctor said. "I'll be right back." He smiled at her. "That coffee smells good."

When Dr. Valentine was settled at the table enjoying scrambled eggs and biscuits, Laina sat across from him. "I need to talk to the commander, and I'm hoping you'll go with me," she said. She outlined her plan, and as soon as the doctor was finished with breakfast, they rose to go.

"I apologize for interrupting your Sunday morning, sir," Laina said as she sat down. She felt nervous, sitting across the massive desk from the uniformed stranger. Of course, everyone at Camp Robinson *knew* the commander, but officers and enlisted men led completely separate lives in the military. Laina had only Granny's encouragement that the commander was "a kind man" to still her pounding heart.

"I . . . I've asked Dr. Valentine to come with me as a sort of character witness," she began. She stopped and swallowed. "Look, sir. I know it isn't considered very polite to really say what a person means. People tend to talk *around* situations more than they talk *about* them." She glanced from the commander to Dr. Valentine. "At least, that's been my experience." She clasped her hands together. "But I'm going to beg your forgiveness this morning and . . . Well, I'm going to be as honest and open about some things as I can be." She stared into the commander's gray eyes, looking for some encouragement, some inkling of a smile. When none appeared, she launched a one-word prayer. *Help.* Taking a deep breath, she told her story. She told the commander everything. About her past, about the dugout, about her changed life.

When Laina paused, the commander leaned forward. "Why are you telling me these things, Miss Gray?"

"Because with Granny Max's and Mrs. O'Malley's deaths, Katie and Becky and I no longer have any association with the military that would officially allow us to stay here. But we all want to stay." She glanced at Dr. Valentine, who nodded encouragement. "It's the only life these girls know," she said. "And it's the only life I *want* to know. I'm hoping you'll let us stay on as laundresses."

"And Mrs. Valentine will certainly want Miss Gray's domestic help when she returns to Camp Robinson in the spring," Dr. Valentine added.

"I see no reason why you can't continue on here," the commander said. "Even if it is determined that you cannot continue as military employees, it would be unthinkable to send three women off toward Sidney until Dull Knife and the Cheyenne who left their agency are rounded up and sent back where they belong." He started to get up. "So, for at least the time being, you and the Misses O'Malley are quite secure in your positions here at Camp Robinson. Now, if you'll excuse me —"

"You need to know something else, sir. Rumors are going to be circling. I'll feel better if you know everything."

"Everything, Miss Gray?"

"I'm going to have a baby," Laina said.

The commander plopped back into his chair. He listened to her explanation and then looked at Dr. Valentine, who nodded yes when asked to confirm what had just been said.

"All I'm asking for is a new start. A chance to earn an honest living," Laina concluded.

The commander twirled the tip of his mustache thoughtfully. He looked from Laina to Dr. Valentine and back again. Finally, he spoke up. "You were quite right, Miss Gray, when you mentioned it isn't fashionable for people to be so candid about themselves." He chewed on his lower lip. "More's the pity," he said, and held out his hand. "I do appreciate your honesty. It took no small amount of courage to walk in here this morning. Even with the good Dr. Valentine as your champion." As Laina shook his hand, the commander said, "I won't be interfering with things over on Soapsuds Row." He stood up. "Now if you'll excuse me, I've got to see to the latest dispatches from General Crook." He nodded and showed them to the door.

"You're early, Private Yates," Laina said as she greeted Harlan. She waved him inside. "Becky and Katie have gone up to the Grubers' to see if they'd like to join us for today's picnic." She smiled at him.

"I'm glad to see Sergeant Boone told you we want to keep up the tradition." She looked past him. "Is Private Jackson coming?"

Harlan bobbed his head. "Yes'm. He'll be along directly. Said maybe this afternoon you could work some more with Wilber. With the horses, I mean. To teach him to behave hisself."

Laina nodded. "That's a wonderful idea." She pushed her hair back out of her face. "It'll give Katie something new to keep her mind off . . ." She sighed and shook her head. Handing him a knife and a loaf of bread, she said, "Thick slices, Private. And don't cut yourself. Granny just sharp—" Laina swallowed hard and blinked away the tears.

"Now, Miss Laina," Harlan said, laying down the knife and patting her awkwardly on the shoulder. "Don't you cry. Everything's going to be all right."

Laina put her hand over his and patted it. "Thank you, Harlan. I know. It's just so . . . fresh." She sighed. "It doesn't seem real. I keep expecting her to come in the back door."

Harlan nodded. "I expect that will be so for a long time to come." He cleared his throat. "The reason I come over early

467

was . . ." He looked up at the ceiling, then down at the floor.

"The reason you came over early was . . ." Laina repeated.

He dropped to one knee. "With Granny gone, Miss Gray, I know you must be wondering what to do. And I was thinking that if —" His voice cracked. He ducked his head. "Well, if you was married, that would solve everything. And we get along good." His face glowed red as he blushed and croaked, "Will you marry me, Miss Gray?"

Dumbfounded, Laina could only slide into the chair next to where Harlan was kneeling. He waited, awkwardly balanced on one knee, watching her. She leaned one arm on the table and, closing her eyes, rested her forehead on her open hand. She shook her head. "Oh, Harlan . . ."

He hopped up. "I know." His voice was miserable. "I was stupid to think you'd want to —"

"Harlan. You're a kind and generous and good man." Looking up, she took his hand. "A woman could do a lot worse than to be Mrs. Yates."

He shrugged. "A woman could do a lot better, too. I reckon."

"You don't love me, Harlan," Laina said

quietly. She squeezed his hand.

"I do," he protested.

"And I love you. If I had a brother, I'd want him to be just like you." She picked up the knife. "Now slice the bread. Here come the girls."

"It's no, then?"

"It's no. But thank you." Laina said.

With a sigh, Harlan picked up the knife and got to work.

It was as if Granny Max's death had opened the floodgates. Within the week after Granny's funeral service, Laina had received proposals from four soldiers. Becky O'Malley thought it was hilarious. "Don't get mad, Laina. When Papa died, Mama had someone propose to her *at the funeral*. You can't blame the men. They're lonely. The only reason you haven't had this happen before is Granny guarded you like a bear protecting her cub. Now that she's gone, the men just naturally assume you need a husband." She giggled. "The funniest one was that Corporal Dorsey." She grimaced. "Can you imagine cleaning up after a man who spits tobacco every twenty seconds?"

"Can you imagine *kissing* him?" Katie chimed in. She made a face. "Yuck."

"But he assured me he can hit the spittoon from clear across the room," Laina said, laughing. "What do you suppose those men would have said if I told them the rest of my story?" She patted her stomach.

"Harlan knows," Becky said. She blushed. "He told me after you turned him down."

Laina studied her expression. "Rebecca O'Malley! Harlan discussed proposing to me? With *you?* He talked about my baby? With *you?*"

Becky shrugged. "I told him it was all right to ask you."

"You did?"

"Well," she ducked her head. "Harlan and me . . . we sort of . . ."

"Yes?"

She grinned. "I knew you'd say no. He just needed to feel like he did the manly thing."

"But how does he know about the baby? Who told him that?"

"Nobody had to tell him," Becky said. "Harlan's got a gentle heart. He notices things. He figured it out. He said he wondered for a long time, but when you started letting out your dresses, that's when he was sure."

Laina took a deep breath. What a relief it was to have talked this over with the commander. What a blessing not to have to wonder what was going to happen when he found out. *Thank you, God.* It wouldn't be long before everyone would know. It was going to be an interesting winter.

"Laina!" Katie came tearing around the edge of the Row and skidded to a stop beside Laina, who was hanging laundry out to dry. "Laina! The Cheyenne. They're coming!"

"Calm down, Katie," Laina said. "Those rumors have been flying around camp for nearly a month now."

"Well, this time it's true!" Katie said. "Private Jackson was helping me introduce Wilber to some of the horses over in the corral — Wilber's getting real good about not chasing them — and Corporal Dorsey came up and said the Cheyenne had crossed the Kansas Pacific Railroad. And they escaped the troops again. And they been raiding and killing white people all over Kansas. And there's cavalry coming to Camp Robinson!" She paused, gasping for breath.

"Sergeant Boone said Camp Robinson

wasn't going to be involved. There's no reason for the Cheyenne to come here now that their agency's been moved," Laina said. "In fact, he was mighty upset about not getting in on the action."

"Well, he's not upset anymore," Katie insisted. "The lieutenant's ordered drills and inspections, and everything has to be perfect for Major . . . Major . . . oh . . ." Katie stomped her foot. "I *knew* I wouldn't remember his name."

"Calm down, Katie," Laina said. "Nothing you've said changes our jobs. We still have to keep the laundry done."

"But it's *exciting!*" Katie said, and tore off toward Gruber's trading post.

"What'll happen to Harlan?" Becky said from the washhouse doorway.

Laina looked over. Becky's face was flushed. Her eyes brimmed with unspilled tears. Laina closed her eyes. *What do I say?* She thought of Sergeant Boone and Corporal Dorsey, of Privates Yates and Jackson, all in the same tangle of fear.

"Get back inside and tend your washpot," she said to Becky.

"But, *Laina* . . ."

"You can't help Private Yates by worrying," Laina said. "But you can help by praying while you do the laundry." Becky nodded and went back inside. Laina was grateful the girl couldn't see how her own hands trembled as she went to hang up one of Private Jackson's shirts.

Twenty-Four

Therefore if any man be in Christ, he is a new creature: old things are passed away; behold, all things are become new.

II Corinthians 5:17

Katie O'Malley leaned on the lower rung of the corral and watched as Private Jackson and some other soldiers drove a herd of decrepit Indian ponies across the snow-covered ground and into the Camp Robinson corral. There were too many horses to all be corralled, but even Katie could tell from the condition of these animals that there would be no danger of them stampeding off somewhere. She ran to the stables and scooped a handful of grain. Running back to the corral, she made the same clicking sound she had heard Private Jackson make when he wanted to get a horse's attention. A pony's head went up. The little mare came over and practically inhaled the grain, then began whickering plaintively and bumping Katie's gloved hand.

"I'm sorry," Katie whispered. "I can't give you any more."

When Private Jackson dismounted nearby, Katie ran to him. "Wilber doesn't chase the horses anymore, see?" She pointed to where the giant white dog sat watching the horses mill around. "Laina and me been working with him the whole month you been gone."

"That's good, Katie," Jackson said. He headed for the stables.

Katie followed. "Did you see the Indians? Are they coming?"

"I saw 'em," Jackson muttered. "They'll be coming soon, I suppose. They don't have much choice." He pulled the saddle off his horse. Steam rose from the animal's back.

"How's Private Yates?" Katie asked. "Becky's been awful worried about him. You've all been gone so long."

"I haven't seen much of Private Yates," Jackson said. He grabbed a brush and began rubbing his horse down. "His battalion went one way, mine went another, most of the time."

"You think he'll be coming back soon?"

"Can't say. They're still trying to negotiate something."

"What's nego-shate?" Katie asked.

"That's when you try to get someone to do something they don't want to do," Jackson said. "The Cheyenne don't want to come to Camp Robinson. They want to go home — up north."

"So how do you nego-shate them to come here, anyway?"

Jackson closed his eyes and shook his head.

Corporal Dorsey rode up. "Orders are to ride back to Chadron Creek," he said. "Looks like there's gonna be a fight. And there's a storm brewing. Temperatures are dropping. Could be a big snow this time. We got to be ready to leave in ten minutes with fresh mounts." He climbed down.

"Hey there, little miss," Dorsey said. He unsaddled his horse and turned it loose in the corral. The half-starved Indian ponies ignored the unfamiliar horse and stood with their heads down. "Most pitiful lot of critters I ever saw," Dorsey said. A stream of tobacco stained the snow.

"We had to shoot over a dozen on the way here," Jackson said. He swore softly. "This isn't the kind of war I signed on to fight — I can tell you that. Women and children —" Glancing at Katie he stopped talking. He nodded at her. "You tell Becky I'll look out for Private Yates for her," he said. "And don't tell Miss Gray you heard me swear."

"And Sergeant Boone?" Katie asked. "Will you look after Sergeant Boone, too? 'Cause she don't say it, but I know Laina worries over him."

Jackson nodded. "Sure."

Calling Wilber to her, Katie trotted off toward Soapsuds Row.

Sergeant Boone dismounted and hurried toward the wagon filled with Cheyenne women and children. When a woman stumbled getting down and almost dropped her baby, he went to help her. She jerked away from him, muttering something under her breath and glaring at him with unbridled hatred. She joined the other women and children. The little girl he'd gotten to know as Lame Deer was among them. She smiled at him as she walked by.

With a twinge of sadness, he remembered the evening he'd met Lame Deer. He'd offered half his rations to a rail-thin Cheyenne child about Katie O'Malley's age and had been surprised when she thanked him in English and told him her name. When he saw her break the biscuit in pieces and share it with about four other children, he'd had to walk away to keep his emotions under control.

Looking at them, it was hard to believe they had crossed hundreds of miles of unfamiliar flatland and eluded the military for nearly two months. One of the troopers, who'd gotten involved in the chase earlier than Nathan had, told him that at least once the Cheyenne had traveled nonstop for three days. "Can you believe it?" the trooper had said, reciting statistics. "Ninety men, a hundred-and-twenty women, and even more children. And it took us all this time to catch up to them."

"The only reason we caught them when we did," Nathan said, "was because Dull Knife probably didn't realize Red Cloud Agency was moved after they left for Indian territory."

The other trooper had nodded agreement. "And we still don't have 'em all. Captain says they found signs that Little Wolf's band separated from Dull Knife down on Whitetail Creek. We'll be going after 'em." He had shivered. "I'm not looking forward to *that* ride."

Nathan felt a sense of relief that Company G was finally back at Camp Robinson with Dull Knife's band. They'd caught up with them in a driving snowstorm. If it was going to practically blizzard in October, he was glad he wasn't among the soldiers chasing farther north after Little Wolf. It made him shiver just to think about the cold days and nights in the saddle. He was glad they had brought a wagon out from Camp Robinson so the women and children hadn't had to walk in the snow.

Nathan felt ashamed. He'd heard more than one of these prisoners echo Dull Knife's sentiment, that it was better to die than to go back South. Some of them already looked half dead. He blocked it out. He'd gotten orders to round up two enlisted men to cook for the captives. If he had anything to say about it, Lame Deer and her young friends were about to be treated to some French-American cooking. As the last of the captives filed into the barracks, Nathan headed off to look for Frenchy Dubois.

I want to master this Book, so the Master of this Book can master me.
Sitting in Granny Max's rocking chair,

Laina reread the now-familiar quotation written on the inside cover of Granny's Bible. In her letter, Granny had said the best advice she could give Laina was written inside her Bible. This was it. Laina ran her finger along the neat row of printing. *I am trying, Granny Max. I am really trying.*

The baby prodded her back. Laina reached behind her to knead the aching away. She shivered and moved closer to the stove, wondering if the Cheyenne captives she'd seen coming in earlier that day were warm inside their barracks. She wondered about Sergeant Boone and Private Yates, Corporal Dorsey and Private Jackson. She'd taken to praying for them more often since they had left Camp Robinson. Now she longed to see them, to see for herself that they were all right.

Becky and Katie came in from the washhouse. Laina could hear them stomping snow off their shoes just inside the back door.

"Brrrrr!"

At first Laina didn't recognize the voice. When Private Jackson came in with the girls, she smiled and started to get up.

"Stay put," he ordered. "You look comfortable wrapped up inside that quilt.

Kind of like a sausage."

"Very funny," Laina said.

"A very cute sausage," he added, winking at Katie.

Laina shivered. "How cold is it, anyway?"

"You don't want to know," Jackson said. "Nobody in Jefferson Barracks told us about the mercury dropping like a stone in *October* out here."

"I don't think this is exactly normal," Laina said.

Jackson nodded toward the back door. "Your woodpile is shrinking. I'll get Yates to help me haul some more up to the back door for you. Sergeant Boone will let that be our morning fatigue duty if I ask."

"When did you all get back in camp?" Laina asked. "Can you eat with us? Can you ask Sergeant Boone and Harlan?" She smiled at Becky.

"We all rode in this afternoon with the wagon. Thanks, but I don't think Yates and I can eat with you. I can't speak for Sergeant Boone, but I'll tell him you asked. They're running things very close to the book these days," he said. "No regulation ignored." He slapped his hands together and held them up to the stove.

"What do you think is going to happen?" Laina asked.

"I don't have any idea. Last I heard, Washington was still saying they have to go back South. And Dull Knife was still saying they'll die before they do that." He paused. "But two good things will happen for the Cheyenne while they are working it all out. Regular rations — which I understand wasn't very common down at Darlington Agency. And a little freedom. Captain says they don't have to be locked up." He smiled. "Sergeant Boone introduced me to a little girl about Katie's age a little while ago — name of Lame Deer." He motioned toward Granny Max's Bible, still lying in Laina's lap. "You spending a lot of time listening to Granny Max's advice?"

Laina smiled. "Morning and evening. Or most mornings and evenings, anyway."

"How you feeling?"

"Good," Laina said. "Really good." She unconsciously reached behind her and rubbed her back.

"Good, except for your back is killing you?"

Laina shrugged. "Part of the territory, I guess. Mrs. Gruber says so, anyway."

"Lean forward," Jackson said.

"What?"

"Hey, Katie," he said. "Would you get Miss Gray a pillow to lean on? I guess she isn't quite as bendable as before." He chuckled.

Katie tossed a pillow at Laina, who took it and put it on the edge of the table. She crossed her arms and leaned forward onto the pillow while Jackson took off his buffalo coat. When Laina was settled, Jackson reached down inside the quilt and began to knead her lower back. "My mama used to make me and my brother rub her back when she was carrying our little sister."

It was the first time Jackson had ever mentioned his family. Laina wanted to ask about that brother and little sister. Instead, she said, "You're hired," as she closed her eyes and concentrated on the release of tension in her aching muscles.

"I already have a job," Jackson replied. "Hauling wood, cleaning stalls, hauling more wood. I expect I'll get the astoundingly fascinating job as sentry inside the barracks with the Cheyenne, too."

"Won't you be afraid?" Katie asked.

Jackson shook his head. "Dorsey did some guard duty up in Minnesota back in '62. He said to expect the men to play cards and smoke while the women do beadwork and make moccasins. Which reminds me," he said, nodding at Katie. "If you'll check the pockets of my coat, there's a couple of packages for you ladies."

Squealing with delight, Katie pounced on the coat and withdrew two packages wrapped in brown paper. She ripped one open and found a pair of moccasins for herself and one for Becky.

"I traded with Lame Deer's mother. I gave her blankets for those," Jackson said. "There's a pair for you, Miss Gray, in the other package." He began to massage her shoulders with both hands.

"You don't have to —"

"Be quiet," Jackson snapped. "I haven't been this close to a warm stove in a long time. This is entirely a self-serving exercise," he said. "So just hush and suffer while I get my backside warm."

Katie giggled. Becky blushed.

"Sorry. I shouldn't have said that," he apologized.

"Do they need more blankets?" Laina asked. "Because we could send a couple. From Lily Boone's trunk."

"That'd be kind of you," Jackson murmured. "They don't have much in the way of blankets. It's always the women and children who suffer most, huh." After a couple minutes of quiet he said, "Well, I best be getting back up to camp. Sergeant Boone only gave me about three minutes to come over here and check on his women." He pulled on his coat.

"You look like a bear with that coat and that scruffy beard," Katie said. "We didn't even know you at first!"

Jackson tugged on his beard. He turned his head so the girls could see his profile. "I let it grow while we were out on patrol. Personally, I think I look rather like Lincoln. Wouldn't you agree?"

"Oh, not at all," Becky said. "President Lincoln wasn't nearly as handsome as you, Private Jackson."

Jackson grinned at her. His brown eyes twinkled. "And now, having finally garnered the compliment for which I was waiting, I shall depart." He bowed stiffly and headed for the door, calling back over his shoulder, "Firewood. Tomorrow."

"Thank you," Laina said.

"What's happened to *him?*" Becky said as soon as he was gone.

Laina shook her head. "I haven't any idea. But whatever it is, I think I like it."

Katie stood on tiptoe and pulled the last wooden clothespin off the line above her, pulling a pair of freeze-dried men's drawers down with it. They were so stiff they wouldn't bend, so she just laid them atop the stack of laundry in the basket at her feet. Wilber, who had been dozing in the sun, suddenly rolled over and raised his head. Ears alert, he thrust his nose into the air. He sat up, thumping his tail as he looked toward the creek. He started to get up, then held back, looking up at Katie and whining.

"What's there, fella?" Katie said, putting her hand on the dog's back and peering toward the creek. But Wilber wasn't looking toward the creek, after all. Katie smiled. "Why, hello there."

A Cheyenne girl about her age stepped out from where she had been hiding around the corner of the Row. She raised her hand in greeting. "Hel-lo," she said carefully.

Wilber stood up. The girl took a step back and pulled the blanket across her shoulders tighter. "Big dog," she said.

Katie glanced down at Wilber. "Yes. He's big. But he won't hurt you." She motioned to the girl. "His name is Wilber. You can pet him."

The girl looked doubtful.

"Come on," Katie said, motioning for the girl to step closer.

She shook her head so hard her long dark braids waved back and forth.

"You have pretty ribbons in your hair," Katie said, pointing to the blue-and-red bows adorning each braid.

"Soldier Jack-Son give," the girl said.

Katie nodded. "That's nice." She took Wilber's collar. "I'll hold onto him. Come say hello."

The girl took a step forward. Wilber wagged his tail. Finally, she extended one hand out of the blanket toward the dog. When Wilber thrust his snout into her hand she screeched with fear and snatched it away. But when Wilber nosed at the opening of the blanket and began to lick her arm, she giggled. Wilber kept licking, literally washing her arm until the girl began to pet him, smiling and cooing.

"My name's Katie." Katie pointed to the back door of Laina's apartment. "I live there." She pointed down at the basket of laundry. "We do laundry for the soldiers."

"Lame Deer," the girl said, pointing to herself. She pointed toward the pine-covered bluffs in the distance. "I live there." Then she gestured toward the barracks across the creek to the east. "Soldiers keep us there."

Katie nodded. "Maybe you'll get to go home soon."

The girl shook her head. "Great Father says no. Says we must go back to Dar-ling-ton." She said the word syllable by syllable.

"You don't like it there?" Katie asked.

"We die there," the girl said. She looked at Katie. "My father die there. My brother, too. Lame Deer and Brave Hand alone now."

"Brave Hand," Katie murmured. "Is that your mother?"

The girl nodded. Her stomach rumbled.

Katie smiled. "You hungry? I have to take this laundry inside." She motioned toward the door. "Laina's making lunch. You could eat with us." When the girl hesitated, Katie said, "You'll like Laina." Katie added, "My papa died, too."

"Soldiers kill white people, too?" Lame Deer asked.

Katie frowned. She shook her head. "Of course not. Soldiers didn't kill my papa. Indians killed him."

"Cheyenne?"

Katie shook her head. "No. Sioux."

Lame Deer made a fist and raised it to her chest. "Killing makes hurt here."

"Yes," Katie said, surprised when tears sprung to her eyes. She blinked them away.

Laina came to the back door.

"That your mother?" Lame Deer asked.

Katie shook her head. "No. My mama died, too. My sister, Becky, and I stay with Laina now." She called out to Laina. "This is Lame Deer. Can she have lunch with us?"

Laina smiled. "Of course."

"Jack-Son say you give us blankets," she said, smiling. "Thank you."

Laina nodded. "You are very welcome, Lame Deer." She motioned the girls inside. "Come in. I have flapjacks on the griddle."

Twenty-Five

But be ye doers of the word, and not hearers only, deceiving your own selves. For if any be a hearer of the word, and not a doer, he is like unto a man beholding his natural face in a glass: For he beholdeth himself, and goeth his way, and straightway forgetteth what manner of man he was. But whoso looketh into the perfect law of liberty, and continueth therein, he being not a forgetful hearer, but a doer of the work, this man shall be blessed in his deed.

James 1:22–25

"You shouldn't be making friends with them," Nathan said one November Sunday evening when he and Yates and Jackson had come over to the Row for dinner. "It's only going to make things harder when we have to move them. And they are going to have to go back South. Orders are orders."

Harlan Yates shifted his weight in his chair. "All due respect, Sergeant," he said, "I realize they can't stay here at Camp Robinson. But why do they have to go south? They're perfectly willing to go anywhere but there. It seems a reasonable request not to want to return to where you just sit and watch each other get sick and die."

"I was there when Dull Knife said 'You may kill us. But you cannot make us go back,'" Jackson said. "And I don't blame him for standing his ground."

"I don't blame him, either," Nathan said. "But I'm a soldier, and I'll do what I'm told. I'll try to do it in a way nobody gets hurt. But a soldier who won't obey orders isn't worth anything to his country."

"A soldier who harms women and children isn't worth anything to anybody," Jackson said abruptly.

"Nobody said anything about intentionally harming women and children," Nathan snapped. "But that doesn't mean we ought to be buying them hair ribbons, either." He glowered at Jackson.

Laina broke in. "Why can't the people giving those orders understand? If those generals had seen them when they arrived — compared to now. Lame Deer was little more than a reed of grass blowing in the wind when I first saw her. And look at her now." She smiled at Nathan. "The results of a few weeks of Frenchy Dubois' cooking are obvious."

Nathan got up and went to the window. He looked out toward the barracks where the Cheyenne were being housed. "Well, you can see those provisions being stockpiled over by the barracks. There's a change coming, that's certain."

"The army can't possibly move them in *this* weather!" Laina said. She rubbed her own numb hands together. "They don't have proper clothing. They'll freeze."

Nathan looked at Laina. "No one's going to deliberately *harm* them."

"No," Jackson interrupted, "we're going to do it more slowly. By sending them back to an unfit climate where measles and malaria can do it for us."

"Well," Nathan said gruffly, "army life isn't all training horses and giving riding lessons to the ladies, Private. Sometimes it means doing things you don't personally approve."

"Who in any name under heaven could ever approve of what's being done to those

Cheyenne?" Jackson blurted out. His face flushed with anger. "We call ourselves a Christian nation. How can any Christian do this to people?"

Nathan glared at Jackson. "May I remind you, Private Jackson, that these wonderful so-called defenseless people you want to give a home murdered over three dozen people in Kansas on their way back up here? Or do you think we should be good Christians about that and turn the other cheek? Or is that not the verse of the week?"

As the conversation got more and more heated, Laina Gray grew more ill at ease. These were not the same three men who had left Camp Robinson to help round up the Cheyenne. They were not the same men who'd been guarding the barracks, either. Yates seemed more sure of himself. Less apologetic about himself in general. She was happy for him.

Jackson was different, too. He seemed more at peace with himself. Apparently he was the one who had given Lame Deer the hair ribbons. Nathan disapproved, but Laina was touched by Jackson's kindness to a child — especially a child whose contact with white people in general and soldiers in particular had undoubtedly created some horrific memories. Laina couldn't see why Granny Max's image of a "funnel of love" from heaven shouldn't operate for Cheyenne children, too.

What did Nathan mean by that *verse of the week* comment? As the men argued over the Cheyenne's fate, Laina watched Caleb, amazed at his self-control. He obviously had intense feelings about the situation, but he was nothing like his old self. His old self would have likely disregarded the fact that he was arguing with an officer and made a point or two with his fists by now. His old self would have probably landed in the guardhouse before the night was over.

But instead of using his fists, Caleb was maintaining control, even while he defended Dull Knife's position. Finally, he raised his hands, palms up. "Hey, Sarge, I've got no intention of refusing to obey orders. I'm just saying it's not right making them go back. And I don't think they will. We're sitting on powder keg, sir."

Nathan walked back toward the table. He snatched his coffee mug up and drained it. "Well, I agree with you about that, soldier. And God help us all when it blows up. Which, thanks to the blind guides back in Washington, it is most certainly going to do."

While an awkward silence reigned in the room, Laina got up from the table and reached for the coffeepot. She bumped the table when she came back, hard enough to slosh Katie's milk out of her mug. "Sorry," she said, blushing. "I don't have a sense of where I begin and end anymore." She smoothed her dress over her bulging abdomen and moved to pour Nathan more coffee. The men exchanged embarrassed glances. "Sorry," Laina apologized again. "I didn't mean to embarrass anyone." *But I did mean to stop the arguing. And between Caleb and me we did it.*

Harlan Yates spoke up. "The men aren't going to let Christmas go by without a hop," he said, looking pointedly at Becky. "You ladies will come, won't you?"

"As long as there isn't a blizzard," Becky said, blushing. "Maybe if we get everyone into one room we'll finally thaw out." She shivered. "I don't remember ever seeing the mercury in a thermometer freeze before. How cold does it have to be for that to happen?"

"Forty below," Nathan said. "And it froze in the thermometer at the adjutant's office just last night."

Laina looked across the room at Caleb. "Many thanks for the firewood, Private."

He nodded back and smiled at her. "A small price to pay for that lined wool shirt you made me. Dorsey wants to know what you charge."

"Mrs. Gruber said the ones she gets from Omaha are a dollar and a half," Laina said. "But tell Corporal Dorsey the girls and I would rather barter if it's all the same to him. If he'll dig us a garden come spring, I'll be happy to make him *two* shirts."

They finished their meal and the men got up to go. Katie and Becky said goodnight.

Nathan lingered. "You keep warm, girls," Nathan said as they slipped behind the quilt curtain he'd helped Granny hang the previous spring.

"You don't have to worry about us," Katie said, with her hand holding up a corner of the quilt. "Wilber keeps us warm. He lies across our feet. It's like having a stove right there on the bed."

Nathan smiled. "I knew that dog would be worth something someday if you could keep him from getting kicked in the head by a horse."

"Oh, he doesn't chase horses anymore."

"Really?" Nathan said.

"Nope," Katie shook her head. "Laina

and me and Private Jackson taught him not to."

Nathan looked at Laina as Katie disappeared behind the quilt curtain. "When was that?"

"Before the snow," Laina said. "While you were out on that first patrol. Caleb showed us how to teach him before his battalion left camp. Then we kept working at it while you were all gone."

Nathan nodded. "Well, good for Private Jackson. Glad to see he made some use of himself besides providing work for the men assigned guardhouse duty."

"I think those days are probably over for Private Jackson," Laina said.

"Yes," Nathan agreed. "Amazing what a dose of self-righteousness can do for a man."

"What?"

"Hasn't he told you? Our old friend Beauregard Preston has gotten religion."

"I thought something was different. I didn't know what."

"Don't ask him about it until you have time for a sermon. He's got a good one all ready for anyone who asks him about it."

"You sound like you've heard it."

He nodded. "It's as good a sermon as Granny Max ever preached."

"I don't recall Granny Max preaching very much," Laina said carefully. "At least not with words. She spoke pretty loud with how she *lived*, though."

"With Jackson, it's more like what he *doesn't* do that preaches the sermon."

"What doesn't he do?"

"Swear. Gamble. Refuse to obey orders. Start fights."

"You sound disappointed. I thought that's exactly what you hoped would happen for him."

Nathan shrugged. "If he's going to start preaching brotherly love and kindness toward the Cheyenne over in the barracks, it's just going to make more trouble for him. He'll be right back where he started. In the guardhouse, serving time for dereliction of duty."

"What he was saying tonight didn't sound too unreasonable to me," Laina said.

"You aren't down in Kansas visiting the graves of half your family."

Laina sat down in a chair. "Did you stay behind to argue with me about the Cheyenne?"

"Of course not," Nathan said. "I just wanted a chance to talk to you without anyone around." He leaned down and put his hand on her shoulder. "I think about you and the girls a lot. I worry about you."

"You don't need to worry about us," Laina said. "The girls and I are doing fine. I'm feeling fine. We have plenty of firewood and plenty to eat and shelter over our heads. What more could a girl ask for?"

"Well," he said, taking his hand away and walking over to stare out the small square window beside the front door. "Most girls ask for a husband at some point in their lives."

"I'm not most girls," Laina said. "And we've already had this conversation. I appreciate what you've offered to do for me. But it just wouldn't be right."

"How can it not be right? Becky and Katie love me."

"They love Harlan Yates and Caleb Jackson, too. But I'm not marrying either of them."

"Maybe you should let them hear you say that," Nathan said.

"What?" She looked at him. He was still staring out the window, but she could see the muscles in his jaw working. "Oh, you mean Harlan." She laughed. "As a matter of fact, I did tell Harlan exactly that. And he was mightily relieved when I turned him down. You and I both know he's going to ask Becky. If he ever gets up the nerve. She's got her acceptance all ready. If he can manage to get his proposal said, I'll be making a wedding dress come spring. She's young, but I think it'll be a good match."

"I wasn't talking about Harlan Yates," Nathan said.

The baby pounded against her bladder, and with a little "Oh," Laina winced and shifted in her chair.

"Hey," Nathan said, stepping away from the window and touching her hand.

"I'm all right," Laina said, standing up. "But I have to . . . um . . ." She felt her face turning red. "I have to go."

Nathan nodded and reached for his coat and hat and gloves.

"You know," Laina said, watching him pull everything on. "The soldiers all look alike now. Except you. You stand out because you're so tall. Add that hat, and Katie says you look like a giant. I'm inclined to agree with her."

"It's good to be back in camp," Nathan said, "even if we're here because of them." He nodded toward the barracks.

"We're all glad to have you back," Laina said, as she moved toward the doorway to the back room. "Becky was so worried about Harlan I was tempted a few times to use some of Granny's sedating tea on her."

"You ever worry about anyone out on patrol?" Nathan asked bluntly.

She paused. "I pray for you every day, Sergeant Boone. I expect I always will."

"What do you pray?"

"Things that would likely make you really mad," Laina said. She winced again as the baby kicked her bladder. "I'm sorry, Nathan, I really do have to *go*." She slipped behind the curtain. When she heard the front door close, she sighed with relief and pulled the chamber pot out from under the bed.

Twenty-Six

A mighty man is not delivered by much strength.

Psalm 33:16

"The only thing I could disguise myself as these days is a whale," Laina joked. "And besides that, I don't think the ladies of Camp Robinson would appreciate me flaunting my condition. Especially on Christmas. I don't think I could dance, even if I wanted to. My idea of a good evening these days is propping my swollen ankles up and enjoying a warm cup of tea as close to the stove as possible." She sipped her tea. "Just like this."

"I still don't feel right leaving you all alone," Becky had protested, even as she dusted her hair with flour to whiten it. She was going to the Christmas Eve masked ball as a shepherdess, thanks to some creative sewing of lace trim to an old dress, a staff made from a cane wired to a stick, and a crocheted mobcap Mrs. Gruber had dug out of an old trunk.

"You *haven't* left me alone," Laina said. "We've had oyster stew with the Grubers and sung Christmas carols. It's been the best Christmas Eve I've ever had," Laina said.

"Are you sure?" asked Katie, who had braided her hair into two long braids and donned a small pair of overalls and a red flannel shirt to transform herself into what she called a country bumpkin.

"I'm sure." Laina smiled. "Except for maybe the night I got locked in the cathedral in St. Louis and had to sleep in a pew."

Katie stared at her. "You did?"

"I did," Laina nodded. "It was beautiful. All golden candlelight and stained glass."

A knock at the door announced Sergeant Boone's arrival. She nodded at the girls. "Be sure you thank Sergeant Boone for escorting you. You both look wonderful." She asked Becky, "Do you know what Harlan's going to be?"

Becky blushed. "He wouldn't tell me. But he said I'd recognize him as soon as I see him." She giggled. " 'Course, unless he dyes his hair, he'll be easy to spot." She opened the door and admitted Sergeant Boone.

"You're not in costume," Laina scolded.

He smiled. "But I am. I'm going as a sergeant in the United States Army."

"Very creative," Laina said. She pulled the quilt up around her shoulders.

"You look comfortable," Boone said.

"I am. And I'm not freezing myself silly walking across the trail and up to the barracks, either, like the rest of you." She smiled at the girls. "You two pay very close attention to everything that happens, because I want to hear all about it when you get back." She waved them out the door. "Dance 'til your feet drop off."

Nathan helped the girls pile on coats and scarves. "They won't be too late," he promised.

"I'm not worried," Laina said, opening Granny's Bible as they left. She closed her eyes and relaxed, her feet propped up on a pillow atop another chair, listening to the sound of Wilber's rhythmic breathing. His paws twitched as he chased imaginary rabbits in his sleep. She closed her eyes, relishing the quiet. But another knock at the door prevented her dozing off. *What now?* She groaned and hoisted herself out of the chair and went to the door. "Who's there?"

"It's me. Jackson. And Corporal Dorsey. We brought you a Christmas present." He stepped inside. "Look out the window."

Scratching the frost off the window, Laina peered outside. Someone waved back from the driver's seat of a sleigh and motioned for her to come out.

"Corporal Dorsey and I thought you might enjoy a moonlight ride."

"He must be frozen solid!"

Jackson grinned. "He's had just enough 'holiday cheer' to warm himself up. And we've put warm bricks on the floor for his feet. And there's some for yours — and mine. But you need to hurry. It won't stay warm for long."

Laina was doubtful.

"Come on. It'll be fun. We won't be gone long. You'd be doing me a favor."

"I can't see how," Laina said, but she was already pulling on her coat and reaching for a scarf hanging on a hook behind the door.

"No one wants to believe Private Jackson doesn't want to drink himself into a stupor tonight." He smiled and shrugged. "This way I won't be around for them to hound me about it. And besides that, we just thought it would be fun to do something nice for you."

"How could I say no to that, after all the work you've done hitching that sleigh up? Where on earth did you find a sleigh, anyway?"

"Oh, Dr. Valentine had it in that shed out back. He had it sent here last winter for his girls. I remembered it from when I was giving them riding lessons. Dinah and I used to saddle her pony out there." He grinned. "Remember the despised side-saddle?" He produced another scarf and a fur muff. "Mrs. Gruber sent these."

"Mrs. Gruber?" Laina asked as he opened the door.

"She thought you might say yes, as long as we had a chaperone." When Wilber jumped up in the back of the sleigh, Jackson laughed. "And now we have two." He helped her up into the backseat and climbed up beside her, shoving Wilber over against the far side of the seat. "You can be a chaperone, you big oaf, but *I* sit beside the lady." Sitting down, he covered their laps with two more buffalo robes. "You feel the heat from the bricks?" he asked. When she nodded, Dorsey slapped the reins and they took off gliding across the snow.

Laina looked up at the starlit sky. The moon shone just above the ridge in the distance, a sliver of light barely illuminating the white landscape with blue light. As they headed west across the valley, the music from the masked ball receded into the distance, and soon there was only the sound of the horse's hooves swishing through the snow.

"I hope you agree I'm at least better company than Wilber," Jackson said after a few minutes.

Laina nodded. "You both went to a lot of trouble." She raised her voice so Corporal Dorsey could hear. "Thank you."

The warm bricks at her feet and the mountains of buffalo robes around them both soon had their effect on her. Laina closed her eyes. When she woke, her head was on Jackson's shoulder, and beneath the buffalo robes he was holding her hand. She could feel his beard against her forehead. He smelled of bay rum cologne and tobacco. When she started to lift her head, he nuzzled the top of her head and whispered, "Thanks for coming."

"Hmm," Laina said, and, relaxing against him, dozed off again.

"Hey, sleeping beauty." Someone was whispering, tickling her cheek.

She opened her eyes and realized with a start the sleigh had stopped outside her apartment on Soapsuds Row. Wilber had jumped down and was waiting beside the front door. Before she could maneuver her belly up off the bench, Jackson slipped his arms around her and lifted her out of the sleigh. She thought maybe she should protest, but she didn't. It was delightful to be babied. And there was that wonderful aroma again of cologne and tobacco. She heard Dorsey say good-night and the sleigh pulled away.

Inside, Jackson settled her back in Granny's rocker, kneeling on the floor in front of her to help pull scarves and robes away before wrapping her up in Granny's quilt. "Snuggle down," he whispered. "I'll stoke the fire and let myself out."

She opened her eyes and said, "That was the best Christmas present I've ever had, Private Jackson. Thank you. It's too bad Charlotte wasn't here to enjoy it instead of me."

Jackson cleared his throat. "I'm quite content with the companion I had." He started to lean toward her but stopped himself and stood up. "I'm going to get out of here before I take advantage of the situation and steal a Christmas kiss from the prettiest girl at Camp Robinson."

Laina chuckled. She waved her hand at

him. "The prettiest or the pitiful-est? You've done your good deed, Private Jackson. You don't have to spin any more yarns tonight."

"Hey," he said, kneeling back down beside her. "I meant what I said about you being the prettiest girl at Camp Robinson."

With her index finger, she tapped the place on his chin where there was a dimple beneath the beard. "You made me feel very . . . special . . . tonight, Private Jackson. That's quite a feat, considering I feel like a bloated cow most of the time these days. Thank you."

He caught her hand and kissed her palm. "Any time you need to feel special, you just call on me." He got up then, stoked the stove, and poured her another cup of tea.

"You mind if I ask you something?" he said.

"Ask away."

"What do you think that verse about a person being a new creation means?" He hadn't replaced the cover on the stove top, and when Laina looked up at him he was staring down into the fire, his features illuminated by golden light. "Do you think it could mean that a person . . . well, say a person like me, with my history, could maybe have a normal life?" He looked at her. "You know. A wife, a family — the whole thing."

"I don't see why not," Laina said. "Why would God talk about a person being a new creation if He wasn't going to let him have a life that reflected the change?"

Jackson nodded and closed the stove lid. "It's just weird lately," he said. "The card playing and the drinking. I don't even want to do that stuff any more. And I *like* reading the Bible. I mean, it makes sense. It's like I just learned to read." He looked at her with a puzzled expression. "I still have trouble with swearing. But when I do, I feel bad. Is that crazy or is that how it works?"

Laina smiled at him. "I think that's how it works, Private Jackson." She asked, "Have you asked Doctor Valentine about writing to Charlotte yet? He's got to have seen the change in you."

"I did. I wrote one letter." He shrugged. "She never answered me."

"Maybe it's just taking a while for the mail to come through," Laina suggested.

He shook his head. "No. I finally worked up my courage and asked Dr. Valentine about it." He tugged on his beard. "It seems there's a Lieutenant Somebody squiring her around town these days."

Laina put her hand on his arm. "I'm sorry."

He pulled up a chair and sat opposite her. "Would you mind calling me Caleb?" he asked abruptly. "I mean, we've shared a sleigh ride. That stands for something, doesn't it? Some new kind of friendship, at least?"

Laina smiled at him. "Of course, Caleb. And you call me Laina. Please."

He nodded. Something in his dark eyes made her feel self-conscious. *Don't be absurd. It's Christmas Eve and he's thinking about Charlotte and that lieutenant. He's just lonely. So are you. It was just a sleigh ride . . . and you always did love bay rum cologne. You're smarter than this. Just control yourself.* But if Riverboat Annie knew anything about men, Caleb Jackson's dark eyes were flickering with something besides just friendship. Just as he leaned toward her, Katie and Becky, followed by Nathan Boone, burst through the door.

"He did it, Laina. He asked her!" Katie blurted out.

"Katie O'Malley!" Becky said.

"I'm sorry," Katie apologized. "I couldn't help it."

511

"Who did what?" Laina asked, hoping no one noticed her flaming cheeks.

Becky hung her coat up next to Katie's. When she turned around, she was blushing, too. "Harlan asked me." She giggled, "He came all dressed up as a *groom*. With a suit and a top hat and everything. And he asked me!"

"Asked what?" Laina teased, relieved that Caleb was leaning back in his chair, acting as natural and calm as if the two of them had just been playing checkers.

"He asked me to *marry* him!"

"And you said . . . ?" Laina raised one eyebrow.

"Yes!" Becky dropped to her knees beside the rocker. "Oh, Laina, I'm so happy, I'm gonna burst!" She threw her arms around Laina and hugged her. "Oh, I *wish* Mama and Papa and Granny Max were all here! I *wish* they knew!" She burst into tears.

"They know, honey-lamb," Laina murmured. "You can bet they know." She took Becky's face in her hands and smiled through her own tears. "Can't you just imagine them doing an Irish jig with the angels right now?"

Becky giggled and nodded. "He took me for a sleigh ride. That's when he asked me."

"Oh, really?" Laina said, looking over Becky's shoulder at Caleb, who held up his hands and shook his head back and forth as if to say, *"Don't look at me. I didn't know anything about that."*

"He said he didn't really plan that part. But he stepped outside and saw Corporal Dorsey driving by on his way to the stables, and Harlan asked him to drive us." Becky giggled. "Isn't that romantic?"

Yes, Laina agreed. It was romantic. She glanced at Caleb again, and then toward the door where Sergeant Boone stood watching them all with a scowl on his handsome face.

"It's Christmas Day, Miss Gray," Sergeant Boone said, stepping into the washhouse. "No one expects Soapsuds Row to operate on Christmas Day."

"You got all your men to agree to going without long johns when it's twenty below?" Laina asked. She arched her back and grimaced. "Becky and Katie are going to take over in a few minutes. The routine is good for all of us. Keeps our minds off all the people we're missing this Christmas," she said. "I let them sleep a little later since they were out so late last night." She smiled. "It took another hour to get them settled down after you left."

Nathan smiled. "When's the wedding, anyway?"

"You tell me," Laina said. "When can Harlan get some leave? He's going to want to take her back East to meet his mother and sister."

He shook his head. "Not until this mess with the Cheyenne is taken care of." He paused, then said, "Sheridan's told Crook they have to be moved back South. By force, if necessary."

"Oh, no," Laina said. "Don't those people back East know what that could mean?"

"Captain says General Crook hates it, too. Says some of the men in that barracks were with Crook last summer as scouts. Now this." Nathan shook his head and swore softly. "It's a shame. I guess Crook telegraphed last night and told Sheridan it would be downright inhuman to make them move now, in this cold."

"And?" Laina asked.

"And Sheridan said move."

Laina closed her eyes. "What are you going to do?"

"I'm going to hope that someone comes up with a better idea. Although I don't know what that could be," Nathan's voice

514

sounded miserable. "Captain's going to do his best to talk them into going without putting up a fight."

"Do you think there's any hope they'll agree?"

Nathan shook his head. "None."

"And *then* what are you going to do?"

"Obey orders. Do the job. Try to keep anyone from getting hurt, if I can." He shook his head. "But I didn't come up here to talk about the Cheyenne."

Just then the back door to Laina's quarters slammed shut. Becky and Katie arrived, greeted Sergeant Boone, and went to work, Becky taking the paddle out of Laina's hand and Katie getting ready to rinse the load of long johns.

"Bring them inside," Laina said. "We'll hang them up in the back room to dry. I'm going to make Sergeant Boone a cup of coffee. I'll save you girls some." She patted Katie on the head. "Maybe some hot cocoa for you when these are hung up."

Together, Laina and Nathan walked through the sleeping quarters and into the kitchen. She set the coffeepot on the stove and got two cups. Nathan rummaged in his coat pocket and produced a small box. "Merry Christmas," he said, and bent down and kissed her on the cheek.

Flushing with embarrassment, Laina opened the box. Nestled inside was a pair of garnet earrings.

"Those were Lily's. I hope it doesn't make you mad. But I want you to have them."

"Oh, Nathan," Laina said, picking up one of the earrings and admiring the deep red glow of the stones. "These are beautiful." She smiled at him and shook her head. "But I can't accept them."

He frowned. "I bet you'd take them if they were from Private Jackson instead of me."

"What are you talking about?"

"I saw the way you two were looking at each other last night. You can't be serious, Laina. You *know* what he is." He was leaning forward, his brows drawn together.

"Yes, Sergeant Boone, I do. He's my friend."

Nathan snorted. "Right." He shook his head. "Wake up, Laina. You know better than to fall for that."

"I haven't fallen for anything." She put the lid back on the box and slid it toward him across the table. "As I said, these are beautiful. But I can't possibly accept them."

"What's so perfect about Caleb

Jackson?" Boone demanded. He took his hat off and plunked it on the table.

"Nothing. There isn't one thing perfect about him," Laina said. *Except maybe those brown eyes. That little dimple in his chin. His laugh. I really like his laugh.*

"So what's the attraction?" He held up his hand. "No. Don't play that game with me, Laina. I *saw.* Everyone at the hop was wondering who it was that got Dr. Valentine to get his sleigh out of the shed. And who it was taking a romantic moonlight ride. It was you and Jackson. And when I brought the girls home I *saw.* What I can't figure out is how a woman who reads the Bible twice a day could possibly have feelings for a man with his history. Even though he has learned to talk religion, you know as well as I — no, you know better than I — what's really inside him."

"I'm not going to discuss my feelings for Private Jackson with you, Nathan. But what's inside him just might be a new creation. Something God promises people who come to Him. And I can tell you one thing that's very attractive about Caleb. He doesn't have any delusions of grandeur about himself. He's trying his best, and he's terrified he's not going to succeed. In fact, he knows he can't change without God's help."

"Well, I'm trying my best, too." He leaned over, resting his hands on the table, staring down at her. "I'm trying my best to watch over the girls and to get on with my life and to take care of you." He tapped his finger on the box. "What do you think *this* is, if it isn't me trying?!"

Laina bowed her head and sighed. "I'm sorry, Nathan. But your best isn't good enough."

"And Caleb Jackson's IS?" He roared the question. "And since when do you call him CALEB, anyway?!"

Laina was trembling with a combination of her own temper and fear of Nathan's anger. "I'll call him Caleb if it pleases me, and it does. And the difference between *your* 'not good enough' and *his* 'not good enough' is he *knows* he's not good enough. He knows that without God, he's hopeless and helpless."

"That's what you want? A man who's helpless?"

Laina put her hands to head and moaned with frustration. "I don't know if I want a man at all. But if I did, I'd want one who knew he was helpless and who had offered God his helplessness."

518

"That doesn't make any sense," Nathan muttered.

"It doesn't make any sense," Laina agreed. "Not to a man who's never once looked at himself and seen *nothing*. Sergeant Nathan Boone sees himself as a man who handles everything on his own. Who doesn't ask God or man for help. Who doesn't need anyone or anything."

"And what good does it do to ask *God* for help? He doesn't *answer!*" He pounded the table with his palms and backed away, glaring at her.

Tears filled Laina's eyes and spilled down her cheeks. "Nathan. Dear, wonderful, blind Nathan. He *does* answer. But sometimes He says *no.*" Her voice was miserable. "Just like I'm saying *no.*"

"I want to take care of you," he said, more gently.

"I know you do." She went around the table and, standing before him, put her hand up and patted his cheek. "I look at you, and I think I must be crazy, but I can't let you take care of me, Nathan. I tried to talk myself into it the last time this came up. I really tried. But I can't do it." She dropped her hand to her side.

"Because of Jackson," Nathan said.

Laina shook her head. "No. Because —"

He snorted. "Because of *God*."

Laina picked the earring box up off the table and handed it to him. "I owe you my life, Nathan. But I can't give you my future. And, yes, it's because of God."

"I won't do it." Caleb planted his feet and stared up at Sergeant Boone.

"Private Jackson, you are being *ordered* to stand guard outside that barracks."

Caleb nodded. "I understand that, sir. But I can't be trusted with the duty. First, captain's orders took away food and fuel. Then water. I won't stand guard over something like that."

"They'll be given everything they need as soon as they comply with the directive to come out and head back South," Boone said.

Caleb nodded. "Right. That's a good solution. Starve them until they agree to go back where they were starving." He pleaded, "It's been four days, sir. They've been scraping the frost off the glass to try to relieve their thirst. Can't we at least try to get the women and children out?"

"We did that while you were chasing after those ponies that stampeded. They said 'one starves, all starve.' "

"What if that was Laina and Katie in

520

there? Would you still follow orders not to let them have any food or water? Would you let them freeze?"

Looking off toward Soapsuds Row, Nathan swore softly. "Get over to the stables and muck out a few stalls. Think about this. Think about the fact that the next time you refuse an order, you're likely ending your career."

"Sir, I could muck out stalls from now to kingdom come, and it's not going to change my mind. Put me in the guardhouse if you have to. Court-martial me. Do whatever you want. I won't be changing my mind about this." He lowered his voice. "And if I could figure a way to do it, I'd smuggle in provisions."

"I didn't hear that," Nathan said. "Now get to work. Stable duty." Nathan could barely keep his voice from trembling as he gave the order. Jackson saluted, spun on his heel, and headed for the stables.

"Well, now, would you look at that." Dorsey, who was stacking crates of provisions in the back of a wagon outside the commissary, motioned toward the Cheyenne barracks.

Caleb, coming out the commissary door lugging another crate of goods, set it down on the ground just in time to see Wild Hog and Old Crow come out of the Cheyenne barracks under guard and head across the parade ground toward the commander's headquarters. Sergeant Boone was one of the guards.

"Maybe they've come to terms," Caleb said hopefully. He handed the crate up to Dorsey.

Before long, there was a commotion from inside headquarters. Soldiers who'd been stationed just outside the building charged through the door. Dorsey jumped down from the wagon, yelping with pain and swearing about his knee.

"Sit down," Caleb ordered and headed for the commander's office just as Wild Hog and Old Crow were brought out in chains and led away. He hesitated and turned back toward the wagon. "Looks like things are under control. Let's get you over to have Doc Valentine take a look at that knee."

Dorsey got up slowly. Just as he started to hobble after Jackson, another warrior came outside the Cheyenne barracks and gave himself up. Several more young men spilled out the door, to be met by soldiers who quickly took up positions in front of and east of the barracks.

Two soldiers came running from the hospital with a litter. Caleb turned to Dorsey. "Did you see Sergeant Boone come out of headquarters?"

"Nope," Dorsey grunted. Just then, the men came out, carrying a wounded soldier toward the hospital.

"You go on," Dorsey said. "I can't run."

Caleb tore across the road and charged inside the hospital just in time to hear Dr. Valentine tell Sergeant Boone that he was a very lucky man.

Twenty-Seven

I said unto the Lord, Thou art my God: hear the voice of my supplications, O Lord.

Psalm 140:6

"Nathan sent me to get you all to move up to the trading post." Private Yates ducked inside Laina's apartment, but not before Laina and the girls heard the unearthly cries coming from the other side of Soldier Creek.

"What *is* that?" Katie asked, clutching Wilber's collar.

Yates pursed his lips. "You don't worry about that, Miss Katie," he said. "You just gather some things in case you end up staying the night with the Grubers."

Becky went to the window and scraped frost away so she could look outside. "There are more soldiers around the bar-

524

racks," she said. "Tell us what's going on, Harlan. Please."

"They're just smashing things inside."

"What things?"

He shrugged. "Don't know. They put blankets over the windows a while ago."

"But they're singing," Katie said.

"That's a death song," Laina croaked. "Sergeant Boone told me." She had hurried to the hospital a while earlier, her heart in her throat, insisting she must see Sergeant Boone for herself, crying with relief when he smiled and squeezed her hand and told her in his own words what had happened inside the commander's headquarters — how Wild Hog had managed to stab him.

"I guess I'm not the big bad army officer I thought I was," he said, coughing and wincing with pain. "Taken out of the action by a half-starved old man."

"Thank God," Laina said, and brushed her hand over his forehead. To her surprise, Nathan blinked back tears. She sat with him until he fell asleep, leaving only when Doctor Valentine insisted that he had far too much to do to be concerned about a premature delivery brought on by her own stubbornness.

While Harlan helped Becky into her

coat, Laina lumbered around gathering her sewing basket and a pile of mending. "Here, Katie," she said, "put these shirts in a sack."

"We're not going to want to do any sewing," Katie complained.

"Well, we're not going to sit up all night staring at each other worrying, either!" Laina snapped. Immediately, she apologized. "I'm sorry. I just . . . I'm not feeling very well."

Harlan grabbed Laina's coat off its hook. "Wind's blowing in, ma'am. It's gonna be a cold one tonight. Best be getting up to the trading post." He patted her awkwardly on the shoulder. Looking around the room, he said, "You ladies ready?"

Laina grabbed Granny Max's Bible off the table and tossed it into her sewing basket. She nodded, took a deep breath, and followed everyone out the back door.

At the trading post, Becky clutched Harlan's hand and began to cry. "Now, Becky," Yates said, with a degree of sternness that surprised Laina. "You stop making such a fuss. If you're going to be a soldier's wife, you got to be brave." He swiped a tear off her cheek. "I been ordered out with the troops going down to help guard Bronson's horses. Captain thinks they might make a run for his ranch first, trying to get some horses before they head north." Kissing her on the cheek, he left.

Mrs. Gruber fussed over Laina, making her put her feet up, fixing her tea, and insisting she was generally grateful for something to do to keep her mind off the horrible sounds coming from "over there."

By four o'clock in the afternoon, things quieted down at the barracks. Mr. Gruber, who'd been keeping an eye on things from just outside the store, came in and reported that Wild Hog and Old Crow had been brought back from the cavalry encampment a mile away. "Looks like they talked their families into coming out," he said. "Saw about twenty of 'em head back down to the lower camp with the guards. That still leaves over a hundred inside, though."

"I hope our soldiers sleep with their boots on tonight," Mrs. Gruber said.

"They did stable call under arms," Mr. Gruber replied. "They're ready."

"At least it's quiet," Mrs. Gruber said hopefully.

"Yes," Mr. Gruber said, "the calm before the storm."

Private Jackson came just before tattoo.

"Sergeant Boone was threatening to crawl up here if I didn't come check on you." He took off his coat and gloves while he talked. "He's resting — if you can call being mad as a hornet about being sidelined resting. Doc seems to think he'll mend. But it will take some time."

"Are we gonna have to sleep here tonight?" Katie asked.

Mrs. Gruber spoke up. "I want you all here with us, Katie. At least for tonight."

Jackson nodded at Mrs. Gruber, then said to Becky, "Private Yates is the lucky one. Bronson will treat those boys well just out of thanks for having his horses guarded."

Laina stopped pretending to stitch the quilt block in her hands and tossed it into her workbasket. "All I can think about is Lame Deer and her mother trapped in a fight . . . or running off into the frigid night." She took a deep breath, trying to relax the muscles across her abdomen that seemed to be cramping. "They won't do that, will they? In the cold? In the snow? With just what they can carry?"

"I hope not," Caleb said. He bent down and asked Laina, "Could I . . . talk to you . . . in private?"

Her heart thumped. *He's got bad news he*

doesn't want Katie or Becky to hear.

Mrs. Gruber spoke up. "Go right through there," she motioned, "into the canteen." She lighted an extra kerosene lamp and handed it to Caleb.

In the deserted canteen, Caleb set the lamp on a billiard table. He pulled a chair out from a nearby poker table for Laina.

"What's wrong?" Laina asked.

Looking around him for a minute, Caleb shook his head. Suddenly, he dropped to one knee beside her. "I don't know if I can do this." He gulped. When he looked up at her, his eyes were brimming with tears. "Can you understand that? I don't want you to think I'm a coward. That I'm just running scared." His hand trembled when he rubbed the side of his jaw. He choked out a laugh. "I finally got to where I do care about things like honor and God and country. But where's the honor in what's been going on around here?"

The anguish in his voice brought tears to Laina's eyes. Not knowing what to say, she grabbed his hand and held it. When a tear rolled down his cheek and into his beard, she pulled him toward her. Putting her arms around him, she kissed his cheek. Her voice broke. "I want to pray for you, Caleb, but I don't even know what to say."

He put his forehead on her shoulder. He was quiet, but Laina could tell from the occasional shudder coursing through his body that he was crying.

Finally, he pulled away, sat back on the floor, and leaned against her knee. Instinctively, she began to comb through his hair with her fingers, something Granny Max had often done to calm her after a nightmare. "One time Granny Max told me that when she didn't know words, sometimes she just pictured the thing or the person she cared about in the palms of her hands, and she'd just silently lift her palms up to the Lord." She opened her hands, palm up, and reached around him to show him. "That's where you'll be tonight, Caleb. Right here." She touched first one palm, then the other. "I'll be holding you and Lame Deer and Nathan and Harlan . . . all night. Holding you up to God. Until we know what's going to happen. Until it's over."

Caleb grabbed her hands. He kissed her palms, the back of her hands, the scars on her wrists and then, rising to his knees, he turned around. Leaning forward, across her bulging abdomen, he kissed her lightly. "Thank you," he said, then stood up and helped her out of the chair.

"Laina, I . . . uh . . ."

She reached up and put a finger over his lips. "Let's just leave things as they are, Caleb."

"Exactly how are . . . things . . . between us?"

Laina thought for a moment. "You used to be one of my best customers," she said, smiling up at him. "Care to take a stint as one of my best friends?"

"I was hoping . . ." he said.

"So am I," she said.

After Caleb left, Mrs. Gruber lit her best hurricane lamp and set it in the center of her table. The women gathered around — Katie and Becky pretending to read and Laina and Mrs. Gruber pretending to sew. They had been there less than an hour when shots rang out. At once, they jumped to their feet, exchanging glances while they listened, every muscle tense. There was more gunfire. Katie grabbed for Laina's hand. Wilber stared at the door, whining.

"Oh, dear God," Mrs. Gruber said, "let them be safe. Let it all end. Oh, dear Lord."

Laina gasped and bent over, resting her palms on the table. "Mrs. Gruber," she said, reaching for the older woman. "What —"

There was a gush, a sensation of warmth, and then the first strong contraction.

At the first sound of gunfire, Caleb leaped off his cot and grabbed his rifle. He had followed Dorsey's example and stayed dressed, but the men charging toward the barracks were a ragtag bunch, most in a state of half-dress, some even barefooted, running through the snow, oblivious, for the moment, to the cold.

"Help! I'm shot!" a guard stationed on the west side of the barracks screeched. Dorsey knelt beside him.

Caleb rounded the front of the barracks. On the east side, warriors were spilling out the windows, guns blazing, forming a line of fire, buying time for the women and children to get away.

"I *knew* they had to have guns hidden in there!" A soldier knelt next to where Caleb had taken cover behind a wagon and cursed. He raised his rifle.

"You might hit a child," Caleb yelled, grabbing the barrel of the rifle.

"One less warrior for the next battle," the man screamed back. When he shoved Caleb away, Caleb lost his balance and hit his head against the steel rim of a wagon wheel. Stunned, Caleb watched as the soldier jumped up and charged toward the barracks. When an old woman fell in the snow, the soldier put a gun to her head and pulled the trigger.

"They're headed for the river!" someone yelled.

"Bronson's!" another voice shouted.

The minute his vision cleared, Caleb took off for the bridge. Just behind the barracks several warriors were putting up a desperate fight, to buy time for the women and children scurrying up the river toward the distant bluffs. As he took cover around the corner of the adjutant's office next to the barracks, Caleb had the odd impression of things happening in slow motion. Cheyenne rifles flashed, war cries filled the air, but then a volley of gunfire sounded from inside the barracks where soldiers had taken cover and were returning fire through the windows. The Cheyenne rear guard toppled, and the soldiers charged out of the barracks and toward the river in pursuit of the fleeing captives. Caleb thought, *It would be a different fight if the warriors had left the women and children behind. They would have crossed the bridge and headed for Bronson's . . . and some of them still might make it before we get our horses saddled and ride after them.*

"Get after them!" someone screamed.

Caleb charged toward the bridge, where he fell into a washout beside the sawmill. His rifle went flying, and he landed with a thud almost on top of two Cheyenne. With his best Rebel yell, he scrambled to his feet, pulling his pistol from where he'd tucked it into his belt, and he launched himself at the shadowy figure coming toward him with upraised arm. He discharged his pistol just as the warrior's arm came slashing down. The warrior crumpled to the earth and lay still.

As gunfire faded into the distance, Caleb whirled around, expecting another attack. Behind him, cowering in the snow, a child pleaded over and over, "Do not kill me. Please do not kill me!"

"Lame Deer?" Jackson gasped.

"Jack-Son. It is you? I begged to leave. They said we would all die together. I don't want to die, Jack-Son. Please do not kill me."

"Where's Brave Hand?" Caleb said, hunkering down in the snow next to Lame Deer.

"I not know," the child said.

"Are you hurt?" he asked.

"I not know," she said, trembling.

"Who is this?" He nudged the body with his boot.

"Pretty Horse," Lame Deer said.

Pretty Horse. The vision of a wizened old man with flowing white hair flashed in his head. He and Caleb had talked, through signs and broken language, of the old man's favorite horse, long since dead. When Pretty Horse learned of Caleb's reputation with horses, he'd insisted they smoke a pipe together. Caleb gulped.

As gunfire blazed around them, he hoisted Lame Deer like a sack of potatoes under his good arm and staggered up out of the washout, heading for the hospital. Halfway there, he stumbled and fell to his knees.

Lame Deer threw herself against him, clutching his shirt. "Don't die, Jack-Son," she screamed at him, pulling on him, trying to get him back to his feet. In the cold air, his left arm felt colder. Wet, he thought. He listened to the shouts and the sounds of gunfire, scowling when he realized they seemed far away. He looked down at his arm. Dark liquid was dripping off his fingertips, staining the moonlit snow. Lame Deer was clutching at his shirt. He thought she was screaming at him, but he couldn't seem to make out the words. The last thing he remembered was a thin line of silver glistening on her cheek as the moonlight illuminated her tears.

Twenty-Eight

And I will give thee the treasures of darkness, and hidden riches of secret places . . .

Isaiah 45:3

Private Caleb Jackson lifted his head off the hospital cot and tried to look around, but even the effort to do that made him sick to his stomach. He lay back down. Closing his eyes, he tried to remember. When it finally came back to him, he couldn't think why he was even here. He'd been carrying Lame Deer . . . to the hospital . . . his arm . . . His memory ran out somewhere near the stables.

He listened to the suffering around him. Doctor Valentine was at the opposite end of the infirmary giving orders about something. Even from this distance, Caleb could hear the weariness in the man's voice. On the cot next to him lay an old

536

man. Jackson thought he'd seen him perform at one of the dances the Cheyenne held in their barracks not long after they arrived at Camp Robinson. *Fort Robinson now,* he reminded himself. The official announcement had come over the wires in December. The old man was asleep. His face was so pale, Jackson wondered if he might be dead.

I wonder if that's what I look like, he thought, and he raised his hand off the cot to look. It felt like he was straining to lift a log. His left forearm was wrapped in blood-soaked strips of white cloth. At the sight of his own blood, his stomach lurched. He closed his eyes again.

Lord. Lord God Almighty. Help. Help us all. He wondered about Yates, assigned to help protect the horse herd down at Bronson's ranch. He doubted any of the Cheyenne had made it that far. From what he could remember, they'd started that way, then had recrossed the bridge and scattered up the river toward the bluffs.

Sergeant Boone. I wonder if he's in this room somewhere, listening to all this. He wanted to get up and see if he could find him, but he couldn't even find the strength to lift his head.

Someone laid a hand on his forehead.

Caleb opened his eyes.

"You all right?" Dorsey asked.

Caleb nodded. "Arm hurts."

"No wonder," Dorsey said. "Doc ain't had time to stitch it up yet." He grinned. "I poured kerosene in it. You had a few colorful words for me, but we got it wrapped up. Bleeding's stopped. Doc'll be back later to stitch it up." He looked around him. "There's others need him worse right now."

"Yates? Boone?" Caleb asked.

Dorsey shook his head. "Can't say. Yates isn't back off patrol yet. Boone's been moved over to the barracks with the ones that aren't so bad. He'll mend."

"You found me?" Caleb asked.

Dorsey nodded. "It's a wonder you didn't bleed to death."

"Lame Deer?"

He shook his head. "Wasn't nobody but you."

Caleb blinked back tears. "She was so terrified," he croaked. He told Dorsey about falling into the washout. "I thought she was shot. Do you think maybe she got away somehow?"

Dorsey looked away. He cleared his throat. "Hard to say. The chase is still going. Sleep if you can. It'll be a while before Doc gets to you."

"Do you know if Laina and the girls are still at the trading post?"

Dorsey grinned. "I reckon they are. Becky came in here some time ago asking for Doctor Valentine to come. That baby's on the way." Dorsey added, "She was more than a little upset when the doctor said he didn't have time for delivering babies."

"Is Laina all right?" Caleb asked.

"I reckon. Doc's been having me go over every so often to check on things. It's taking some time, but women know about these things. She'll be fine."

Caleb struggled to sit up. "Help me get up. I wanna go to her . . ." His head swam, and he fell back on the cot.

Dorsey was stern. "You're not goin' anywhere until Doc Valentine says it's all right, soldier. Now you lay back down." His expression softened. "That little gal's made of iron. Think what she's been through. Birthing a baby's nothin'." He patted Caleb's shoulder.

Had Laina Gray heard Corporal Dorsey's opinion of birthing a baby, she would have resurrected a Riverboat Annie phrase or two. As it was, she was struggling not to scream her insides out. Katie and

Becky were clearly terrified. Mrs. Gruber was worried. Laina's emotions rocketed between fear, worry, and complete exhaustion. Just when she thought she'd endured the strongest contraction possible, another one left her panting and breathless. She'd begun the ordeal perfectly at peace with God's timing, more concerned with what was happening with the soldiers and the Cheyenne than herself. But as the hours wore on, as the contractions increased, as all her efforts at control and trust failed to birth a baby, she grew afraid.

Twenty hours into the ordeal, Laina no longer cared about any of the things that had worried her before. If Katie and Becky couldn't handle her moans, they could leave. If Doctor Valentine didn't get here soon, she was going to die, never knowing whether the baby looked like Josiah Paine or not. She didn't care anymore. She just wanted things to be over.

When Caleb next awoke, it was daylight. He lifted his arm and realized there was a new bandage. Apparently he'd been stitched up and never realized it. The throbbing was terrible. He tried to sit up.

"Whoa, there, soldier." Dorsey was immediately at his side. "You lost a lot of blood. It's going to be a while before you're back in the saddle."

"Is it . . . is it over?"

"It will be soon enough," Dorsey said. "They're holed up on Soldier Creek. Every time Wessells gets them in a tight spot, he calls a cease-fire and begs them to give up. Then somebody else gets killed or gets his horse shot out from under him and they retreat back here." He shook his head in disgust. "I just heard he's going to take artillery out to negotiate a complete surrender."

"Is it a girl or boy?" Caleb asked.

Dorsey chewed on his moustache. "Baby hasn't come yet." He held Caleb down. "Now you listen here, sonny. I've got better things to do than scoop you up off the floor. You rip that arm open again and gangrene is going to be the only friend you care about. Doc Valentine went on over. Unless you think you know more than him, you'd best stay put."

"How long has it been?" he demanded.

"Becky said things started up for Miss Gray right about the same time they started up for everybody else." He thought for a moment. "Guess that makes it nearly a full day. Sun's setting outside."

"Does it always take this long?"

Dorsey stared at him like he was crazy. "You think I know the answer to that?" He paused. "Doc'll send word. He knows Sergeant Boone and you both want to know."

"Any word about Lame Deer?" Caleb asked.

Dorsey shook his head. "Sorry, son."

"Help me up," Caleb said. "Please. Just help me get over to the trading post. I don't care if you lay me out on a billiard table. I want to be closer."

Dorsey started to protest, then relented. "All right. Here we go —"

He was conscious for about ten seconds.

It was dark outside when Caleb woke again. Lifting his head off the cot, he could see Dorsey sitting in a chair on the far side of the hospital, his head leaning back against the wall, his mouth hanging open.

On the cot next to him lay a Cheyenne child. *The old man must have died.* The child, a little girl with two long braids tied with bright hair ribbons, was lying on her side with her back to Jackson. When she turned over, she smiled at him.

"You saved me, Jack-Son."

Caleb's eyes filled with tears. "How? I fell in the snow."

She nodded. "I run away. Hurt leg. Go

542

to Soapy Row. No one there."

"Are you hurt bad?" he asked.

She made a face. "Not bad."

Caleb forced another smile. He tried to get up, but realized he wasn't going to get far alone.

"You sleep," Lame Deer whispered. "Doctor-man take care of you."

Nodding, Caleb closed his eyes.

"Wake up, soldier. There's news."

Caleb opened his eyes and looked up at Dorsey. It was daylight.

"I'll help you get over to the trading post now. She's asking for you."

Caleb frowned. "Asking for me? Why? Is something wrong?"

Doctor Valentine came into view. "There is nothing wrong, Private. But it was a long haul. Breech. Almost lost them both." He sighed. "The keyword, Private, is *almost*. Go on over so you can see for yourself."

Dorsey helped him sit up.

Lame Deer was sitting up in bed, too, eating a bowl of grits. She smiled at him.

"I'll be back," Caleb said.

Dorsey leaned down. "Stand up slow. You're gonna be dizzy. Put your good arm over my shoulder, and do what you can yourself. My knees haven't gotten any better since you tackled me." He reached into his pocket and took out a small silver flask. "Now don't give me a sermon about the evils of drink. One swig won't kill you, and it might get you over to the trading post without me having to haul you on my shoulder. This is no different than taking a dose of Granny Max's medicinal whiskey."

"I haven't heard any bugles," Caleb said when they got outside into the sunshine. "What time is it? What day?"

"It's about seven. Sunday."

They had to stop twice and wait for Caleb to get his breath, but by the time they reached the trading post, Caleb had let go of Dorsey and was walking, albeit slowly, under his own power. He stopped just outside and took a deep breath, trying to still his nerves, wondering if, now that the baby was here, things would change between him and Laina. Dorsey had said she asked for him — she wanted *him*. He was almost afraid to find out what that meant. He wanted her, too, but he wasn't sure if they both meant the same thing.

Sergeant Boone was at the trading post, sitting at a table with Becky and Katie playing cards. Jackson stammered a string of questions. Nathan held his hand up. "Hey. You look terrible. Get yourself in there before you pass out on us." He pointed over his shoulder, then he said, "She was happy to know Lame Deer is all right. But that didn't settle her much." He smiled sadly, "I don't understand it, personally, but it seems she wants *you*."

His heart pounding, Caleb felt his way along the counter towards the door that led to the Grubers' sleeping quarters. He paused at the end of the counter to catch his breath before continuing into Mrs. Gruber's kitchen, past the table and stove, toward the doorway that stood open, revealing just the foot of a bed. He swept his hands across his hair and wiped the sweat off his forehead with the back of his hand. Instead of going in, he leaned against the door frame and peered around toward the head of the bed.

When he saw how pale she was, his heart lurched. But then she opened her eyes and smiled at him.

"They . . . uh . . . they said you wanted to see me." He suddenly felt shy in her presence.

She nodded. "Come over here and sit down before you collapse."

He sank onto the bed beside her.

She touched the edge of the bandage on his arm.

"It's all right. I just lost a lot of blood. Makes me feel weak as a kitten." He swiped his hand across his forehead again. "Dorsey tells me he poured it full of kerosene. Sure to prevent infection."

"Dorsey's a good man."

Caleb nodded. "He helped me get over here."

"I'll have to thank him."

The awkward silence between them was broached by a faint mewling sound coming from a drawer behind him. As he turned and looked down, Laina said, "She's hungry. Again."

Caleb glanced back at Laina. "She?"

Laina nodded. Her green eyes misted over. "I miss Granny Max."

Caleb lay his hand on her cheek. "I know you do, honey-lamb." The endearment had just slipped out. He wondered if it would somehow hurt her more to hear Granny's pet name for her come from his mouth. But then she raised her hand to his and nuzzled his palm.

The baby's complaints took on a more strident tone.

"Think you can pick her up?" Laina asked. "If it hurts your arm, we can call Katie. She's hardly put her down since she was born."

Caleb reached into the drawer and lifted the infant out, barely needing his wounded arm. He looked down in wonder at the tiny creature with the wrinkled face, so swathed in blankets he could see nothing save a nose and two eyes. "She just fits," he said, cradling the baby in his right hand.

"You'd think she could have arrived with less of a fuss," Laina said, moving to her side to snuggle the baby next to her. When she stroked her cheek, the infant turned and began to mouth the knuckle of Laina's little finger.

Caleb looked from the child to Laina and back again. His heart pounded. He cleared his throat. "You're really pale. You gonna be all right?"

She nodded but didn't look at him as she said, "Thank you for coming. I just . . . I just needed to see for myself." Her cheek flushed with color.

"See what for yourself?"

"You," she said. Her voice trembled. When she finally looked up at him, he saw tears glistening in her green eyes. She croaked, "I just wanted you."

"You did?" he asked, brushing the hair away from her forehead.

She nodded. "That night after the sleigh ride — before the girls came in — I thought . . ." She looked up at him and bit her lower lip. "I thought maybe there was something . . ."

He tucked the long braid of auburn hair behind her shoulder. "There was. For me. But I didn't know about you. That's what I was trying to talk about that night in the canteen. When you said to leave things as they were. Not to say anything more."

"I didn't want to take advantage of you," Laina said.

He chuckled. *"You* didn't want to take advantage of *me?"*

She smiled. "I guess that is kind of funny when you think about it . . . considering. But it's true." The smile disappeared. "People can do crazy things when it seems like the world's going to h—" She bit her lip and corrected herself. "— falling apart. That's not a time to say things or promise things you might regret later." She looked down at the baby. "I've no right to expect . . ." She left the sentence unfinished.

Caleb cleared his throat. "Is that a hint of red I see in her hair?" he said, moving aside the blanket.

Laina nodded. "I was so afraid the baby would look like *him.* I thought I'd hate it." She blinked back tears, then gave in to her emotions and let them come. "I don't. I love her so much it hurts." She looked up at Caleb, tears streaming down her cheeks.

He nodded. "The good Lord just funnels it down from heaven. Isn't that what you told me Granny Max used to say?"

Laina nodded.

He touched the baby's hand. When she latched on to his little finger, it was his turn to tear up. He wiggled his finger, thrilled when the infant didn't let go. Then he looked at Laina and smiled. "The Lord started funneling long before this lamb was born. He's been funneling love for you into my heart for a while now. But you wouldn't let me tell you the other night." He slipped his finger away from the infant and lifted Laina's chin, waiting until she looked into his eyes. "I love you, Laina Gray. So much it hurts."

His heart nearly cracked while he waited for her to say something. She closed her eyes. Tears slid from beneath her eyelids and coursed down her face. When she finally opened them, her eyes were shining with joy. "I love you, too," she said. Her voice broke. "But, oh, Caleb . . . I don't deserve . . . I don't deserve any of it." She was almost sobbing.

"Didn't you tell me once that's what God is about — giving love to people who don't deserve it?" He kissed her, then asked, "Will you marry me?"

She nodded. "Yes."

He smothered her next sob with a kiss. Pulling away, he stroked the baby's cheek. "So what will we name the baby, Mrs. Jackson?"

"Joy," Laina said. "We'll name her Clara Joy."

And I will give thee the treasures of darkness, and hidden riches of secret places, that thou mayest know that I, the Lord, which call thee by thy name, am the God of Israel.

Isaiah 45:3

About Stephanie

A native of southern Illinois, Stephanie Grace Whitson has resided in Nebraska since 1975. It was when she was teaching her homeschooled children their state history unit that Stephanie became interested in the lives of the women who settled her adopted state. What she likes to call "playing with imaginary friends" eventually became her first book, *Walks the Fire*, published in 1995 by Thomas Nelson Publishers. Stephanie's books have appeared on the ECPA bestseller list and been finalists for the Christy Award (*www.christyawards.com*). She founded a home-based inspirational gift company (*www.besttoyou.com* — see Burden Bear) and has also been involved in quilt pattern and sewing-related jewelry design (pewter at *www.lorarocke.com*). Widowed in 2001, Stephanie now pursues a full-time writing and speaking ministry from her home studio in Lincoln, Nebraska. Visit her at *www.stephaniegracewhitson.com.* You may also contact her at: WhitsonInk, 3800 Old Cheney Road, #101–178, Lincoln, Nebraska 68516.